The Unholy Angels

The Legends of Pangaea: Book Four

I.D. Marie

Editing by Stephanie Canto. Cover and special characters by Lunaris Falcon Studios. Fonts: Aldrich, EB Garamond

ISBN Paperback: 979-8-9896472-7-9

ISBN Hardcover: 979-8-9896472-8-6

First Edition: February 2026

To the love of my life, whoever you are,
I'll move continents for you, just like the characters in this book.

Content Warning

The Legends of Pangaea Series is an Adult-rated series. This means there will be content unfit for some readers including:

Adult sexual content

Trauma around death of a loved one

Drug and alcohol usage

Domestic abuse

Graphic violence

Cursing

Depictions of PTSD, depression, and anxiety

Human trafficking

[[Mission Files]]

Keston Leroy, Empire of Pangaea, Year 2552

[[For context of the following report :: list of known operatives related to mission]]

[[The Empire of Pangaea, European Continent]]

Capital City: Paris, Old France 48° 51' N, 2° 21' E
   Ruler: Leon Murray
   Objective: One of the six continents that make up Pangaea. The Empire strives to create global peace and order after the chaos of the Great Disaster and Last War. A world united under the rule of six Commanders is the best way to maintain global homeostasis.

Known Operatives:

Leon Murray (status: ALIVE) – *Pangaean Commander, Europe* – Reagent of Europe, controls all of the continent's armies and citizens. Serum-enhanced psyche: every bit of Pangaean knowledge has been directly downloaded into his brain. Known descendants: Arianne Murray and Pandora Richards.

Cassius Leroy (status: ALIVE) – *European Lord Advisor* – Reference all the records of the bullshit this man pulled. I'm not reliving all my family events for a file no one is going to read. Known descendants: Keston Leroy and Genevieve Leroy.

Keston Leroy (status: ALIVE) – *Heir to Leroy Family Title* – You know everything about me, I'm not writing about myself in this damned report.

Genevieve Leroy (status: ALIVE) – *European Lord Advisor in Training* – Genevieve is currently in school to succeed her father as European Lord Advisor. I'm also not talking about her. Next.

Hera Richards (status: ALIVE) – *European General of Scientific Warfare* – Matriarch of the Richards family, reagent of the United Kingdom. Also moonlights as a mad scientist who has a frequent flier card to my nightmares. Known descendant: Pandora Richards.

Pandora Richards (status: UNKNOWN) – *Heir to Richards Family Title* – Bitch. I hope she reads this. **Don't approach if you value any part of your body**

Sensatia Wolfe (status: ALIVE) – *Media Manager for European Inner Circle* – At a young age, her rapid rise to fame is still under investigation. Sensatia forgoes personal safety in the name of the next top story. When I say she doesn't care about her personal safety, she does not. ***Approach conversations with caution***

[[The Selvian Tribe]]

Capital City: Moon Warren, Old Norway 60° 03' N, 7° 21' E

Ruler: Sygrid of the Selvian Tribe

Objective: Create a civilization that protects and honors mutant abilities and lives one with nature. As one of the oldest tribes in the world, Selvia aims to protect the tribal way of life in Pangaean politics, interference in global events, and their own culture.

Known Operatives

Sygrid of the Selvian Tribe_Champion name: STRIX (status: ALIVE) – *Ductor of the Selvian Tribe* – Touted as the hero of the Selvian War, Strix goes by many names including The Silent Death. After the death of her mentor and Ductor, Cervi, Strix is now the figurehead of the war. *Fera* mutation positive: owl wings, silent flight, cold resistance, and advanced abilities.

???_Champion name: PHOENIX (status: ALIVE) - *Selvian Champion* – Absolute nightmare. I don't think you need me to spell it out to you if you've been conscious for the past six months.

Jin Kayda_Champion name: BLUE KRAIT (status: ALIVE) - *Selvian Champion* – Formally owned by the Richards family, Blue managed to escape during the skirmish in Madrid after Andre Murray's birthday party. Highly skilled in espionage. *Fera* mutation positive: neurotoxic venom, advanced agility, hyper-mobility, and advanced abilities.

William Adams_Champion name: RHINO (status: ALIVE) – *Selvian Champion* – Formally a member of the Pacific rebellion, Rhino escaped Citadel Island's destruction and chose to become a Selvian with his newfound, and old friends. *Fera* mutation positive: increased durability, bulletproof skin, increased strength, advanced abilities.

Khari Sarr_Champion name: Pharaoh (status: ALIVE) – *Selvian Champion* – First-born son of African Commander, Kajari Sarr. This asshole pisses me off. *Fera* mutation positive: electric shock, aquatic adaptation, advanced abilities.

Kristopher of the Selvian Tribe_Champion name: SATYR (status: ALIVE) – *Selvian Champion* – Only known grandson of Cervi, Topher is sometimes regarded as Tribal royalty, though he works to ignore it. *Fera* mutation positive: goat-like legs, increased vertical range, horns, advanced peripheral vision, and advanced abilities.

Lova of the Selvian Tribe_Champion name: BLITZ (status: ALIVE) – *Selvian Champion* – Originally from Africa, Lova joined the Circus of Artemis after terrible treatment as a mutant. When her abilities attracted the attention of the Selvians, she was recruited to train as a Champion in the tribe. *Fera* mutation positive: speckled skin, super-speed, balance tail, rapid reflexes, and advanced abilities.

[[United Colonies of Pacific]]

Capital City: Nassau, Old Bahamas 25° 06' N, -77° 35' W
  Ruler: Caesar Ortiz
  Objective: Create a democratic republic in defiance of Pangaea's monarchy. Pacificans believe people should have options for government instead of being forced to adhere to one single global empire.

Known Operatives:

Andre Murray-Ortiz (status: ALIVE) – *Former European Heir Apparent* – After discovering the true cause of his mother's death—and his genetics—Andre defected from Pangaea to live in Pacific. Known descendant: Roulette Ortiz (mother unconfirmed).

  Jaya Bahri (status: ALIVE) – *Pacifican Major* – Pangaean Empire refugee. Hero of the Battle of Leonueva and earned both a military promotion and island celebrity status for her actions. *Fera* mutation positive: skin and hair color manipulation, advanced abilities, and wall climbing. Citadel Academy graduate. Known relative: Kalinda Bahri

  Kalinda Bahri (status: ALIVE) – *Registered Nurse* – Pangaean Empire refugee. Current occupation: Caesar's personal nurse. Known relative: Jaya Bahri

  Haris Cadmilus (status: ALIVE) – *Research and Development Corps Officer* – Top island engineer, specialty: coding and electrical mechanics. Citadel Academy graduate. *Fera* mutation positive: quill hair, quill projectors, increased dexterity, and advanced abilities.

[[Miscallaneous]]

Imani Azikiwe_ Codename: ACE (status: UNKNOWN) - *Former Queen of the Underground* - Also fuck her.

Colla of the Circus of Artemis (status: ALIVE) - *Ringleader of the Circus* – Having forgotten the first quarter century of his life, Colla rebuilt his life with the aid of the Selvian Tribe and the Circus of Artemis. After spending years with the Circus, he became the group's leader when the former owners passed. Currently uses his performances to help rescue and rehome endangered mutants. *Fera* mutation positive: super reflexes, clawed hands, and advanced abilities.

Kajari Sarr (status: ALIVE) – *Pangaean Commander, Africa* – Suspected ally of the mutant cause due to recent history of allowing Pacific rebel encampments to be built on his continent. Known descendants: Khari Sarr, Koda Sarr, Kenda Sarr, Kuron Sarr, Kasim Sarr, and Kya Sarr

Alvaro Smith (status: ALIVE) – *North American Heir Apparent* – Secretly a *Fera*, Alvaro has hidden his mutation for the entire time he's been in the public eye. Cautious of the position, Alvaro has declared his nephew as his heir to spare his children the burden of Commandership. Set to Ascend to Commander this January after the death (assassination) of his father. Known descendants: Miguel Smith (nephew), Alexis Smith (daughter), Armando Smith (son).

Zhou Qin (status: ALIVE) – *Asian Heir Apparent* – After surviving an assassination attempt as a teenager, Qin suffered paralysis on half of his body and the lost of his twin brother, Khan. While the details of the assassination are a close-kept secret, it is well known Qin's strict and royal demeanor only intensified after surviving.

Mori Sora (status: ALIVE) – *Asian Princess* – The daughter of Commander Lang's second marriage, Sora is the half sister of Qin. It is unknown why her mother passed her up for consideration for the Commandership, but there are some whisperings that Sora has flirted with the idea of giving *Feras* rights in Asia.

One Week Ago

E ven she wasn't crazy enough to believe what she was about to do was a good idea. But Pandora Richards, the rightful heir of Europe, was out of options. Her mother would tear her apart for her failures, and her father might finally wash his hands of her.

Close. She'd been so close. Then her actions started an uprising she'd been too incompetent to quell. She'd lost Oslo. She'd lost Leon's good graces.

Now all she had was her fists, her nerves, and Ace's outrageous plan.

"I'm convinced I'll never meet an agreeable Murray in my life," Ace grumbled behind her. "You're all miserable, brooding brutes just royal enough to convince the world your volatile moods are a sign of tortured leadership, not anger-management issues."

Kill her, she's insulted your family for the last time.

Pandora huffed, ignoring the furious urges her mind had grown accustomed to producing. After almost a decade of killing and experimentation without consideration or recourse, she'd found the filter most people had to keep the more volatile thoughts at bay had nearly all but deteriorated in her. She'd become a being dominated by whim, doing whatever she desired without consideration for the consequences, because, why not? There was nothing she could do that she hadn't already done.

There was no punishment she hadn't already withstood.

But Pandora ignored that specific urge and focused on watching the Caribbean Sea lap underneath her. She wasn't interested in arguing with—or killing—the kingpin. She was hardly interested in staying alive. Unfortunately, there she was. Alive. But as long as there was breath in her lungs, there was opportunity. Her mother taught her that, though she doubted those teachings ever came from a place of love.

Either way, she was still breathing, so she had work to do. Frustration stung with its molten heat in her chest. If she couldn't convince Leon she was worthy enough for his throne, she had other avenues to explore.

She stole a look at Ace. The Underground Queen stood behind the mahogany wheel of her cabin cruiser, directing their small boat toward an island approaching on the horizon. Ace was a master at hiding the venom that pumped through her veins like blood. To any unknowing onlooker, she could be a fashion model. Perfect skin, stunning style, and a frame that would make any designer swoon. With her obsidian eyes concentrated on the water, the typical malice in her expression was replaced by a passive contentment.

In rare moments like that, Pandora could see herself falling in love with her.

But similarities became kindling to a flame in her line of work. Two malicious souls could never live in symbiosis. They would tear the world to bits and then concentrate their energy on each other until they imploded. There would also never be a moment of trust.

Not that Pandora had ever trusted anyone in her torrid existence. Not since Arianne, and that'd left her alone to the whims of her parents. And with one less arm. Maybe she'd given a fraction of that trust to Blue, but that had turned to bite her in the ass–more accurately her tongue–almost as painfully. Pandora winced at the reminder of how foolish she'd once been.

Love was not something that protected her. It weakened her. Hence why she was more than willing to give Ace's newest scheme a chance. There was no love involved, and she got a shot at the birthright that should've been hers.

The boat slowed, the island still three kilometers in the distance. Pandora turned to Ace in confusion and was met with one of her insufferable smirks. The cyborg rolled her eyes and looked back at the lapping waters in distaste. So early in the season and so far from shore, the water would be freezing.

Not that Ace cared.

"You didn't think I would risk getting too close to Pacific's defense systems with you in tow, did you? You're going to have to swim from here—if all those cybernetics *can* get wet."

"This plan better fucking work," Pandora said as she balefully considered the waves.

Ace's chuckle was sensual, almost provocative. "It will work for me. Let's just hope you're lucky enough to land in Pacific's good graces."

Grumbling, Pandora ripped off her jacket and jeans. She wordlessly stripped down to her undershirt and underwear, unwilling to tolerate both frigid waters and the feeling of wet denim on her legs. Scanning the distance, she suspected she could use her rocket boots to get her a third of the way, but that still left a couple of kilometers of swimming ahead of her. The thought of so much physical activity churned her stomach.

She might be up and moving after Blue's venomous kiss, but she was certain so much swimming would be close to her current limit. From her past experiments with Blue's venom, her body was usually compromised for about a week, and that was when she'd only taken moderate doses.

The dose Blue had given her that day in Oslo *should* have been enough to kill her.

It seemed like Arianne wasn't the only Murray resistant to death.

You'll never be as good as Arianne.

Refusing to wait around and listen to more intrusive thoughts, Pandora dove directly into the frigid waters. She wouldn't be using rocket boots this time; she needed the shock of the cold mixed with the sound of water rushing past her ears. Arianne was dead, and the dead never deserved a moment of her consideration—especially her sister.

Pandora's enhanced muscles and cybernetic tendons made quick work of the water. Years of perfecting her body in the gym—and the laboratory—had turned her into something her human genetics did not have the right to be. It was one of the few things about herself she was proud of. Her movements were perfectly mechanical as she swam, and she lost herself to the rhythm of her arms and legs slicing through the waves.

This was why she was so obsessed with the next mission: it gave her something to concentrate on.

She reached the island of Nassau in fifty minutes. Hardly her best work, but better than the most elite human athletes could boast. Shivering, she walked onto the sandy shore and ran under a collection of palm trees twenty meters away. From the looks of it, she'd arrived on a stretch that might've once been a public beach. Now the white sands were overgrown with brush and speckled with seaweed, rocks, and other sediment delivered by the shifting tides of the sea. The uneven ground earned a couple of curses from her as she ran for cover, one or two rocks and broken seashells finding their way into the bottom of her feet.

Even though her feet were retrofitted with rocket boot cybernetics, there was still sensitive skin.

Pandora didn't have to wait long for the second phase of Ace's plan to commence. Minutes after securing her hiding spot behind palms and thick ferns, two figures walked down the beach—precisely on the agreed-upon schedule. She squinted, activating her ocular implants to magnify her vision. As expected, her internal database recognized Andre and Caesar, complete with their detailed profiles.

"*Caesar Ortiz,*" her database reported in her ear with its robotic, feminine voice. "*President of the former terrorist organization known as* The United Colonies of Pacific. *Legal Status: Wanted Terrorist. Last Recorded Status: Alive. Previous Recorded Location: Madrid, Old Spain. Update current coordinates for database?*"

"Denied," Pandora whispered.

She didn't need to give Pangaea any free favors.

The implant continued, "*Andre Ortiz, formerly Andre Valentino-Murray. Former Heir Apparent of Europe. Legal Status: Exile. Last Recorded Status—*"

"I got the gist," the cyborg hissed, muting the application.

Caesar and Andre drew closer, and Pandora ducked behind the trees once more. It took them a while to reach her thanks to the uneven ground and Caesar's prosthetic leg. When they didn't reach her in the expected time, she snuck a glance around the palm and watched the Pacific President as he wobbled forward, his balance shaky as he relied on his cane in the shifting sand.

The president had declined rapidly since the last time she'd seen him on Citadel Island. He looked older, more ragged. If there was a part of her that cared, she might've felt an ounce of pity.

"—just some ideas I had for the continued transition to the mainland," Andre was in the middle of saying. His voice was hardly enthusiastic, but it was far more animated than Pandora ever remembered.

"Leave that up to Kalfas and General Lyn," Caesar replied blankly.

"But I can help, this kind of management was something I did often back in Pangaea—"

An ounce of fire lit in the President's tone as he cut off his son. "This is not Pangaea. Learn from what happened to your sister and mother, and stay out of things that do not concern you. Let the elected officials handle it, Andre."

"I've been working with Kalfas for weeks. You would know that if you participated in anything anymore."

Caesar let out a deep sigh. "I didn't come on this walk to talk about this."

The extended silence after the President's reply was heavy with disappointment. Pandora was familiar with that particular brand of reaction.

She waited, curious how the former princeling would respond. She risked looking out toward the beach with one eye. Andre had stopped in the sand and had a carefully constructed neutrality on his face, but Pandora caught the frustrated clenching of his fists. Andre looked more like Caesar than ever with his glasses and the tropical sun darkening his skin, but his controlled annoyance was something straight out of Leon's handbook.

Ace was right. Andre was losing patience with Pacific. All he needed was a little push.

Pandora took that as her cue. Pushing off the trunk, she stumbled out of the grove and back onto the beach. It wasn't hard to lean into the exhaustion from her long swim. She took advantage of her ruined clothes and bleeding feet as she tripped and staggered across the sand, attempting to look as disoriented and compromised as possible. If she played her part right, she could convince Caesar she was an injured runaway too close to death to be any threat.

He'd certainly fallen for that bit before. Twice.

Pandora let her eyes start to flutter shut as she approached Andre. When he subtly nodded, she allowed herself to drop limply in the sand as one plea escaped her lips: "*Help.*"

Letting her head roll to the side, Pandora feigned unconsciousness as Andre convinced Caesar to take her into military custody for healing and questioning. She had to fight to keep a smile from coming to her face as Caesar hesitantly agreed.

Phase One: complete.

Hopefully, they didn't kill her. How exciting.

Part I

Opening Pandora's Box

Chapter 1

Keston

G one.

Keston was gone from the world, and he didn't want to come back.

His mind spun in a whirlwind that blurred his surroundings, and his feet struggled to find footing. A euphoric smile spread across his lips as he landed on a U-shaped leather couch. His fingertips numbly grappled for the woman at his side. A name rose on his tongue amidst the haze: *Sensatia*. She extended a hand to him, her blissful smile deepening as her eyes fluttered shut. Pounding music had become a lull in the background. Above it all was a thick haze of sweet-smelling smoke, the color of electric green.

Aside from slaves, Slime was Cartel's signature product. With Keston in charge, it'd taken over the European drug market. Naturally, a good businessman runs quality checks on his products. One could consider that night a business meeting of sorts.

"Another hit, Kes?" Christos Drakos, his band's bassist, asked. A light green haze emitted from the man's sweat-glistened skin—a side effect of Slime.

He also offered the pipe to Joshua, their drummer, but the man quietly shook his head.

Keston was fairly certain he took several minutes to react. After what felt like an eternity, he extended an arm and took the smoking pipe from Christos. A giddy chuckle escaped just before his deep inhale, the smoke like sugar on his tongue and liquor warming his lungs.

He wasn't aware of much after that.

As usual, he woke up the following day in his bed.

As was *not* usual, four guests were sprawled across the mattress.

Christos and Sensatia were the only ones he recognized. The other two were strangers. It wasn't hard to piece together what'd happened the night before. The utter lack of clothes said enough.

Heart racing, Keston used his *Fera* stealth to sneak from the crumpled covers. Wincing, he jumped into a pair of sweatpants and crept out of the room. As soon as the door closed behind him, he sank to the floor and descended into a slight panic attack.

"Oh, God. *Oh, God,*" he heaved, hands raking through his hair. He was unable to erase the image of the four bodies sleeping naked in his bed. "I didn't do that—did I?"

He didn't need his stellar sleuthing skills to determine there was no possible way he *didn't* do that.

Fortunately, his loyal valet arrived moments later with a steaming cup of coffee. The older man patiently lowered the mug, not an ounce of judgment to be found in his elegant demeanor. "Don't worry, Master Keston. Everyone has one of those nights every once in a while."

Keston paled, mug quivering in his hands. "What did I do, Warrane?"

"Oh my, you don't remember. The better question is, what *didn't* you do?"

Fuck.

Dancing, flashing lights, and random faces flashed in his memory. The images were a jumbled mess—nothing he could understand. He faintly recalled the buffeting winds atop the Eiffel Tower as he leaned over the edge, a half-empty bottle in his hand.

Keston massaged his temple, wishing his nausea were simply from a hangover. But as he'd learned in the past few weeks, his *Fera* metabolism was too fast for those. Maybe he couldn't run from his existential dread, but he could certainly run from the physical consequences of a night out.

"Don't feel too bad. You were quite entertaining." With a knowing raise of his eyebrow, Warrane held out a newspaper. "Somehow, you made a brassiere look very appealing."

Fighting a rising sense of dread, Keston took the newspaper. He unfolded it to see his face plastered across the front page, titled: *Keston's Sensatia-nal Night Out.* Fortunately, the article had enough photos to help him piece his night together. Unfortunately, the image of him sticking his tongue halfway down Sensatia's throat would be plastered on news channels all across Europe. Looking at himself, it was clear that the lights had been on, but absolutely no one had been home.

He buried his head in the papers. "God fucking damn it."

"Keston!"

Warrane turned toward the shout and frowned. "I would run, Master Keston. He's not too pleased with you."

Cassius Leroy charged down the hallway, an identical paper bunched furiously in his hand. Warrane excused himself without a word.

The Lord Advisor of Europe, reigning Elite of Paris and Northern France, and Keston's very own father stomped up to him, bearded face screwed up in rage. Still sluggish, Keston didn't heed his valet's warning, remaining slumped and shirtless on the floor. He was well aware he looked like a hot mess.

The crumpled paper slammed to the floor. "Care to explain?"

Keston chuckled darkly. "Even if I wanted to, I typically need to have a thorough understanding of a story to explain it." He nodded to the floor. "As it stands, I know as much as you."

"*Bordel de merde*," Cassius cursed in French, kneading his brow.

"Tell me about it."

Before Keston could scramble to stop him, Cassius burst into Keston's room and threw open the curtains and yanked open the windows. Bright, snow-amplified sunlight washed into the room along with the chilling winter air. Keston could only watch in horror as the light illuminated the only room Warrane had not yet cleaned.

Every inch of nighttime debauchery looked horrific in the morning sun. Discarded pipes and empty bottles littered the room, every surface was slick with suspicious liquid, and the four naked guests stirred awake—some obviously still drunk from their slurred complaints.

Keston was ready to keel over and die.

"All of you, out!" Cassius shouted. His green eyes landed on Sensatia, who quickly scrambled to cover herself in blankets. "You're supposed to meet with General Richards in fifteen minutes."

Sensatia attempted a charming smile through a wince. "Daylight Savings must still be getting the best of me."

Keston's palm met his face. It was December. Daylight Savings was a month ago.

"Out!" Cassius screeched.

All of them hastily threw their clothes on and filed out of the room. Christos flashed Keston a daring smile. "That was great last night. And that thing you did with your tongue—"

"I *really* don't want to hear it," Keston interrupted, almost passing out from his father's withering glare.

The silence of the empty room was excruciating. As Cassius patrolled the crime scene, Keston shuffled back and forth, unsure what to do with himself. But embarrassment flared into panic as his father grabbed the half-full bottle of those strange blue pills from the nightstand.

He frowned, turning the bottle over. "'*To take the edge off*,'" he murmured, reading Hera Richard's note on the side. His eyes met Keston's. "What are you doing with medication from Hera? I thought your immunosuppressant treatment was over."

The immunosuppressants had kept his body from rejecting the numerous implants he'd received a year earlier: upgraded bones, muscles, and even cybernetic connectors piecing his body back together. Thanks to Hera, Keston was now as powerful as a Level Two mutant. Unfortunately, he'd done many terrible things with those new powers, and he wasn't too good at addressing those things.

Welcome to the next level of his treatment: numbing it all.

"New experimental trial."

Please don't take it away.

Suspicion clouded Cassius's eyes. "What *kind* of trial?"

Even Keston hadn't pieced that together. Hera had never technically explained how the strange blue pills worked. When he'd taken the first dose two weeks prior, he'd discovered his metabolism slowed enough for him to feel the effects of alcohol and drugs—the weeks since then had been a blur of euphoria. The strange pills wore off when he slept, allowing his mutant metabolism to wash away the effects. Then he woke up and did it all over again.

"Not certain." He dug his palms into his eyes, still trying to wake up. "All I know is I'm much more fun when I take those things."

Cassius squeezed the prescription vial so hard his knuckles turned white. "You're telling me you took drugs without knowing what they did?"

"Looking at the list of stupid things I've done, that doesn't even scratch the top ten."

"I'm taking these," Cassius concluded, heading for the door.

Keston stumbled forward. "No! Come on, don't take those."

The Lord Advisor abruptly turned with a deep frown. "You're going to be the Reigning Elite of Paris soon. It's time to start acting like it. I will not have my heir ruining our family reputation." He waved the vial, and those beautiful blue pills rattled in the orange plastic. "Especially using something made by Hera."

"At this point, every piece of me is made by Hera. What's the difference?"

Keston debated tackling his father before he left the room—there was no denying the fight would be over in seconds. But he thought better of it. Like it or not, Cassius was responsible for his *and* Genevieve's safety. Even if Keston wasn't on speaking terms with his sister, he couldn't compromise that.

Genevieve's words returned to him from the day he'd woken up in the hospital from his bout of hysteria: *I am truly sorry you were made the villain.*

"Stop thinking about that," Keston hissed to himself.

"What?" Cassius asked with an expression that could almost be described as concern.

"I need those," Keston croaked. "I don't want to think about... everything."

For a split second, he could have sworn he saw his father pause. There was a softness in the Lord Advisor's eyes as he glanced at the bottle. The look was strangely reminiscent of Jaleel—Keston's *actual* father, who was trapped somewhere in Cassius's mind thanks to his dissociative identity disorder mixed with the Serum. It was in split seconds like those that almost drove Keston as mad as his father.

Jaleel was right there, just inches out of his reach.

The look was gone as quickly as it came. Cassius straightened and pocketed the vial. "No Leroy is going to touch something made by Hera—not until I know exactly how it works. Besides, Ascension Day is a week away, and you're supposed to be one of Alvaro Smith's honored guests. You need to be on your best behavior. Do your damn job—you've had enough time to mope."

Alvaro Smith. Ascension Day.

The only reason Alvaro would Ascend to Commander was because Keston had *assassinated* his father, Denzel Smith. Hanging limply from the doorframe, Keston watched his own father walk away with the only thing that'd made life bearable since. Denzel's assassination had started the cascade of terrible events that'd sent Keston's life into an even faster downward spiral than before.

The assassination, Genevieve's supposed kidnapping, the New York massacre, the Siege of Oslo, and Arianne... Arianne was *alive*. She hated him. He'd killed her mother and then abandoned her, just to lead the battle against her people.

Your fault. Your fault. Your fault.

The guilt was crippling. Before he could think any more about Arianne's rage or the feel of her hands closing around his neck, he crawled back into bed and passed out.

His damn job could wait another few days.

Chapter 2

Arianne

"On second thought, this was a terrible idea," Arianne murmured.

Handcuffs snapped into place around her wrists, and the blue, impenetrable light of the cuffs shone up into her face. Arianne took a moment to look around: she was surrounded by Wards, who were escorting her to a specifically sinister Pangaean jet waiting on the tarmac before her.

Arianne and Lova were led into the belly of the jet. She had to suppress her nerves as she exchanged a silent look with her mission partner and friend. No matter how dire the situation, she needed to be professional. This was her first mission as the leader of her team of Champions. She wouldn't fail–even if it looked like she was well on her way there. She looked up as she was dragged deeper into the jet, just in time to see a particularly thin Ward disappear into the cockpit.

The cockpit that had access to the Pangaean intranet.

Time for phase two: the part where Arianne put on a show.

The gangplank door closed behind them, the faint hum followed by the dimming of the outside light. Arianne was left in the shadows of the small hallway, her and Lova's cuffs glowing blue in the sudden darkness. The distinct weightlessness of the jet taking off caused her stomach to drop as they gained altitude. No going back. A pair of hands shoved them into the main cabin, and they fell forward on their knees—just helpless savages.

Arianne smirked to herself as one of the Wards guffawed. Let them assume defeat. She'd dealt with far worse.

The main cabin was more luxurious than the ones Arianne had known in Pacific: windows taking up the entire ceiling, leather couches, and even a furnished mini-bar. But she'd expected that. A luxurious jet meant a Pangaean Officer governed it, and Officers had access to more juicy intel to steal.

"Sir! We brought the savages," said the Ward posted at Arianne's side. He saluted before giving her a swift kick to the ribs.

It was almost impossible to suppress her gasp of pain as the air left her lungs. She stared with narrowed eyes at the floor, fighting to suppress the destructive urge to snap the Ward's leg off.

Not yet. One alarm and we're in bigger trouble than we already are.

The Officer rested on a cream leather couch. His bright red cape splayed around him like a pool of blood. He was older with a trimmed white beard. A glass of amber liquid swirled in his hand—celebrating too soon. His dark eyes roved over his fresh catches. "You know, I fought in the Selvian War," he hummed in a thick northern European accent. "I didn't think they would be dumb enough to try again."

"Seeing as we've conquered all of Norway in two weeks, I don't think we're the stupid ones," Arianne laughed, making sure to use her best Selvian accent possible.

The Officer's upper lip curled. He stood and walked in her direction, his shining boots making deliberate thumps on the floor with each slow step forward. Arianne glared at him, hoping her painted face put an ounce of fear in his heart. But apathy, not fear, dominated his face as he stopped in front of her kneeling form. With a frown, he tipped his glass and poured the remaining contents over Arianne's head.

White hot rage burst to life inside her, like thousands of needles stabbing out of her stomach. Her jaw clenched as she stared through the droplets of liquor falling down her face. Her body shook as something more sinister than anger stirred. Her fingers curled, and a growl emanated in her chest—

Lova's tail swept once over her backside, cooling her fury just enough to quell the growing explosion.

"Oh, I'm certain you think highly of yourselves for taking the Old Norway territories," the Officer sneered. "But let me tell you something: as reigning Officer of Stockholm, your little rebellion ends here. Did you think I wouldn't expect savage scouts in my city?"

"You'll have to try harder than just pouring liquor on my head to make your death memorable to me."

"And you'll have to do a better job at hiding your savage friends."

The Officer nodded to the Wards at his side, and they lunged at the large officer behind Arianne. Rhino, hidden in a Ward's uniform, cried out in surprise as three Wards overpowered him and threw him to the ground. The jet shook with the impact and Rhino's bellow of outrage. At the same time, the Officer pointed a blaster at Lova's head. Rhino—despite his size advantage—stopped his struggle.

Arianne gritted her teeth, her element of surprise crumbling. *Come on,* she prayed silently, *any time now.*

The Officer smiled down at his three captives. "Now, we only need one of you to interrogate. Which one should I take?" His dark eyes settled on Lova with interest. He kneeled and lifted her chin with a finger. "Aren't you a stunning little *Fera*? You'll make a great addition to my collection."

Lova bared her elongated canines.

"How about you back the fuck up," Rhino rumbled.

The Officer didn't take his eyes off Lova as his hand slid to his hip. "Do you know what I do to people who interrupt me?"

Rhino scowled. "You'll have to enlighten me."

The Officer aimed his blaster at Rhino's temple.

Lova lunged forward, biting hard on the man's hand. Blood splattered. The Officer cried out in surprise. The blaster fired, piercing a hole in one of the other Wards. Screaming echoed off the walls of the jet. As the other Wards scrambled for their weapons, Arianne took a deep breath and accepted that the mission was about to take a nosedive.

She hadn't meant that *literally*, but the universe had other plans.

"Attention, passengers, this is *not* your captain speaking," came Blue's voice over the jet's intercom. Miraculously, the cabin paused to listen in confusion—everyone in various stages of bloodlust and weapon-drawing. "It looks like we're about to experience some turbulence. So, if you could sit down, buckle up, and quit shooting my friends, that would be greatly appreciated!"

And then the jet went into a nosedive.

Every passenger released a collective scream as they became weightless, carried to the back of the cabin as they plummeted. Arianne, used to the feeling of her stomach rising to her throat, recovered fastest. Adjusting her body, she kicked her legs toward the back wall, gathered her strength, and pushed to the nearest Ward. The woman was too busy panicking to see the attack. Hands still bound, Arianne lunged head-first, hammering her forehead into the woman's temple.

The jet's automatic adjustment systems came online, righting the aircraft just enough to slow their crash landing, but it wasn't enough to reverse whatever setting Blue had put in place. They still plummeted, albeit slower. Everyone else tumbled on their hands and knees at the rapid change of momentum. The *Feras* recovered faster than the Wards, jumping up and continuing the attack.

Blue snuck out of the cockpit, mask removed and a wry smirk on full display. Arianne intercepted her by the emergency exit. "You call this turbulence?" she demanded.

Blue pulled on the exit door. "I call it giving you a window. Now help me open this." She freed Arianne's wrists with a key card.

With one hand holding the inside of the jet and the other opening the exit hatch, they finally unleashed the lever. The door went flying into the sky beyond. The ripping wind pulled at Arianne's braids, but she lingered long enough to see another jet hover next to them. Topher leaned out of the open gangplank, an arrow attached to a rope and ready to fire.

"Do you have the data?" Arianne asked.

Blue nodded, pointedly stuffing a flash drive into her bra beneath her combat leathers.

"Go, I got the others," Arianne ordered.

Onto phase three: escape.

Topher fired, his perfect aim striking home right next to the exit hatch and connecting the two jets by a rope. With a Ward-issue nightstick, Blue sucked in a breath and jumped into the open air. Stringing the nightstick over the rope, she slid down the impromptu zipline to the safety of the other jet.

With the information secured, Arianne focused on friend retrieval like the only sober participant on a night out.

Even with the reduced angle of their crash landing, the other cabin members struggled to maintain balance. The fight was more reminiscent of a scramble than any form of combat.

"Rhino, Blitz! Exit! Now!" Arianne screamed over the wind and the blaring low altitude alarms.

Lova struggled for a moment to pull herself out of the scramble with her hands still bound, but her feline grace made up for the lost balance. A Ward tried to crawl after her, but Arianne smashed a boot downward on his head. She grinned as his skull crushed like a pumpkin.

Her maniacal smile faded when she heard blaster fire, followed by Rhino's cry. The jet shuddered as he fell, an ugly flash of red splattering on the side of his temple. Arianne's eyes found the silver-bearded Officer, braced behind a leather couch with his blaster still trained on Rhino. He met Arianne's gaze with a broad smile.

And then she saw *red*.

He fired again, and its scorching plasma burned an ugly wound into her shoulder. But she didn't feel a thing. Instinct allowed her to close the final few feet before he could fire a third time. The otherworldly calmness made the world move in slow motion, and Arianne sighed with euphoria. She hardly felt the downward tilt of the jet anymore. All she felt was rage and desire.

Arianne pinned the Officer against the wall by his neck, her hand squeezing his soft flesh as her fingers broke through the wall behind him to hold him in place. He was easily two hundred pounds, but he felt like little more than a picture frame she was nailing to the wall. Struggling below her, his breath came out in ragged gasps as his pupils narrowed to pinpoints.

There it is. There's the fear.

The Officer grabbed at her hand, his fingers clawing at her wrist as his eyes bugged. She watched in silent satisfaction as his oxygen-deprived skin turned purple.

"*Who's the stupid one now?*"

"Phoenix!" Rhino wheezed.

She didn't hear. Squeezing harder, she savored the salty-sweet scent of fear. The Officer kicked and wheezed, desperate and terrified. But he didn't scream. How could he? She'd crushed his windpipe.

"*You called us savages. I'll give you savage.*"

"Phoenix!" Weaker, Rhino said, "Arianne, help..."

At the sound of her name, the world returned to focus. The Officer slackened in her hand. She almost buckled as the pain from the blaster wound in her shoulder returned. Dropping the Officer, she turned toward her friend, who was still on the ground, ear bleeding and face contorted in pain. Her throat closed up.

The jet's alarms were insistent now. One look out the window showed they could only be a couple of thousand feet in the air.

Arianne lunged toward Rhino, lamenting Instinct's strength as she helped him stand. He leaned on her heavily, struggling to stay upright. From the look of his bloodied right ear, she could only assume the blaster had damaged his vestibule, which controlled his balance—the jet's nosedive wasn't helping. Though Arianne was patient as she guided him to the exit, her heart thundered in her chest.

Every second they delayed was a second closer to the ground.

"Come on!" Topher screamed over the ripping air currents. "We're running out of time!"

As long as that rope bound the two jets, their escape craft would continue to nosedive at that same life-threatening speed.

"Rhino, you need to jump."

"Systems down for the count, Ari," he slurred.

Arianne's anxiety was a living thing threatening to crawl out of her ribcage. She ripped the arrow with the rope out of the jet. The ground was dangerously close now. She didn't need raptor eyesight to make out individual branches on the trees. Shaking, she shoved Rhino's large hands around her nightstick, connecting him to the rope. She swallowed hard.

They didn't have time for him to slide across.

Only one idea remained.

"Satyr, hold on tight! Tell them to gain altitude! *Now!*"

Without another moment to overthink her Hail Mary of a plan, Arianne shoved Rhino out of the crash-landing jet. The second they hit open air, she unfurled her wings and shot up with every last bit of her strength. The line she held with Rhino pulled taught, and her shoulders screamed in protest as she flew upward despite his weight.

With Arianne clutching one end of the rope and the other end tied to the escape craft, they hauled Rhino out of the crashing Pangaean jet. Her mouth went dry as it smashed into the trees below, erupting in an angry plume of smoke and fire. Rhino dangled on that perilously thin rope between herself and the escape jet, his grip dangerously light.

"Satyr!" Arianne strained, her wings screaming at her with effort. "Tell Pharaoh to drop the jet!"

"What?"

"Drop the goddamn jet!"

The escape craft lowered a dozen feet below her, and she sagged in relief. Rhino slid down the last stretch of the rope and onto the open gangplank, where the others pulled him on board. Arianne tumbled after him and collapsed against the wall, shoulder throbbing.

Her team devolved into a screaming match.

"Maybe a warning next time?" Khari demanded, crashing in from the cockpit.

Blue pointed a threatening finger. "*You* don't get to say shit after the stunt you pulled in Oslo."

Cloven hooves clanking on the metal, Topher paced back and forth. "The jet was supposed to be *stable*. Do you know how hard it is to hit an accelerating target?"

"Things don't always go as planned," Blue said, defensive.

"So you decided to test if we can survive a thirty-five-thousand-foot drop?" Topher barked.

From the ground, Rhino moaned. "I'm durable, but not that durable."

"People started blasting," Blue argued, yellow eyes blazing. "We needed to destroy the evidence of involvement. I didn't have many options."

"All right, all right!" Arianne shouted, halting the cacophony of arguments. "We barely survived—let's not kill each other now."

With one last eye roll and a grumble, Khari disappeared into the cockpit to navigate back to Moon Warren. Lova rushed to Rhino's side, her clawed hands reaching toward his bloodied ear.

As the tensions settled, Arianne banged her head against the wall, blaming herself for everything.

She hadn't taken control. In fact, she'd *lost* control of herself. Arianne stared forward, the noise of the engine fading as she thought back to those last minutes on the jet and the rush she'd felt at the Officer's life fading in her arms. Her stomach flopped like she was back in freefall, eyes focusing on the large figure on the ground before her.

Rhino, her oldest friend, almost died because she'd lost control.

Arianne wrung out her wrist, fighting to eliminate the sensation of the Officer's neck in her hand. Bile rose in her throat.

One hell of a first mission as a leader.

Sure, they got the data they'd come for and destroyed the evidence in the crash, but that was hardly a clean success. Two teammates were injured, including herself. Almost three casualties, including herself. That was hardly a stellar performance.

Sygrid was going to kill her—after she lectured her about her lackluster self-preservation skills. Guess Arianne hadn't learned from the last three lectures she'd received.

Chapter 3
Andre

"I don't like it." Vice President Kalfas, former Pacifican General, frowned into the laboratory-turned-prison cell. His olive eyes narrowed in suspicion.

Andre joined him at the mezzanine railing that looked down into the lab. Everything in the laboratory had been emptied, with thick security detail posted along every possible exit. His long fingers curled around the railing's cool metal as he followed Kalfas's gaze to the examination table bathed in bright white light. And resting on that chilling table, in a medical coma monitored by Kalinda and Dr. Ike, was Pandora.

Technicians Officer Haris Cadmilus worked diligently at Pandora's bedside, his square-rimmed glasses glinting in the examination light. His fingers were a fury on his laptop, which was connected to Pandora's head by a series of wires. Haris had been trying to hack into the network embedded in her skull for three hours. No luck.

Major Jaya Bahri watched from Kalfas's other side, her skin a light shade of blue in anticipation. When Kalfas ordered Kalinda to participate in the procedure—she was already privy to much of Pacific's classified information—Jaya almost outright refused. But even Andre knew she'd never disobey an order from a superior, especially from Kalfas.

That didn't mean Jaya was happy about her sister being so close to Pandora Richards.

"I don't like it either," Jaya mumbled. "There's no way the deadliest human in the world just surrenders herself to Pacific."

Andre fought to keep his face neutral. He'd told no one about his meeting with Ace the week before—he was still processing everything. Chiefly, he still hadn't decided if he believed a word the Underground Queen had said.

Despite his apprehension, he couldn't get the picture of Roulette's round face out of his mind. Could she be his daughter? He was still waiting for the blood tests.

"Andre," Kalfas said, stern voice breaking through his thoughts. "You grew up with Pandora. Is there any reason why she would hand herself in?"

Pandora goes where she wants to go. If you're not concerned, then it's too late.

Andre could've said that the only reason the Richards heir was anywhere near Nassau was because she was a peace offering. But he held his tongue. His relations with the rebellious remainder of Pacific were tenuous at best, and word that he'd had contact with two representatives of its enemies wouldn't be good for his reputation.

It wasn't like he'd agreed to any craziness Ace and Pandora tried to throw his way. Yet.

"Growing up, Pandora was put under a lot of pressure, being an illegitimate daughter of Leon," Andre recalled. "Whenever she failed a test or a mission, she would disappear for a week. When she returned, there was always a part of her that was... different. Hera hated failure, so every time Pandora lost, her mother would modify another part of her until she was perfect."

Andre stared forward, his haunting memories of the labs beneath the Murray Monument coming back in chilling flashes. "Pandora lost a critical battle when the Norwegian tribes laid siege to Oslo. Knowing Hera, I would run too."

The only reason Pandora would cooperate with Ace was if she didn't want to go home. Even if that meant she was running from one laboratory to another. It wasn't a stretch to assume Pacific's researchers would be far kinder to her than Hera.

Andre studied the cyborg below. Her bleach-blonde hair had been shaved off for better access to her skull. Her bald head now shone pristinely in the light. Her eyes, though open, were gray instead of their typical glowing turquoise, looking like an unplugged neon sign. A prickle of guilt gnawed at him for the girl he'd once believed was his sister. In her skintight test suit, picked-apart cybernetic arm, and wires connected to her head, Pandora looked more like a decommissioned Puppet than a woman.

Granted, a ticking time bomb might be the best description.

"Last time Leon sent one of his children to Pacific, it was to take us down." Jaya's untrusting, fluorite eyes bored into Andre. "Even if they were a sleeper agent."

Again, Andre kept quiet. If his relationship with the Pacificans was tenuous, his relationship with Jaya was volatile. She didn't trust him. He wasn't a fan of how she'd abandoned Arianne in her last months of life. Unfortunately, they both cared about Kalinda, so they were stuck in hesitant co-existence.

Calling on his practiced skill of calmly ignoring people he didn't like talking to, Andre turned his head away, directing his attention back to the laboratory floor. "Fortunately, as long as Pandora's unconscious, she's not a problem."

Kalfas nodded. "Haris is having trouble breaking through the Pandora's Box coding that allows her to talk to Puppets, but he did manage to turn off her location tracker and external communication. We can't see what's happening in Pangaea, but they can't see us either."

"I'm glad we learned from last time," Jaya said, with another pointed look at Andre, eyes roving down to his inner wrist.

He massaged the scar he'd received from the removal of his subdermal tracker. Another stab of guilt made his insides flop. Thanks to a tracking device planted unknowingly in his wrist, he'd led Leon right to Citadel nearly a year ago. Jaya was right to blame him. He blamed himself. There were still nights he lay awake with memories of that damaging MRI scan that revealed his unwitting betrayal.

Still, fuck Jaya for bringing it up. She didn't know him—she didn't try to know him.

Not like Kalinda. Kalinda was patient, understanding, and the complete opposite of her sister. On nights when the sounds of the Pacific Hospital collapsing on Arianne startled him from his sleep, she was there to soothe him. He couldn't stop a soft smile from growing on his face as he stared down at the nurse decked in navy surgical scrubs positioned below, monitoring Pandora's vitals.

"Technicians Officer Cadmilus!" Kalfas called. "How much juice do you have left?"

Haris looked up, his fine quilled hair bouncing softly at the sudden movement. "I'm pretty certain I've lost feeling in my fingers, sir."

"All right, get the cyborg into the stasis chamber. We'll call it for the day."

A set of Pacifican soldiers filed around Pandora's examination table, carefully moving her as Kalinda unhooked the wires and IV lines. A steel pod looking strangely like a one-man sauna waited just feet away. The soldiers loaded Pandora inside the chamber and closed the hatch. Her sleeping face was visible through the small glass window for a few moments before it fogged over.

"You never told me why you have a stasis chamber," Andre said slowly, hating his own guilt.

Kalfas's face took on a haunted sheen as he gripped the railings before him. "For Arianne."

Jaya swayed. "Arianne?"

The Vice President pursed his lips. "We noticed it when she was a child and still recovering her memories. I've never seen anything like it. Her eyes would pool to black like she was going feral, and she would become as powerful as a fully grown *Fera*. We knew we needed a failsafe—especially as her abilities grew."

"Instinct," Andre remembered. "It was a result of her dual mutations—if I remember Hera correctly. Her sect of scientists hypothesized that when Arianne fully matured, she had the potential to be the most powerful being on the planet. That's why Leon was obsessed with turning her into his weapon."

His teeth clenched as an uncomfortable concoction of guilt, grief, and anger bubbled inside of him. He hated that he'd been jealous of a tortured girl. He hated that his sister had been reduced to a weapon. Most of all, he hated that he was thinking about her in the past tense.

Arianne spent her life surrounded by fear—fear of her secrets, fear for her life, and weathering the fear others felt for her. And then she died while drowning in all those fears at once. It wasn't fair.

Kalfas's strangely gravelly voice broke the tense silence. "She did turn into a weapon—and Leon killed her when he realized he couldn't control it." His eyes burned with morbid finality. "No one could control her in those final months, and she hadn't even grown into her full power yet."

The conversation stalled, and Andre could only assume they were all thinking about the trail of destruction Arianne had caused in her last months alive.

"Don't say it," Jaya choked.

"I miss Arianne as much as both of you," Kalfas breathed. "But there was a reason we didn't tell her about her potential. There was a reason we kept her on Citadel. If she grew into those powers—and still found no interest in being controlled—Ancestors save us."

Chapter 4

Arianne

A small army of Wards stood outside Dara Cave.

Arianne and Khari slowed when they spotted the squadron of Pangaeans dressed in inky black and red skirts, armed to the teeth. The skirts notified her the squadron was from Africa, their allies, but worry still pricked her gut. Wards in Moon Warren were never good, no matter which Commander they worshipped. Whatever conversation awaited her and Khari in that cave was not one she had the energy for. From the crackle of energy at Khari's fingertips, he felt the same.

The frontmost Ward stepped in front of Arianne's path into the cave. She was an Amazon of a woman with corded muscles and dark skin. She gave Arianne a severe frown. "No one enters this cave without Commander Sarr's permission."

So Commander Kajari Sarr was here. Annoyance bubbled, exacerbated by Arianne's exhaustion. "Do you know who the fuck I am?"

"I don't care."

Arianne barred her teeth and prepared to strike, but Khari stepped in front of her. "Zuri," he said sharply. "Stand down. Phoenix is a Champion of Selvia and Strix's apprentice."

After another charged glare, Zuri stepped back with a respectful nod. Arianne didn't pay her any mind as she strutted past.

She hated Wards.

"You didn't have to step in for me," Arianne grumbled as they ducked into the cave. Now she had three reasons to be pissed: subpar mission, an unwelcome meeting with a Commander, and *Khari* had to fix her problems.

"I was just trying to help."

"The only way you could help is if you tell your father to get the hell out of our village."

Moon Warren had become her safe space. A home disconnected from the world, where she could decompress after months of fighting the growing global tensions. And now those global tensions had just invaded that space. She didn't like it one bit. With an annoyed hiss, she sped off into the complex systems of underground tunnels and away from Khari.

Might as well get that day from hell over with.

The set of deer antlers above the Dara Cave's entrance cast drastic lines of light and shadow across the floor from undying torches—the symbol of tribal leadership. Every tribe's Ductor created a crown of ivory in honor of their progenitor, Cervi, who'd borne the antlers of a stag.

Looking at them still felt strange. They reminded Arianne of how much Selvia had lost, and how things would never be the same again. It was haunting to think about how many secrets hid in those walls. War-starting secrets. Empire-ending secrets.

So many people had already died. How many more would she lose? And Commander Sarr's presence only warned of conflict on a grander scale to come.

The Commander of Africa stood against the cave's majestic stalagmite backdrop. He looked slightly out of place. Rather than regal skirts and jewels like a god of gold, he wore a modern Pangaean style: a dark trench coat and burgundy three-piece suit. Even Kajari's graying dreadlocks, which he usually kept down and adorned with jewels, were tied back in a simple knot atop his head.

"I smell blood. Care to explain why you were wounded on a *covert* mission, Arianne?"

Without the entire tribe packed inside, the Dara Cave's dome-like structure was cavernous, so the voice echoed off the stone with bone-rattling power. The source came from the island in the pond on the far side of the cave. Though barren for winter, the oak tree in the middle was as magnificent as ever, with its vast network of twisting branches reaching to the skylight above—their tribe's Dara, representing strength, family, and preservation.

The white-haired figure rose from her meditation beneath the Dara, her stunning wings unfurling as she flew toward her apprentice. Strix—Ductor of the Selvian Tribe, the Silent Death, and leader of the tribal rebellion—landed before them. It'd taken a couple of weeks for her to embrace her new role as Ductor, but now she wore the ivory crown with pride. To most, she was a Legend; to Arianne, she was simply Sygrid.

Sygrid reached out to Arianne's wound. "I did smell blood." She shook her silver head. "Why are you here? You should be getting treated."

"Ringtail told us to meet at Dara Cave when we got back from our mission," Khari said.

Arianne ignored her mentor's fussing. "We have an important guest," she said with a pointed look toward the Commander. When Sygrid continued her motherly inspection, Arianne pushed her hand away.

"Since all parties are present, it's time for a meeting," Commander Sarr announced, hands folding regally behind his back.

Sygrid straightened, the cold she reserved for leadership freezing over her orange eyes that'd burned with warmth just moments ago. "Come, we can meet in my private quarters."

Only tribal leadership resided in the Dara Cave. As Deputy, Sygrid had opted to live in a treehouse closer to the sky. But as Ductor, she'd moved to the cave. The tribe's Lyre and Master of Stories and Ceremonies, Saga, also lived somewhere in those tunnels—her music echoing through chambers from time to time. Ringtail's quarters were there, but he was too secretive for Arianne to know where they were.

It was rumored that only Sygrid and a handful of other Champions even knew Ringtail's birth name.

Cervi's distinctive evergreen-and-soil scent struck Arianne the moment she entered Sygrid's quarters. Even after weeks, the space still carried the presence of the female who'd called it home for over a century. The Ductor's cave was comfortably worn and lived-in—a fire pit burned in the center, moss and lichen crept along the walls, and clusters of bioluminescent mushrooms added a soft light outside the hearth. At the back, a raised platform held a bed and a lounging area, layered with colorful blankets and pillows.

Safe. The Ductor's quarters felt safe.

Sygrid's face was grim as she gestured for everyone to sit around the central fire. "Make yourselves comfortable." She lit an incense stick. "Or as comfortable as we can be discussing a subject like this."

For the thousandth time that day, Arianne's adrenaline spiked.

She *hated* it when Sygrid spoke like that.

The Commander let out a long breath. "Slavery is legal in both Europe and Asia. Pacific is drowned. Cartel is under new leadership. A new Commander is to Ascend in North America. Cervi is dead. The Librarians are dead—their knowledge supposedly hidden within the Leroy girl. And now a rebellion led by the ancient Selvian Tribe marches through northern Europe."

Staring into the fire, Sygrid's eyes reflected the flickering flames. "Congratulations, Commander Sarr. You've summarized our current predicament well."

"Predicament?" he demanded. "We're one diplomatic incident away from a world war. We're talking about a crisis unlike anything Pangaea has ever seen."

"You must know that was always Cervi's plan. Don't tell me you chose to ally yourself with us without knowing these tensions would eventually devolve."

The Commander tensely cracked his knuckles. "I was hoping we could find a path to *Fera* acceptance that didn't involve global conflict."

Arianne laughed. "When did you realize that would never happen? Before or after my father decimated Selvia to a tenth of its population? What about the economy? Did you think Europe and Asia would *willingly* shut down their most lucrative market?" She scoffed, uncaring that a Commander—a god—glared at her. "I thought the Serum was supposed to make you smart."

"What Arianne means to say," Sygrid said, shooting her a look, "is that history repeats itself. Cervi witnessed it once. While I'd love to believe we could do this without conflict, I've come to see we don't have a choice." She shook her head. "Even if I wanted to, it's too late to stop now. We've attacked Oslo—wheels have been set in motion."

Khari lowered his head. Ultimately, it was his former mentor who initiated the attack. For better or for worse, Selvia was at war, and Sygrid was forced to navigate it.

"This Leroy girl, Genevieve," the Commander hedged. "She's supposed to have unparalleled knowledge. Maybe she knows a way without war."

Sygrid lifted her palms in a slight shrug. "I don't know what she knows, but we can't risk retrieving her. If we capture her, we either escalate the conflict or reveal that she's more important than she seems."

The Commander stared into the fire for a long time, his handsome face so still he could've been a statue. It was strange to be able to watch a Commander with so much unflinching interest—Arianne had never been able to stare at her father like that. How did the Commanders think? How did the Serum change their brains? Did they see the world through a Serum-induced lens?

He finally spoke. "I've played out the variables in my head many times. Whether we start a world war or find a way to isolate this conflict in Europe, there is one thing we can do to stabilize our position and mitigate risk in eighty-five percent of my projected potential outcomes."

Straightening, Sygrid tilted her chin in distaste. "You know my opinion."

"And you know Cervi was the one to propose it," the Commander countered. "You claim unyielding loyalty to her in one breath and reject her plans in the next. What is it, O' Great Strix? Are Cervi's words scripture only when you want to follow them?"

The tension in the room grew warmer, and Arianne glanced at Khari in question. His blue eyes met hers with a subtle shrug. She frowned—both heirs were in the dark.

"It's too soon to play that card." Sygrid's curled lip was a warning that she was near the end of her saint-like patience.

With a daring smile that displayed striking white teeth, the Commander leaned forward. "Ascension Day is in one week. Every major player will be in Mexico City vying for the new Commander's favor. You don't need the Serum to see that a world war could be initiated or delayed based on the events of that day. This is the *only* card we can play to mitigate risk and shield us against potential chaos."

"She's not ready," Sygrid snapped.

All eyes in the cave turned to Arianne. Her mouth dried out. "Ready for what?"

After a long breath, Sygrid steadied herself from her outburst. She walked to the back of her quarters and returned carrying a beautiful red dress with the reverence a priest would have for a relic. She sat back down in silence, expression full of longing as her fingers ran along the smooth fabric.

"This was my Mating Ceremony dress. '*Red is for love, the connection of two,*'" Sygrid whispered, voice cracking at the end. "Dancing with Erik in this dress on our Mating Day is one of my fondest memories."

Arianne reached out and squeezed her hand.

Sygrid stared back at her, the warmth in her gaze making Arianne's heart flutter. There was a time when the only thing she'd seen in her mentor's eyes had been annoyance and contempt. Only over months of thawing each other's frozen hearts had they learned they both craved one thing: love. Not love to replace what was lost, but love strong enough to promise light after so much darkness.

"You don't have to do this if you don't want to," said Sygrid.

"Do what?"

It was Kajari, not Sygrid, who filled the heavy silence. The Commander cleared his throat. "Africa and the tribes must form a bridge. They must be a united front to deter conflict and guarantee protection. This solution is the only way to ensure this connection. To protect Selvia if they lose and protect my family if Pangaea retaliates against me, or if *Feras* win this conflict and turn on Commanders like me."

Khari's eyes widened with realization. "Father—"

"The bond is *sacred*," Sygrid spat, clutching her dress to her chest. "I will not defile it for human politics."

"Human politics may determine whether or not the world believes your people continue to have human *rights*," the Commander shot back.

His words were a shock—not just what he said, but how he said it. There was genuine fear there. Fear that, win or lose, they could all face ugly consequences. She turned to Sygrid and saw an emotion equally as powerful as fear plastered on her face: heartbreak. The dueling potent emotions backed Arianne into a corner, making her feel weighed down and claustrophobic.

Two very powerful people were very wary of whatever decision Arianne had in front of her.

With a cautious look at Sygrid, Arianne turned back to the Commander. "And how did you and Cervi propose we make this bridge?"

"You will be betrothed to Khari," he responded, as simply as if he were ordering at a restaurant.

"*What.*" Arianne's eyes shot to Khari, but his gaze was unfocused as he stared at the ground.

"Think about it!" The Commander stood and extended his arms majestically. "Arianne Murray, princess of Europe. Khari Sarr, prince of Africa. Two powerful *Feras*, two powerful *warriors*, people can unite behind. A pairing that the world would have to take seriously. If we lose, Selvia can be protected in Africa with your union. If we win, Arianne will Ascend as Commander with a pro-mutant heir as her husband. No matter the outcome, we'll better our chances with the two of you united."

Arianne's jaw hung open.

Hauntingly quiet during Kajari's impassioned speech, Sygrid's shaking voice broke the silence. "He's looking at this like you're models on a board—not actual people." The Ductor looked between her young Champions, a dark cloud of uncertainty settling around her. "You would both give up your chance to love the person of your choice. And that's not even the worst of it."

"We would be lying about being mates," Khari whispered.

The typically unaffected prince looked mortified.

"The tribes don't recognize marriages." Sygrid frowned at the Commander. "Arianne and Khari can't simply fake it like you can with humans. They would have to convince the tribal world they're mated."

Khari still refused to look up. "A mating bond is sacred. If people ever discovered we were lying—"

"Social suicide is putting it lightly," Arianne finished, suddenly feeling very cold despite the fire.

"And since there's no royalty in the tribes, Arianne would have to become my Deputy." Sygrid's hands flexed in dismay. "Which is a burden I don't want to thrust on her yet."

Arianne knew she was speaking from experience.

The Commander shook his head, seemingly confused as to why everyone else in that cave was frightened at the idea. "This has been the plan for quite a while," he said. "Arianne becomes the Heir of Ivory, the Deputy of Selvia. She gets betrothed to my son. Africa stands behind him, and the tribes stand behind Arianne. They become the most powerful pairing in the world—untouchable. If Europe doesn't back down, we set ourselves up nicely to weather the storm."

Khari raised his head for the first time since realizing his father's plans. If losing his respect in Selvia's social circles after Cavalier's betrayal hadn't snapped his confidence, this impossible choice certainly had. Arianne held his gaze, feeling every ounce of confusion and hopelessness reflected in herself.

"This was the plan all along," she numbly repeated, hugging herself. "That's why Cervi was molding me into a leader. That's why she let me come here in the first place."

The coldness inside her grew. Cervi never lied to her. She'd always said Arianne would have a more significant part to play. But was it so wrong to want to be wanted for *her*, not her blood? For so long, she'd believed she'd finally found a home that valued her happiness and healing.

It was painfully evident that she'd always been just another princess pawn.

With a squeeze on her knee, Sygrid pulled her out of her darkening thoughts. The Ductor's familiar voice steadied her with its tranquil power. "I will *not* force this on you. Your worth is far more than your blood. It's wrong to ask you to give up your chance to find someone you love, or expose your existence to the world when you've found peace in hiding."

"But," Arianne said, looking at Khari again, "if we don't..."

Will people die? Will we lose the war?

The questions she was too terrified to ask hung in the air. Could she be so selfish as to say no? What was one life over millions, maybe billions? What was her life worth—one she'd been so content to throw away a year before?

Sygrid shook her shoulders, forcing their gazes together. "It's too soon. You don't have to make a decision now—or *ever*. You deserve to heal in peace. You deserve to gain your footing in the tribe before we thrust leadership of it on you. Most of all you," she said, turning to smile at Khari, "both of you, deserve to be with someone you love. Whether they're a mate or simply a life partner."

"We should make this decision before the Ascension Ceremony," the Commander insisted.

"Give them some time," Sygrid growled at him. "I will not rush a decision that lasts a lifetime."

A lifetime... Arianne sucked in a breath as the room began to spin around her.

The Commander seemed displeased at the Selvians' hesitation. He marched toward the arching cave exit and waved, unamused. "War isn't a fairytale. In real life, the princess marries the prince because the prince has armies, not because they have butterflies in their stomachs. You know how to reach me when you decide."

Arianne watched Commander Sarr leave. Her stress headache, anxious churning stomach, and still-throbbing shoulder wound combined to make her want to pass out. On paper, she agreed with everything Kajari had said. But why was every part of her rejecting the idea? She was terrified, confused, conflicted, and ultimately resigned.

What did it make her if she chose herself over the alliance? Selfish. Really fucking selfish.

She'd always believed power meant freedom. It was funny how, to become part of the most powerful pairing in the world, she would have to give up her freedom.

On days like those, she regretted ever letting Ringtail pull her out of that riverbed a year before.

Chapter 5

Keston

"We should cut his hair," his stylist muttered to Sensatia, who was overseeing Keston's interview preparation. "It's getting quite long and not exactly the popular style. People might say he looks unkempt."

Keston scowled at the stylist. "You touch my hair, and I cut off something far more important to you," he said before Sensatia could respond.

He got an ounce of pleasure from watching his stylist pale in the mirror.

Keston's eyes drifted to his reflection. He rarely did that anymore. He hated what stared back—hated seeing what Pangaea turned him into. Fortunately, that time, he saw that he'd reclaimed a fraction of his old self, even if it was frowned upon by everyone around him.

Thanks to Hera's modifications, his hair was still black, but it was back to the length he'd favored in Cartel. Though the strands were not quite as long as they were in Greece, the feeling of his hair curling around his ears again was comforting.

A pink scar also slashed across his left cheek and through the bridge of his nose—a remnant of the wound from Arianne during the Siege of Oslo. The stinging pain and the drops of blood had been what woke him up, what'd made him realize she was *alive*. That wound had changed everything for him.

In the days following the battle, Keston picked at the scabs that formed over the wound until even his mutant healing couldn't stop the scar. When he looked at his face, he didn't see perfection; he saw a small reminder of his old self: vile, broken, and in love with a female he could *never* have. That scar was what he deserved—what he needed. He'd started feeling like himself again.

He still felt like shit, but at least he felt like shit as *himself*.

His stylist settled on tying the top of his hair back, allowing the lower strands to curl around his neck. After a few layers of makeup, she'd covered his scar and added extra color to his face, still pallid from weeks of partying. Looking at himself in his suit, cape, and makeup, he was disappointed that he couldn't recognize his reflection again.

He glanced at the mirror one last time on the way out of the dressing room to ensure his smile looked genuine. The stage lights struck him with their humming intensity as he made his entrance to the simple set of two chairs with a small table in between. He almost wished he'd worn sunglasses.

Sensatia bounced up. While she'd become the head of media in Leon's Inner Circle in the past year, the public still knew her as Sensatia Wolfe: star journalist and reporter. Most would consider a manager interviewing their client a conflict of interest.

Leon saw it as a perfect way to control the narrative.

"Welcome, Keston Leroy!" Sensatia shook his hand with impressive grace in her six-inch heels and extremely tight pantskirt. "Thank you so much for making time for another *European Exclusive!*"

"I can always make time for you," Keston purred, even if flirting with her on live television was the last thing he wanted to do.

After the photos of his night in Paris got out, Cassius and Leon decided to play into the sensational rumors.

For some reason, he sorely hoped Arianne wasn't watching. His stomach flipped at the thought. He almost lost his composure. *I am not supposed to be thinking like that.* But the more he scolded himself, the more the idea of Arianne—who already wanted him dead—seeing him with Sensatia clouded his thoughts.

"So, Keston!" She clapped her hands together, yanking him from his daze. "It's been a year since you came into the public spotlight. I thought a recap of your journey to stardom would be interesting."

They settled into the plush chairs, and he fought down a grimace as the narrow back squeezed his wings. "It's certainly been an interesting year," he chided.

"Modeling deals, named the most eligible bachelor below thirty, your own world tour, and a heroic survival story during the Siege of Oslo. Interesting is an understatement! It's a year for the record books."

The chaos of the past four months flashed across his mind in excruciating detail. Denzel Smith dying below him as Alvaro watched. The countless bodies that Pandora's Bubblegum Battalion left behind during the raid *he'd* sanctioned in New York. The Siege of Oslo. The horde of tribespeople rushing into the city. The falling skyscraper, brought down by his hand, and countless people crying out in pain as he assaulted them with his sonic voice at Pandora's abomination of a concert.

Arianne, with death in her eyes, slowly squeezing his life out...

"Keston?"

Sensatia's prompting drew him back to the interview for the second time. He shook his head, knowing he was dangerously off his game. With an awkward chuckle, he rubbed the back of his neck and smiled. "Sorry, I'm just exhausted, that's all."

That's an understatement.

"How do you juggle it all?" The reporter leaned forward. "The concerts, your family, and—need I say—Leon?"

The first response that popped into his head was: *You don't.* Naturally, he couldn't say that.

Closing his eyes, Keston allowed himself one deep breath. They could cut out his hesitation in post-production anyway. As he breathed, the melody from his most recent piano session came into his head. His fingers began to passively play on ghostly keys. The movement soothed him, clarifying his thoughts as he transported himself back to his soundproof music room.

"Music," Keston finally replied. "Music has been a part of my life since I was young—it's therapeutic." He thought about those nights in his hometown of Mende, where he would play the piano while his mother sang. He remembered practicing dances with his sister while his parents played together. "When I play, everything else fades."

Everyone he played with faded as well. His mother, *real* father, Pépé, and Arianne... all gone. Genevieve was not the girl he'd lived with in Mende and Porto Cheli. Pandora used his music for power. Even *The Black Sails*, Pacific's most famous band, had died because of him. Their last member, Christos, was a crumbled shell of himself.

"How about your family? I bet they help keep you grounded."

The question struck him. He exchanged a charged glance with Sensatia; the pursing of her lips told him she knew what she'd just asked. The expectant raise of her perfectly tweezed eyebrows told him enough. He needed to lie again.

"My family means the world to me," Keston began, uncertain how much he could say before eagle-eyed viewers saw the tension in his brow. "My sister and I have always been close. She's busy with her studies and plans to start her junior courses in the fall. She's set to graduate by next summer as the youngest graduate from the Paris University of Pangaea. I'm very proud."

Always promote the family. Always take the opportunity to remind the masses that an Elite was cut from a different cloth.

"And your father? Jaleel Leroy?"

"My father is busy with his responsibilities as Lord Advisor, so I don't see him much. Still, I admire his work ethic and hope to replicate it one day."

Lie, lie, *lie*.

Glancing down at her notes, Sensatia's red lips parted in an uncharacteristic moment of hesitation. Keston tilted his head at her, concern surging in his gut. He recognized that look: it was the one she gave as she geared up to test the boundaries. Doing so was precisely how she'd risen from commoner to international sensation, but it was also a great way to get killed.

Keston would know.

"Speaking of Jaleel," Sensatia paused again, her blue eyes scanning her notecards. "Can you discuss the rumors surrounding his...condition?"

Keston's mouth dried out. "His condition?"

"Some reports say Jaleel suffers from Dissociative Identity Disorder. The rumors started after the car accident that claimed his parents and sister when he was a child. Whisperings followed him through university, and his strange twenty-year disappearance from the public eye."

Blinking at the camera crew in disbelief, Keston saw they were still rolling. His eyes roved over the staff—*Sensatia's* staff—and realized the only one blindsided was himself.

What is going on?

After a few moments to collect his celebrity composure, he responded, "My father didn't disappear for twenty years. He was trying his hand at private sector business. After having my sister and me, he realized he wanted a stable legacy as an Elite, so he returned to his duty to serve as Lord Advisor of—"

"Private sector business," Sensatia interrupted. "The Leroys had plenty of wealth and influence. Your father hardly needed to pave his way like a commoner. If his condition wasn't what removed him from the public sphere, what did?"

The urge to clench up magnified, but he covered the reaction, falling back on the years of controlled emotion he'd learned from Ace. Instead of arguing, he flashed his charming smile, trained to make Europe swoon. "What can I say, Senny? I'm part of a family of trailblazers. We don't take the typical route. But the method speaks for itself. Average actions only create average people, and the Leroys always aim to go beyond that."

"Trailblazers." There was that look again. As Sensatia glanced up from her notes, he prepared for the worst. "That's certainly a good word for it. On all accounts, your family is *different*. For example, you've never elaborated on the accident that took your mother, Celine Leroy, or injured your sister."

"Car accident," Keston ground out.

"*Another* car accident?" Sensatia gasped.

He frowned at her, sweat making his makeup pile up in sticky droplets on his brow. What was she *thinking*? Leon wouldn't simply kill her for asking questions like that; he would make Keston watch—or force him to do it.

If Sensatia sensed her impending doom, she didn't heed the warning. She continued onward, smelling blood in her interviewee's proverbial waters. "And what grievance would assassins have on the Leroy family?" she pressed. "Elites are common victims of such events, but your family was out of the political scene at the time—what could other Elite families hope to gain?"

Keston squeezed his eyes shut as the deadly blast that'd erupted over Mende like a dying sun slammed into his memory. Pépé throwing him down the basement steps. Flashes of his mother, crushed and virtually unrecognizable under the rubble of her home.

His body shook. He remembered unburying Genevieve's bright red hair, a beacon of life amid so much death.

"People claim that your mother was a savage, like the horde that attacked Oslo and killed thousands of Pangaeans. How can the public expect to trust the Leroys when they'd actively fraternized with the very savages tearing our empire down?"

Savage. Like his mother was filthy, uncivilized, and monstrous. Savage, as if his mother hadn't breathed life into his childhood with her kindness and music. Savage, as if she hadn't made the ultimate sacrifice for Genevieve.

"You know what?" Keston stood and ripped the mic from his tie. "This interview is over."

He didn't wait for Sensatia's response as he marched off the bright set and toward his dressing room. The questions repeated in his head, working him into a growing fury. He hated the balancing acts, the anxiety, and the lies. How could he sit there and take relentless reminders of everything he lost? How could he smile while his family was audited for all of their misgivings?

And the best part was he would get in trouble for everything: Sensatia's rebellious questions and his responding humanity. He wasn't supposed to feel emotion in front of the camera. The world was supposed to see him as divine—a demigod gracing mortals with his presence. Instead, he let cameras record him being the emotionally dysregulated *boy* he actually was.

Keston's shoes pounded down the hallway of the Chateau de Ramboulette in a fury, uncaring what servants saw him. He heard Sensatia calling for him, her heels clicking after him as fast as she dared in those gaudy shoes and skirts. He didn't listen. All he wanted was to be left alone for five *fucking* minutes.

Slamming the doors to his quarters behind him, he realized he wasn't about to get that reprieve.

Genevieve sat in the leather chair, her back to the grand arching windows displaying the castle grounds. His sister had that strange sereneness on her face, the look she'd adopted since waking up from her abduction in New York. It unnerved him—she was present and five thousand miles away all at once. He'd been able to read her before, but now her expression was a riddle worthy of one of Ace's games.

It was one of the reasons he avoided her.

"You shouldn't have left the interview." Her green eyes were unblinking as she stared at him.

Keston blew a couple of stray hairs out of his face. "And shouldn't you be back at school?"

"There's nothing of importance at school."

"That's the point," he barked back. "Nothing of importance means *safe*."

The doors were thrown open behind him, and Sensatia rushed in, brown hair frazzled. She hung on the open doors, catching her breath. "Keston, we need to go back in there."

"So you can keep asking questions that will kill us both?" he demanded. "No, thank you. Go home, Sensatia."

To his surprise, her eyes tracked to Genevieve in...confirmation.

He bristled. "All right, what the fuck is going on?"

Genevieve fixed the cuffs on her jacket. That's when Keston noticed her marked fashion change. Long gone were the bright-colored dresses and flower accessories. She wore a well-fitted plaid pantsuit of red and tan, the colors both complementing her complexion and making her look ten years older. Or maybe it was the expression that aged her. He couldn't tell. Her hair, once an unruly mane of red curls, was tied back in a tight ponytail. She'd used to wear her hair down, vibrant with a touch of wildness, like she'd once been.

"I gave her those questions," Genevieve answered plainly.

Keston looked between the two women in astonishment. "Excuse me? Has anyone else been *conscious* when Leon's around? Are you that eager to piss him off?"

"Leon's busy with his war. Cassius, too," Genevieve said. "They appointed Sensatia for a reason. They don't have the time for publicity anymore. I designed the questions to be civil enough to fly below their radars. You did great, Keston. We can feed this to the news cycles and start spreading unease. It is not the ax that breaks the rock, but the slow trickle of water over time."

With a hesitant look into the hallway, Sensatia closed the doors. "We still have questions to highlight the slave trade."

Genevieve waved a freckled hand. "I was going to ask you to delete those questions in editing. Those might be too inflammatory. This will be enough for now."

"Can someone tell me what's going on?" Keston burst out.

Sensatia hugged herself, her jaw working as her foot tapped nervously. "They're asking me to cover up slaughter," she whispered. "Dozens of riots burst out after Pandora killed Selvia's Ductor, and dozens more after Oslo. Puppets killed hundreds—maybe even thousands—across the continent, and I'm the villain who has to erase their tragedies from history. And to make matters worse." She looked away, eyes welling with tears. "I can't keep seeing stories landing on my desk and pretend they're not happening. Families are getting ripped apart. *Feras* are murdered in the streets out of fear. They're stealing *children*, Keston."

"So, what's your plan?" Keston demanded. "Are you so eager to join them?"

Sensatia shrank from him. "I'm a reporter. I observe global events. I know better than most how history will see us. I don't want my name remembered like that. I–I can't live with it."

He cast a side eye at his sister. "Be careful. Gen is going to tell you some stupid shit like you being evil is actually for the greater good."

Her words from the hospital still burned him, even weeks later. He hated what Pangaea had turned him into, that he'd led an assault that devolved into a massacre, all by his sister's design and manipulation. That she'd *known* Arianne was alive and kept it from him so he'd fly into battle like a good little caged bird.

All those lies stemmed from Genevieve's belief that Keston needed to be the bad guy that the heroes could rise against.

"Exactly," Genevieve's voice was eerily emotionless.

Keston bristled at the word. He whirled on her. "I never asked for this, Gen," he screamed. "I *never* wanted to be the bad guy! I wanted to run away, retire, and let the world forget I existed. I would have been happy living in a hovel by the beach." He gestured around him. "I didn't want the riches and the fame. I just wanted to stop covering my hands with blood. I just wanted my family."

Pépé. Genevieve. Arianne.

He looked at his hands and could've sworn he saw blood falling from his fingertips. Against his best efforts, tears pooled in his eyes. "And then I was forced to choose, and I chose family. Or whatever was left of it. And now that family—the family I've given *everything* to protect—is throwing that protection out the window. To make it worse, they're feeding into my pain over the person I became, and are asking me to perpetuate the cycle no matter what it does to *me*."

For a fraction of a second, the Genevieve he once knew returned. Her freckled face softened, and Keston was reminded of sun-bleached days on the beach and nights spent singing in beer-soaked bars. Then the look faded, replaced by whatever had possessed her in the days following New York. What'd Selvia shown her? What'd happened to her?

Between himself, Cassius, and Genevieve, Keston was starting to fear his family was suffering a fate worse than death. They were physically alive, but the souls that'd called their Mende cottage home were long gone. They were walking corpses, husks of themselves, possessed by demons.

"I'm sorry, Keston," was all she offered.

Keston couldn't look at his sister anymore. Instead, he turned his wrath on Sensatia. "And what about you? I thought you just wanted to crawl up the social ladder—screw morality as long as you got your fame."

For the first time since meeting Sensatia, he noticed a diamond ring on her left hand. She twirled the stone around her finger. "That was before Pangaea started ripping families apart." The ring twirling stopped, and a muscle ticked in her fine jaw. "I became a reporter to look for the truth, not hide it. I think the glitter of fame blinded me for a time."

Keston frowned. "There's no glitter in a torture chamber. I'll guarantee that."

She lowered her head.

Genevieve cleared her throat. "Senny, can I have a minute with my brother?"

"Oh, so you two are on a nickname basis now?" Keston squeaked, feeling oddly betrayed.

Sensatia opened the door but gave Keston one last long look before she stepped out. Her eyes said she was sorry, but the set in her jaw told a different story.

"Do you know the name Sebastian?" Genevieve asked.

In the room's silence, Keston's rage started to deflate. "I've probably killed quite a few Sebastians in my life."

"He was her husband," Genevieve replied. "Sebastian Wolfe. There's no word of him in pop culture. I assume she's attempted to hide his existence, but there's no deleting a marriage record."

"*Was*," he sighed.

"Sebastian was a *Fera*. One day, he disappeared into thin air. You can assume the rest."

"Cartel."

"Or some minor slave trading subsidiary." Genevieve glanced at a glass tablet resting in the chair at her side. "The subjects of Sensatia's early investigative articles are quite telling. Dates tell a story, too."

Keston took the tablet from his sister, dread rising in his gut as he swiped through the profile.

Married in 2547. Sebastian Wolfe was officially declared dead in 2548. The cause of his death was unknown, with no body found. *The Dark Secret of the Underground,* Sensatia's first investigative report, aired in 2549. But the one that made her big break a year later was a twenty-minute op-ed: *Within the Elite Halls.*

Keston watched the video in shock. Most must have been transfixed by her stunning beauty and flirtatious interactions with the Elites she interviewed—cementing her in the gossip industry—but he saw beyond the flashy outfits and even flashier residences.

She'd found a way to publish a documentary showcasing *Fera* slaves working in Elite palaces, two years before slavery was legal in Europe. Now, with his eye trained for editing and camera angles, he noticed specific rebellious choices. A camera angle cut slightly too wide to display a reptilian *Fera* wearing a control collar standing behind the Elite being interviewed. A tour of the kitchen, the staff packed with exhausted *Feras* with clawed hands or slit pupils. Each destination wasn't meant to be an exotic tour of a luxury household for commoners to see; it was a cinematic missing person poster.

The documentary was Sensatia's call out into the void, a desperate attempt to show families missing loved ones that they were alive. Because Keston could only assume Sensatia hoped someone would do that for her husband. Or, she wished she would find him along the gilded halls of her interviewees.

"I had no idea," Keston said, lowering the tablet.

"By design," Genevieve replied. "Sensatia is a gifted manipulator, which is precisely what Leon hired her for. But her behavior—favoritism—toward you didn't make sense. So, I did some research and discovered her soft spots. That's why I approached her. From now on, she's a part of our team. Trust her decisions as you trust mine."

Keston shook his head. "But I *don't* trust you, Gen. I have no idea what's going on. What happened to you? Why are you acting like this?"

The only reason he felt safe enough to ask those questions was because they were locked in his quarters. He'd removed hidden cameras within days of moving into the palace and checked for replacements multiple times a week.

"I'm sorry, I can't explain everything just yet. I'll remind you of what I told you in the hospital: trust everything I do is for the greater good."

"I need more than that. You're risking your life, and you won't tell me why. I'm supposed to protect you."

I promised Mom I would protect you.

Genevieve's green eyes were cold, no longer reminding him of the summer meadows of Mende. "I didn't ask you to protect me, Kes."

"You didn't have to. I'm your older brother. Let me do my damn job."

"I don't need your protection anymore."

The sentence was like a punch to the gut. Keston wanted to bark back, shout at her over all the times he'd saved her ass in the past year, but he bit his tongue. He'd already done a stellar job at ruining everything in his life. The last thing he needed was to cut the fraying thread between the last family member he could interact with.

"Fine," his response was strained. "But you're asking me to blindly follow you while you make me the villain. I'm not okay with that."

"That's why I came here today." Genevieve's smile was heart-wrenching: so sweet, so deceiving.

He shook his head. "Stop with the riddles. I'm not an idiot, but I'm starting to think you're trying to confuse me on purpose."

She looked down, a strange flicker crossing her face. "I'm sorry. I'm not used to all the thoughts running around in my head. Sometimes, I forget everyone else isn't following."

"Gen," Keston began in concern. All his annoyance washed away, leaving only brotherly protectiveness. "What's going on? How can I help—"

"Alvaro Smith is in danger," Genevieve interrupted. "I need you to stop the Ascension Ceremony. Time to be the hero, Kes."

Chapter 6

Andre

Roulette squirmed in Andre's arms. He grumbled as he adjusted her on his knee, glaring at the mother with rising annoyance. "And why did you decide to meet here?"

Folding her ring-studded hands in front of her, Ace rested her chin on top as she observed him with smug interest. "With Pandora captured, you can't leave the island without turning heads. So I came to you."

Andre glanced around at the gloomy dive bar at the edge of some shipyard docks. A certain level of protectiveness surged inside him at the sight of the heavily tattooed dock workers and sailors crowding the grimy space. Without thinking, he felt his grip tighten around his daughter, pulling her closer to his chest.

Yes, Rou *was* his daughter—blood tests confirmed it. He wasn't about to suffer Leon's fate by raising a child that wasn't his. Well, he didn't quite know what *raising* entailed, seeing as he wanted nothing to do with the mother. Yet he refused to let Rou endure growing up without her biological father in the picture.

"Why did you send Pandora?" Andre frowned.

Ace leaned back, looking strangely at home among rickety wood benches, flickering lights, and liquor-soaked air. Even before the Underground riches, the Cartel boss must've been well acquainted with the backwater corners of the world. Even now, despite the exquisite leather jumpsuit and golden jewelry, any wandering eyes snapped in the other direction with one obsidian glare. With her characteristic tattoo hidden behind a thick layer of makeup, the deference she received from that flickering bar was from her aura, not her reputation.

"Pandora is a peace offering," Ace purred. A motherly frown crossed her face—a strange look on her. "Give Rou to me. You're holding her wrong."

Hesitant, he eyed Ace and said, "I have half a mind to take another peace offering."

Ace laughed out loud. "You think she's safer here? A refugee colony run by a catatonic president, almost as washed up as his rebellion?"

"She'll be safer here than with a mother who made her as a bargaining chip."

The overwhelming affection he'd felt at seeing his daughter for the second time had been unanticipated. The moment he'd looked into her light brown eyes, he'd been hypnotized. He didn't care about the hostility he would receive if he brought her home. He didn't care if he risked his relationship with Kalinda, Caesar, or Pacific—he didn't want to let his baby go.

"I've come to talk about that bargaining chip." She crossed her thick arms, not bothering to deny his claim. "You don't expect me to believe you intend to linger here? Where's the fun in that? Don't you want Rou to have a strong name to protect her?"

"You and your *names*," he huffed. "Pick whichever you want if it's so important to you. Murray, Valentino, Ortiz—you have plenty to choose from."

Ace leaned forward, practically glowing with her hunger for a deal. "So *boring*. Have you been paying attention? The world is in chaos. It's a playground for people like us."

"I am nothing like you."

"Darling, you're *everything* like me," Ace sang. "We've both tasted the sweet nectar of power, but have been told our blood isn't regal enough to deserve it. We've been pushed aside, buried, despite our talents and ambitions. Well, I say, let them bury us. There's enough untapped power in the Underground to turn the world over."

Opening her palm, Ace gestured to the bar around them. During their conversation, Andre had missed the influx of hundreds more patrons. But the crowd wasn't a random collection of drunkards. It was organized.

A rally.

A hooded figure walked to the front. Conversation died as the figure climbed onto the counter and turned to address the group, baited with anticipation. Andre was thankful for the reclusive nook Ace had chosen toward the back, where he could watch while hidden behind booths shadowed by the low light.

The figure removed their hood. Andre's breath caught as he recognized the male's quilled hair. Haris Cadmilus: Pacific's top engineer, trusted ally to Kalfas and Caesar, and one of Arianne's oldest friends.

Haris—timid Haris—looked almost unrecognizable. Gone were his classic square-rimmed glasses, and his unobstructed blue eyes were harder than Andre had ever seen. He'd changed a lot while Andre was in Spain. Before, Andre had been too caught up in his turmoils to notice the quiet male, but now, slight differences stacked up to make an entirely new person.

Haris's quills, once pure brown, were striped with white. His form was sturdier, and he seemed to stand a few centimeters taller. His jaw was set in uncharacteristic hardness.

Andre wondered if the changes he saw were from Haris maturing as a *Fera*, or from the year of secrets and loss he'd endured—presumably a mix of both.

"Hello, everyone," Haris began, an ounce of his former sheepishness returning as he scanned the crowd. "Thank you for coming."

He couldn't say more before the audience cheered.

A ghost of a smile appeared on the Porcupine's face. "For our newest recruits, I'll start from the beginning. Arianne Murray-Ortiz was my oldest friend. We grew up together. I knew her better than she knew herself sometimes. I loved her like a sister." Andre's stomach flopped at that. "And I *know* her exile was wrong."

The audience roared in agreement. Some shouted, others cursed, and most threw their fists in the air.

"I lost my father in Leonueva thanks to the repeated betrayals of Bradley Shaw—the man Arianne *justly* removed from our shores when Pacific chose to do nothing. I was there during the Drowning of Pacific. I watched as our evacuation efforts were delayed because Pacific didn't listen to Arianne. And I fought beside her as she risked her life to protect the very people who shunned her."

Andre felt himself wilt. He looked down at Rou, babbling in his arms as spit bubbles rolled down her chin. His heart broke as he imagined Arianne's excitement at meeting her niece. She would've loved to be an aunt.

And all that was taken away because she didn't get help fast enough. She'd *died* fighting to protect friends and family who were content to call her the villain, including himself.

Then came that all-too-familiar ache. A potent mixture of anger, regret, love, and loss. He replayed those moments in the hospital when he held his baby sister for the last time, relishing in the warmth of their reunion. Those critical moments with Leon. Everything he *should* have done.

He'd let his emotions overwhelm him. Tied to a tree, he'd been sentenced to watch his sister's demise. Powerless, just like all those years in the Murray Monument watching her experimentation and torture.

He'd been a shit brother to Arianne his entire life.

"I remember those days following our graduation," Haris continued. "Arianne was frustrated because she rightly deserved to fight for her people. She was the best graduate from our academy, and Pacific still kept her on the island like a prisoner. All because they were scared of her blood. Instead of embracing her heritage, they doused her flame. This world would be entirely different if Arianne were allowed to thrive—to challenge Pangaea for her birthright. She was the only rightful heir to Europe. She *would* have enacted Empire-wide change if she were in charge—something Pacific has proven they cannot do."

The crowd cheered again, and Andre finally realized what Ace had led him to.

"This is the Peregrine Pacific," he whispered.

Ace's grin wasn't reassuring. "Now you're catching on."

After Arianne's exile and the Drowning of Pacific, the Pacific had fractured. The Loyalists—two-thirds of the rebellion—believed the actions of the Head Chair and Senate were just in exiling her. But the other third, the reclusive Peregrine Pacific, saw history in a different light. To them, Arianne, whose mutations resembled those of the peregrine falcon, had been the path to global change. The Peregrine Pacific saw her exile as a mistake. They believed Pacific should've championed her as a citizen and warrior and used its power to lobby for her right to serve as the Commander of Europe.

Whispers and unease surrounding this shadow faction had spread throughout Pacific's refugee colony, Nassau. Caesar's safe return from Madrid had quieted some growing unease for a while, but that calm period seemed to be nearing its end.

Andre's lips parted in shock. Haris was working on Pandora. He *knew* Pacific was housing a dangerous Pangaean. If there was a catalyst to cause enough unease to bring the might of the Peregrine Pacific into the light, it was Pandora's presence.

The bar was silent as Haris continued, voice growing more powerful, "I understand you may feel wronged by the very country you placed your trust in. I must emphasize that mistakes do not make the Loyalists evil, just as Arianne's mistakes did not make her evil. No matter what we discuss tonight, I implore you to keep the peace."

As Haris jumped off the bar and began greeting the crowd and personally welcoming new guests, Ace sat back in satisfaction. Andre eyed her warily.

Always relishing in leaving people guessing, Ace simply shrugged. "Something to consider."

She gave him that classic smile, the one that showed her unyielding confidence—the same one that ultimately got her in his bed. As if on cue, Rou babbled: the result of such a manipulative pairing.

"What is your play?" Andre asked flatly.

If Rou was any evidence, he had to approach every interaction with Ace assuming that she'd determined every detail long before she'd arrived. She'd seduced him over weeks to sleep with her enough to give her a child. With that evidence, he could only assume she was playing another long game.

Ace twirled one of her braids around her clawlike fingernails. The diamonds on her golden rings twinkled in the bar's low light. "Come now, Andre. You know the ingredients required to rise to power better than most—I would argue that was your major in university." Her finger dropped her braid, pointing toward Haris. "Every king needs people ready to fight for him."

"And I'm Arianne's brother."

Ace stood and scooped their daughter into her arms. "And Caesar's son, giving you significant sway in Pacific. Not to mention, you have a non-Murray heir who could Ascend after you. You might not be Arianne, but you might just offer the Peregrine Pacific the uprising they need to change Europe."

The former Cartel boss didn't wait for a response. With one last wave, she strutted out of the bar. Andre was left watching her leave, his mind reeling with the possibilities. Only once Ace was gone did he let himself look back toward the Peregrine Pacific gathering with an ounce of interest.

For the first time since learning about his parentage, the desire to become Commander stirred in his gut.

Chapter 7

Arianne

"Two squadrons," Sygrid said, analyzing a map of Mexico City projected from one of the spatial map generators they'd stolen in Oslo. The Ductor's crown of antlers cast her face in sharp shadows, and her words echoed off the walls of the Dara Cave. "Alpha Team is with me at the Ascension Ceremony. Beta Team is with Phoenix and will monitor the periphery. Ringtail will remain behind and lead the war effort in my absence."

Ringtail, who reverently stood by Sygrid's side, nodded silently. Since the Siege of Oslo, he'd stepped down from active missions. Keston's sonic voice in the stadium's echo chamber and the communications unit in his ear combined to blow out one of his eardrums. The Master of Shadows had lost all hearing in his right ear and most in his left—medically deaf. In close quarters, whatever was left of his *Fera* hearing compensated enough to hear, but it was improbable he would ever be mission-ready again.

That didn't mean Ringtail wasn't the best Shadow that Selvia could offer. No one knew stealth, strategy, and espionage better than the Lemur. Under his command, Selvia's network of Shadows was still thriving, including Tyrell and Treena: Arianne's former friends who'd gone under deep cover almost a year ago.

"Alpha team," Sygrid continued. "Ursa, Luna, Mouse, and Pharaoh." Khari's Champion name hit Arianne like one of his electric shocks. "Our job is simple: mingle. We must show face. We are now an active participant on the global scale. Missing this ceremony would reflect negatively on our image."

Blue scoffed. "I can't believe Prince Perfect gets Alpha team after everything he's done."

Arianne tried her best to hide her flinch. Their meeting with Commander Sarr still weighed heavily on her mind days later. That *Prince Perfect* could be her fiancé...

She quickly shook her head before thoughts of that clusterfuck made her lose focus. "Exactly," Arianne quickly retorted, knowing her silence would only egg Blue on. "Khari is a prince. He needs to be there. And if he's mingling with Selvians, it will be enough to remind my father that Africa has a soft spot for the tribes."

Leon. Arianne felt her jaw tighten. What if she saw him in Mexico City? She had no idea what she'd do. Fortunately, her job was to stay *away* from the ceremony.

"We didn't need a *prince* on our last mission," Blue hissed. "You still brought him."

"Khari is a talented Champion." Arianne felt she was convincing herself, not her friend. "He proved his loyalty during the Siege of Oslo. Sygrid agreed: taking him on missions will help him regain his confidence. Plus, he can fly a jet better than most of our team."

After supporting a coup with his mentor, Cavalier, throwing Arianne to her death, and watching Cavalier die at Sygrid's hand, Khari was far from the male he'd been a month before.

Blue rolled her slitted snake eyes. "Like this world needs Khari with more confidence."

Ringtail's yellow eyes scanned the Champions gathered in the war room. "This is a strategic mission. North America formally invited us—we must show we're a willing ally *and* prove to Europe we are not easily intimidated."

He spoke softer than ever. Arianne felt a pang of guilt. Because of Pangaea and *Keston*, one of Selvia's best warriors had lost a crucial part of himself—a Master of Whispers who could no longer hear them.

"Beta team," Sygrid continued. "Phoenix, Blitz, Satyr, Rhino, and Blue Krait." The Ductor's attention landed on Blue. "As our only Shadow on this mission, you'll serve as the interface between Alpha and Beta." A nervous chuckle rose in Arianne's throat as Sygrid focused on her. "Beta team is *strictly* surveillance. If everything goes to plan, you shouldn't need to engage. No more international incidents. Understood?"

The question was blatantly pointed. Arianne coughed.

"Guess she heard about the turbulence," Blue hummed.

Sygrid frowned. "I heard about the turbulence."

Blue eyed Arianne expectantly, but she didn't return with another quip. She was too busy staring across the projection table toward Khari. He stared back at her, his face cast in the green sheen of the map. She wondered if he'd heard Blue's comments. She wondered how much Khari hated her and the destruction to his reputation—and future—she represented.

Arianne was well aware that the moment she arrived in Selvia was the moment Khari's comfortable place in the world had started to crumble.

"Meet with your separate teams. We leave for the Ascension Ceremony tomorrow morning. Don't stay up too late partying in the Valhan. Understood?" Sygrid finished.

The war room of Champions barked their affirmative, and their Ductor waved them out. Khari was the first to leave. Arianne waited for the older Champions to go before she moved toward the exit. Her team quickly flanked her as they navigated out of the cave toward the primary tunnel system that led outside.

Lova was the first to speak. "What's our plan, Ari?"

"Hide," she said. "Be ready to strike at a moment's notice."

Topher flexed his toned arms. "I've already marked the best positions to set up. I'll have a clear line of fire toward the crowd."

Arianne shook her head. "The Commanders will have those areas heavily guarded."

"I have plenty of encrypted bank accounts," Blue smirked and passed Arianne a hotel key card. "I bought this room months ago with one of them—a perfect visual of Constitution Plaza, the location of the ceremony."

"Fitting name," Arianne muttered, taking the key.

If she knew anything about Pangaea, there would be *nothing* constitutional about the upcoming Ascension Ceremony. She felt it in her gut.

Rhino raised a hand. "I'm psyched I got a spot on the field trip, but I'm hardly a surveillance guy."

"He said it, not me," Blue chuckled, earning a shove from Rhino that sent her careening into the rock wall.

Arianne's stress grew as her friends—now teammates—pelted her with information. She rubbed her temples. "Rhino, you're coming in the very likely event this becomes more than surveillance."

He cracked his knuckles. "Nice."

To add to her growing spiral, a specific male was lingering at the edge of the water. The older Champions had already crossed the slick rock path over the river and out of the cave system. But not him. His blue eyes were fixed on her, confirming her worst fear.

Khari wanted to talk to her.

Arianne slowed, waving at her friends. "Rhino, save me a couple of oatmeal raisin cookies, okay?"

Her old friend snapped his fingers at her. "I'll make sure they're fresh out of the hearth."

Arianne tried her best to smile as they left, but all she felt was the chilling spray of the waterfall, which seemed to worsen the growing chill around her heart. With one last concerned glance, Blue moved to follow the others.

Only when she was alone did Khari approach her. They hadn't spoken since Commander Sarr's proposition three days ago.

"I didn't get a chance to thank you for your help on the mission," Arianne strained as she broke the silence. "If you hadn't flown our jet so well, Lova, Blue, Rhino, and I wouldn't have escaped."

He nodded tightly. "I'm a Champion. I did my job—there's nothing more to it."

Something was growing in Khari: that rigid loyalty and militaristic mindset that'd turned Cavalier's entire personality to stone. Cavalier had fallen on his warrior status and duty to the tribe after Sygrid's rejection. Was the loss of Khari's mentor and his disdain for her pushing him down a dark road? She feared Khari could follow in Cavalier's shoes, shutting down his personality until only honor and duty remained to guide him.

"You still deserve recognition for your efforts," Arianne said.

Ire sparked in his eyes. "What, from you?" he huffed. "In case you've forgotten, I've been here *far* longer than you." He pointed to where Beta Team had disappeared. "Just one year ago, they were supposed to be my team. Now I have to watch you lead them."

Fighting the urge to bark back at him, Arianne took a deep breath. In that momentary pause, she could feel his pain. The rage faded, leaving empathy in its formerly destructive wake. "I know." She sighed. "I know."

She closed her eyes, calling on the pain she felt when Pacific shunned her. Killing Bradley Shaw had been wrong, traitorous. But when she'd acted, she'd believed she was doing the right thing. That didn't make her evil. Blinded by emotion, yes, but not evil. Like Khari, who'd followed his beloved mentor in a move he believed was protecting Selvia from Arianne Murray: City Crusher, the Tyrant's Daughter.

"Do you?" Khari pressed, his handsome face twisting into an ugly, all too familiar emotion. "Do you really know?"

Arianne didn't hesitate. "You saw my condition a year ago. You saw the hole I crawled out of—bleeding fingers and all. If we want to keep a record of wrongs committed to each other, our mentors' rivalry will continue to us. And I thought you were committed to breaking that cycle."

His frustration cooled. They both seemed to remember a similar conversation on the battlefield as they watched their mentors claw to the death. Sygrid and Cavalier's dominance battle had torn the tribe apart—something Selvia couldn't afford again if they wanted to win that war. An Arianne from another lifetime would've been content to crush Khari in any attempt to prove herself above him. But now, all she saw was his potential.

"If you think you need to prove yourself to this tribe after Cavalier's betrayal, I'm here to tell you you don't—not to me." She managed a genuine smile in the direction of her rival.

"People question my Champion's name," he whispered. "I hear them. They think my Championship was a scam by a false Ductor."

Arianne moved to reach for him but stopped herself. With everything going on between them, physical contact felt far from appropriate. "Then let's prove to them beyond a shadow of a doubt you're worthy of your Champion's name."

The frustrated tension between them since the Siege of Oslo cracked, leaving an oppressive air of sadness. In a very un-Khari-like fashion, the male shuffled his feet in uncertainty, blue eyes focused on the water-slick floor. He didn't look up as he spoke. "What are we going to do about my father's proposal?"

Arianne's stomach flopped more than when she dropped into a free fall. It was her turn to avoid the prince's gaze. She'd tried her best to distract herself from the massive elephant planting its ass in her psyche since Commander Sarr's discussion. Lova's dance classes, long nights at the Valhan, even longer hunting trips—but there was no avoiding a subject of that caliber.

She'd been hoping Khari would reject the proposal, saving her any grief in decision-making.

Turning from him, she couldn't look at him lest she have a mental breakdown before her biggest mission since Oslo. She hated how she could recognize Khari's scent almost as well as she could recognize another particular male—the one who was *supposed* to hold her heart forever. Khari's scent of static and river water was a mockery of her squashed dreams.

"Let's get through this mission, and then we can figure out what we need to do," she choked out.

Maybe a marriage between them wouldn't be needed. Maybe tensions were improving. The Ascension Ceremony could mark a new beginning for tribal and Pangaean relations.

Sure. That was as likely as Leon walking her down the aisle at her wedding.

The Valhan was bursting with life. Selvia's green-skinned Lyre, Saga, orchestrated upbeat music from the central pyre. One of the band members included Topher, looking straight from a fairy tale as he danced across the stage's beams and artfully played the wooden flute. Rhino and Lova joined the dancing crowds around the heat of the fire.

The dancing was wild, passionate, and energetic as dozens of younger tribesfolk crashed into each other, shouting excitedly. Tongues of flames licked the indigo sky, surrounding the snowy Valhan in crackling firelight and the dense, smoky smell of burning oak. Even the late December chill was shielded by the half dozen raging pyres and moving bodies.

Typically, as soon as Arianne heard the excited screams of her tribemates, she would itch to join the celebration—especially since earning her Champion's paint. But that night, she watched her friends and sat on a tree trunk bench, a mug of hot chocolate warming her scarred hands.

Her reeling mind made it impossible to feel the urge to dance. Rhino and Lova beckoned her a few times, but she shook her head, making some excuse about wanting to finish her drink. Not one sip later, she was down to the last chocolaty dregs. With a groan, she stood to refill her excuse.

At least the vitality of the Valhan was better than being left alone to her thoughts in her treehouse.

The tribe's chefs had erected the hot chocolate stand next to a smaller fire. Reaching to open a pot and ladle out another serving of the Selvian delicacy, she barely filled half her cup the lid slammed down on her hand. Arianne looked up, annoyance poking through the strange numbness that'd taken over her since her conversation with Khari.

Blue frowned at her, her lithe hand still fastened over the lid. "Talk."

Arianne tried to move the lid, only to find Blue's grip was far stronger than anticipated. "I'm about to shovel snow down your bra."

"Oh," she said, raising an eyebrow. "And what do you plan to do after? Fight me, or fuck me? Because that's an interesting initiation for both."

"Not right now, Blue."

"Something's definitely wrong. You usually have a much better response to invitations to my bed." Her venomous fangs flashed in a flirtatious smile.

Arianne finally pried Blue's hands off the lid and quickly poured herself another cup. "It's not really an invitation when the bed's in the same room I sleep in," she muttered. "It's more of an update to the roommate agreement."

Blue's hands slowly curled around Arianne's shoulders as her forked tongue flicked past her ear. "Sounds like a *fun* update."

"I don't need to be spit-sisters with Pandora. I already have to deal with her as a real sister."

"There's the comeback I was looking for." Blue stepped away from her friend. "But a little late—you're off, I can practically smell it."

Arianne looked around, searching for eager listeners. Since earning her Championship, her social status in the tribe had skyrocketed. That also meant more eyes—and ears—eagerly followed her. A group of particularly nosy farmers nearby barely hid their sideward glances in her direction. She grabbed Blue's hand and dragged her from the Valhan into the surrounding evergreen grove.

Removed from the bonfire's heat, nothing stopped the forbidding northern chill. Arianne shivered, shoving her hands into her wolf-fur jacket, her wings fluffing up behind her for an extra boost of warmth. Blue, little more than skin and bones, quickly covered her blue-streaked hair with a woven hat.

"You listened to my talk with Khari," Arianne said. "I smelled you lingering just beyond the waterfall."

Blue shrugged. "Left my Mist in the treehouse."

Mist was one of Pangaea's newest anti-*Fera* inventions. Anyone who wore the perfume-like liquid became virtually invisible to a mutant's sense of smell.

"What did Khari mean by the Commander's proposal?" Blue pressed.

"I was going to tell you, I just didn't want to bring it up until I knew what to do." Arianne sighed deeply, her breath clouding her face. "Commander Sarr had this plan with Cervi." She paused, searching for the best words. "Basically, if we want to guarantee Africa's aid, I must marry Khari. We're meant to build a bridge between the tribes and Africa—a mutual protection alliance."

"That's a very one-sided bridge." Blue shook her head. "Tribes don't recognize Pangaen marriages."

Arianne winced. "There's the kicker: we would also go through the mating ceremony in Selvia."

Sygrid's red mating ceremony dress popped into her mind, and the loving softness on her face when she held it. Arianne knew she'd be defiling a sacred ceremony with her lies. But that lie could save millions of lives.

"What did Strix say?"

"She's against it."

"And you?"

Arianne raised her hot chocolate mug to her face, distracted by its enticing scent and warm steam. "I don't know, Blue."

She blinked away the unnecessary flash of Keston lying next to her in bed, amber eyes shining against the sunrise trickling in through their villa's windows. With a sip of her drink, she focused on its burn as it slid down her throat instead of the burn in her chest.

"Mating is sacred."

"I know."

Crossing her arms, Blue leaned on a snow-painted pine tree. "It's not an average political marriage. You can't just hold hands in public and fuck whoever you want behind the scenes. The mating bond is special for a reason—it literally links biology."

"I'm aware." Arianne massaged her brow, the stress that'd been at a low simmer all day growing to a boil. "The bond only happens when your body recognizes a physical equal paired with an emotional connection. It's a crapshoot—no one knows the science."

"Even Hera couldn't figure out the biological pathways. Don't tell me you plan on trying to mate with Khari."

"*I don't know*," Arianne hissed.

"Two things." Blue did her best to seem severe, but a smirk was rising on her angular face. "One: you and Khari? Never going to happen. Two: biological connection means–"

"I know what biological connection means. I wasn't born yesterday."

The smirk came full force. "Then you know if you're going to claim he's your mate, but don't *actually* mate with him, you're fucked—literally. Mates' smells mix. If you want to even attempt to convince a civilization full of people with advanced sniffers, you'll have to sleep with him. A *lot*."

Arianne stared at the snow, wishing she could hide underneath the layers of ice crystals. "If I'm forced to sleep with someone, I could do worse than Khari."

Whatever optimism she'd hoped to portray with that statement fell flat.

"And you can't sleep with anyone else."

The image of Keston propping her against a tree, his powerful shoulders outlined by moonlight, inadvertently snaked into her mind. It was quickly replaced with an image of him bleeding and broken underneath her.

I'm sorry we lost our After, Princess.

"Shouldn't be a problem," she blurted, shoving the butterflies out of her stomach.

Blue didn't look convinced. Nor was Arianne, but she didn't have the emotional bandwidth to deal with it the night before a critical mission.

As usual, her *amica* read her perfectly. She patted Arianne on the cresting bone of her wing. "Come on. Let's dance it out."

She allowed Blue to guide her back to the Valhan. Finding Rhino and Lova was easy, thanks to him standing a head above most of the crowd. They welcomed her with an excited shout. She quickly fell under the music's hypnosis and the celebration's warming flames. Her worries went out the window, and her tribe danced late into the night.

She may be nothing more than a pawn to be positioned in the worldwide chess game, but right then, she let herself forget it all. Everything awaited her in the morning, but the later she danced, the further away that morning felt.

Chapter 8

Keston

A lvaro would go insane.

The second the Serum touched his brain, he might be lost forever. Though Genevieve neglected to explain how she knew, the reasoning didn't matter. In two days, the Alvaro that Keston knew—the male who'd become somewhat of a friend—could lose his mind, memory, or life. It was unknown how he would react, but there was one guarantee: it wouldn't be pretty.

If North America lost Alvaro, they would be vulnerable to influence from other continents, like Europe. While Keston was forced to follow the Commander's orders, he understood better than most that the last thing the world needed right then was Leon with more power.

Time to be the hero. Unfortunately, he didn't have much experience in that category.

With a deep breath, he stepped out into Cartel's private underground hangar. It was as large as two warehouses: the heart of Keston's aerial force hidden just below Paris.

Jokers in Techwear saluted as he passed, their faces shielded by masks and hoods. Jamie—Texas Hold'Em—was long gone, having escaped in the chaos of the Siege of Oslo. Keston couldn't care less. Whatever use Jamie had been in rounding up the last of Ace's strongholds was long worn out.

Keston was the King of the European Underground now. Jamie was the last of the old guard. The little shit was fortunate he escaped when he did because Keston was fairly certain he would've killed him already.

Silence filled the cold space built of concrete, stale air, and fear. Keston was the harbinger of that ripe scent of dread assaulting his nostrils. He knew what he looked like with an armored black tactical suit, an obsidian headpiece holding his growing hair back, and a flowing black cape lined in red.

"Prepare the jets," he ordered the squadron of twenty Jokers he'd recruited. "Follow ten clicks behind the royal jet. Do not engage until explicitly ordered."

The Jokers clasped their hands together to form a spade and held the symbol over their eyes. Keston stilled. That was Ace's salute. Too often, he'd been another Joker standing in a line like the one before him, hands forming that perfect spade in solidarity. It was still hard to disentangle his internal image as a follower from the leader he'd become.

Maybe it was because he was still just another follower, just to a stronger master.

"Blackjack, what is our mission?" one Joker asked.

"Mission parameters still unknown," he responded, fighting against the chill at his Cartel name. "Current objective is to remain on standby. Await further orders."

The Jokers pounded their chests, the resounding thump echoing throughout the hangar. He tried not to look at their ace-of-spades tattoos. He tried to ignore the burning of his own on his inner forearm.

Before Pandora's disappearance, Keston had relied on Puppets, and sometimes Wards, for backup to avoid suspicion. He operated on the idea of out of sight, out of mind. The less he used his Underground forces, the less he reminded his father and Leon that he had an independent organization loyal only to him.

But if he was about to commit treason—*again*—he needed operatives that wouldn't run screaming back to Leon like preschoolers snitching on their classmates.

Now, he just needed to figure out what he was going to do.

From Keston's experience, there was only one way to make Leon Murray more intimidating: hiding something from him. Unfortunately for Keston, he'd developed a stellar habit of doing just that.

The towering Commander hadn't been around much since the battle in Oslo had expanded conflict across northern Europe. Leon was a boots-on-the-ground leader, so he was frequently away from Paris overseeing the various battlefronts. This meant Keston didn't have much experience hiding certain nuclear-sized truth bombs from him in person.

Including the plan to ruin Pangaea's most sacred gathering and—oh, yeah—Arianne's current status of *not dead*.

He stood as Leon boarded *The Artic,* his signature jet, flanked by Hera and Cassius. Since the war began, the Commander had forsaken his three-piece suits. Now he wore just his military uniform, which could only be described as a Ward's uniform on steroids. Like them, the base fabric was black with red trim, and it was lined with fiberglass armor plates in the chest, legs, and shoulders. But something about the array of medals across his breast, the half-shoulder cape, and the black polyester material that absorbed light made his uniform seem cut from divine cloth.

His scared face, perfectly slicked-back blond hair, and broadsword strapped across his back made him look like a god of war.

Keston's mouth dried out. He'd decided to keep secrets from *that*. Despite knowing Leon couldn't scent the fear on him as a mutant could, he was terrified the Commander could feel it like a sixth sense. Indeed, as those blue eyes landed on him, one crystalline and the other foggy with scar tissue, Keston felt stripped raw.

"Swallow a feather, Leroy?" Leon asked.

"Of course not, Commander. I was just debating if I would look half as good in that uniform."

"Flattery is a new strategy for you."

Keston eyed the broadsword, debating whether Leon would kill him quickly or leave him to bleed out. He offered a charming smile. "Worth a try."

With a frown, Leon turned to the back of the jet, already bored. Cassius followed, always the loyal lapdog. But Hera remained behind, sitting down in the booth next to Keston. His anxiety quickly turned into annoyance.

"Can I help you?"

Keston never liked Hera. He hated her conniving smile, one born from the gloating pleasure of knowing more than everyone around her. He hated her for letting a monster such as Pandora roam free. And most of all, he hated how she turned him into a Frankenstein of an experiment, a collection of favorable parts stitched together.

That insufferable smile was plastered on her face now. She leaned in. He leaned back. The slight smell of sterilizing alcohol followed her around from the never-ending hours spent in her labs. The scent burned his nose and reminded him of the very place that'd ripped his body from him.

The scientist General looked more General than scientist that day in her military uniform. She adjusted her red-laced sleeves. "How has my *gift* been treating you?"

Keston's palms grew damp. *The pills*. He shifted uncomfortably, missing the blissful effects of a night's debauchery. He certainly wouldn't mind a drink to get through that flight.

"Confiscated," he said, waving her off. "Go talk to your buddy, *Cassie*."

Hera's light eyes traced to the back of the jet, where Cassius presented a tablet to Leon. She frowned. "He's always ruining my fun." In those moments, she resembled Pandora, and it was apparent where the cyborg had gotten her, well, *everything* from. Hera's attention returned to him. "How did you like them?"

"You and I both know you saw the news."

Hera hummed. "*Keston's Sensatia-nal Night Out*. That was certainly a fun read." The clang of the gangplank closing caught their attention as Sensatia boarded the jet. The scientist General winked. "Speak of the devil."

Keston ignored her attempt to distract him. "What was the point of giving those pills to me? Because it's obvious you didn't do it out of the kindness of your non-existent heart."

"Certainly not."

"Go on," Keston said, his annoyance steadily rising.

"Access to the Serum has fast-tracked my research. I can now isolate the genes involved in *Fera* expression. Most of my learnings are not quite ready to show, but these?" She pulled out a familiar prescription bottle filled with blue pills. "These are the most developed of my recent experiments. A temporary *Fera* ability suppressor."

"I thought it only suppressed my metabolism."

Hera gave a long-suffering sigh, tired of needing to explain her science. "Metabolism suppression is *one* side effect of the medication. I'm curious about the other effects."

"I'm not your lab rat."

The bottle rattled in her hand. "But do you want them?"

Pursing his lips, Keston quickly swiped the bottle and shoved it in his suit's inner pocket. He looked toward his father and heard the phrase *diminishing returns*. Wanting nothing to do with economic bullshit, he excused himself to his room to get high.

He barely made it through the door before he opened the bottle and swallowed one of the blue pills. Then he dug an edible out of his pocket. From experience, the pills took about fifteen minutes to kick in. During that time, his fast metabolism would process the edible so it would take effect just as the pills lowered his metabolism. Keston flopped onto the small bed, the room's shadows doing little to hide his shame.

Was it wrong to be so eager?

Bracing himself, he waited for the first effects to take place. The sudden chill that spread throughout his body was a major tell that his metabolism was slowing down. His internal furnace wasn't burning as much fuel, which meant his body produced less heat. It was well known that mutants typically ran hotter than humans. The side effect was mainly in his fingers, now ice cold. Then, the room, once easy to see, was almost too dark to navigate.

Standing, he turned on the soft white wall lights that lined the room, chalking his vision to exhaustion. He refused to believe a drug he'd used as a crutch could suppress his abilities.

Then relaxation suddenly shot down his limbs. With an audible sigh, he removed his uniform and stepped into the shower. The steam, hot water, and mind-numbing high lessened the tension in his shoulders. There, braced against the wall, scalding water sliding down his neck, he pushed all thoughts of Pangaea from his head.

"You know, I always saw this shirt in your room. I did some research. I could never find a *Citadel Academy* in the Pangaean record."

He jumped in surprise as Arianne's blue and gold academy t-shirt was pressed against the foggy glass shower door. He almost slipped on the water-slicked floor, staring dumbly at the shirt. The t-shirt he slept in. The t-shirt he'd retrieved from his villa after he lost Arianne. He registered Sensatia through the dense steam. He must not have heard the door open. With a mortified choking sound, he quickly wrapped his wings around him to cover his modesty.

"*Senny*," he wheezed, his mind too hazy to deal with questions about his ex-dead ex-girlfriend.

The reporter sat on the toilet seat, blue eyes unamused. "Keston, I've seen you naked hundreds of times."

He glared at her, making a point to inject as much attitude as possible into turning off the shower.

"So, where's Citadel Academy?"

"It was disbanded."

"Did you go there?"

"No."

"Whose shirt is this, then?"

Keston rubbed his eyes, now painfully dry. He pretended not to hear the question and wrapped a towel around his waist.

Sensatia tapped her foot on the floor. "It's known that you were a Joker in Cartel until the Fall of Leonueva. Then, you disappeared off the map for six months before joining Leon's Inner Circle. Those six months are a black box. No one will tell me anything about them, including you. You can see why I'm curious."

Those six months were the best months of his life.

Keston wiped some fog from the bathroom mirror. Gripping the sink, he stared at his broken reflection—bloodshot eyes, dripping back hair, and lifeless frown. He didn't take his eyes off it as he said, "Those six months don't matter."

"You're a good actor, but not that good."

He turned from the mirror, but he moved too fast, making him dizzy again. "Why are you here? Did Gen send you?"

"You and I both know what's about to happen. We need to stop it." She looked down at the crumpled shirt in her hand. "I was hoping we could still trust each other."

Alvaro. Keston thought about the brief time they'd spent together. While their relationship had been strained from the beginning, he had to admit he liked the Heir Apparent. That meant he'd blame himself if anything happened to him—even if ruining the most sacred ceremony in Pangaea was next to impossible without getting caught.

"We?" Keston pressed. "Senny, you refuse to punch someone because it'll ruin your nails. There's no we. I have to stop this."

Sensatia twirled a few strands of brown hair. "I don't know how to fight, but I do know how to light a fuse."

"Excuse me?" He shook his head. "I need you to be a little clearer. I'm too high for this."

"Well, with a fuse, you can set up an explosion without being there when it goes off."

"I know how a fuse works."

She shrugged. "Is there anyone you can think of who might want to ruin the ceremony? If it's canceled, we'll have another year to figure out how to stop Alvaro from taking the Serum."

Keston's eyes tracked to the Citadel Academy t-shirt. A mischievous grin grew on his face. He could think of one winged creature of chaos who was always eager to crash a party.

And he was willing to gamble that she would be there.

Chapter 9

Arianne

"So, who do you think will do it?" Blue asked, gazing out at their hotel room's view of Constitution Plaza in the center of Mexico City. The world's most high-profile individuals crowded into the heavily guarded ceremony.

"No one's going to do anything," Arianne said.

"You sound in denial, but those swords strapped to your hips say otherwise."

Arianne grumbled.

"Europe, Africa, Asia, and Selvia are all mixing to make a delicious soup of chaos," the Snake continued, her excitement growing. "There's no question of if, only when, and who."

The sound of Topher's hooves clacked into the room. His calming presence and easy smile were just enough to keep Arianne from snapping. "Everything's going to be fine. Blue just paid for a fun vacation for us, you'll see." He winked at the Snake. "I'll remember your private bank accounts next time I'm craving Thai food."

She stuck her forked tongue out, but Arianne couldn't help but notice a slight blush on her cheeks. Stepping out of the room, Arianne gave the pair a moment alone. She had no idea what was going on between the two. Granted, they probably didn't either.

Lova and Rhino sat in the suite's common space. The couch looked plush and welcoming, and Arianne plopped down between her friends to watch what was on the projection television. She quickly discovered why the room was so eerily quiet.

"–thank you so much for taking the time for another *European Exclusive*!"

The camera panned to Keston Leroy, dressed in a double-breasted dark green suit. The color brought out the green flecks in his eyes. She swallowed hard as she conceded how handsome he looked. And how much like *himself* he seemed. His hair—still that dark shade with splashes of indigo—was long again, and that classic flirtatious smile had returned to his face.

But that smile wasn't directed at Arianne. It was directed at *her*, that brown-haired reporter he'd been dancing with at Alvaro's *Dia de los Muertos* party. Arianne flinched at the ounce of hurt she felt.

"I never liked him," Rhino growled in an uncharacteristically dark tone.

She ignored the comment, locking in on the news segment. It jumped back and forth between recaps of the recent interview. Keston was notably the poster boy the world recognized him as, but Arianne knew him better than the rest of the world. Even after a year, it was reassuring to see that he hadn't completely changed.

Keston was charming, yes, but it was an act.

Was his affection for the reporter an act? Did Arianne want to find out? *Why* did she care?

At some point during the segment, Blue and Topher arrived, only noticeable from Blue's sarcastic low whistle. "Well, look at that piece of work."

She shared a sympathetic look with Rhino.

"All right!" Arianne exclaimed, feeling her friend's incoming intervention like winds before a storm. "I get it, Keston's on the news. I don't need a counseling session."

"She's not over the breakup," Rhino whispered to Lova.

"Breakup?" Arianne wheezed. "One: there was no breakup. Two: I'm over him! In case you idiots forgot, I thundercunted him out of the sky! That's how over it I am—whatever *it* was." She crossed her arms defensively. "I could have killed him if I wanted to."

The corner of Blue's mouth quirked. "Then why didn't you?"

Arianne's cheeks burned. "Because keeping him alive was the *strategic* choice."

"I'm so glad that you think so, Princess."

The room promptly erupted into chaos.

Topher and Blue immediately palmed their weapons as Lova dashed to shield Arianne. Rhino flipped the couch over as a tiny blockade. Admittedly, Arianne was left frozen in utter shock. Keston Leroy casually watched the explosive reaction with thinly veiled amusement, looking far too comfortable leaning against *her* bedroom doorway.

"Cute," he drawled, glancing at their weapons with a smirk. "The infamous Champions of Selvia. I got to say, I'm a little disappointed."

Rhino balled his fists, his face red with rage. "Give me one good reason why I shouldn't smash your skull in right now."

Keston's amber eyes raked up and down the towering male, assessing and bored. "Simple," he hummed. "Because you wouldn't be able to touch me."

Rhino's grumble was a warning that he would attempt to prove the pompous ass wrong. Still speechless, Arianne could only hold her hand out to stop him. No matter how shocking, Keston had hunted them down for a reason. Despite the raging firestorm of emotions inside her, she knew he wouldn't have confidently stepped foot in that room if he didn't have something to say.

"Oh, look, he's trained too," Keston sang with a taunting grin.

Rhino huffed like a bull facing a matador, but he didn't dare charge past Arianne's hand.

"How'd you find us?" Blue questioned.

"Funny you ask," Keston pointed to her. "You think I didn't do an audit after our hang-out session in Madrid? You showed me you wanted to be a player in this game, so I built a profile that included all your fun little bank accounts. You can understand my curiosity when one of those accounts purchased a room with a view of the year's most important event. You're lucky I was the one who noticed."

Blue's mouth was agape, rendered speechless.

He shook his head. "Seriously? Am I the only professional here?"

Sliding around the toppled couch, Arianne extended the left half of her double-sided sword, *Horizon's Edge*. A deep scowl settled on her face as she pointed the heated blade toward Keston. "I want you to take a long minute to consider what I told you last time we saw each other."

Keston's charming facade faltered for a fraction of a second.

"I said," Arianne said, taking another shaky step, "if I ever catch you again, I will kill you."

"Why do we always end up at this point?" Eyes burning in challenge, Keston moved forward until her blade was inches from his throat. He leaned in to whisper, "Good thing I've always liked the game of chase."

"Unlike the Darwin Zone, you have nothing to offer me to appeal to my *kinder* nature."

"Are you sure about that?" Keston leaned even closer, his knowing grin so familiar and enticing.

Maybe it wasn't rage making her shake. "Why are you here?"

He grinned in delight. "Well, this certainly isn't a booty call, Princess. I have a contact book full of desperate women—and men—for that purpose." Arianne hated that her stomach flopped. To her dismay, Keston noted her flinch, which only seemed to delight him more. "Come on, be a little more creative for me. We're boring our audience."

He walked around her blade, hands casually in his pockets as he closed the last few inches between them. His breath fanned her face ever so slightly. His scent of sandalwood wrapped around her, and it took more willpower than she could admit to keep a neutral face. He still used the same deodorant. For some reason, that had her head spinning. Arianne's heart thundered as she fought to remain still amidst the onslaught of memories and emotions that scent brought up. She was intimately aware of her teammates' eyes on her, but the only eyes she cared about were his—paralyzing amber.

"Seeing as your favorite pastime is stabbing people in the back, I assume you want to do something that will really piss my father off." Arianne was proud of how bored her voice sounded. "And what better proxy than his disowned daughter?"

Keston snapped his fingers. "You're getting warmer."

"Enough games."

His hands were as tender as she remembered as he ran a hand up her sternum, to her chin, and lifted her eyes to him. She should have killed him for that. Instead, all she did was let out a shaking breath. Keston caught her reaction easily. "I thought you liked games," he said just loud enough for her to hear.

"How about you take a few steps back," Rhino warned, breaking whatever spell they'd found themselves trapped in.

Cold and collected again, Keston took two straight-legged steps away from Arianne in a movement mockingly reminiscent of a ballet toy soldier. He raised his hands in surrender. It struck Arianne that he looked far from the pleading and defeated male she'd fought weeks before. And then she realized that, while his hair had grown long and his face was scarred once more, this wasn't Keston standing before her.

It was Blackjack.

Blue interjected, "As much fun as it was to watch whatever *that* was." She glared at Arianne, blade still raised. "You've outstayed your welcome, Leroy, which is funny because you were never welcome in the first place."

Keston paid her no mind, staring at Arianne. "Lose the friends and the sword, and maybe we can have a civil conversation—for once."

Topher drew back his bow. "I don't like it, Phoenix."

The tension was thick. "Satyr, lower the arrow," Arianne said.

A challenge rose in Keston's expression. "No, go ahead, I want to see if he's fast enough to hit me."

"If he's not, I certainly will be." Lova's tail flicked.

Considering her friends, Arianne knew they were right to question Keston's unexpected arrival. The right thing to do would be to send him on his merry way, maybe with a wound to match the one he'd given her mother. Usually, it was easy to give in to her destructive impulses, but every time she thought of raising a hand toward the winged male, something stopped her.

He could play dress up and pretend he'd changed, but she knew he would always be the same person deep down. The person she'd fallen for. And that person only risked his life if something important was at stake.

"You have ten minutes," Arianne growled. "Blue, get in contact with Alpha. Let them know there might be a change in plans. The rest of you do a perimeter sweep of the hotel—I don't want any more Pangaean surprises."

Keston smugly watched her team leave the hotel suite, taking the liberty to settle himself on her couch. With the extra distractions gone, she could finally focus on him. He'd always had a passive beauty: the organized chaos of his hair, the overly alert eyes, and the muscles visible beneath any outfit he chose. But this Keston, the Elite celebrity, was not one she'd gotten to know. This Keston was a demigod, a beauty that screamed for the masses to see him.

Elite Keston wore clothes tailored specifically for him, effortlessly hugging him in all the right places. Though she missed his chestnut hair with hints of red, she had to admit the indigo black was striking with his black eyeliner. It gave his features an angelic sharpness.

The only thing that remained of the Keston she'd known was his look of uncertainty. Arianne told herself the male still hid underneath, but the longer she stared at him, the more she feared the male she'd loved had truly disappeared.

Keston touched the bridge of his nose where that one imperfect scar cut across his olive skin. "This is the wound you gave me during the Siege."

"That should have healed by now," Arianne said, averting her eyes.

Why did she suddenly feel guilty?

"I didn't want it to heal."

She looked up, lips parted, but no words came out.

Suddenly, his eyes were elsewhere. He leaned forward, his wings freeing themselves from his cape to stretch out. "I think about that fight every day."

Arianne's hands felt numb. The same hands that'd closed around his neck. She took a step back, her feelings a mixture of uncertainty. She *should* hate him. She *should* be happy that she tried to kill him. But looking at him, sitting in her hotel room with all his walls down, made her more confused than ever.

Keston always found a way to blur the lines that should have been petrified in concrete.

"We're not here to talk about us—whatever is left of it," Arianne spat. "We're here to talk about why you're committing treason to recruit my team."

"Right." He pinched the bridge of his nose like he was fighting a painful headache. "Personal clusterfuck has been tabled for later discussion. Political clusterfuck takes precedence."

"In case you forgot, your *politics* don't interest me."

Keston laughed at the ground. "Same old Arianne."

"Then you remember what happens when my patience runs thin."

"Alvaro Smith is in danger."

Her breath caught. "What?"

He looked up at her then. "The Heir Apparent—"

"I know who he is."

"Then you know he's a mutant." He stood. "I don't know if your people know this, but the Serum reacts negatively to *Fera* anatomy. If the Serum reaches his brain, we lose him."

Suddenly, Arianne recalled hearing something similar when they visited the Librarians in New York. But with the day's chaos, she presumed no one remembered that small detail—or thought to apply it to Alvaro. She ruffled her wings as she fought a shiver.

Keston held his hands out in surrender. "I can't interfere. If Leon finds out I was involved and, somehow, doesn't arrest me for treason, he might punish my sister. My hands are tied."

"So you want us to—what? Blow up the ceremony?"

Despite a heavy coat of stress blanketing the room, Keston managed a classic smirk that made her toes curl. "From what I recall, that's your specialty, Princess."

She started to pace. "You better not be bullshitting me, Keston."

If they lost Alvaro, they lost a valuable ally and Continent.

If they interrupt the ceremony, tensions deteriorate further.

Of course, Keston was the one to deliver the news that messed up her day.

He watched her pace for a moment, his eyebrows pinching together. Finally, he broke the tense silence. "Alvaro is a friend. Don't trust my political motivations. Trust that. Have I ever lied to you?"

Arianne halted, that terrific fire of annoyance blazing in her stomach. She glared at him and took pleasure in his flinch. "You never lied to me, but you have a knack for keeping things from me."

"If I had known she was your mother—"

"You what?" she cut him off with a bark. "You what, Keston? You wouldn't have pulled the trigger?"

His shoulders sagged. "Leon was messing with my head. It was my life or hers. He was using it as insurance. And if I didn't shoot her, someone else would've."

The response was like a punch to the gut. She stared at him in disbelief, tears welling in her eyes. "And that makes it any better?"

"Arianne, I'm sorry."

Her upper lip quivered. "'Sorry' doesn't bring my mom back."

She hated how she pictured him standing above her dying mother, smoking gun in hand. Arianne's fists clenched so tightly she drew blood. Conflicting images flashed across her mind. Her mother's body. Keston kissing her neck. The howling alarm as the heart rate monitor flatlined. Flying over the waters outside their villa. Keston walking away from her, leaving her to die.

She didn't notice Keston reaching toward her until his hand pressed to her shoulder. The touch sent electricity shooting up her arm and down her spine. "Arianne," he began.

Those three syllables shot her to another time. To sun-kissed days at the beach and long mornings in bed. Her name was spoken so softly on his lips that it almost paralyzed her.

Almost.

Warm tears dripping down her cheeks woke her up. She slapped his hand away. "It's *Phoenix* now." The voice that spoke wasn't her own. "I don't know what made you think it was okay to touch me, to even breathe my air, but I'll make this perfectly clear. *You* kept secrets from me. *You* let me fall for you, knowing I wouldn't if I knew the full story. *You* killed my mother. And in the end, *you* abandoned me to die. Don't forget that."

Each sentence landed on him like a blow. She enjoyed watching the mounting pain on his face at each reminder of his betrayal.

"That's the first and last thing I think about every single day, Princess." Keston didn't look up, his words more delicate than fine china.

Before she could say more, the hotel room doors burst open, and Arianne's team returned. Rhino barreled in first, quickly placing his body between her and Keston. Topher and Lova followed, weapons raised and scanning for anything out of the ordinary. And lastly, Blue, a hand to the earpiece planted in her ear, most likely on a call with Sygrid.

"Have a nice talk?" Rhino smiled humorlessly.

In a flash, the Keston from before disappeared. Emotionless Blackjack remained, as still as a shadow. His expression in those moments was unnerving: perfect and blank like a fresh sheet of paper. Regarding the Selvians coolly, he tilted his chin up as he shoved his hands back into his pockets. "Don't worry, I was just leaving," he said, amber eyes landing on Arianne.

She braced herself against Rhino's back. The vertigo she felt at so many rapidly changing emotions made her ready to collapse. She returned Keston's stare, terrified that he would see something other than hatred in her eyes when he looked at her.

"Don't forget, Princess, you kept plenty of things from me." His voice was unaffected. "You may treat me like the villain, but you're not too far off."

Before she could respond, Keston waved to her team and sauntered back toward her room, jumping out the open window he'd climbed through.

Topher lowered his bow, his eyebrows almost high enough to touch his horns. "Anything you want to tell us?"

Arianne shook herself, the remaining effects of Keston's hypnosis on her fading the longer he was out of her sight. She processed the question and slowly nodded. "We might need to make a slight change in our plans."

Tapping her earpiece, Blue put her call on speaker. Sygrid was cautious as she said, "I'm not sure I like the sound of that."

Arianne quickly relayed the information Keston had told her, and she was met with an uncertain silence. No one questioned the intel's legitimacy, but no one came forward with a brilliant way to avoid an international incident. They all stared at each other, dumbly waiting for Sygrid's orders.

Finally, the Ductor sighed. "Alpha Team cannot get involved. We must represent Selvia so the blame doesn't immediately fall on the Tribes. It's your team, it's your call, Phoenix."

Great. Just fucking great.

Arianne felt the weight of her team's stares. Her decision could put their lives at risk or doom a good leader to a life of insanity. Before her nerves could get the best of her, she shrugged. "Sure, let's try it. What's the worst that could happen?"

"Ancestors give me patience," Sygrid muttered.

Chapter 10

Andre

Andre had been watching Pandora's sleeping face for half an hour now. He should leave the lab before anyone asked any questions. But he couldn't look away. The motion lights had long since turned off, and he was left standing in the passive glow of the stasis chamber.

Arianne's stasis chamber.

"Something tells me this entire war could've been prevented if the three of us were locked up years ago," he whispered to the cyborg.

Leon was nothing but effective. Obsessed with power, he'd turned his three children into agents of pure chaos. Andre, Arianne, and Pandora had caused more trouble for Europe—and the entire planet—than any other group of siblings in recorded history.

And he knew whatever guilt he felt wouldn't stop him. He was bored. History already reflected what happened when one of Leon's children grew bored.

"There you are."

The laboratory lights flickered on as Kalinda, still in her navy blue surgical scrubs, padded toward him. A smile grew on his face at her approach. Dark bags swelled under her eyes—restless days spent monitoring Pandora were taking their toll. Still, she shone like honey caught in a beam of sunlight.

Kalinda laced her fingers with his. "Come on, everyone's gone home. Jaya's making beef curry for dinner."

"Go on, I'll catch up."

"Caesar was asking for you." Her voice was careful.

The jolt of hurt he felt at the comment surprised him. "That's new," he muttered.

In the few instances where Caesar left his home office—and the Simulator inside—he spent more time with the Bahri sisters than with his own son. Andre had taken it personally for their first few months in Madrid. Now he was numb to it.

Just because he showed up on Caesar's doorstep, sharing his blood, didn't mean he deserved a relationship with the man.

"I know he's struggling." Kalinda squeezed Andre's hand. "But he's the best man I know. He was the only family Jaya and I had growing up. He wants a relationship with you, Andre. You just need to give him time."

Andre felt his upper lip stiffen. "I've given him a year of time."

And now he had new prospects. He wasn't the type to wait around.

Kalinda pulled away. "Dinner is at seven. Don't be late."

Then she was gone.

Minutes later, the laboratory doors scraped open again. Haris walked up to Andre's side, face conflicted as he looked up at the stasis chamber. "You asked to meet?"

"What's your opinion on Pandora?"

Haris's jaw worked. "I'm glad she's asleep."

"You're the only one who's ever been able to deprogram her," Andre recalled the tales of the Drowning of Pacific, where Haris had successfully cut Pandora off from her infamous Bubblegum Battalion. "We might have people who can go toe-to-toe with her on the physical plane, but you're the only person in the world who can combat her on the digital."

"You're not thinking about waking her up, are you?"

Andre kept his face neutral. "With control comes power. If we can control her, we can use her."

"Pacific would never take that risk," Haris warned.

"What about the Peregrine Pacific?"

Through the reflection in Pandora's chamber, Andre witnessed the shift in Haris's face. The once friendly male switched on a dime, and darkness overcame his once bright blue eyes. He slowly removed his glasses.

"I haven't needed these for months." Haris smiled. "I wear them to keep people comfortable. Just innocent little Haris, right?"

Found you.

Andre understood. The same way he'd worn contacts for the first quarter century of his life was why Haris continued to wear glasses. In a game where every slight advantage—including eyesight—could mean life or death, players needed to present the best version of themselves. Andre couldn't show weakness in front of Leon. On the other hand, Haris played to his weaknesses to ensure people overlooked him.

"My question still stands."

Shifting his attention back to Pandora, Haris's assessment was no longer of a researcher but of a leader. He was silent for a moment, eyes darting between the cyborg and the former prince. When he finally spoke, his words were careful: "If you intend to overthrow Pacific leadership, I'm afraid I cannot help you."

"I would never unleash Pandora on innocent Pacificans," Andre returned vaguely.

"Then what is your question?"

Andre smiled. He'd done his research since the Peregrine Pacific gathering. The movement was a couple thousand strong, full of eager, battle-ready rebels. Most were fighting age. Most were ready for change, no matter what form it took. And Haris, loyal as he was, wouldn't rise against Caesar and Kalfas. But he was also sick of doing nothing to avenge Arianne.

"I hear Madrid is lovely this time of year. Fortunately, I have a place to stay. Maybe we'll make our way to Paris afterward." He turned to leave the lab, grinning regally. "Let me know if your people are interested in a new direction with a Murray who *isn't* a Murray."

Caesar didn't come to dinner.

As had become the new normal, Andre, Kalinda, and Jaya spent their dinner grinding through painful stunts of small talk. Their dining table was on a porch facing the Caribbean Sea. The sound of crashing waves dominated most of their meal, punctuating how little the sewn-together family spoke.

Wind buffeted Andre's face, carrying the strong scent of salt and the chili of Jaya's curry. If the sight of the beach wasn't so beautiful—and the food so delicious—dinner might've been unbearable.

"Jay, stop staring at him like that," Kalinda's voice finally broke the tense silence.

Jaya's purple hair fell over her face as she looked down and focused on sawing through her beef. "Is no one going to talk about how Andre's been disappearing at night?"

Annoyance poked at him, and he sat up straighter. "Do we have a problem?" He glared at the Chameleon. "I didn't know I needed to report my whereabouts to you."

The tips of Jaya's fingers turned red. "Just because you're Caesar's son doesn't mean—"

Andre stood up abruptly. "I think we all know Caesar doesn't pay me any special privileges." He dropped his napkin on his plate. "It seems I'm not welcome at dinner."

It was becoming apparent he wasn't welcome anywhere. He kept a cool indifference on his face as he disappeared inside, sliding the glass door behind him. Was this how Arianne had felt in Pacific? Afraid of rejection from the people she craved love from, but too terrified to return to Pangaea?

He could see how, over a decade of such treatment, it could become maddening.

Maybe he needed to pave his way. Arianne had figured that out too late. He wasn't too keen on repeating her mistakes.

He stalked through the two-story beachside house. The sun set behind him, casting the white walls and furniture in shadow. Still, his training made it easy to detect movement in the kitchen. Andre slowed, recognizing Caesar's figure lingering by the fridge, brewing most likely his tenth coffee of the day.

He survived on coffee and leftovers. Andre assumed the sugar from the coffee provided most of Caesar's calories those days.

Content to ignore his father, he didn't say a word as he passed the kitchen, hoping the sound of the brewing coffee would cover the sound of his footsteps.

"Andre."

The former prince slowed with a grumble. "I see you've managed to miss dinner again."

"I wasn't hungry."

Andre turned. Caesar, like him, had always been on the lean side, but the months following the Valentinos' deaths had marked the difference between lean and emaciated. As strained as their relationship was, Andre hated watching him decompose before his eyes.

Once stately and composed, Caesar hardly found the energy to maintain his appearance anymore. His salt and pepper scruff had grown into a scraggly beard, and short-cropped hair had grown into jaw-length dreadlocks. Even the pressed two-piece suits that had once been his staple had been replaced with sweatpants and t-shirts.

"I wasn't hungry either," Andre said, moving to the room he shared with Kalinda.

Was this his life? Walking the line between loss and hatred? Were his only options working with people who didn't trust him, or fading away like his father?

Shoving his bedroom door closed behind him, he went to the window overlooking the sea as the sun descended over the water. He braced the windowsill, letting the sea breeze fill his nostrils. He knew he should reject the part of him that was drawn to Ace's machinations, but, but, *but...*

He'd tasted the ichor of royalty, and its golden glow seemed like a guiding light out of the surrounding darkness. Could he continue to drift through life worrying over what once was? Or would it be worth risking the peace he'd found for a chance at something better?

Stasis, or the thrill of the game?

A game he could play well.

The answer came when his mobile phone buzzed. Andre eagerly reached for it. Haris Cadmilus had only sent him two sentences, but they were the most valuable two sentences he'd read in months:

The Peregrine Pacific is behind you. Awaiting orders.

Chapter 11
Keston

The hours directly following treason always felt strange.

Everything proceeded as usual, yet a powerful sense of dread pressed on him everywhere he went. Keston desperately wanted a drink to calm his nerves, but even he knew that would be stupid after unleashing a team of superpowered operatives on Mexico City.

To make matters worse, his most recent run-in with treason—it was sad he was building a resume in that category—wasn't even the main thing on his mind. His thoughts repeatedly went back to one thing, one *female*.

Arianne. Arianne was *alive* in front of him. Witty and combative as ever. She'd been wearing civilian clothes, not those foreign battle leathers he'd seen in Oslo. She looked like the Arianne he'd lost. It was almost enough to drive him insane.

Especially in those fleeting moments when she didn't look like she wanted him dead. It made him crazy enough to think there was a chance.

A chance for what? He was trying to figure that out.

Well, he was still breathing, which was never guaranteed when dealing with any Murray. Keston numbly walked through the growing crowd of Elites. The afternoon sun beat down on his overwhelmed senses, leaving him strangely disoriented. He survived Arianne. Now what?

His eyes went to the ancient cathedral on the far side of Constitution Plaza, where a stage had been erected. Alvaro. He needed to find Alvaro.

Built in the center of Mexico City, the Plaza was massive. The entire square, typically flooded with street vendors, was sectioned off by a battalion of Wards, massive barricades, and military vehicles. Elites with VIP invitations entered the venue in controlled waves. Keston was among the masses pushing closer to the front, where another partition was erected for the special guests: Commanders and their inner circles.

Unfortunately, Keston's field trip meant he hadn't entered with the rest of the Europeans. He took advantage of the time swimming through the crowd to devise an excuse for his tardiness.

A giant clock stood on the central pyre of the cathedral, and he kept his eye on it. Eleven in the morning. Less than an hour before the Ascension Ceremony began. Could he reach Alvaro in time? Would he even be allowed to see him? Tension twisted his gut. If he couldn't warn Alvaro, or if Arianne refused to help, he was about to have a massive problem on his hands.

"Keston Celieneson."

The voice was chilling, stopping him in his tracks. There was power in how she spoke his name, like a priestess summoning an ancient demon. The crowd pressing against him faded. There was only one person on that planet who'd called him by that name before, and the last time she'd spoken it, she'd threatened to kill him.

Find yourself on the proper path, or I will send you to meet your mother myself. That's a promise.

Collecting himself, Keston turned to face his childhood hero, the warrior he'd looked up to when his town was nothing but ash with his mother buried beneath it. The bright desert sun caught her white hair in an ethereal glow. Up close, she was shorter than he expected, yet it felt like she was staring down at him. And those bright orange eyes... they could absolutely rip his soul apart piece by piece.

"Strix."

The winged warrior inclined her head, strangely calm amidst a bustling crowd. She wore a deep green tribal tunic with a white belt, a direct match to the antler crown on her head, and white paint scattered on her face and arms. Her wings were like her hair: unbound and ivory, hanging behind her shoulders. The stories of the Legend clashed with who stood before him. This was Strix, the Silent Death, the warrior who redefined how dangerous a *Fera* could be. But staring at her now, he saw nothing of her rumored rage and lethality. Instead, she was serene, refined, and controlled.

Strix extended her wings just slightly, parting the crowd around them for some space. That's when Keston noticed three more tribal warriors surrounding her: a towering female with dark brown hair, a shorter mouse-haired female, and a grey-haired female with a lupine smile. Each warrior had a tribal tunic similar to Strix's and had their faces painted artfully with black designs.

"Find our seats," Strix ordered, never removing her eyes from Keston. "I will join you momentarily."

The three Champions ducked their heads and disappeared in shocking unison, as if operating on a hive mind.

The corner of Strix's mouth tilted up. "You're wondering why we're here."

"Among other things."

Part of him was still amazed to be talking to his hero. The other part was figuring out why she hadn't yet killed him for what he'd done in New York.

"We were invited, of course," Strix said. He realized that she spoke so softly that only his sensitive ears could hear. Amidst the rush of passersby, they were virtually silent to humans.

In plain sight and surrounded by thousands of bustling bodies, they were in their most secure meeting spot possible. It was apparent now that she had not bumped into him by accident.

"You followed me."

"You just asked my Champions to endanger their mission." Strix shrugged. "Contrary to what your Commander believes, the Selvians came to this event with peaceful intentions."

Keston scanned the crowd for unwanted Pangaean eyes. "And what are your intentions now?"

"It brings me no comfort to admit that peace is no longer an option." A strange look of regret fell over her expression.

It suddenly struck Keston that he stood on the opposite side of Strix in that war. He took a careful step back. It didn't matter if he believed himself to be one of the most powerful fighters in the world. That past year had taught him to treat Legends with some deference.

"And where does that put us?" he asked slowly. "You called me Celineson..."

The rest of his question fell flat between them: *Did you know my mother?*

Strix nodded slowly. "I didn't know you were alive until recently. I believed Celine's children died beneath the rubble of Mende. I was tired of so much loss that I couldn't will myself to witness more. I didn't look for you when I should have. For that, I am genuinely sorry."

The ground felt like it was shaking beneath him, only for him to realize the only things shaking were his legs. He looked back up, unable to meet the Selvian's eyes. "No, but that doesn't make sense. My mother was—"

Cutting himself off, he realized he'd never known who his mother really was. A Pacifican and a musician, yes. But Pacific was only a few decades old, and music wasn't a nationality. His lips parted as the pieces came together—all those years of Ace alluding to his 'savage' blood, and Cassius's disappointment at his impure heritage.

"Your mother was many things," Strix said with careful deference. "Celine of the Montagne Tribe, Songbird of the Selvian Tribe, then Celiene Leroy. She was a daughter, sister, friend, rebel, mother, and the most talented Lyre in history."

"And what was she to you?"

"My *amica*—my best friend."

He could barely take a breath. "My mother was from the tribes? She knew you?" He shook his head. "Why didn't she tell me?"

Uncertainty crossed Strix's face. "Your mother suffered a lot of discrimination. And when you were a baby, she had to watch as her tribe was massacred. I can only assume she wanted to protect you and let you choose when you were ready. You were always a son of two worlds—worlds that have been at war for generations. Such a decision shouldn't be thrust on a child."

"I could have grown up in Selvia?"

The pain lacing his words shocked him. His mother was tribal, a mutant. He could've been raised shielded from the world: no Mende, no Leonueva, no machinations and power plays. He could've grown up embracing his powers, not hiding them.

"I'm so sorry," Strix said, voice cracking at the end. "What I said in New York still stands. I take responsibility for not finding you sooner. As your mother's *amica*, I was meant to be—what's the English phrase—your godmother." She reached into her tunic and produced a mobile phone. "This was your mother's, encrypted with Pacific shielding. If you're interested in learning more about your *Selvian* birthright, you know how to contact me."

He took the phone like a delicate egg. He didn't know if he'd ever held something so precious. That small rectangular device held a key to a past he'd thought was lost forever—a key to his mother.

The real question was whether he was brave enough to open the door.

"What about my sister?"

Strix paused, considering. "Genevieve chose what world she wanted to be in. It seems you've yet to make that choice."

Pangaea or Selvia. Was it just a simple choice? He wasn't so sure.

"Is that why you took her back in New York? Because she's Celine's daughter?"

Strix smiled, shifting back into the bustle of the crowd with one last wave. "Genevieve is Jaleel's daughter, and you are Celine's son. Something tells me she is exactly where she needs to be. If she has not explained further, then it is not the time."

"But what does that mean?"

"Goodbye, Celieneson. You have an event—or should I say an *attack*—to attend. We'll be in touch."

And then Strix was gone, disappearing into the dense crowd like an island fading into the mist. Keston was a rock lodged in a stream, the masses pushing past and diverting waves of people around him. Still, he didn't move.

Strix was his *godmother*. It all made sense now: his mother's endless stories, her reverence for the *Song of the Feras,* and her love of the nature surrounding their mountain home. And now he had a lifeline in his hands, a tether to a slumbering part of him he'd always felt was there but could never name.

Tucking the phone into the secret pocket of his jacket, right next to Hera's prescription bottle, Keston pushed his way to the front of the crowd. Strix was right. His latest existential crisis had to wait. He had a riot to pretend he didn't plan, a Commander to betray, and a Heir Apparent to save.

"Look who finally decided to show up."

Leon's rumble sent a shiver up Keston's spine as he lowered himself into his assigned seat beside his father. They were positioned directly in front of the ceremonial stage, adorned with turquoise flags, orchids, and ancient Aztec art. The ceremony's setup was stunning. Too bad Keston was too fixated on ruining it to marvel at the vast display of wealth.

He shifted uncomfortably in his chair, wings pressing into his backside. "You want me to be your celebrity? Well, I was out doing my job."

That wasn't a lie. He'd spared some time to mingle with the crowds on the way to the front, smiling for a camera or two. Thanks to his newest cape design, inspired by Native American designs and a poncho cut, he expected to appear on the front page of every fashion column for the next few weeks. A European Elite wearing North American designs was a subtle way to show their continent's growing alliance—that specific fashion would dominate the Elite halls until spring.

Leon crossed his legs, still in his military uniform. "My apologies. I just presumed you wouldn't want to miss a moment of the ceremony you orchestrated."

His eyes bore into Keston, and he tried not to flinch. The insinuation was obvious. He knew Leon was trying to get a rise out of him. Keston had killed Denzel Smith, clearing the way for Alvaro to Ascend. Sure, the former North American Commander had been comatose, but that didn't relieve the guilt.

Alvaro had been a good person, and Keston killed his beloved parent. Just like Arianne.

He suddenly got the urge to snap his wings out and fly as far away as possible.

Then, the Pangaean anthem echoed across the square. Blood-red Pangaean flags rose to the trumpets, followed by a thunder of feet as everyone stood. As the music rose to a crescendo, the doors to the cathedral opened, and Alvaro strode out with his family behind him. To his right were his brother and nephew: the soon-to-be Heir Apparent, Miguel. Alvaro's wife walked hand in hand with him, followed by their two toddlers, with a graying woman Keston could only assume was their grandmother.

The former First Mother of North America, Denzel Smith's wife, a widow, thanks to Keston. He knew it didn't matter, but he applauded even harder.

The North American royal family sat on the stage, and the former First Mother stepped toward the podium. She still wore mourning black, her face half-shrouded in a veil. Still, she addressed the crowd bravely, "Today marks the five hundred and second anniversary of the Ascension of Pangaea. On this day of Ascension, we may present our Heirs to rise to the ultimate servants of Pangaea. On this day, we create a Commander."

The audience burst into thunderous applause. As Mexico City and the world cheered, five figures rose from the front row and walked toward the stage. Keston felt the breath escape him as the five gods who'd graced the ceremony approached to greet their newest member: the Commanders of Pangaea.

Leon Murray was first, always the tallest of any group, but in a rare moment, not the most intimidating. Each Commander behind him carried an equal, though different, brand of oppressive power.

Hana Lang, a woman hardly larger than one hundred twenty pounds, wore a stunning deep red hanfu with golden trim. The skirts rained behind her like feathers as she ascended the steps. Though the smallest of the five, she carried a delicate power like a diamond that adorned a ring: beautiful but unbreakable. A man and a woman waited behind Hana, presumably her children: Zhou Qin and Mori Sora, from two different fathers.

Ansley Williams, the oldest of the Commanders, reigned over Australia. Many regarded the woman as the matriarch of Commanders, with her short, gray hair and her favored traditional pant suits. Rumors of her retiring in the next few years had spread before the conflict in the Big Three escalated. She left a large group behind, including many heirs and grandchildren.

Luiza Angular was the only Commander who'd brought no family. From the reports Keston had read, the man beside her was her general. Luiza, with curling Brazilian hair adorned with Amazonian beads, was the most secretive, favoring an almost anti-Empire nationalism. But she participated just enough in worldwide events—such as that Ceremony—to stave off suspicions.

The last Commander to stand, pointedly as far away from Leon as possible, was Kajari Sarr. While Leon seemed carved from Viking mythology with his golden hair and militaristic clothing, Kajari was molded by an entirely different pantheon. He looked like an Egyptian god with his golden breastplate, jewelry, and long locs of hair beautifully adorning his perfect face. He walked with confidence despite Leon's noticeable glare.

Keston looked toward Kajari's family, only to find the eldest son staring directly at him. Prince Khari's eyes narrowed as they locked gazes, and Keston couldn't help but bristle. Still, he managed an insufferable smile that made the prince scowl. It seemed neither male had forgotten their meeting at Alvaro's *Dia de los Muertos* celebration, or how they'd both been in New York.

Watching the African Commander, it was easy to see where Khari got all his insufferable confidence from—and beauty. He was joined by five younger siblings and the First Mother of Africa, who notably stood as far away from him as possible.

Then Keston remembered: Khari's mother had passed years ago, making the current Queen his stepmother—another *Fera* heir, paired with a rival mother vying for her children's favoritism.

Maybe Europe wasn't the only continent with a healthy dose of conflict in the halls of its royal family.

Alvaro's mother continued once the five Commanders had lined up on stage and the applause had died down. "I am proud to present my son, Alvaro Smith, as my husband's successor to the Commandership of North America."

The former First Mother presented an ancient tome with worn leather binding and yellowing pages: the Pangaean Constitution. Keston had always heard stories of the book created by the founders of Pangaea, but he'd never seen it before. If he hadn't known the book was the Constitution, he would've assumed it was just another dust-covered manuscript that crowded the private libraries in Elite palaces. It was strange to think such a mundane book could contain the words controlling the largest empire in Earth's history.

The ceremony descended into reading passages from the Constitution, preaching about the importance of worldwide unity and how Pangaea had saved this world from itself five hundred years ago. Keston stopped listening. He'd heard enough propaganda to rot his brain cells five hundred times over. Instead, his eyes locked on Alvaro, cursing himself for failing to warn the Heir Apparent. Alvaro looked eager and proud as he recited his mother's words—a well-bred leader ready to carry the weight of a continent.

If he only knew what insanity was waiting for him.

Cautiously, Keston scanned the audience. He was fortunate to be on a raised viewing platform; he could see the sea of people flowing for blocks behind him. There were easily tens of thousands of people, all eager to witness the birth of a god. Sweat broke out in his clenched palms. Whatever distraction Arianne had planned would cause a riot on a scale he'd never witnessed.

That was, *if* Arianne chose to help him.

Where was she?

The more Keston stole glances toward the crowd, the more his anxiety grew. There was nothing out of the ordinary. Finding a team of rebel insurgents in such a mass would be next to impossible, but he tried anyway. Alvaro—the entire continent—was counting on this ceremony going down the drain.

He searched. Still nothing.

The sea of people behind the viewing platform parted, and Keston's head immediately whipped to the source. Hera Richards, donning her finest hooded lab coat, carried a crimson-red pillow. Resting on top was a needle, syringe, and the glowing turquoise liquid of the Serum. As was the custom, the Continent with the most recent Ascension would protect the Serum Creation Protocol until another Commander needed to Ascend. That continent would then be the one to deliver the Serum to the newest Commander as a sign of good faith.

Keston's mouth dried out. Hera's head was held high in pride. She *never* did anything in good faith.

For the first time since Genevieve's warning about Alvaro's reaction to the Serum, he wondered if Hera and Leon *knew* what would happen. Keston squinted, analyzing the European Commander, but he never gave anything away that he didn't want people to see.

"You're fidgeting more than usual," Cassius said.

Keston pursed his lips. "A lot of noise. It's bothering my ears," he lied.

"Then put your earplugs in."

Hera's earplugs limited his hearing for situations like those, but he wasn't about to explain that there was no way in hell he'd wear them right now. He needed all his senses for what was coming.

Arianne, where are *you?*

Alvaro's hand was on the Constitution, completing his final recitation. "I shall uphold the Constitution and the pillars on which this empire stands. I, Alvaro Smith, accept the Serum and pledge silence of its secrets as I take on the name Denzel Smith."

A shadow shot past the sun, too low to be a jet. It dropped out of the sky, surrounded by feathers and the flowing fabric of a poncho. The figure slammed between Hera, gearing up to inject the Serum, and Alvaro. Though a sombrero and red bandana shielded the person's face, Keston knew it was her.

His Princess had come after all.

Arianne extended one of her burning blades toward Hera, looping her hand around Alvaro and pulling him to her like he was her captive. Her voice was distorted, most likely by the Ward's mask hidden underneath her bandana, when she spoke: "Gee, I do love crashing parties."

Explosions rocked the square. Billowing plumes of flame shot to the sky and blew the barriers around the ceremony to crumbling fragments. The whole city shook. As Keston lunged to shield his father from the raining debris, he was taken back to Oslo, where a similar tactic had been utilized. Arianne's team—only five strong—just convinced Mexico City that they were under attack by a much larger insurgent army.

That's when the screaming began.

Chapter 12

Arianne

Alvaro needed to crowned Commander first. They needed to thread the needle, bide their time for the crucial period between Alvaro becoming regent of North America and receiving his dose of Serum. This way, he kept unrestricted control over his continent *without* losing his mind.

It wasn't a long-term fix, but it would have to do for now.

"Now is not the time for one of your scenes," Alvaro spat in her grip, recognizing her scent.

"My timing happens to be *impecable*," Arianne said. "Whatever you do, don't let that needle touch you."

"Or what?"

"You get a one-way ticket to crazy-ville. Trust me, it's not a fun ride."

The only reason the Wards storming the stage didn't pepper her with lead and lasers was thanks to her human—or more accurately, mutant—shield. The shield she was trying to save. It sounded absolutely absurd, but that was her life.

Alvaro yanked again, but his efforts were strictly for show that time. "What do you know?" he screamed louder. "Let me go!"

"Congratulations, Your Majesty, we're kidnapping you!"

Through the chaos assaulting her senses, Arianne hadn't taken notice of the one Commander who hadn't hastily exited the stage. Whether it was from pure confidence in his aim or a lack of care if he hit Alvaro, Leon Murray fired at her. A shooting pain pierced her shoulder. She fell backward, feeling the awful recoil of the bullet digging through bone and muscle. And, of course, it was precisely on her unhealed blaster wound from her previous mission.

Thanks, Daddy-o.

As she fell, she allowed herself a couple of moments to bemoan the awful irony of her existence. Even when he believed her dead, Leon was still trying to kill her.

Alvaro ran out of her grip toward Leon. Arianne recovered moments after hitting the ground—a bullet wound was the least of her worries with the risk of a feral *Fera* on her hands. Her eyes locked on her father, muscles tensing to spring at him and rip his head clean off. He was inches away. She could do it. *She would do it.*

Before she could rocket toward her father's jugular, the Wards finally converged on her. She barked more in annoyance than fear as the first two rushed forward with their military-issue swords. *Fera*-skewers, she liked to call them. Arianne ignited her blades—people would call them Ward-skewers once she was done with them.

"Love to stick around and play, but I don't have time for appetizers right now!" she said through her mask's modulator, her voice far deeper.

She charged at the Wards, one eye on their blades and another on Leon escorting Alvaro off the stage. Even with her attention divided, the Wards didn't stand a chance. She jumped ten feet in the air as the five officers converged on her, spinning in a death tornado of flaming metal and feathers. She landed with ease. With one last twist, she killed the remaining Ward.

Five down. And she hadn't even lost her sombrero.

She looked up. Leon and Alvaro ran toward the cathedral where the other Commanders had retreated. That must've been their evacuation plan. She turned and watched as her team fought through the rampage of terrified citizens toward the stage, weapons ready.

"We got this covered. You get Alvaro!" Topher shouted in English, careful to conceal their tribal relations.

Arianne barely had a moment to nod before her team dove into the fray. She smiled proudly at her team, and sprinted toward the cathedral. She barely made it behind the cover of the stage when she ran into a wall of feathers so dark they shone like obsidian in the sun.

"Keston!" She stomped her foot in frustration, more like a disgruntled toddler than a deadly operative.

He didn't budge. His huge frame blocked the cathedral doors, unreadable like a sphinx, wings and all. He shrugged. "Appearances, Princess."

Her stomach dropped. He looked like Blackjack, like he betrayed her. *Again.* Was this his plan all along? To incriminate the Selvians and pull her out of hiding?

How could she be so stupid? She screamed in rage and connected the dual blades of *Horizon's Edge* at their handles, making a gnarly double-sided blade.

Keston wanted a fight? She would give it to him.

"It appears I've trusted you for the last time, Pangaea Boy." She extended her weapon, marking her target.

He winked, and for a brief second, she could've sworn the male she'd fallen for stood before her. The moment passed before she was sure of what she'd seen, but it was enough to make her waver.

Keston drew a Pangaean military sword from his hip and pointed it at her in welcome. "Trust that if you beat me, you'll still have time to save him." He flicked his chin ever so slightly toward a camera erected on the cathedral wall.

A dance, then. An act for the ever-present cameras. She'd show him just how good at dancing she was. A small smile quirked on her lips. Good thing her lower face was covered; she didn't want any evidence that she might be enjoying herself.

"You were always my favorite dance partner," Arianne said.

Then she attacked.

They locked blades. Sparks flew as the molten tip of *Horizon's Edge* ate through his steel. Keston didn't flinch from the impact, weathering the full strength of her attack. Arianne gave him an ounce of credit—his power had grown since they'd called themselves lovers.

But so had hers.

"Try not to step on my toes," he said, throwing her off him and slyly dusting off his boots. "They're North American grass-fed leather."

"Here, I'll give you a taste of Selvian leather!"

Keston slackened. "Wha—"

She cut him off with a flap of her wings, a twist, and a *satisfying* kick to his lower jaw. He stumbled back, hand cupping his face. A trail of blood trickled down his cheek, turning his lips bright red.

Arianne bit her lip, somehow aroused at the sight.

Body a blur of motion that she was almost too slow to follow, Keston closed the space. She threw her blade up to block, cursing her distraction. Unless he'd hired a master swordsman to train him every day that past year, there was no *way* he should be able to match her favored form of combat.

"I thought we agreed to pull our punches," Keston smirked, his amber eyes glittering with challenge.

"I never agreed to that."

Without warning, Arianne disconnected *Horizon's Edge* and palmed twin swords. The sudden shift caught Keston off balance. She took the offensive, her arms a fury of attacks punctuated by the orange glow of metal. He was impressive for someone with a lesser blade and lesser abilities. His speed and strength kept him in the fight, and she was forced to admit that someone *had* been training him.

An uninitiated swordsman wouldn't be able to hold a candle to her bonfire.

As they traded blows, a shadow shot past overhead. Both winged fighters looked up to see Sygrid rocket toward the closed cathedral doors. Flipping around, she delivered a two-booted kick at the entrance, the doors flying open upon impact. Locked or not, no door in the world could withstand Sygrid on a mission.

"Look, now you've gotten Sygrid involved," Arianne moaned in annoyance. "Let me inside!"

Keston deflected her ambitious jab. "That's what I was planning on saying to you later, Princess."

With a scream, she swung down at his head. And not the head on his shoulders. The one that seemed to be thinking for him those days. Keston yelped and fumbled backward. Even such a momentary call of surprise from his sonic voice threatened to burst her eardrums. She buckled at the high-pitched note, her swords clattering to the ground.

"Shit!" Keston shouted, genuine concern in his voice.

Her head spun as he ran toward her. She felt the vibration of his feet on the ground more than heard him in her daze. It was obvious he hadn't meant to hurt her. She knew he was rushing to her aid.

But she was *pissed*. Most importantly, they had certain appearances to uphold.

The ringing in her ears slowly ebbed. As soon as his shadow covered her, she shot upward. Her wings carried her into the sky, and her knee connected with his lower jaw, shooting his head back.

Flipping back and landing limp on the ground, his lights were instantly off. Arianne told herself she didn't care. She told herself he deserved it. But, despite every reason, she didn't fly after Sygrid. Instead, she knelt and checked him for signs of life.

Nothing.

Her breath caught. Thinking quickly, Arianne stole the blaster from Keston's hip and fired three shots at the camera that had caught their fight. The camera saw her beat him, he would have an alibi for his treason. Now, she just needed to ensure she hadn't killed him—Pangaea didn't need to see that part. Even she didn't want to see that part.

Removing her sombrero, she leaned over him. Placing a hand over his bloody lips, she prayed for that hot air he was always so full of. She couldn't detect anything. Leaning closer, their faces were now inches apart.

"Come on, Pangaea Boy, I thought your skull was thicker than that," she muttered.

One amber eye opened just slightly. The other was swollen shut, the skin already a bright shade of purple. A small smile cracked Keston's lips. "You always held the trophy in the thick skull category, Princess."

"Seeing as you're not dead, I'm going back to hating you."

Dashing off, Arianne shoved her hat back on as she darted past the intricate artwork lining the cathedral's hallways. She had tunnel vision, following Sygrid's scent toward the Commanders. It wasn't a long run. The church opened into a cavernous sanctuary with colorful stained-glass windows and a grand golden altar. Arianne slowed, realizing she'd never been inside a church in her life.

God—or whoever was supposed to watch over the place—probably wasn't happy with her actions that day. Not that the alternative was much better.

While most Commanders and their families had wisely evacuated, five particularly curious masochists remained behind. Leon Murray, Hera Richards, and Hana Lang stood with Kajari and Khari Sarr on the raised altar. Sygrid faced their half-circle, hands raised in surrender. And in the middle of it all was Alvaro. Though the young North American Commander attempted to look collected, it was apparent he was confused by how his head whipped around in assessment.

Shoulders squared, Leon seemed incredibly proud of himself. "Just as I suspected, Selvia has decided to take their terrorism international."

"It brings me no joy to concede that Commander Murray was correct." Hana frowned at Sygrid, her dark eyes freezing cold. "Can we expect your scourge to cross into my borders, savage?"

Kajari remained silent. He watched his rival Commanders with interest but didn't attempt to sway the conversation. Only Khari seemed to notice Arianne's arrival. His eyes flickered toward her for a fraction of a second before returning to his loyal vigil behind his father.

Sygrid paid the three Commanders no mind. Her orange gaze remained locked on Alvaro. "We did not start this. Ask Europe why they're so eager to inject you with that poison."

"Poison?" Leon rumbled. "Unless you know something we don't, this Serum will make him a god. Don't you want to join our Pantheon, Alvaro Smith?"

Hera stepped out from behind him, the Serum syringe prepared in her hand.

Ducking behind a pew, Arianne's frustration went from simmering to boiling. She itched to shoot across the church and kill her father *now*. The version of her from a year ago might've taken the risk. But attacking Leon would only make that very delicate situation worse. Fists clenched, she bided her time.

Sygrid was silent. Did Leon know about Alvaro's genetics? What were the chances that he knew what that Serum would do to a mutant? Such secrets were too valuable to risk spilling, but they were the only way to convince Alvaro to side with Selvia. If Arianne were Sygrid, she would've started swinging. But that was why she wasn't in charge.

Alvaro pointed a finger. "We invited your people in good faith, Strix."

She ducked her head. "That is why I am returning your kindness. Everything I do today is in good faith." Looking up, her eyes locked with Leon's. "We all know he's incapable of such consideration."

That gave Alvaro pause. "This ceremony is already ruined. It would be against tradition to receive the Serum now: away from the Constitution and out of the eye of my people. I am Commander, so I command that we complete this ceremony as intended next Ascension Day. We'll have a year to work out the *kinks*."

"I agree," Kajari risked injecting.

Something shifted on Leon's face. Arianne's mouth dried out. She'd learned to recognize that change from a very young age—it was one of the few reasons she'd survived long enough to escape. All regalness in him was gone, replaced by burning contempt. He was a lion cornered by people he considered gazelles. The following kills were no longer for survival. They were for pride.

This vicious predation was Leon's true nature, not that dignified mask. This was what lingered underneath the European Commander's composure.

"I don't think so," Leon said slowly, stepping toward Alvaro. He extended his hand, and Hera placed the vaccine in his open palm. "You are not Commander until you take the Serum." Again, he looked at Sygrid. "Unless there is something we should know?"

She clenched her jaw, body rigid with hatred.

Hana Lang nodded, agreeing. "North America cannot remain stagnant for another year. We are doing this ceremony *now*." Her hand snaked toward a blaster at her hip.

Khari narrowed his eyes and stepped protectively in front of his father.

Alvaro turned to Sygrid cautiously. "I trust you—"

He couldn't finish. Leon lunged with an all-too-familiar warrior's speed, tackling Alvaro to the ground. The needle sank into Alvaro's neck before they hit the floor.

Arianne and Sygrid screamed in tandem as the entire vial of turquoise liquid drained into Alvaro's bloodstream. The color crept like a glowing river through the arteries up his neck and into the base of his skull.

Sprinting from behind the pew, Arianne didn't make it two steps before Alvaro began convulsing on the floor. Sygrid jumped over his body, battle axes ready, as she ran toward Leon. More than ready to join her in cutting Leon in half, Arianne pumped her arms faster.

She barely made it up the altar's first step before a powerful soundwave assaulted her ears. Collapsing to the ground, she and Sygrid screamed in pain. Another distant thud: Khari. Gritting her teeth, Arianne fought to find the source until she registered a small device in Hera's hand.

A high-pitched sound emitter that only affected *Fera* ears.

Hera placed the device on the ground before she and Leon ran.

Kajari and Hana didn't escape with their European counterparts. Instead, they both lunged for the device. Kajari reached it first and immediately flipped the switch. The three *Feras* sagged in relief. Arianne's ears still rang, but she could finally think.

Hana Lang barked in annoyance, stepping back to fire at the African Commander. Khari jumped in front of his father, reaching out to intercept the plasma shot like he was catching a ball. Though deflecting the blast, he hit the ground with a bark in pain, clutching his burnt fist to his chest.

"You always had a soft spot for *Feras*," Hana seethed at Kajari. "It makes sense now. Your son is one of them! You're a *traitor*. You don't deserve your position as Commander."

Maybe Arianne's cover wasn't the one being blown today.

She realized too late that she had focused on the wrong Commander. Sygrid screamed, forcing Arianne's attention on Alvaro. The Ductor had the North

American in an arresting hold, her arms looped under his shoulders as she held him to the ground. His body continued to writhe and shake.

The African and Asian Commanders were in a standoff. Two Pangaean heirs faced exposure. And the Selvian Ductor clutched the North American Commander in a chokehold.

Diplomatic disaster, indeed.

"Come on, Alvaro," Sygrid said. "Fight it. You need to fight it!"

"*¡Tienes que luchar!*" Arianne screamed, praying Alvaro would hear his native tongue.

She would remember the moment he opened his black eyes for the rest of her life.

Feral. Too late.

Sygrid still struggled to hold the writhing male down. "Stay with me!" She didn't notice the shift, and if she did, she couldn't have prepared for Alvaro's assault.

With unreasonable strength, Alvaro twisted in Sygrid's grip and delivered a swipe down the left side of her face with his clawed hand. Her left eye rolled across the bloodied altar.

Arianne was lost in a trance, staring at her mentor's orange iris as it rolled to her boot. Each heartbeat, each pound of blood in her ears, stretched for eternity. Maybe her hearing was still damaged, but all she heard was sharp ringing, drowning out the chaos.

Lifting her eyes from the eyeball, there was Sygrid, her mentor—her *mother*—lying in a bleeding heap on the ground.

This is Leon's fault.

Her heartbeat raced. Her breathing, once deep and slow, became shallow and fast. Sweat pooled out of every pore, making her skin feel like it was on fire.

This is my father's fault. This is my *fault.*

Arianne roared. That ember of Instinct inside of her became hellfire. She barely registered Hana Lang standing over Sygrid, emotionlessly holding a blaster to her head. She barely heard her own screams as she dove into the line of Hana's fire. She barely felt the impact of the blaster plasma as it tore into her abdomen.

Only feral excitement remained as her blades cut the Asian Commander in half from shoulder to hip.

Consequences didn't exist in that state. She wasn't thinking about Alvaro as a friend or worrying about angering Asia. Sygrid was hurt, and Hana was attempting to kill her. Everyone involved would *pay*.

Commander Hana Lang slumped to the floor, the top half of her body sliding away as the bottom half buckled. No blood spilled. The heat of Arianne's blades cauterized the wound that had cleanly slashed the Commander in two. Only when she was certain Sygrid was safe did she focus her crazed attention on the other feral creature in the room.

Khari was fighting to keep Alvaro's rampage away from his father. Arianne took her chance. With Alvaro's back to her, it was easy to grab him by his jacket collar and throw him across the room. The North American Commander rocketed into the back wall of the altar, his shoulder impaled by the edge of a cross on the wall. Arianne didn't slow. She leaped into the air, ripping him from where he hung. His shoulder made an ugly squelching noise as she tugged him free and threw him onto the ground. The cathedral shook with the impact.

Arianne landed, ready to put down the feral creature that'd possessed Alvaro. Her wings surrounded her, casting her and her infernal mission in shadow. All she felt was rage and vengeance.

"Stop!" A familiar voice cracked her fury. "He's down! We're restraining him."

Blue. Her friend's arms wrapped around her midsection, hugging her tight. Arianne almost threw the Snake off her, but Lova suddenly materialized, orange eyes wide with concern. The Cheetah didn't say anything, just extended her arms in a hug, completing the circle. As Arianne breathed in the familiar scents of her friends, her frenzy faded.

And she was left with the aftermath.

Instinct had left her, but her anger hadn't.

"Sygrid!" Arianne cried out, tearing herself from the embrace and landing beside her mentor.

Sygrid was breathing, her right eye open, but dazed. The Selvian Ductor barely registered Arianne as she scooped her up and held her in her lap. Arianne's hands were shaking as she stroked Sygrid's white hair in an attempt to soothe her.

"Sygrid?" Arianne's voice wavered. "Sygrid, come on. I'm here. It's over."

Behind them, her team of Champions had managed to restrain Alvaro. Eyes still black, he continued to fight, but his struggles were subsiding.

Arianne didn't care if her team *killed* Alvaro. All she cared about was Sygrid. "Come on," she whispered. "You're all right. You're all right."

Sygrid's breathing evened out, and her remaining eye lost some of its fog. "Arianne?"

Arianne sobbed. "You're okay. You're okay."

Even though her face was a bloodied mess, Sygrid managed to smile. She raised a hand, and Arianne took it fervently. "That's my girl."

"You're okay," Arianne said a third time.

Because she needed to guarantee it was true. She couldn't think of a world where Sygrid was not in it with her. A tear slid down her face as she pressed Sygrid's hand to her cheek. They sat there, crying in relief and terror.

They'd almost lost each other, all because they'd risked themselves to maintain peace with an Empire that had no interest in returning the favor.

Kajari let out a low whistle, forcing Arianne to raise her head. He was staring down at what was left of Hana Lang, kneeling to close her lifeless eyes.

Slowly, he stood. "This isn't good."

Arianne squeezed Sygrid's hand. "She raised a blaster toward my Ductor. Her death was faster than she deserved."

Silence answered. Everyone in the cathedral stared at her now, the implications of her crime coating the air with tension. But Arianne found she didn't care. She didn't care if Hana was a Commander. She didn't care if she'd pissed off Asia in the process.

Leon stole Alvaro's sanity. Hana almost took Sygrid's life. They ruined what should've been a hopeful ceremony crowning a good male as a leader—the world's final shot at peace.

She refused to let Pangaea keep taking. She refused to keep apologizing for her actions when Pangaea *started* the conflict.

It was her turn.

Arianne slowly stood, the weight of her decision settling on her like a comforting blanket. They'd played Sygrid's game. No longer would she hold out for the *humanity* of her opponents. It was time to match them blow for blow. It was time to play like a Commander.

And, like it or not, only Arianne knew how to do it.

Arianne pointed at Blue. "Give Alvaro enough venom to neutralize him."

Blue nodded, carefully walking over to him and sticking one of her venom darts in his arm.

Once Alvaro's struggles ceased, Arianne pointed to Rhino. "Keep Alvaro restrained. Put him on the jet and bring him back to Selvia for observation.

Hopefully, we can rehabilitate him. If the insanity from the Serum is permanent, we can use him as a bargaining chip. Blitz, Blue, Satyr. Take our Ductor back to the jet. I want medical intervention immediately."

Sygrid was conscious enough to smile proudly at Arianne. "Are you sure you're ready?"

Sygrid had grown insanely adept at reading Arianne. Maybe it was because they were too similar for their own good. Despite Sygrid's best attempts, Arianne needed to follow the path her mentor had walked twenty years ago. She just hoped this time it would work.

Arianne solemnly watched her teammates collect their fallen Ductor. "I don't think we have a choice anymore."

As Sygrid and Alvaro were carried out of the sanctuary, Kajari folded his arms behind his back. He hardly seemed phased by the day's events. "I'll await news from your Ductor once she's recovered."

"No need," Arianne replied. "You'll receive communication from me from now on."

"Oh?" Kajari's eyebrow quirked.

When Arianne's eyes landed on Khari, she was surprised to see understanding there. Slowly, he ducked his head.

He agreed.

"No more half measures. No more fear. War is upon us. We must move forward unflinchingly if we want to survive." Arianne forced herself to stand straighter, even as the weight of the responsibility she was stepping into was already attempting to crush her. "I hereby accept your proposal, Commander Sarr. From this moment on, I will be Deputy of Selvia. Khari and I will be betrothed and make an uprising unlike anything this world has seen."

Commander Kajari Sarr's smile stretched from ear to ear. He extended his hand adorned in gold. Arianne shook it. The only way to beat Leon was to play like him. She was ready to become the monster if it meant she would win.

"We have a deal, Phoenix."

"We will burn our enemies to the ground."

Chapter 13

Andre

"Are you sure about this?"

Haris's warning barely registered. Staring at Pandora's stasis chamber, Andre's reflection melded with the murky image of her sleeping face behind the glass. He knew better than most what kind of monster he was unleashing. But it didn't matter. His mind was made up, and he was not the type to turn back on his decisions because of *nerves*.

The Ascension Ceremony terrorist attack the day before only solidified his plans. The empire was unstable. Power vacuums were spawning left and right. If there was a time to take power of his own, it was now. Ace was right: he was the perfect mix of rebel and Elite blood.

"Do you have her shutoff protocol figured out?"

Haris nodded. He reached into his pocket and produced a small control panel. "She thinks of herself as a puppet master, but now we have her strings."

"Let her out, then." Andre clasped his hands behind his back. "Then get to the airport and ensure your forces are ready."

At that, Haris hesitated. "We agreed on a *peaceful* evacuation. Waking Pandora up puts that at risk."

"Then make sure you're not in this room when she wakes up. I'm the only person on this island who won't set her off. We need her in case things go south."

Andre also had to ensure he wasn't walking into one of Ace's traps. Waking Pandora would allow him an opportunity to compare notes *before* he staged a coup that took one-third of Pacific's forces.

Without another word, Haris typed a code into the stasis chamber's computer. His fingers were a fury of motion as he bypassed dozens of security systems—ironically put in place by him to avoid that very situation.

But things had changed since Pandora had landed on Pacific's shores. The world was ripping itself apart. If Pacific refused to address it, Andre would take matters into his own hands.

There was a sharp hissing noise as the stasis chamber depressurized. The coffin-like pod started to rotate onto its back. Haris hastily collected his personal tablet, several loose-leaf notebooks full of blueprints and notes, and a few prototypes. Backpack stuffed to the limits of its zippers, the male turned to look out over his laboratory one last time.

Andre realized this was the first time Haris had ever left the safety of Pacific's borders.

Haris tossed Pandora's remote to Andre, his lips tensed. "We'll see you at the runway in twenty minutes." His blue eyes flickered to Pandora's vitals monitor, watching as her heart rate started to rise. "Not a drop of Pacific blood spilled, or we do not have a deal, Andre."

"What good is a king if you cannot trust his promises?"

His thoughts instantly went to Caesar. His father built a powerful rebellion with the promise of freedom and victory, only to let the society he'd created rot away after one loss. Andre would not be like him, like either of his fathers. He would be better. Driven, not cruel. Robust, not apathetic.

He would succeed because he'd seen the ruin in Leon's wake. He wouldn't quit because he'd seen the oppressive fog of Caesar's hopelessness.

The chamber hatch finally clicked open. Smoke billowed out, built of humidity and stimulants to pull her out of her death-like stasis. The cyborg looked like a vampire rising out of a century-long sleep.

Pandora's eyes burst open, her robotic irises flaring neon blue. She sat up slowly and deliberately, her hands rising to her face as she assessed herself with a disconnected curiosity. Maybe she was too dazed to be cautious, or maybe she no longer concerned herself with whatever threats awaited her.

When you're the most dangerous human in the world, you typically don't concern yourself with whether or not you'll win a fight.

"Did you finally decide to kill me?" Pandora sang, not even looking at him.

Andre's hand crept to his double-bladed sword strapped to his back. "If I had, I would've saved myself the trouble and killed you in your sleep."

She tipped her bald head back and laughed. Without her hair, the cybernetics lining her skull were far more visible, some glowing the same shade of blue as her eyes.

She jumped out of the pod, adorned in a jet-black experimental bodysuit. Her cybernetic arm traced the outside of her stasis chamber with sensuous tenderness. "Ace sure is convincing, if she's managed to get you to work with *me*. My mother did orchestrate your mother and Arianne's deaths." She shrugged, eyes flickering up to him. "And your grandparents... Well, I'll take full credit for that one."

Andre stiffened.

"But you need me," Pandora continued, cracking her neck with a satisfying pop. "At this level in the game, the past means nothing compared to the future."

"*We* need each other if we want to rule."

Pandora advanced on Andre so quickly that he feared an attack. But she halted a few heart-stopping centimeters from his face. She tilted her head just enough to cast her face in shadow and then snapped her fingers. "Exactly," she said darkly. "*Perspective*. We can keep tearing each other to pieces, but that only means someone else inherits the throne. And then we both lose."

"Andre?"

His stomach bottomed out when he recognized Kalinda's voice. When he turned, it was as he'd feared. Kaldina stood at the lab doors, sides heaving from running, and face cast in white terror.

Jaya was with her, skin and hair bright red in outrage. "I told you we couldn't trust him!" she bellowed. "He was sneaking out at night for *something*."

A terrible smile grew on Pandora's face as she crouched. "Look at you, Andy. You even brought me a warm-up match."

Andre's mouth parted, brain too slow to process the rapidly devolving situation. He barely shot an arm out to stop Pandora before she attacked. "Don't move. No Pacifican blood will be spilled today."

Kalinda stepped toward him even as Jaya fought to hold her back. "Andre, what's happening? Please, there must be an explanation."

Staring into Kalinda's eyes, his gut twisted in knots. He'd hoped to return to the island in a few weeks and explain everything to her. He'd hoped she would understand and agree to join him when the dust settled. In all of his calculations, he'd always thought Kalinda would come with him. He'd never considered her looking at him like *that*.

Like he was a traitor. Like he was the villain.

But what could he do? He'd grown up learning his purpose in life far outweighed any feelings he built for others along the way, regardless of how powerful they were. Leon had prepared him for that predicament since he was a child. Leaders sacrificed for their crowns.

Jaya stepped in front of her sister and pointed a blaster at Pandora. "There's no explanation in existence that can justify letting that *monster* free."

Pandora stared hungrily at Jaya, fingers twitching with anticipation. "Hello again, Little Chameleon." She tilted her head slightly toward Andre. "They're going to alert the entire island. If you want to avoid more bloodshed, we must silence them."

Andre's chest tightened. The Bahri sisters had shown him immense kindness in the year since he lost his position as prince. Sure, Jaya had been abrasive, but she'd allowed him to exist in her family. And Kalinda...

He couldn't harm Kalinda.

"Take them," Andre ordered. "Not a drop spilled, Pandora."

"Boy, do I love a challenge."

Without warning, Pandora dashed. In the time it took the cyborg to close the distance between them, Jaya fired off two blaster shots. Neither hit as Pandora had changed directions with inhuman efficiency.

Kalinda's screech would haunt his nightmares. "Andre! What are you doing?"

Jaya was no match for Pandora. She was pacified in seconds. He had to look away as Pandora converged on Kalinda. If he saw the cyborg lay a hand on her, the image would be seared into his brain, too.

"You'll understand soon, Kal. Please trust me."

It would all make sense soon. It would all be worth it when he was in control.

The throne room doors in the Madrid Royal Palace burst open. Leon Murray stormed in, flanked by his Inner Circle. Andre sat back on his throne, a delighted smile coming to his face as Hera, Cassius, Keston, Genevieve, and Sensatia approached.

One year ago, those insufferable Elites had discarded him. Now, he got to watch as they came to *him*.

Pandora grinned, her hand resting on his right shoulder. Leon had brought his court, and it was time to introduce them to Andre's. He was surrounded by his closest confidants: Pandora, Haris, Texas Hold'Em, the captain of the Madrid Wards, and Rou, sleeping in his lap. Even Jaya and Kalinda were in attendance—though Jaya had been forced into one of Pandora's collars, and Kalinda hadn't spoken to him in days.

But Andre's power extended far beyond who was seated at his side. Since Leon never publicly disowned him, staking his claim to the Ortiz estate had been a bloodless affair. It helped that Andre had three thousand Peregrine Pacific forces—all eager for revolution. The Wards in Madrid, loyal to his grandparents, pledged their allegiance just as quickly. That throne room was packed with a healthy mix of both factions, all kneeling before their new lord.

Leon's Inner Circle was forced to walk through the narrow aisle that parted his sea of loyal warriors. Andre might lack his family's showmanship, but he'd still learned how to turn heads.

Just before the steps to Andre's throne, Leon came to a stop. Though his face was calm and regal, thinly veiled rage simmered beneath the surface. The Commander frowned. "I see you've grown a backbone, son."

"Son," Andre spat. "Are we still playing that game, *father*?"

Ace spoke through his earpiece. "Your palace is surrounded, prince. Don't instigate too much. May I also remind you that my daughter is in your hands?"

He ignored her. Leon didn't respect people who tiptoed around him. That lesson had been learned the hard way a year before. If he wanted Leon's attention—and to retain his claim as Heir Apparent—he needed to demonstrate that he wasn't afraid of being burned by Leon's flames.

Leon folded his muscled arms behind his back, dangerously close to the broadsword, *Lion's Fang,* strapped there. A small smile came to his lips as he looked between Hera and Cassius at his sides. Finally, he shrugged. "I think we're still playing, seeing as you've just become a *far* more interesting participant."

Andre casually crossed his legs, looking at Pandora. She nodded to him. *So far, so good*. If Leon weren't interested in a deal, he would've already blown that palace to bits.

"I presume you want to hear my demands."

"Always to the point," Leon said. "Just how I raised you."

Andre considered the Commander's court. Though packed with financial, political, and intellectual power, they were severely lacking in heavy hitters. Keston

Leroy was the only legitimate threat if Leon wasn't interested in bloodying his sword. And in a war against the Selvians, a lack of powerful operatives could quickly become a problem.

Not to mention that Leon was getting older, with no one on his court related to him.

"Let's start with Madrid." Andre decided to target the easiest piece first. "By blood or by birthright, this territory is mine. As the last of both Ortiz and Valentino lines, I presume we do not need to argue." He tapped his chin in thought. "That is, unless you want to open the position and have an Elite power struggle on your hands along with your current conflict."

Historically, such affairs were bloodbaths, destabilizing a region for years as Elite families who regulated the economy assassinated each other in their palaces. Southern Spain supplied a large share of Europe's food, so such a disruption would compromise the war effort.

The Commander did an impressive job of being nonchalant when he replied, "I'm glad your mourning period has ended, and you're finally willing to take up the role, son."

He always made things sound like they were his idea—projecting confidence even when backed against a wall. Andre had valued his father's confidence growing up, but now it irked him. Even when he won, Leon's calm demeanor took away any joy of victory.

Perhaps Andre just needed to keep winning.

He gestured to the cyborg at his side. He'd noted Hera had been unable to look away from her daughter, probably out of fear that Andre had turned her into an enemy. Fortunately for everyone in that room, Pandora understood that grievances needed to be forgotten to acquire power.

Which was precisely Andre's next talking point.

"As you can see, Pandora and I have put our pasts behind us," he continued. "An example of goodwill we wish to extend to you."

"Goodwill," Leon scoffed. "Like a continent in the Big Three needs charity."

"I am still publicly Heir Apparent."

Disdain contorted Leon's features for the first time that meeting. His lip curled. "Because the only thing more humiliating than having your bastard blood in line for *my* throne is announcing to the world how that blood got in your veins."

"You got cucked by a rebel, Daddy." Pandora mocked a look of concern as her hands cupped her face. "Oh, the *pain*."

Leon drew his broadsword and pointed it at the cyborg. "And you were grown in a test tube because your mother couldn't get anyone to fuck her, isn't that right?"

"Murrays are spiraling," Ace warned in his ear. "We all know what happens next. De-escalate, or you can kiss that pretty palace goodbye."

"The past doesn't matter," Andre raised his voice just enough to return the room's attention to him. "What matters is that we need each other to guarantee our futures. The savages are conquering the north. Africa's favoritism for mutants grows by the day. North America's Commander went insane and murdered Asia's Commander—and now their continents are without leadership. Asia is experiencing destabilization for the first time in decades. And now, the mighty house of Murray is reduced to an aging Commander and a bastard daughter. I think we can agree that the last thing we can afford is infighting."

And just like that, Leon sheathed his sword. Pride came to the Commander's face, an expression that made Andre's heart race—a remnant of the decades he'd spent crawling for such a look of approval.

"And what future do you envision?" Leon asked.

Andre lovingly stroked his daughter's curling brown hair. "Everyone, I want to introduce you to Rou—my daughter." He took a moment to appreciate the shock rippling through Leon's Inner Circle. He gestured to Kalinda. "Though I am not married to the mother, I am now a prince with an established line of inheritance."

The glare Kalinda gave him was harrowing. He did his best to ignore the stab of guilt. To guarantee her, Jaya, and Rou's safety, he had to link them. The lie also ensured Rou's true parentage remained hidden.

"And that child has no Murray blood." Leon bared his teeth. "I will not recognize her."

"You don't have to, so long as the word does. Making me your heir strengthens your position—your enemies now see three Murray generations to cut down instead of one. You become immortal in their eyes. Harder to defeat."

And now for the final nail that would cement his position as heir.

Andre reached behind him and intertwined his hand with Pandora's. "But that's only a temporary fix. Pandora and I will marry and produce a new generation with Murray blood. You get a legacy without the embarrassment of infidelity. You get the stability of my support *and* a Murray Commander after me."

The air left the room, and everything went still. Pandora's grin had grown wild. Even Hera couldn't conceal her excitement at the possibility of her daughter becoming the First Mother of Europe. Sensatia had already started frantically typing on her tablet. The only person seemingly dissatisfied was Cassius, who turned to his children in shock. Keston cursed.

Only Genevieve seemed unmoved. Her green eyes were slightly unnerving as she stared him down. While the rest of the room pressurized with his proposal, she appeared content.

While Andre was distracted by Genevieve, Leon stalked up the steps to his throne. The towering Commander stopped once he stood over him, casting the usurper in shadow. Andre had to fight not to flinch. But he realized his father had extended a hand, not a sword.

It was the most beautiful thing Andre had ever seen.

He rose, satisfied that he stood a few centimeters taller than the tyrant. Leon's large hand grasped his own with burning heat. But Andre didn't flinch from his fire—for the first time in his life, he unapologetically basked in it.

"I'm happy to be back in service," Prince Andre Murray said with a bow.

Part II

Hades, Persephone, and the Underground

Chapter 14

Arianne

"Satyr, if you don't have another set of charges ready, so help me!" Arianne bellowed into her communications unit, wind whipping past her ears.

Two Pangaean jets screamed behind her. She cut hard to the right, praying the brick buildings would shield her. Wings tucked in tight, her eyes focused on the alleyway shooting past, hoping with all her might that she wouldn't crash. Face-planting into the side of a building going one hundred miles an hour would certainly complicate her day.

And they'd been building up to that attack for two months. Everything had to be perfect. *She* had to be perfect.

Clearing the alleyway, she snapped out her wings and twisted back toward the warzone above her head. Topher. She needed to find Topher, and *fast*. She was out of explosives and had only lost one jet in her maneuver.

"I'm at your six o'clock!" Topher reported back. "You got a tail."

"Well aware," Arianne gritted, diving near the street and forcing the jet to weave through the buildings.

The sharp hiss of a lit fuse was audible through the comms line. "Bring them to me. I got a gift for them."

Arianne smirked, happy to oblige.

Months on the front lines of Selvia's war with Europe had turned her into an ace in aerial combat. Though not as fast as a Pangaean jet, she could outmaneuver them all day long. Movements that had once given her pause were second nature to her now, her wings as agile as her own two legs.

She flew beneath a bridge for cover and shot straight out the other side. Clearing the buildings, her raptor vision caught sight of Topher on a rooftop across the river.

Angling herself down, Arianne used gravity and the aerodynamic shape of her wings to produce enough speed to stay just outside the jet's firing range. Months of fighting had taught her the importance of memorizing that critical distance.

Seeing how she was still alive, she'd gotten pretty good at the specific calculation.

She'd also become intimately familiar with Topher's firing range. Inside his danger zone, she risked a spin to look at her Pangaean pursuer one last time. She flipped the pilot the bird for ironic measure. And then Topher shot that motherfucker to smithereens in a fiery display of orange.

"I love it when you do that, Satyr," Arianne shouted, running as she landed on the rooftop with him.

Her friend stroked his goatee with a small smile. Instead of responding, he strung another arrow and fired, taking out a group of soldiers on the rooftop next to them. Topher had an extended range of vision like the mountain goats he'd taken after. Because of that, he very literally had eyes in the back of his head.

"The airport is down," Arianne reported, slightly breathless from her flight. "Just need the last round of charges for the shipment port, and we'll cut them off from naval support."

Topher quickly gave her the last backpack. She took the empty one off her back and threw it onto the rooftop. One last bombing and Dublin—and the entirety of Old Ireland—was theirs.

Arianne tapped her communications unit. "Blitz, report!"

Seconds later, Lova appeared from the staircase leading downstairs and skidded to a stop before her Deputy. Her typical crown of curls had been pulled back into dozens of braids that now reached the bottom of her neck.

"We're holding the building. Blue got into the barracks' intranet. They've lost communication with the mainland."

"News on River Liffey?"

"Rhino led the brute squadron to take out the first three bridges from the port. There'll be no naval support inside the city." Lova smiled. "From my reconnaissance, we're winning, Phoenix."

"It's not over yet," Arianne warned.

She tightened her grip on her bag, checking for the charges her trusted explosives expert had packed. If Topher was right, there should be enough to decimate the remaining military vessels in Dublin's harbor.

Arianne chose to bomb cities herself rather than trust the task to pilots for one reason: unpredictability. Radar would detect a jet's arrival. People could hear them—see them. And they could only fly in very specific patterns.

But not Arianne.

She could carpet bomb a city's airport before they even saw her coming—throw them off balance before her forces even attacked. And she was *damn* hard to catch. Why risk their limited air force when she could do it herself?

She'd earned the name City Crusher for a reason—time to remind everyone why.

"Help get Blue out of the combat zone," Arianne ordered Lova, then looked to Topher. "Contact Rhino and the other brutes. Bring them back to this building. We hold this building on the river until we win. Meet at the rendezvous point once I send up the flare."

And with that, she took off. It was a relief to have a team she could trust. Months of combat had taught her their strengths and weaknesses, but it'd also strengthened her already powerful confidence in them. If she ordered something, they did it, no questions asked.

It made completing her tasks a hell of a lot easier.

Tapping her temple, her mask snapped over her face. She turned on the eye protection setting and watched as the blue shield materialized over the black polyester mask.

So late into the battle—they'd already been in open combat for eight hours—the jets circling Dublin's sky were fewer and fewer. Red still flashed sporadically as the city fires rose and mixed with smoke and fire from the jets, but nothing like the start.

After bombing the barracks and sneaking Blue Krait inside to hack the systems, the battle devolved from there. A mess of European and African jets had clouded the air, and Arianne had fought on the ground with her team until the sky became less of a death sentence.

And now, as the combined African and tribal forces overwhelmed the occupying military, Arianne was alone up there. She still flew low, feet above the river, just in case she made any more friends with two wings and a target system primed for her.

The ocean materialized beyond the river, and the harbor stretched alongside her. Gametime. Checking her surroundings one last time, Arianne shot skyward. Four Pangaean naval vessels lingered just offshore. Perfect. Time for the new trick she'd been working on. Building speed, she dove below the waves and shot like a torpedo through the bay toward the first vessel. Anyone monitoring for enemy attacks wouldn't have noticed her dip below the water, and their sonar sure as hell wouldn't have picked up on her.

Those multi-billion-Unit vessels were sitting ducks for the Shark lurking below.

Arianne carefully placed one explosive charge after another on the underside of the ship, thankful for her webbed hands, which helped her with extra precision. She repeated the procedure for the following two boats. Unfortunately, the last one was too far from the rest—she certainly didn't have time to swim.

The sooner the battle was over, the better.

Swimming back to the surface, Arianne propelled herself out of the water. Her wings caught her and quickly carried her back into the clouded sky. Water droplets rained from her, and she grinned, proud that her new trick had worked. Spinning in a corkscrew to free herself from remaining moisture, Arianne flew to her final target.

Alarms blared just as she managed to place the first charge on the ship's hull. The sirens pierced her ears and lit the darkening day with fiery red. She cursed, attaching another charge.

Of course, I couldn't have one battle go off without a hitch.

That thought barely left her skull before cannons appeared off the side of the boat, aimed directly at her. With a shout, Arianne pumped her wings to escape the firing rage. Too late. The cannon fired, and she had a split second to spin away as a large ball of plasma shot past where her head once was.

She was alive, but that relief was short-lived. An agonizing pain shot down her wing, like a hot iron pressing down, burning the skin and crushing the bone. And then she was falling.

Needless to say, a *lot* of creative curses left her mouth on her way down.

The world spun as the deck of the ship drew closer. She fought like hell to right herself, pushing away the blinding pain long enough to focus.

Pain later. Right now, crash landing.

With the remaining strength in her wings, Arianne managed to slow her fall and roll across the deck. Her explosives scattered in a broad arc around her. Not good. She stood to dozens of sailors staring at her in shock.

Also not good.

Arianne sighed, drawing the twin batons of *Horizon's Edge* and extending them into their burning blades.

Guess guerrilla warfare was over—time to party.

"I'm down," Arianne reported to her communications unit in Latin. "I'll need backup if I'm still alive in five minutes."

She barely finished before three dozen sailors in white naval uniforms screamed and dashed at her. Fortunately, none of them had been prepared for combat so far offshore. Unfortunately, the wound in her wing had black spots filling her vision.

Arianne mowed down about ten of them before anyone could get a hand on her. And then someone delivered a blow to her ruined wing. She roared in pain.

Instinct took over.

Suddenly, it didn't matter that she was buried in a sea of white uniforms—she quickly turned them all red. Any pain was replaced with gleeful laughter. She was having *fun*. Each kill gave her an intoxicating dose of euphoria.

As usual, giving into Instinct, she questioned why she'd ever let go.

She kept killing. It was a massacre. But she didn't care. These were *Pangaeans*. All they did was take. Was it wrong to take in return? Besides, they shot her out of the *sky*. They deserved this.

Even when she could've run, even when she killed enough to make a window to escape, she remained. Reinforcements with blasters and *Fera*-issue swords arrived—but that was just a challenge for her now. Arianne picked each sailor off one by one, using shipping containers for cover and then taking up blasters for herself.

Was she running low on blood? Maybe. But she couldn't feel it, so full steam ahead.

Time lost meaning as she held off the hordes of sailors. What was once a battle had become a game. She hardly registered the powerful thud that rocked the vessel as Rhino landed behind her, rushing in to wipe out an oncoming assault of five sailors with one mighty swing of his battle hammer. Lova zipped behind him, cutting down whoever dodged his attacks. And hanging out of one of Selvia's helicopters above them was Topher, shooting down at a line of artillery cannons.

Even possessed by Instinct, Arianne recognized her team. She knew they had her back. So, with an eager battle cry, she lunged to get back into the fight. But she barely leapt into the air before a hand yanked her down—the one female who always managed to sneak up on her, even in that state.

"You won. Time to retreat," Blue Krait whispered in her ear.

Arianne struggled against her grip. Instinct wanted to rip Blue's arms out of her sockets, but she loved Blue too much to be tempted to try. Still, she managed a growl. "*It's over when I say it's over.*"

"You can come back to us, Arianne, or you can get your medicine," Blue warned.

"*No. I'm drowning this fucking boat.*"

She stroked Arianne's long braids. "You've left enough explosive charges on here to drown a fleet. Let's get airborne so we can press the button."

Arianne bared her fangs. "*I am your Deputy. I am City Crusher. I am Phoenix. Commander's blood runs through my veins. You do not command me.*"

"Goodnight, Arianne," Blue sighed and stuck a carefully measured dart of her venom in her neck.

She passed out in her friend's arms.

Arianne sank into the steaming waters of her personal recovery pool. Lavender and sandalwood incense mixed with the steam, leaving the atmosphere cloudy and thick to breathe in. Her body savored the water's soothing touch, her skin darkening to grey as she adapted to the new environment. Eyes closed, she could almost feel her wounds starting to stitch back together.

With all her body submerged, save her face, Arianne breathed deeply, hoping the incense did its job and calmed her nerves. Spanish guitar played faintly on speakers around her, accompanied by the soft ripples of the water. She concentrated on the familiar sounds, fighting to *fucking* relax.

But she couldn't.

Another battle won, yes, but another time she lost control.

Arianne squeezed her eyes shut. She had to stop thinking about that. Her heart rate was already rising. With another deep breath, she imagined lavender blanketing her anxiety and the hints of sandalwood easing the tension in her shoulders.

Breathe in. Breathe out. Just like Cervi taught her. *Breathe in. Breathe out.*

But those stupid lessons weren't working anymore. Her eyes shot open, slapping the water with frustration. "Fucking Cervi," she spat. "Had to go get herself killed. Had to die without telling me how to control this bullshit."

She regretted the outburst immediately. She sighed, looking up toward the palm trees. As much as Cervi's secrets were frustrating, Arianne still missed her. As the only other Level Two mutant she'd ever met, her former Ductor was supposed to teach her how to control the beast inside her.

Instead, Cervi was killed, and Arianne was left as clueless as the rest of the world. And as the end of her maturation approached, Instinct was only getting more challenging to control.

She flinched, remembering the ship. All those sailors. She hadn't been able to *stop*. And yet, even without Instinct, she didn't feel as bad as she knew she should have.

The doors to her spa opened. She didn't look to see who arrived.

"Blue is stress-eating chocolate cake, and you've got your fancy incense going." Khari's voice. "Instinct pay another visit?"

Arianne finally lifted her head to frown at the male—her *fiancé.*

Khari was handsome as ever. The front lines had done wonders to his beauty: he favored a clean military cut and had let a scruff take over his face. But the most prominent change was his authority. Khari's father had put him in charge of a specialized African force made strictly of *Feras.* Months of leading—proving himself without the stain of his mentor's mistakes—brought back his confidence. He looked older. He looked like royalty.

Granted, they both did.

Arianne distantly drew patterns in the steam with her fingers. "The healers *claim* the incense is supposed to help with Instinct and my dreams, but I'm starting to think it's a load of bullshit."

If Instinct haunted her waking hours, her dreams had returned to haunt her sleep. Needless to say, she was exhausted. Not that she could tell anyone that.

Arianne was Phoenix: Deputy of Selvia. She was the leader of the most elite team in their war, a team their forces had taken to calling the Ivory Court. They'd overtaken the territories of Finland, the United Kingdom, and Ireland in nine months. They were making good progress, and the world was just starting to take her—and Sygrid's appointment of her as Deputy—seriously.

She couldn't afford to slow down. Not now.

"Well, I come bearing good news," Khari said. "My forces have cleared out London. We have a captive arriving soon. I just got off a call with my father, and it's official—the Tribal forces control the Old United Kingdom territories, with Ireland quickly falling into the fold."

Arianne continued to stare forward. "And to think Ireland should have been mine by birthright. My grandfather, Patrick McGrath, was the reigning Elite of Dublin before he married my grandmother."

Khari removed his royal dashiki. Finally turning, she watched him pull the fabric off his torso, revealing his toned abs, beautifully accentuated by his dark skin. He caught her watching and smiled as he slowly stepped out of his pants. "Stop looking so sad. It's time to celebrate. We've won the campaign, Ari."

She allowed a slight smirk as he removed the last of his clothes without breaking eye contact. The prince was slow as he waded toward her in the pool, his skin turning into a mosaic of browns and tans as it adapted to the water. Arianne didn't move as he converged on her. She was no longer shy when it came to his body or the relationship they needed to have together.

Khari was beautiful, and he knew how to make her feel good. He was a duty, but he'd also become her distraction. She'd grown to see nothing wrong with enjoying the fate thrust upon her.

Especially when such fate was *very* good at thrusting.

Though they weren't part of the same division, they needed to make a point of being seen together as often as their responsibilities allowed. To solidify his position as an African prince, Khari spent more time with African forces, while Arianne did the same with hers. The first few months of their engagement had been awkward, even forced, but as time went on—and as the battles grew particularly bloody—they'd both found comfort in a familiar body.

Khari was a release like a massage or lounging in a sauna. There was no passion or endless need to see each other. If she didn't see him for a month, she didn't particularly miss him. But when they were together, she found herself thankful for the thoughtless moments where they were just two bodies exploring each other, warding off the loneliness of war.

Arianne told herself that's all she needed—even when Khari's lips brushed her neck a specific way, and she was caught imagining an*other* male's lips on her like that. Sometimes, she even fed into the fantasy of that other someone kissing her. Why not?

Keston Leroy was from another lifetime—a lifetime when she was just an island princess, and he was just a bounty hunter.

But, no matter how often she told herself that story, she always caught herself scanning the enemy lines, trying to catch a glimpse of his dark feathers shining in the sunlight. She never did. Ever since Mexico City, he'd disappeared off the continental grid. Arianne would know. She'd ordered some of Selvia's Shadows to keep tabs on him. As far as the reports went, Keston hadn't been in Europe for nine months.

Sometime after Arianne and Khari had their fill of each other—activities underwater were certainly entertaining for two *Feras* with water adaptations—the door to the spa opened again to reveal Ringtail. Arianne straightened in surprise, lifting herself from where she lounged in Khari's arms.

Modesty in the tribes was very different from that in civilization. Ringtail didn't so much as react at her bare chest when she sat up. He simply ducked his head in greeting. "Phoenix, my Deputy. It's been some time."

Arianne paused. She'd grown used to the reverence she received from others as a Champion and Deputy of Selvia, but Ringtail had always been like a mentor to her. Seeing him bowing to her was strange, even if she wasn't entirely opposed.

"Ringtail." She smiled. "What brings you to the front?"

Khari sensuously dragged his finger across her back.

As Ringtail prepared to answer, the doors opened again, and two of Khari's men dragged a blond-haired man in Elite dress. The prisoner looked disheveled as the men pulled him across the ground, too beaten up to raise his head.

Khari snapped his fingers. "We're in a meeting. Leave him."

"Leave him?" one of Khari's soldiers asked. "He's not bound."

Arianne raised a hand, and both soldiers blushed at her naked body. Their embarrassment gave her an exciting rush of dominance. "He's no threat to us. Let him think he has a chance. They're more exciting that way."

Ringtail frowned as he watched the African soldiers leave, his orange eyes drifting to the Elite prisoner before returning to Arianne. "That was hardly necessary," he said, risking scolding her.

Both Arianne and Khari laughed.

Pursing his lips, Ringtail continued. "Strix requests that you and your team return to Moon Warren once you're all healed and ready for travel."

Arianne stiffened. "What?" She shook her head. "No, that can't be right. We're doing good work out here. We're ready to take on the mainland. We're primed to squeeze Europe from the North and West—you can't be sending us back now!"

She was so close to glory. So *close* to marching on Paris and punching her father in his perfect teeth—

"We're not ready to take the mainland," Ringtail retorted. "Europe is too powerful to attack in its power center right now. And," he said, tail flicking nervously as he looked around the spa, "you and your team need a break."

Outrage bubbled inside her. "A break?" she demanded, voice squeaking. No, he couldn't be shutting her down. She was *fine*. They were winning. Couldn't Sygrid see that? "No. I don't need a break. I need to win, Ringtail. Let me do that."

"Orders are orders, Phoenix." Ringtail's mouth was a hard line. "You've done good work. Don't ruin it by overworking yourself now." He took one last look at her spa. "Incense and Khari will only patch up the holes for so long. Moon Warren, three days."

Arianne's annoyance burned so hot that the water might start to boil. Khari laughed at her reaction, the sound tickling her ear as he leaned in close to her side. "Why is it so hot when you talk back to them?" he whispered.

"Not now, we have a guest," Arianne grumbled, her withering stare going to the Elite, still shivering on the floor. She pointed at him. "And what's your name?"

Khari kissed down her chest now, making his way under the water. "Come on," he moaned. "I thought we said no politics in the bedroom.

With Sygrid's summons, Ringtail's painfully accurate warning, and their newest Pangaean guest, the last thing on her mind was indulging in Khari's obnoxiously high sex drive. She shoved him off her, grumbling, "We have an arranged marriage. Our politics *are* the bedroom."

Arianne rose from the water, uncaring that she wore nothing as she approached the Elite. She wanted him to be intimidated. She wanted him to look at her body, scarred and covered in muscle after years of fighting for her life, and be *terrified*. His people had turned her into the weapon she was. She had every right to remind him of that.

"He's the hostage my troops captured," Khari groaned. "He's going to some prison in Egypt. Who cares?"

"Your name," Arianne said again, wading to the end of the pool.

The Elite stopped his quivering long enough to look up. "Reginald Richards."

She perked up, her annoyance at being sent home dissipating momentarily. "Richards, as in Hera Richards?"

"She's my sister."

Arianne shrugged as she stepped out of the pool and approached the Elite. "Good enough for me."

Then she grabbed her sword and cut that nightmare-fuel-for-a-scientist's brother in half. She watched blankly as blood spilled into the water. "Look at that. I feel better already."

Chapter 15

Keston

Neon green smoke filled his lungs, and his eyes rolled back into his head. Keston leaned back in his seat as the Slime filled his system, delivering just enough sweet venom to remove the sharp edge of his anxiety. *Fera* servants shuffled around him, their movements blurred. A green-scaled female was about to carry a tray of dumplings away, and he gestured for her to leave the platter on the table.

"Are you even listening to me, Keston?"

He sat up toward Sensatia's full-body projection next to him. A retort itched his tongue that he hadn't heard her due to being in a nightclub with deafening music, but he reeled it in. If it was important, she'd repeat it.

Otherwise, he couldn't be bothered.

Sensatia crossed her arms in annoyance, her projection bringing a soft blue glow to his private booth at the club. "Selvian and African troops have secured the Norwegian and United Kingdom territories. North America just announced that Miguel Smith will Ascend this January."

That got his attention. "No sign of Alvaro?"

"Ghost story," she admitted, looking down. "The best my sources can say is that he's being held hostage by Strix and Phoenix—*if* he's still alive."

Keston took another hit of his pen, green smoke floating around his face.

Phoenix... Arianne...

Try as he might, thinking about her still hurt. He replayed those fleeting moments with her that day in Mexico City. She'd been just as feisty and beautiful as he'd remembered.

And for a few heart-wrenching moments, she'd looked at him like she might still love him.

"Any word on Ari—uh—Phoenix?"

"They're calling her the Firebird. City Crusher. Everywhere she goes, her forces dominate on the ground while she holds the sky, decimating every strategic stronghold with explosive charges. No jet can catch her." Sensatia shook her head. "She's a demon, Keston. I'm uncertain how you managed to survive her twice."

He looked out toward the crowded dance floor and flashing neon lights. Despite himself, he laughed. "She wasn't always a demon."

He closed his eyes, picturing the mornings spent cooking waffles with her—whipped cream somehow always ending up in his hair. But he erased those thoughts and grabbed his glass of Japanese whiskey, quickly downing the contents. Arianne may not be dead, but the version he'd mourned might be.

Well, the version of him she'd loved was dead, too.

Sensatia's projection leaned forward, her love for digging up dirt making her eyes light up. "She wasn't always a demon?" she repeated. "Did you uncover any fun information on Strix's prodigy?"

Standing to refill his glass, Keston was careful not to reveal anything on his face. "I've only heard rumors. Even in this corner of the world, people talk about Pangaea's newest Legend."

There'd been Strix, the Silent Death. And now there was her *daughter*: Phoenix, City Crusher. The world was captivated. And as someone intimately used to the public eye at that point, Keston understood that captivation led to obsession. Everyone was throwing their hat in the ring about who the masked Phoenix, leader of the deadly Ivory Court, truly was.

All of the speculations were wrong, of course.

But even Keston hadn't been able to predict the true story: that Phoenix was the vengeful ghost of a princess once deemed a monster by her family and island home.

The curtains of his private booth opened, and Keston was half expecting one of his bandmates to join him for a smoking session. But to his annoyance, Texas Hold'em stepped through.

The Joker dipped his hat in greeting. "Apologies, boss. Ya' have a guest requestin' a meeting."

After Tex's triumphant return with Pandora and Andre nine months ago—and plenty of apologies for disappearing when the cyborg fled instead of doing his damn job—Keston took the idiot back like a make-up after a bad breakup. Ever since then, the Joker had become a model Cartel citizen. So Keston had let him live.

Shaking off the worst of the Slime and alcohol, Keston grabbed Sensatia's projection caller and stormed up to Tex, adjusting his cape to hide his wings. "This is my nightclub. Who the *hell* is summoning *me?*"

"I'm Sorry, Blackjack," Tex replied, guiding Keston through the club's packed halls. "The Wards were extremely convincin'."

Outside of his private booth, Keston had to turn on his earpieces to drown out the background noise. Usually, his ears were highly acute—even in loud environments—but Hera's experimental drugs had suppressed his abilities to human standards.

It was a risk, but a necessary one for a slower metabolism. His life would be intolerable if he couldn't numb it all with nightly vices.

Sensatia's projection phased in and out of focus as they passed through party-goers. Fortunately, her voice was clear in his earpiece. "So, when can I come visit you?"

There was hope in her voice. He needed to crush it.

After his repeated failures in Oslo and Mexico City, and especially with the return of Pandora and Andre, Keston had effectively been demoted. Thanks to his Saudi heritage through his great aunt and grandparents, he had Elite relations on the Asian continent. So, Cassius had dropped him in Tokyo and said, *"Have fun."*

And to add to his credibility, he used this Saudi family name. Say hello to Keston Leroy Al-Fayed. Whatever. He'd had plenty of names in his life. What was one more?

On the surface, he was building a strong European-Asian connection by social climbing with the Elites and all that. Behind the scenes, he was doing what he did best: taming the Underground.

If his thriving nightclub was any indication, he was doing a damn good job in his exile. But it was still an exile, and one he intended to adhere to. After the scheming and betrayal in Europe, he wanted to remain far away, including maintaining distance from any previously involved parties.

Like Sensatia.

"Keston, I asked if I could come visit you," the reporter pouted. She raised a hand to his shoulder, the projection's blue light passing through his cape. "I miss you."

He tightened his jaw. Even his lover had become an untrustworthy part of the games, the politics. He was so tired of it all. Against his will, he pictured sunning himself on the beach outside his Grecian villa. How did it all go so wrong? He'd been *retired*. He'd been *happy*.

At least in Tokyo, surrounded by unfamiliar faces, politics and games didn't feel personal.

"And are you still working with my sister?" Keston asked.

Sensatia paused. That was answer enough.

Up ahead, Tex slowed at another private booth where he spoke with two Asian Wards who wore the traditional samurai uniforms known as kamishinos. They kept the typical Ward black-and-red, giving them a domineering, sleek look. The flowing fabric was lightweight and flexible, not great for defense, but an extra layer of thin body armor hid underneath. The Asian Wards were more bulletproof than their fancy uniforms let on—a mistake Keston's Jokers had made their first few weeks on the continent.

"Look," Keston said, holding up a hand before Sensatia could speak again. "I've got to go and deal with whatever Elite thinks they can order me around in my territory. I don't have time to explain why I need more time away from Europe—including time away from you."

She looked wounded. "I'm sorry Genevieve and I went behind your back. But we're doing good work—"

"I don't care, Senny. Unlike you, I've moved on from manipulating the people I care about." He hung up the call and walked through the curtain Tex held open for him.

Keston did his best to look unfazed when he saw who waited in a cloud of hookah smoke: Zhou Qin, Heir Apparent to the most powerful continent in the empire.

The prince lounged on a red velvet sectional, surrounded by two *Fera* dancers. His robe was open, exposing a thin chest and a collection of dark blue veins that extended toward the paralyzed right side of his body. As Keston entered, the prince adjusted the robe, covering the veins.

When Qin was a child, there had been an accident that had killed his twin brother and left the right side of his body paralyzed. Despite months of digging,

Keston had been unable to discover more about the incident. Many speculated an all-too-common Elite assassination attempt.

But he didn't know about any assassination methods that left behind dark blue veins.

Standing alert at the end of the sectional was an Asian woman in her late twenties with long black hair and matching eyes. Her mother's black eyes. Mori Sora was as thin as her half-brother, but Keston could sense decent muscle tone beneath her executive pantsuit. He recalled the princess, who'd been passed over as heir, was now a professional dancer.

Keston quickly bowed to the royals. "And to what do I owe the pleasure of finally being graced with your presence, Your Highnesses?"

He'd been trying to get an audience with the Heir Apparent for months, only to be rejected each time. Whether it was a power play or if Keston's distant Asian Elite heritage was too insignificant for Qin to care, was still up for debate.

Sora narrowed her eyes but didn't speak.

Qin tilted his chin up at Keston, the gesture doing an excellent job of displaying his apparent disgust. "Keston Al-Fayed. Or Leroy? I've lost track. Not that I care." His eyes raked up and down the winged male. "You are pretty. I would expect nothing less from Europe's whore. First, you sell yourself to the masses out West. Now look at you, being a good little playboy for my people. It must hurt to be disowned by your family, just to be replaced by your baby sister."

"I missed the part where being insulted was a good use of my time." Keston smiled balefully. "If you need someone to degrade, I can offer you a list of my employees you can pay for such a service." He opened his hand to the two escorts at the prince's side. "As for me, my fees are too high—even for a prince."

Qin didn't flinch. He twisted a ring around his finger with mild interest. "My, you have a sharp tongue for a courtesan. I would think a social climber like you would know how to kiss ass a little better."

"I don't kiss ass if someone deserves an ass-kicking instead, Your Highness."

Sora reached for the whip hanging at her side. "You dare to threaten the Heir Apparent?"

"Hardly." Keston shoved his hands into his suit pockets. "You would've brought *far* more security if you thought I would even attempt such a thing." He returned his attention to Qin. "Still, coming here is a risky move, I'll admit. Seeing that you knew how to find me here, you know what business I operate. Meeting me here would require you to step out of your domain."

"Every square inch of Asia will be my domain come January," Qin gritted.

Keston openly laughed. "Then you have no clue how the Underground works."

"And you do?"

Taking that as his cue, Keston sat down, delighting in how Sora bristled at the casual gesture. To add salt to the wound, he snapped his fingers, and the escorts sitting with Qin stood and fetched him a drink. When his drink fell into his hand, he took a long sip before slowly placing the glass down. Qin looked ready to boil over. Only then did Keston speak, enjoying the heir's annoyance.

"Let me make a few things abundantly clear." Keston held up a finger each time he counted. "One: only scared small boys with even smaller dicks start a negotiation with insults. Two: this playboy has played with far scarier mother-fuckers than you. If you think you hold a candle to any of them, I can't wait to watch you shit your pants like the rookie you are. And three: I've been here nine months, and Cartel already controls a fifth of your Underground, which means I know what I'm doing, so put some respect in your goddamn tone when you come down here to *my* domain."

That gave Qin pause. Keston smiled through the smoke. He'd dealt with kings, queens, mutants, monsters, and everything in between. An untested Commander, hardly in his thirties, didn't even make the top ten on his danger radar anymore.

Finally, the prince chuckled low. "What makes you think you can talk to me like that?"

"Simple. You pretended I didn't exist for months, then showed up at my door once you discovered my talents go far beyond performing at fancy parties. You need me. So out with it. You're ruining my buzz."

It was only a matter of time before he got the Heir Apparent's attention. And while Leon specifically wanted Keston to ease tensions between their continents to forge an alliance, something told him Qin was the type of man who walked all over people he didn't respect.

Sora finally replied, "Your control over Asia's Underground is precisely why we came. Shanghai may be the capital, but Tokyo is where all the power lies. Our mother focused security on the capital, leaving Tokyo to run rampant. Now we're faced with a beast that could threaten my brother's reign."

Bingo.

"You assist me in taming my continent's Underground," Qin said, "and I will entertain your Commander's advances when I Ascend."

Sora's head whipped toward her brother, her sleek hair shimmering in the low light. "We agreed it would be safer for our people to uproot the Underground—not attempt to control something that clearly does not want to be contained."

"I am Heir Apparent," Qin snapped. "Know your place, or you can remain in your dance halls."

Sora scowled but didn't respond as she stepped back from her brother's sectional.

The apparent tension between the siblings made Keston perk up. While he wasn't too keen on doing more dirty work to tame the rival factions of Asia's Underground, he couldn't deny the opportunity to get closer to the prince and princess. He smelled weakness, which was just as dangerous as a shark smelling blood. Weakness meant he had something to exploit—a crack to manipulate. The possibility was enticing.

"I'll see what I can do," Keston hummed blissfully. "Now, if you'll excuse me. I have a performance with my band to get to."

Qin grabbed his cane, pushing on the handle to sit up in outrage. "Where do you think you're going? You have not been dismissed!"

Keston hung on the curtains leading toward the hallway. "Your research obviously failed to tell you some very important things about me."

"And what is that?"

"You might be a Pangaean prince, but I'm an Underground King." Keston swung on his curtains and danced out of the room with a cackle of delight. "Also: I stopped giving a fuck a year ago, babe!"

Chapter 16

Arianne

"You know what I want you to do."

Leon's voice echoed through the dark concrete room. Arianne felt painfully small in her father's shadow, and she was too terrified to turn and look him in the eye. The view before her was not much easier to bear. A tribal female stared unflinchingly up at her, the dirt on her face and ripped clothes doing little to tarnish her unflinching bravery. With a whimper, Arianne looked away from the prisoner, unable to process her father's request.

In desperation, she turned to her brother and mother, who watched the scene with barely suppressed sobs.

"Don't look at them. Look at the traitor!" Leon bellowed. Hands curling around her shoulders, he leaned down to whisper, "I want you to *see* the form your enemies can take, Subject One."

The sword's weight in Arianne's hand was heavier than the oppressive sorrow in the room. Leon's words danced around her psyche, the desire to please her father mixing with the childish innocence that begged her to stop. The tribal female before her had been a friend of Josephina, a kind servant and companion throughout Arianne's short memory. Even now, the female's face didn't contain anything but compassion.

Though Arianne still didn't quite understand the difference between right and wrong, something was screaming at her that this had crossed the line into wrong a *long* time ago.

"Griffin!" Josephina pleaded, face red. "She's a *child*."

"That's where you're wrong," Leon muttered, and Arianne heard the distinct sound of leather slithering across the ground. "She's my weapon. It's about time we start sharpening the blade."

"M-mom," Arianne whimpered. "I can't."

Josephina's arms shielded Andre from the sight, her hazel eyes bright with tears. "I know, baby," she whispered. "I know."

Before Arianne could cry out for her, there was a distinct *crack* as the whip broke the barrier of sound milliseconds before it broke the barrier of her skin. Arianne shrieked as her knees slammed to the ground. Agony, like a burning fire, coursed up her back, and her body threatened to give out. But something else took over, shielding her from every ounce of aching emotion in an impenetrable layer of numbness.

The scientist researching her had started calling that numbness Instinct.

"Subject One," Leon said, voice sending the child into a deadly trance, "you know what I want you to do."

"*Yes, father.*"

Josephina screamed, but the weapon no longer heard her.

The rise of her sword lasted an eternity. The tribal female didn't flinch as the princess with eyes like a demon approached her, the sword meant for her neck simply an extension of the weapon carrying it. An eight-year-old girl shouldn't know the correct angle required to sever the carotid artery, but Arianne had trained that particular strike on practice dummies for years.

As her sword cut through her target's life force, Arianne realized the movement felt no different than it had in practice.

The chaos slowed. Suddenly, she felt like she was watching the scene outside her body. She remembered that day now. Her first kill: Mila, the secret tribal servant caught attempting to take Arianne from Leonueva, on Josephina's orders.

Then, the bodies started to pile up.

Mila. The other sixteen whom she killed under Leon's command as a child. The tribal hunting party in the Darwin Zone. Wards in the Murray Monument. Bradley Shaw. The killing sped up; individual faces blurring together until she could only recall cities, not singular souls. Oslo. Mexico City. Stockholm. Edinburgh. Manchester. London. Dublin.

Bodies after bodies. Pools of blood. Fire and ash.

And to think, just two years ago, she'd been terrified of growing numb to such carnage. Now, she craved it. Death was a drug, the only thing making the screaming rage in her head stop. The more she conquered and killed, the more she proved to her enemies, her father, and the *world* that she was worthy of the life she kept stealing.

Arianne was no longer afraid. Phoenix was a monster to match Leon. It was *his* turn to be afraid.

The flames of the cities she burned rose to meet her, setting her wings ablaze like the very creature she'd claimed as her Champion's name. Time moved backward, the flames slowly consuming her body as the Pacific hospital collapsed on top of her, burning her arms and reducing the old version of herself to ash. The memory of the agonizing pain of fire melting her flesh made her scream.

And then she was writhing, lashing out for anything that could draw blood. Her father was there. She could feel it. If only she could cut him down—

"Arianne!"

Someone held her shoulders to the floor while another hand slapped her cheeks. She opened her eyes, voice hoarse from screaming. She'd been sleeping. At least, her eyes had been closed. She wasn't sure if fitful nightmares could constitute any form of rest. As her vision cleared, she recognized Khari, naked, holding her down. He was bleeding from four scratches down his cheek. Arianne didn't need to feel the skin bunched under her nails to know she'd been responsible.

"Come on, Ari, calm down. You're okay." Blue. The Snake had been the one slapping her awake. Now she sat at Khari's side, soothingly stroking Arianne's hair. "Breathe in, breathe out. Come on."

Arianne closed her eyes, listening to her friend's calming voice. Her heart thudded painfully against her ribcage, and her gills fought for air. She concentrated on breathing through her nose, reminding her body it was on land. Air filled her lungs slowly, and she felt her dizziness recede as oxygen reentered her bloodstream.

Only when her breathing slowed did Khari release his vice grip on her shoulders.

It took a few moments for a conscious thought to enter her head. For a while there, she'd been trapped in a terrible purgatory between her nightmares and her bedroom. Sitting up, she could still hear the screams of Pangaean citizens as she dropped barrage after explosive barrage on their city blocks. She did her best to drown it out.

I'm in Moon Warren. The war is far away. I'm in Moon Warren. I'm safe.

"Khari." Arianne put her bloodied hand to her forehead. "Khari, I'm so sorry." Her voice cracked, and she realized it hurt to speak after screaming.

The male retreated to the far corner of their shared tree house, shaking as he cupped his face. He refused to look up.

"I heard you screaming," Blue sighed. "I came as quickly as I could."

"Not quickly enough," Khari muttered.

Arianne braced the floor.

"What did you see this time?" Blue asked.

"More of the same." Arianne reached to pull back memories of what she'd seen. "Bodies. Blood. Fire. *Screams.*" She raked her hands through her hair. "It's just getting *worse.*"

She'd hoped the more she fought, the more she won, the more her pain would fade. But the opposite was true. The horrors of the recent battles only mixed with those from years before until it all became one monstrous amalgamation of torture.

With a hiss, Khari stomped around the room, throwing on his tunic and boots with frustrated and jerky movements. "I can't do this anymore." He pointed at Arianne. "This is insanity. You need to tell Strix. I'm not hiding this for you anymore."

Arianne stared forward, numb. Her recent nightmare blurred her thoughts, making it hard to focus on her fiancé storming out of their home. Finally, Khari's manic packing pulled her out of it enough to say, "Where do you think you're going?"

They needed to be a united front before the tribe. People couldn't see them sleeping in separate quarters. She hated how her first thoughts went to her public image, not her mental state.

"I'm bunking with Topher," Khari spat, pulling on his cloak. "I've tried so hard to help you, Ari, but you're not just a danger to yourself." He pointed to his bleeding cheek, and she flinched. "Now you're a danger to me."

"I'm sorry."

Khari's blue eyes softened as he looked between Blue and Arianne. "I'm sorry, too. I'm glad Strix took you off the front lines. You need a break. Maybe we need a break, too."

Arianne didn't respond as he left. Eventually, she became aware of Blue stroking the top of her wings—a soothing mechanism her friend had learned after months of helping her through sleepless nights. Leaning into the touch, Arianne focused on her breathing, unable to fill her lungs with her thundering heart.

"I'm falling apart," she whimpered, eyes stinging.

Blue stood, moving to light the lavender candles the Healers had erected around the room. "We already knew that," she quipped, but her voice was missing its classic bravado. The candles gave the dark room a soft orange glow. Finished, she sat back down and started wiping Khari's blood off Arianne's hand. "What else did you see? Come on, give me specifics."

"Blue, I don't want to talk about it," Arianne said, upper lip stiff.

"You have to. Remembering your childhood could be the answer to this madness."

"I got a new memory," Arianne admitted. "My first kill. Her name was Mila. She was a friend of my mother's." She pulled her hand away, clenching it painfully. "The death wasn't the hard part—it was seeing the way my mother looked at me. She was *afraid* of me, Blue. People have been terrified of me my entire life." Her eyes went to the blood still caked under her fingernails. "And all I do is keep proving them right."

Blue's yellow eyes glinted in the candlelight. Just a year ago, her eyes had been terrifying with their eerie glow and slit pupils. Now, Arianne found strange comfort in their intensity. Those were the eyes of her *amica*, of someone she'd never been able to scare away. They were the eyes of a female who understood how it felt to have the entire world see her as a monster and still strive to be *human* despite it all.

"The memories are hard, but they're helping you piece everything together," Blue offered. "One day, you might understand what happened to you."

Arianne shook her head. "They're still just fragments."

No matter how many memories her fractured mind conjured from her childhood, more blank spaces seemed to form. It was maddening: the flashes, moments of happiness, anger, and pain. And above it all, there were no answers, no continuity.

"I still have no idea how I escaped. I have no idea how Leon convinced me to become his monster—and I don't know how I finally got the courage to run. It's all missing." She buried her head in her hands. "The only thing I have left is to take him down. If he's dead, none of this matters."

Blue frowned in concern. "But is it worth breaking yourself all over again?"

"It has to be."

Aurum Hill was as morbidly beautiful as Arianne remembered. The golden grass brushed against her wings as she walked toward the grove of birch trees that stood against the rising sun. The leaves were starting to turn yellow with autumn, the first hints of winter's rapid approach.

Winter meant struggle: less food, frostbitten troops, and snow squalls that delayed advances. If Selvia's forces wanted to make landfall on the main continent from England, it had to be soon.

Arianne had only been back in Moon Warren for two days, but she already knew she needed to return to the front. Winter waited for no one, so neither could she.

She recited her battle strategy in her head as she walked. She'd already met with her team and Khari. They all agreed, and Khari had already left for Egypt to speak to his father. All they needed was Sygrid on board.

With European naval vessels, they'd sail to Amsterdam and pinch Leon's forces with the help of northern tribal reinforcements. They'd claim all the old territories of the Netherlands and Belgium. Meanwhile, Khari's troops would travel up the Artery from Morocco and overwhelm Spain—her brother was untested in open battle.

Uniting in France, they would take Paris with pure, unrelenting force. If the war didn't end there, Leon would be forced to move out of his capital city. Selvia's forces would control all of Europe's largest cities, squeezing Leon's remaining armies and resources.

That should be enough.

Once Europe was weakened, Arianne would announce herself and claim her rightful title as Leona Murray. No one would question her, seeing as she would've done something her father never had to do: conquer the territory she intended to own. War over. *Feras* safe. And if need be, she'd take her fiancé's forces with her and march on Asia.

She didn't want to be Commander. But she couldn't live in a world where Leon was.

"Why do I always come across you while you're brooding, Young One?"

Arianne slowed. She hadn't realized she'd entered the birch tree grove until Colla's question stirred her from her thoughts. The Lion stood against a thin trunk, the tree hardly older than a sapling—the outer edges of the grove always held the youngest trees as Selvians planted new offerings for their recently deceased. While most people in her circle had aged since the war broke out, Colla looked the same as when she'd met him two years ago. He teetered on the edge of middle age with handsome silver streaks in his hair and a youthful face brushed with the first signs of wrinkles. Though Arianne knew he was in his late fifties, he hardly looked forty.

Granted, forgetting half a life meant he had fifty percent fewer memories to stress over.

"There's a lot to brood about." Arianne tried to laugh off the heaviness of her words. "What brings you to the grove?"

Colla's Circus had spent a lot of time on the front with her team. As such, Colla and her had fought together in several skirmishes since January. She'd always felt at ease around him, and the ease had grown into a close friendship over the past months. But the Lion had another duty lately. His memory loss made him a perfect chaperone for a specific Commander in their custody.

Colla crossed his arms, claws sinking into his muscled biceps. "He remembered his name, but we haven't had another breakthrough in months. Sygrid was hoping meditation in a new place might trigger something."

Through the trees, her stomach lurched when she spotted Sygrid seated at the bottom of a small hill. Alvaro Smith sat at her side. The North American Commander looked far different from when she'd first met him. He'd forgone his dark-haired wig, and now his hair's natural light-red shade was on full display, along with his pointed ears. Instead of cowboy hats and sports coats, he wore classic tribal robes of neutral hues and green. There was also a new aura about the male: a strange calmness had replaced the mischievous comedic side he once held dear.

The Serum had turned Alvaro feral, but unlike naturally going feral, the effects had worn off after a day. But when the insanity was gone, so were his memories. Naturally, Sygrid had employed Colla to dig through Alvaro's fractured psyche carefully. Still, that task had proven more complicated than initially anticipated. They couldn't tell Alvaro anything, or they risked harming his ability to remember things naturally. The only thing Colla had been able to guide Alvaro into remembering was his birth name. He didn't even remember his crowned name, Denzel.

"We're running out of time," Arianne sighed with another glance toward Alvaro. "We need North America's help. Miguel is too young to be an effective Commander."

"Leon will manipulate him," Colla agreed.

"He probably already has." She shook her head. "The circumstances of Alvaro's disappearance don't do us any favors. The entire world, including Miguel, thinks we abducted a hostage."

"Come January, Leon gets two young Commanders with a bone to pick with Selvia."

Miguel in North America and Qin in Asia.

"Precisely why I intend to end this war before they get the chance," Arianne said.

Colla's hand went to her shoulder, stopping her from advancing toward Sygrid. "You look tired, Young One."

"We're all tired."

"You more than most."

She sighed. "The sooner we end this, the sooner I can rest."

Colla frowned. "I only ask because I care."

"I know," Arianne relented, leaning into his touch. Colla had become like an uncle to her over the past few months. She'd come to value their talks, even if they mainly consisted of how quickly their worlds were closing around them. "How's your memory going? Working with Alvaro must have helped."

He managed a half smile. "Still a black box. You?"

Her nightmares from the night before came back to her. She shivered. "Quite shitty, thanks for asking."

"I'm sorry."

"I still turn into a rage monster whenever I remember something with a little too much spice. We're workshopping solutions. Candles are the current experiment. I'm sick of lavender now," she tried to joke, but Colla's frown made her half-hearted chuckle die between them. She massaged her temples. "A black box might make me less of a hazard."

His gold-blue eyes drifted to where Alvaro sat, surrounded by a ring of incense Sygrid burned. "A black box isn't fun."

"Maybe it's time to consider you both got your black boxes from the same place," Arianne said, wincing as the words left her lips.

She'd thought about it for months, but the implications had been too terrifying to touch. Alvaro's circumstances were eerily similar to Colla's: waking up without memories, covered in blood from apparent chaos. There was a chance Colla had a run-in with the Serum that'd turned him feral and erased his memories.

"I think about that every night." For someone so large, Colla's voice was frighteningly small.

"Does it help with your memories?"

He shook his shaggy head. "It's maddening. Like a word on the tip of your tongue. But no. I try to think about those labs you told me about, hoping they might spark a memory. Still nothing."

"You think Hera experimented on you?"

"We know she experiments with the Serum. Who knows when she started? Maybe she attempted to make her own before Leon Ascended." Colla looked up at the yellow and red leaves, the combined colors similar to his hair. "How else could I access it if that wasn't the case?"

Arianne shook her head. More mysteries. More manipulation. She wanted answers more than anyone, but it was becoming clear that winning a world war might be easier than uncovering decades-old secrets.

The undergrowth rustled, and Sygrid and Alvaro appeared, smelling of rose incense—something the Healers associated with memory. Every day, Sygrid looked more like Cervi, from the ivory staff that never left her hands to the regal green skirts and fabrics that dominated her wardrobe. A strange serenity had also taken hold of her as the weight of leadership settled on her shoulders. Almost immortal, weighed down by generations of struggle.

But the one thing Arianne couldn't ignore was the eye patch strapped across her mentor's face. Her stomach churned at the reminder of the attack that'd almost taken Sygrid's life—avenged by Arianne killing Commander Hana Lang.

No, she would never regret her retaliation, no matter how many world wars it started.

"I would advise the two of you to employ *whispering* next time," Sygrid raised an eyebrow.

Colla blushed. "You heard everything?"

The Selvian Ductor smirked at him. "Super hearing is funny like that."

Arianne's eyes darted between the two. "Excuse me, what's happening here? Please tell me I didn't just witness old person flirting."

"Alvaro, you can head back to Moon Warren. I trust you know the way?" Sygrid said, deftly ignoring that comment.

"Thank you for your help," The North American Commander said. Turning, he ducked his head toward Arianne. "Phoenix, it was lovely seeing you again."

"Arianne is fine. Only people below me need to use my Champion's name," she fumbled, still not used to such deference from Pangaean royalty.

Alvaro blinked. "I'm hardly your rank."

Her breath caught, remembering he had no idea he *was* Pangaean royalty. She quickly bowed to him. "Forget I said anything."

Once Alvaro was out of earshot, which was painfully long, thanks to his highly acute hearing, Sygrid sighed loud enough for Selvians in Moon Warren to hear. "All right, Arianne, what have you been plotting?"

"Plotting? I've been *strategizing*," Arianne corrected. "I've already consulted my team and Pharaoh—he's heading to Egypt to relay the plan to Commander Sarr now."

Sygrid simply crossed her arms and raised her white eyebrows. Arianne relented and relayed her plan. Colla and Sygrid listened intently as she described her strategy. She was even convinced she'd done the impossible: impress her mentor.

Her hopes were short-lived.

"Colla, get word to Pharaoh and tell him that he's not to discuss this plan with his father," Sygrid said.

With one last regretful look at Arianne, Colla took off down the path toward Moon Warren.

The Deputy stared down her Ductor. "I don't understand."

"No, you do not."

Arianne's hands clenched at her sides. "Care to elaborate? We have momentum. Do you suggest we slow down now? Europe is on its heels. We need to take them!"

"And war has consumed you." Though Sygrid spoke softly, her words were stronger than steel. "Do you think I haven't heard about your outbursts? You are cracking. I will not push you until you break, Arianne."

Arianne's upper lip curled. "So you're benching me?"

"We're *maintaining*," Sygrid corrected. "Commander Sarr agrees." She stepped toward her apprentice with a calming hand on her shoulder. "You've done brilliantly. As winter approaches, it's time to hold the territories we've gained until warmer weather."

"That's insane. We strike now while they're caught off guard."

"You've been on the front too long—you only look at war through the lens of a soldier. I need you to look at it as a leader." Sygrid produced a mobile phone from her pocket. "Do you think our successes in recent months have been from superior battle strategy alone?"

Arianne frowned. "I attributed the success to my team. The Ivory Court has performed admirably."

Sygrid waved the phone. "And they have—I won't take that away from them. But I've sanctioned attacks in Stockholm, London, and Dublin because we had *intel*. My contacts on the inside knew these cities' weaknesses and relayed them to me. They cannot do the same for the larger European cities without compromising their positions. We would be going into highly fortified cities blind."

"So be it," Arianne growled.

"All right. Let's say you choose to assault the major European cities without intel. You'd be facing beasts you've yet to see. Leon has concentrated his forces and resources on the major cities surrounding Paris—a circle of protection. These territories won't be taken as easily as the ones in the mostly forested north and the islands. You'll be stuck when winter hits—exposed and lacking the resources to keep your troops alive. Face it: Pangaea is better prepared for winter. We would be needlessly exposing ourselves to pursue your pride and bloodlust.

"Not to mention, without North America's air force, we have no hope of taking Paris. The city is sprawling. We wouldn't stand a chance with ground movements. Naturally, Paris has advanced air defense systems because it knows the air is the only way attackers stand a chance. Even with air forces capable of overpowering their defenses, we would still be going in blind without intel. It's all out of the question, Arianne."

Sygrid spoke with the certainty of someone who'd gone to war before. Arianne felt herself deflate because, no matter how much she hated to admit it, her mentor was right.

"I once wanted nothing more than to spill Pangaean blood," Sygrid finished with a knowing expression softening her face. "And my eagerness cost me the war, and my family. I will not repeat those mistakes."

Arianne ducked her head. "Understood."

When she looked back, her Ductor was smirking. "I didn't say you wouldn't get to have some fun. Just that you needed a break from the front lines."

"I love it when you make that face," Arianne said, perking up. "It means you want me to get into some trouble."

Sygrid raised a hand adorned in bracers and rings. "Not too much trouble. Just enough to keep things interesting."

"Come on, you're killing me. Out with it, or I'm telling everyone you have a crush on Colla."

A bright blush spread across Sygrid's cheeks. "There will be none of that." She quickly adjusted her silver braids. "*Anyway*, I am hesitant to assault the mainland with the impending threat of Asia. The last thing we need is to push Europe east and inadvertently combine their forces with Asia's."

Excitement stirred in Arianne's gut. She started bouncing on the balls of her feet. This was precisely what she needed: a distraction, time away from the war where she could still make a difference. Her mentor knew her so well.

"Your Ivory Court—that's what everyone's calling them now, right?"

Arianne smiled as she gestured to Sygrid's head. "Well, we serve the Ivory crown worn by a Ductor with ivory coloring, do we not?"

"I suppose." Sygrid waved her off. "We're getting off track. Your Ivory Court will head to Tokyo to meet with the Jin family. From there, you'll meet my contact. I need you to kill Heir Apparent Zhou Qin. *Covertly*. Can you do that?"

"Did I ever tell you how much I love you?"

"That's not an appropriate response to being assigned an assassination mission, Arianne."

Chapter 17

Andre

Another painfully silent dinner.

Andre's knife scraped loudly on his plate. He winced as the sound pierced the silence. Looking up, Kalinda's eyes were on him. He smiled at her. She hastily looked back down and continued her meal.

He'd been eating dinner with Kalinda every Thursday for months now. She'd neglected to speak a word each time. Andre frowned as she shoveled chicken masala into her mouth. She was trying to get out of there as quickly as possible.

Their dinners only had one rule: remain until the plate was empty.

"I got a chef from Old India specifically for you," Andre said in an attempt to fill the silence. "I thought you would enjoy some authentic food."

Kalinda didn't respond.

He hadn't heard her voice since Leon crowned him Heir Apparent. He'd be convinced the woman was a mute had her hand servants not attested to the opposite. The prince suppressed the urge to shout. He didn't need to explain himself to her again. If Kalinda didn't understand he was doing this for her, there was nothing else he could say.

So they continued to eat in silence—the second generation of a prince and his rebel commoner lover. Everyone knew how well that pairing worked the first time, yet Andre was still crazy enough to try.

He looked across the impossibly long dining table. The dining room was dark, and the candles lining the table provided just enough light to illuminate two miniature feasts on each end. Andre enjoyed returning to the comfort of Elite life. Kalinda seemed out of place.

Giving her a double-take, he realized she was crying.

He sprang to his feet, pulling out his maroon pocket square as he moved to the opposite side of his ten-meter table. Closer, he could see tears lining her beautiful green eyes. Andre knelt beside her, extending the pocket square to her as his heart constricted.

Why was she crying? Sure, they were in a rough patch, but she never wanted for anything in the Madrid Royal Palace. Personal servants, any cuisine she could desire, weekends in the countryside, a personal stylist, and her own wing in the palace. If Kalinda desired anything, she had it in ten minutes or less.

This was the power of the Heir Apparent. Couldn't she see that?

"Kal." He raised his pocket square to brush a tear off her cheek. "Why are you crying?"

She ducked away from his arm. Sniffling, she avoided his gaze.

Andre's chest tightened. The distance between them had grown grating. Usually, his busy days reigning over Madrid, his responsibilities as Heir Apparent, sitting in on war councils, and time with Rou left him too busy to notice the space that had grown between them. But, on their nights alone together, when the silence seemed louder than a grenade, Andre couldn't ignore the strange pain he felt at her constant rejection.

He raised a hesitant hand to her shoulder. He hadn't even *touched* her in months. She pulled away with another sniffle. Andre almost stumbled backward like she'd struck him.

"Kalinda, talk to me. Please. I don't understand—"

After a moment of tense silence, Kalinda finally said, "Where's my sister, Andre?"

Blinking in surprise, he was unsure what to say. Last he'd heard, Jaya was in London with Pandora, helping to evacuate the troops that hadn't been captured or killed. But Kalinda wasn't supposed to know that. As part of his *engagement* with Pandora, he had minimal power over her. Pandora had taken one look at Jaya and claimed her as her own.

And it was better not to think about it.

"She's making a difference," Andre said.

Kalinda's face contorted into an ugly mix of fury and tears. "*You put a control collar on her.* When was the last time she had *free will*?"

Nine months ago.

Andre blinked. "Who's putting these thoughts in your head? Jaya is safe."

If being safe meant fighting on the front lines next to Pandora and her Bubblegum Battalion.

Kalinda pushed her chair away from the table, no longer making eye contact with him. Her upper lip twitched in disgust. "You can't even tell me the truth."

"Why are you mad at me?" Andre shot to his feet to follow after her. "I've given you everything you could want!"

"I want my sister, Andre."

He stopped abruptly, frustration finally taking over his affection. Did she want to shun him? Fine. The prince spoke through clenched teeth. "I cannot give her to you."

"How about you get me a man who says he loves me, says he would never do anything to hurt me, and actually *means it?* How about a man who isn't engaged to a psychotic cyborg? A man who could marry me, not keep me as his mistress?"

That's it.

Andre darkened, his mood finally matching the gloom of the room. "I've done nothing but protect you. You're a rebel, a terrorist operative. The only thing you deserve is execution. I made a different call. I treat you like royalty—far more than you should have ever deserved."

"How *noble* of you." Though she wasn't facing him, her clenched fists said enough. "You treat me like your guest, but I know the truth: I'm your trophy prisoner." She finally turned, tears cascading down her cheeks. "How could you ever think I could be happy?"

Because you were happy with me in Pacific when I wasn't happy. Now I am happy. Now we can both *be happy.*

But those words didn't leave his mouth. He was Prince Andre Murray. He was the Heir Apparent to the second most powerful continent in the world. He wasn't allowed to grovel to a commoner.

When Andre looked back up, Kalinda was walking away. With her dark hair left down and her flowing blood-red dress, he was almost convinced it was Josephina's ghost. Kalinda reached the hidden door, one of those designs found in ancient European palaces, seemingly carved out of the wall art. She stopped, slightly turning her head to face him. "Haris told me what Pandora is doing to her. I'm not the only one tired of being your prisoner."

And then she left.

The door had barely clicked shut before Andre rushed to his seat, downed the rest of his wine, and charged off to the barracks attached to his palace. There, the

Peregrine Pacific resided under the watchful eye of their leader. A leader Andre just discovered he no longer trusted.

Haris Cadmilus was hunched over his computer in the darkness of his stateroom, as usual, face illuminated by blue light. He'd forgone his guise of needing glasses months ago, and now his crystal blue eyes reflected the engineering specs on the screen perfectly.

Andre scowled, turning the bright lights on without an ounce of remorse. Haris screamed like a vampire caught in the sunlight, hissing as he ducked his head under his hood. "I give you a free ride, and you disrespect me behind my back, Cadmilus?"

Haris had the intelligence to get out of bed. His face hardened. "I'm sorry, I made a mistake. I shouldn't have disrespected you behind your back. You turned my best friend into a slave. That's worth disrespecting you to your face."

He spat on the ground.

Andre had half a mind to discipline him on national television. But that would cost him the Peregrine Pacific—a division that'd given him an edge in the power structures of Europe.

So, like the prince he was raised to be, Andre made a decision that would clean up as many loose ends as possible.

He snapped his fingers, and three Wards rushed into the bedroom. Haris barked in surprise as the Wards held him down, cuffing his arms behind his back. He struggled, but the male was far from a mutant with developed strength or martial training. He managed to shoot a set of quills from his head toward a Ward, but it was too little and too late.

Andre was careful to stand out of the firing range of the male's quills, watching in satisfaction as the traitor was pressed to the ground. He scowled. "I shouldn't be surprised. You were born as a traitor to Pangaea, and then you betrayed Pacific. Shame on me for thinking you could change your nature."

Haris gritted his teeth as the Wards pressed his head into the ground with their shining boots. "Shame on me for thinking you would be any different than Leon."

"I will be far better than my father," Andre promised, pacing the room. "But I have no tolerance for someone hacking into my servers and then spreading dissent behind my back. And weakness is the last thing you can have at this level of the game—that doesn't make me Leon. That makes me a survivor."

"Kalinda deserves to know the truth."

Andre shrugged. "And you deserve to die. Unfortunately, you're too brilliant to kill. I can think of someone who would love to have you. Lucky for me, it will buy me a favor."

"That savage bitch cut Uncle Reggie in half like he was a medium-rare sirloin!"

Andre covered Rou's ears against Pandora's outburst. His daughter squirmed, and he kissed her on the forehead. That was enough to calm her down. Ace had disappeared months ago, seemingly bored with Elite politics. She'd left two things behind when she disappeared to re-tame the Underground: a written contract guaranteeing her a spot in Andre's Inner Circle when he became Commander, and Baby Roulette.

Apparently, the cutthroat Elite halls of Pangaea were safer for a toddler than the casinos and tunnels of the Underground.

"And you lost London. Did you think they wouldn't take prisoners?" Andre asked incredulously.

Reginald Richards, Hera's brother, had been left in charge of London while Hera remained in Paris as part of Leon's war council. When the opposition claimed London, they'd taken its reigning Elite as a trophy. But instead of using Reginald as a hostage, they'd killed him in cold blood like the savages they were.

Reports said Strix's daughter, Phoenix, had become an even larger nuisance than her mother. Phoenix was hellfire. Something told Andre she killed Reginald for no other reason than because she *could*.

The leather chair Pandora sat in squeaked as she slid down it in painful defeat. She'd met Andre in his drawing room. The calming space had become his favorite spot for meetings. He still had fond memories of spending long evenings with his grandparents there. It'd been where he'd smoked his first cigar with his grandfather. Even now, the sweet smell of smoke hovered in the room. Andre didn't have the heart to let his servants clean in there, lest the scent deplete.

Cigar smoke was among the few things he had left of them.

"You act like I *wanted* to lose London," Pandora muttered.

Annoyance prickled in his gut, remembering his grandparents' killer currently lounged directly across from him. He quickly pushed the vile emotion down.

Hating Pandora for what she'd done would only complicate things. He needed Pandora if he wanted his plans to succeed. That was all there was to it.

That was politics. Sometimes sacrifices had to be made—something Kalinda and Haris obviously didn't understand.

"Have you spoken to Leon about this yet?" Andre asked.

Pandora rolled her eyes. "I'm taking a page out of your book: I'm hiding in Spain. I don't want to deal with Daddy right now."

"We both need to report to Paris in two days." He was dreading the visit almost as much as his fiancée. He enjoyed operating in an *out-of-sight, out-of-mind* policy with his father, especially when war had made Leon's temper even shorter than usual. Andre kneaded his brow. "With these repeated losses, I think Leon wants to take the offensive. Confront Africa's forces."

And Spain held one of the most significant stretches of the Artery: the narrow span over the Mediterranean, linking Europe to Morocco. Whoever controlled that bridge controlled movement in that region. With the savages' recent success in England, Africa might grow confident enough to attempt crossing and starting a campaign in Spain.

"Just like old times." Pandora's smile returned as she rubbed her hands together. "Look at us: Europe's power couple. I can get Sensatia to film our campaign—we'll have everyone anticipating our wedding once we become war heroes."

Andre's gut twisted at the thought. Allying with Pandora was the *strategic* choice, but any mention of an actual marriage always made him hesitate. Fortunately, to Hera's never-ending annoyance, Leon had yet to announce a date.

"We need to win the campaign first," he said.

Pandora waved him off. "Good thing I've gotten a good hold of my newest toy. She'll make a great addition to our team."

That's when he noticed Jaya lingering in the back of the drawing room. Pandora had instructed the female to remain invisible: hair and skin matching the room's shadows like a wraith. Thanks to her color-changing tactical suit, most wouldn't have even noticed she was there. But Jaya's expression was the most jarring: emotionless, with eyes staring forward at nothing. A blank slate. She looked like one of Pandora's Puppets waiting for orders.

You put a control collar on my sister. Kalinda's accusing words cut into his mind, making him flinch.

"How did you get Jaya to cooperate?" Andre asked slowly, realizing the more he stared at the former Pacifican, the more unnerved he became.

From his previous experience with Blue Krait, the control collar historically acted as a powerful nudge—one Blue was already predisposed to follow. On the other hand, there was no way Jaya would ever willingly cooperate with Pandora.

She gestured to Jaya. "Come here, Changeling. Show and tell time."

Jaya's colors returned to normal: purple hair, light brown skin, and sparkling green scales dusting her cheeks—a new result of her maturation. At the same time, her tactical suit shifted from black to olive green. She mechanically walked up to the cyborg's side, eyes still distantly trained on the far wall.

"My mother's newest control collar," Pandora explained. "She's combined it with technology from the Simulator and a new experimental injection she derived from the Serum. It puts *Feras* in a beautiful dreamscape while giving us control of their bodies and abilities."

Andre's jaw dropped open. Guilt slithered its way through his professionalism before he shoved it back down. Still, he felt compelled to ask, "Does she feel any pain?"

"Trust me, the bitch is having the time of her life in there," Pandora reassured him. "We take their memories and track their chemical receptors to keep them in a manufactured dreamscape that brings them joy."

With a swipe on her tablet, she brought up a video that almost looked like security footage. It was from Jaya's perspective. She ran on the beach, purple hair streaming across her eyes and a surfboard held under her shoulder. And running beside her was Arianne, wings concealed by a turquoise wetsuit as she carried her surfboard toward the water. They seemed to be laughing. Andre's heart lurched as Arianne turned to face Jaya. He saw his sister's smile, bright as the sun, painful as a sunburn.

Arianne... happy...

At least some version of his sister could live on forever, enjoying the beaches of her home with her best friend.

He shook himself, bringing his composure back. He knew he couldn't give Pandora an inch. So, Andre sat up in his seat, lit a cigar, and did his best to look the picture of content, just like Leon had taught him. "As long as you can keep your newest toy under control, that's all I care about."

"Then we're prepared to meet with Leon in Paris." Pandora got ready to leave—her attention span had always been short.

"Not so fast." Andre smiled as the cyborg paused. He took a deep drag of his cigar. "You didn't think I would let my betrothed leave without a wedding present, did you?"

There was nothing human in Pandora's smile. "Oh, *dearest,* you shouldn't have."

The doors opened, and Wards dragged Haris inside. Andre forced himself to return the male's venomous stare, commanding the Wards to let the Pacifican go with a casual flick of his hand. They threw Haris to the floor, right at Jaya's feet. Still in a trance, Jaya didn't so much as flinch as her best friend fell on her boots in chains.

Haris whimpered when he saw her. "Jay?" His voice cracked. "Jay!"

"She can't hear you, hun," Pandora cooed, spinning her pixie-cut hair around a cybernetic finger.

Haris lunged at her with a cry. "What did you do to her?"

In a cruel twist of fate, Jaya was the one to subdue her friend, her fluorite eyes eerily glassy and distant the entire time. Haris whimpered against her grip but didn't struggle further.

Rou cooed and clapped in Andre's hands. It seemed his daughter had developed a specific taste for violence over the past few months. Maybe he needed to stop bringing her to his meetings. Andre tapped Rou on her forehead and couldn't help but scrunch up his nose at her adorable giggle.

Haris sobbed, leaning his forehead forward to touch his unresponsive friend. "Jay."

Jaya didn't react.

Pandora watched the pair, her glowing blue eyes bored. "As much as I like watching a good drama, I have a flight to Paris to catch. What is your gift, Andre?"

Looking away from his daughter, Andre was suddenly disinterested in the meeting. He nodded at Haris. "A peace offering for Leon and Hera to soften the blow of your failure in London. I think your mother would appreciate another talented researcher in her labs."

Haris paled. The look he gave Andre was one of straight betrayal. "Hera's labs? You're sending me to *her*?"

"Since you wore out your welcome here," Andre responded blandly. "It's time to see if you have uses elsewhere."

"The Peregrine Pacific—"

"Belong to me now," Andre cut in. "I don't think they'll take kindly to you attempting to throw out their best chance at revolution *or* my stellar accommodations and munitions."

Haris reddened in rage. "You're a *monster*."

"No, I'm an Heir." Andre corrected. "And I intend to do everything in my power to stay that way this time—whether people call me a monster or not is inconsequential."

Chapter 18

Keston

The moments after *Cinderella* hit his system were the most disorienting, especially when he was in public.

As Cartel's influence spread across Asia, so did Keston's *pharmaceutical* market. Along with the classic brands of drugs, and Ace's signature Slime, Hera had asked him to inject her metabolism-suppressing drug into the Underground's *Fera* groups. Avid users had taken to calling the drug Cinderella—Cindy for short—because, much like the classic fairy tale, the drug gave them a party for a few short hours. When the clock struck midnight, so to speak, they lost their sparkly highs and returned to the dullness of their *Fera* immunity.

Keston gripped the bathroom sink, focusing on his balance. Maybe he'd been too eager to get high in his first few uses of the drug, or maybe he hadn't been aware of the effects. He could feel them now. Cindy didn't just lower his metabolism; it undoubtedly turned off his other abilities. Sight, hearing, sense of smell, and balance. Hence, the need to grip the sink. Even his wings started to prickle with pins and needles beneath his cape. He didn't know if he had lost the ability to control them—he was too scared to find out.

Logically, when he was high off his ass, he didn't dare try flying.

Looking in the mirror, he tried to avoid how his vision blurred. He reached into his bag and put on his glasses to compensate for his human eyesight and cover his bloodshot eyes. Next, he took a rip of his pen. The weed numbed his system. With one last look in the mirror—it was far too luxurious to deserve idiots doing drugs in front of it—he was ready.

Zhou Qin had invited him to a performance as a royal guest. If he wanted to survive the night without picking a fight, he needed to have enough drugs coursing through his system to numb an elephant.

Sora waited outside the restroom, her flowing red halter-top dress succeeding at making the scowling princess look somewhat agreeable. "If you're going to smoke in the bathroom, at least do a better job of concealing it."

"Care to join me?"

She grumbled and started walking. Keston took that as his cue to follow. Keeping two paces ahead, she didn't turn as she spoke. "My brother invited you as a sign of goodwill between the royal family and the Underground. I would have assumed you would want to do your best to present yourself."

Keston chuckled, enjoying the slight tingling in his fingers as the high took hold. "Trust me, this version of me is far preferable, Your Highness."

No one wanted to see the version he had to suffer with in the silent moments. He couldn't even tolerate it. That version was quiet, introspective, and unbearably miserable. In the rare times he found himself sober and alone, all the regret inched through his perfectly crafted facade. It was debilitating. He was forced to remember the critical moments when he *should* have made different decisions, the images crashing against his temples like a splitting headache. And when he wasn't reminiscing about his mistakes or the things he'd lost, he was met with every traumatic memory his mind could conjure.

He'd followed Sora upstairs, unaware she'd been talking to him as his inebriated mind drifted lazily from thought to thought. He tuned in again as they reached a set of curtains guarded by Wards. "It's nice to sit in the viewing box every once in a while," she said, holding the curtains open for her guest. "Usually, I'm the one on stage."

He hardly registered her words, focused instead on the wound on her upper arm, which she'd almost succeeded in concealing with makeup. It looked like a sword wound. As if in response, the scar on his nose gave an unpleasant *zing*. Keston stopped halfway through the door and nodded to Sora's arm. "That looks like it hurt."

The princess quickly dropped the curtain, leading him into the viewing box. "Practice accident. I use many props in my act: flags, whips, banners, fire, and swords."

Keston put his hands in his pockets. "For a second, I thought you might be more interesting than just another pampered Elite."

"'Interesting' gets people like me killed."

"Then make yourself harder to kill."

He hated that an image of Arianne, face painted with avenging fury, flashed across his mind.

Before Sora could respond, Qin snapped his fingers from his lounger. "Someone get my friend a drink. It looks like he's thinking far too much for a Friday night." The Heir Apparent's demeanor had changed drastically from the week before—granted, Keston was worth something to him now. Qin looked almost excited to see his Underground guest sit in the chair beside him. "I see you put on my gift."

Like Qin, Keston had on a flowing Japanese kimono that hid his wings perfectly. While the prince favored the black and red Pangaean colors, Keston received a royal-blue design with a stunning pattern of orange koi fish. He'd even tied back his hair in a matching ribbon. Fortunately, the mid-autumn evening was cold, giving him an excuse to wear the kimono's matching cape.

A drink materialized in his hands from Qin's *Fera* servants as Keston gazed over the theater below him. He passively sipped the sickeningly sweet beverage, still smoking from the dry ice on top, as he analyzed the seating and six exits. Once an operative, always an operative. Naturally, no other guests were close enough to be a threat to Qin and Sora—the circle of Elite viewing boxes rested a story below them.

The only threat was the rafters above the stage.

"You know, after our first meeting, I was half expecting to wake up to your assassins attempting to break into my penthouse," Keston began mildly, swirling the ruby-red contents of his drink.

"You should have," Qin replied. "Unfortunately, none of my men made it past your Jokers. Those who escaped barely made it back to my palace with enough blood in their veins to tell me what happened before they died."

Keston was thankful for his high. "I know. I was checking to see if you'd admit to it."

That'd been an interesting dilemma to wake up to five days ago. Tex had burst into his room, reporting on a group of ten ninjas making their way up the tower toward Keston's penthouse. Qin's description of the events was mostly accurate, except for the missing detail where Keston managed to kill half of the assassins himself.

The morning after, Keston woke up to his brand-new kimono carefully wrapped with a royal invitation to the theater. He'd almost forgotten how people in his business made friends.

"I have no use for someone who can't survive my assassins," Qin said.

Keston grinned. "Would you like me to give you the same test?"

Sora reached for the whip placed casually on the table next to her. Keston winked at her. For *just* a dancer, she really liked reaching for weapons.

Qin's eyes narrowed, amusement fading from his face. The prince didn't break eye contact with Keston as he picked up his unmoving right arm and let it drop down at his side. "Someone attempted to kill me years ago. Let me remind you that I'm the one still breathing, and they were wiped off the map."

Keston bit back on the retort that the assassin had been three-quarters successful. Qin's twin brother, Khan, was dead, and Qin had lost the right side of his body. Something told Keston his new frenemies wouldn't find a fraction of that joke funny. He laughed to himself at his internal pun.

Fortunately, the stage curtains opened moments later, saving Keston from a response, and he shifted to the edge of the balcony for the best view of the stage. He slung his arms casually over the edge, trying to convince the room—and himself—that he was comfortable.

What was more comfortable than being in a foreign country, attending an event with the man who'd attempted to assassinate him? Elites were so strange. At least in the Underground, if someone wanted you dead, they were upfront about it.

A performer in a red ringleader's outfit stepped out into the spotlight. A Lion's mask covered the top half of his face. Keston sat up straighter. Up on the rafters, performers crawled into position with acrobatic ribbons and trapeze equipment. Keston's palms grew damp. Then the Lion Ringleader opened his clawed hands and smiled broadly enough to display his fangs.

Keston was out of his seat and rushing toward Qin as the ringleader began to speak: "First, there were Seven. From these seven *Feras,* all the tribes were born. Come with me and my Circus of Artemis as we dive into the journey of Legends. For Artemis was the goddess of Beasts, and this is the story of the greatest beasts to ever walk this earth."

The Circus of Artemis was *there*.

Qin frowned at Keston. "What are you doing? Sit down. The show has just begun."

Sora lunged into his path. "How dare you approach—"

"You need to get out of this theater *now*." Keston pushed the princess aside. "Like, you should probably bury yourself in a bunker kind of *now*."

That got Qin's attention. The prince sat up straighter in his seat, his left hand reaching for his cane. "What do you mean? It's a mutant warm-up act. I don't possibly see the problem."

Keston gave a wary glance back toward the stage. Smoke machines had started filling the theater with crawling clouds of fog. The crowd applauded as tribal music mixed with the smoke and low lights, creating a mythical effect. But Keston wasn't clapping. That fog wasn't for the performance—it was meant to disorient. Was it just him, or were the acrobats in the rafters climbing closer?

"Let's just say I've seen this episode before," Keston responded cryptically.

Sora was helping her brother stand, her hand rising to her face so she could shout orders to her Wards through her watch. "Are you coming?" she asked Keston.

As much as he wanted to avoid the clusterfuck brewing below, he'd put too much effort into his alliance with Qin. He wasn't about to throw that down the drain because the Circus of Artemis wanted to intervene. With a long-suffering sigh, Keston pulled out two brass knuckle gauntlets and strapped them to his fists. "I'll hold them off. You two get out."

"Thank you," Sora said breathlessly.

Keston gave Qin a shit-eating grin. "You owe me one, asshole."

The royals dipped out the back of the box, flanked by their squadron of Wards. Keston waited for the curtains to settle before raising his watch to his face and calling the one contact on his device he was explicitly instructed *not* to call. He couldn't summon his Jokers—something told him Cartel wouldn't take lightly to his unorthodox relations. He was out of options.

The call was answered almost immediately. They were curt, voice mechanically distorted. "I thought you didn't need assistance tonight?"

Keston rolled his eyes. "The Circus is in town. Didn't think to tell me?"

"We had no idea."

"Interfere now before another diplomatic incident takes a hot shit on nine months of my hard work."

As he spoke, he pulled out his bottle of Cindy and began hastily smashing the pills into a fine light-blue powder. At the moment, he was outmatched with the drug coursing through his system. He prayed that if he could make an inhalant out of it, he might be able to bring his mutant assailants down to his level faster than the usual digestion period. He didn't like to admit that his experience with drugs had taught him that trick. Anxiously eyeing the performance below, he winced when he recognized a speckled female in a cheetah's mask and a male with the legs of a satyr.

Yes, he'd *undoubtedly* seen that episode before.

Mashing the pills faster, he hoped his hunch was correct.

The voice on the call wasn't promising. "Christos and Joshua are supposed to be performing ten blocks away. It's a public event. They could risk being grouped in with the incident if they don't show. It will risk our cover."

Naturally, the remaining members of his band had joined him in Tokyo. Keston had done his best to keep Christos and Joshua out of his Underground activities, only allowing them to associate with his nightclubs for partying and performances.

Three performers suddenly walked through the audience. Most people applauded as the unitard-clad *Feras* interacted with the crowd, but Keston knew they weren't performing. They were searching.

"We don't have a choice." Keston hissed. "I can't hold the Circus off for long. *Call him.*"

"This shouldn't be hard for you."

He took a concentrated breath. "I'm not sober."

"*Keston.*"

The winged male relented as he scooped the crushed Cindy into his hands. "I *know*," he hissed. "I'm sorry."

"Your backup is coming."

"Thank you."

His contact's voice was flat. "Don't use this number again. It's compromised."

The call ended.

The rafters above the box begin to shake. He braced himself.

A female dressed in a stunning red singlet and matching skirt swung down from the rafters and landed in a deadly crouch on the railing of the open viewing window. Her hair was laced with sparkles and curled for her performance, but he still recognized the golden brown that faded to bleached blonde at the tips. Her wings surrounded her, a cape of feathers covered in smoke. When she raised her face, it was covered by a feathered silver-and-red circus mask.

"We need to stop meeting like this, Princess."

Before Arianne could attack, he opened his palm and blew the crushed-up Cindy at her face.

Chapter 19

Arianne

"Keston—"

A cloud of glittering blue powder shot into her face, cutting off her outburst. It filled her mouth and nose, and she stumbled in surprise at the painful sting. Arianne caught herself and rolled into the Heir Apparent's viewing box, hating that she started sneezing immediately.

When the stinging pain faded, she shot off the ground. She prepared to rip that *motherfucker* to pieces. But Keston was gone. For a moment, she was convinced she was only seeing things. But his scent circled the room—as familiar to her as the smell of her lavender candles. Arianne reoriented herself, needing to brace on a barstool to stand.

The Circus was still performing. No alarms blared just yet. Still, Zhou Qin was gone. She pounded her fist on the nearest hard surface. Somehow, Keston had gotten wind of her ambush, or—she barely wanted to think about it—he was close to the prince and had been visiting with him.

Which meant Europe already had Asia in a vice grip.

Having only landed in Tokyo the day before, Arianne had hoped to take care of Qin quickly. An easy, successful mission was precisely what she needed to show Sygrid she was still on her game. It'd been easy for Colla to inject his circus into the opening act, granting the Ivory Court a shot at Qin—no months of scheming needed. Asia wouldn't have even known what hit them until it was too late.

And, of *course,* it was Keston getting in her way.

With a flashlight attached to her hip, Arianne signaled a series of flashes to Blue behind the stage curtains. It translated to: "*First attempt failed; pursuing target. Backup needed.*"

Arianne drew the twin batons of *Horizon's Edge*. She didn't extend the blades just yet, hoping to maintain her performer disguise for as long as possible. Cracking her neck, she dashed out of the viewing box after Keston.

"Time to see what barbecue sauce goes well with Keston wings."

Tracking his scent was like following a neon arrow pointed in his direction. As her sense of smell matured, she'd learned just how easy it'd been for the tribes in the Darwin Zone to track her and Keston down during their first journey together. A mature *Fera's* sense of smell acted as another set of eyes. After nearly two years of training, she could form a black-and-white image of that room's past or present state in her mind.

The trail led to the private parking lot behind the theater. She almost threw the exit doors off their metal frames with her desperate momentum. Sprinting onto the pavement, illuminated against the night by one flashing street light, she was disappointed to find the parking lot empty.

Blue's reconnaissance from an hour before had reported that was where Qin's stretch limo had been parked. Instead of a limo, a lone figure stood on the pavement. He stood strategically between her and the entrance to the lot. Keston.

Arianne bared her teeth as she extended her Selvian steel blades. "*You*," she spat. "Always *you*."

Keston raised his hands. "Okay. This time, I can explain—"

Arianne screamed over him. "I'm sick of your *explanations*. Let's go for an *ex*ecution instead!"

Jumping off the steps into the theater, she flapped once, twice, then tucked in her wings for a corkscrew offensive. But her body didn't respond. She twisted mid-air and started falling, her wings suddenly numb. A strangled cry escaped her as she tumbled to the ground, her skin scraping across the asphalt.

With a groan, she tried to lift herself from her embarrassing fall. Her vision started to blur around the edges, the night suddenly shades darker than it'd been just a minute before. Had her body always been this heavy?

Arianne had a sinking feeling that whatever Keston had blown in her face wasn't just glitter.

"Sorry, Princess. Had to even the playing field. Couldn't have you killing me."

Standing, Arianne held her arms out for balance. "What did you do to me?"

Keston's honey gold eyes flashed. "Welcome to your first dance with Cinderella."

He threw off his kimono to reveal an armored tactical suit, wings tucked tight to his body. With a smile, he punched his fists together, brass knuckles bursting to life with a bright purple glow. Three claws of burning purple plasma extended eight inches from each hand. It produced a sharp-looking edge, but the sparkling blades dripped purple, as if they were made of viscous liquid.

Well, that was certainly a weapons upgrade.

Flicking on the heat of her own blades, Arianne smiled maniacally as their gunmetal grey turned molten orange. "Get tired of me kicking your ass?"

Keston flashed his new blades. "Like them? I call them *Talons*, a fun invention from some of my associates. They're based on the Japanese Takagi shuko claws." He waved the brass knuckles. "They let me keep my street-style fighting while giving me something to fight *Feras* like you. And the best part? My hands remain free for my preferred weapon: firearms."

"Wow, talk any longer, and you might have a good old-fashioned villain monologue."

She didn't wait for his response. She attacked, even though her body moved in slow motion. Calling on her muscles to sprint, a block stopped her from going to that next level. Was this how she'd fought back in Pacific? She was practically stuck in molasses.

But that had to do.

Abilities intact or not, she knew how to kill, even if it had to be in slow motion. Swords locked with Keston's Talons, she realized he moved just as slowly.

Had he *voluntarily* taken the drug?

Plasma sparked purple between them. He pushed upward against her momentum, throwing her off balance. Taking advantage, he jumped, his right arm targeting her exposed shoulder. Arianne rolled under him, managing to swipe one of his boots, but he recovered quickly enough to deflect her second sword.

Arianne took a defensive position, smiling at him, slightly impressed. He'd found the one thing Selvian steel couldn't cut through: non-solid matter. She was almost thankful for the challenge—not a single opponent had lasted more than a minute against her in months. And there Keston was, matching her not just blow for blow, but weapon for weapon. Slower than usual, yes, but still far faster than the average human.

It was invigorating.

The two winged warriors assessed each other, winded without their *Fera* stamina. Keston extended a right hand, beckoning her. Extending her blades, she rushed him, swinging her arm in a wide arc. He blocked. She turned to intercept, but Keston retracted his Talons, and her momentum continued until she was off balance. Re-extending his Talons just as fast, he jabbed at her midsection. She just managed to vault backward and avoid a deadly kidney shot.

Arianne blew a few curling strands of hair out of her face. "You missed, Pangaea Boy."

Keston smiled. Then her skirt dropped, leaving her in just her unitard, cut like a bathing suit. She felt the color drain from her face, suddenly more exposed than she'd ever wanted to be on an assassination mission.

"I think I was right on target." He winked. "Think of it like strip poker, except with weapons."

He looked so much like the Keston she'd come to love. A shit-eating grin that still managed to be undeniably handsome, long curling hair tied back, and glistening eyes that welcomed playful challenge.

It only pissed her off more.

"Not my problem if you want to die with your balls out."

She attacked again.

They exchanged a few more blows, equal with every strike and parry. If she hadn't been so annoyed, she might've complimented him. Dangerously close to having fun, when presented with an opportunity at his inner leg, she didn't take it. Instead, she swiped upward, slicing at his waist.

A deep-bellied laugh escaped her as his pants dropped, exposing his hot pink boxers.

With more grace than a male caught with his pants around his ankles deserved, Keston rolled out of her range, sliced himself free of his pants, and resumed a defensive stance. Somehow, he'd kept a straight face.

Keston Leroy, Europe's most deadly operative, stood in front of his opponent in pink boxers and tactical boots. Arianne almost curled up in a fetal position on the ground with laughter.

"Well played, Princess." The corner of his lips curled. "If you wanted to see me without my pants, all you had to do was ask."

She hated that she smiled back at him. "You know I always liked removing them myself." She nodded to his boxers. "Pink looks good on you."

"There was a time when Arianne looked good on me, too."

A roaring in her ears drowned out everything else. She stared at him, forgetting she was in the middle of a fight. Against her will, she was brought back to the top of that skyscraper, tangled in his arms with only the sky to bear witness. They'd sat together, watching the sunset as his hands ran through her hair. She remembered what she'd whispered to him in those moments, like she'd just said it yesterday.

Whatever happens between now and After, we'll find each other. I promise.

Somehow, annoyingly, she'd kept that promise.

He seemed so different from the male she'd said those words to. Yet, she couldn't help but feel like the past two years had faded away. Alliances or betrothals didn't matter. There, eyes locked together, they were just Keston and Arianne. Years of heartbreak separated them, yet why did it feel like *nothing had changed?*

In her daze, an armored SUV swerved into the parking lot. The gunfire barely registered in her ears. The building could have exploded next to her, and she would've still been fixated on Keston. Like a rookie, she didn't even think to dodge. Luckily, Rhino's muscled frame filled her vision, shielding her from the onslaught of bullets. From behind his shoulder, the SUV squealed up to Keston. A masked Joker trained a semi-automatic on their position until Keston escaped inside.

Arianne struggled in Rhino's arms, the world returning to focus now that she was away from Keston's hypnotizing stare. They needed to chase after him. This was their only chance. She needed to kill Qin—

"Phoenix." Rhino always used her Champion's name on missions. "Phoenix, we can't pursue!"

"They're getting away!" Arianne struggled harder, hating that a few of her heartstrings were pulled as Keston's SUV sped away.

She couldn't explain it, but she *needed* to follow. It'd been nine long months, and he was gone in the blink of an eye. Again. What if another nine months went by before their blades crossed?

She told herself she shouldn't care. But she did.

"Are you okay?" Rhino asked in the resulting silence.

"I lost him," Arianne said, slumping against her friend's embrace.

"We'll get Qin another day."

She couldn't take her eyes off where the SUV had disappeared. "Right. Qin."

"What Rhino forgot to mention is that pursuing Qin tonight would be a bad idea," a new voice said.

Arianne straightened. She knew that voice, though she hadn't heard it in ages. Looking up, Rhino was smiling despite the mission's failure.

"Treena," Arianne realized, turning. Sure enough, she stood at the theater's exit, looking no different than the day she'd left for her mission almost a year and a half ago. Arianne shook her head, correcting herself, "Or should I call you Whisper now?"

Treena's Champion name—a perfect match for her echolocation abilities. Treena and her brother Tyrell, who'd earned the name Echo, had disappeared off the grid on what Ringtail had insisted was a top-secret Shadow mission collecting intel for Cervi. And now, years later, they'd reappeared in Tokyo.

The rust-haired female smiled. "And I should call you Phoenix now."

Despite Arianne's reservations about the twins' roles in faking her death, years apart had numbed the pain. And after countless difficult decisions of her own, she better understood the painful decisions the twins had to make.

Stepping forward, she hugged her friend from a lifetime ago. Treena accepted the embrace, head falling on her shoulder. With a whimper, Rhino wrapped his arms around them both, picking them up effortlessly. For a few fleeting moments, Arianne closed her eyes and let herself pretend she was still on Citadel Island, meeting her friends outside of Shipwreck for a night of dancing.

Things had been so simple back then.

When Rhino finally set them down, the remaining Ivory Court had arrived to surround their newest addition. Topher and Lova were still in their performance uniforms, the sparkles on their outfits twinkling in the streetlight. Blue, wearing her tribal leathers, regarded Treena with a slight flick of her head.

After a minute, Arianne finally asked the question everyone was thinking: "What are you doing here?"

Treena smiled, looking so familiar it almost hurt. "I could ask the same question. I was waiting for you dim-wits at the Okazaki Estate. You were supposed to meet with the Jin family, remember?"

"I got intel Qin would be here tonight." Arianne shrugged. "I thought I would just get the damn thing over with."

"Impulsive Arianne." Treena laughed. "I'm glad to see some things don't change. Sorry for the confusion. I couldn't reveal my identity until you made it to Tokyo." With a passive glance around, she waved for the Ivory Court to follow her. "Come on, this area's not secure."

The drugs hadn't worn off yet.

Trying to steady her breathing as she sat on her cot, she assessed her hands. Though she didn't look different, everything felt different. Weaker, *reduced*. Even her eyesight was worse. In the gloom of her room—it was more of a closet—she could barely see her hands in front of her face.

What had Keston done to her? After the thrill and anxiety had faded, Arianne was left with the deep-seated fear of being unable to access her abilities. Without her advanced senses relaying the world around her, she felt exposed. Had this been how she'd been during her first missions away from Pacific?

She'd been so *weak*. How did she survive?

Arianne looked toward the rickety door she'd hastily closed behind her once she'd arrived at Treena's shack-like safehouse. She'd yet to explain to her team that her abilities were M.I.A. If the problem persisted into the morning, she would bring it up. For now, they all needed rest after their failed mission.

Treena's safehouse was on the outskirts of Tokyo: an abandoned single-family shack left to the unrelenting hands of nature. Even without Arianne's abilities, she could smell the rot and mold that had taken hold of the house's foundation. But she wasn't in a position to complain. Their failed mission had put a target on their backs, and Treena was kind enough to give them a place to lick their wounds for the night. Until they were certain they hadn't attracted a tail, they couldn't go within three miles of the Okazaki estate.

Minor setback. At least the only thing that died was her pride.

Arianne might have removed Keston's pants, but he'd effectively caught her entire team with their pants down. She cracked her knuckles as she recalled the fight, hating how her heart skipped a beat at the thought of his mocking smile. Keston was a roadblock she hadn't anticipated. What did it mean to her mission?

Keston always found new ways to complicate her life.

There was a knock on the door. Moments later, Blue let herself in. "Thanks for taking the blow for me," she said, closing the door tightly behind her.

Arianne shrugged. "'Impulsive Arianne,' it was an easy enough sell."

"I just—" Blue paused in a rare moment of uncertainty. "I wasn't ready to see my parents again. I'd hoped we could get this finished without involving them."

"I'm sorry."

"No, I'm sorry. I shouldn't have asked you to risk the team on a mission like this," Blue relented.

Arianne stood and took her friend's hands. "You can always sit this one out, Blue."

"I need to rip the band-aid off. It's scary, but I need to do it." Her fingers squeezed, yellow eyes wide with fear. "I made a *major* mistake as a kid, Ari. I still don't know if I can face it."

The mistake that'd made her start calling herself Blue Krait. The mistake that'd had Ringtail running halfway across the world to shield a little girl from the wrath of a continent that hated *Feras*. Though Blue didn't talk about her past much, something significant had happened to rip her away from her family and force her to hide in Selvia. Arianne knew a thing or two about ugly secrets, and she knew enough never to press.

"We'll face it together," she promised.

Another knock came on the door. Lova.

The Cheetah seemed strangely quiet, her speckled tail wrapped around her hips—her usual sign of discomfort. Arianne's gut twisted, hating that the failed mission was affecting more people than just her.

"Did the Circus of Artemis get out all right?" Arianne asked.

Adopting her from a particularly *Fera*-unfriendly region of Africa when she was an infant, Lova had grown up with the Circus. While also a Champion of Selvia, a large part of her heart still belonged to Colla and the rest of the company.

She sank down on Arianne's cot, eyes strangely distant. "Yes. Colla just sent word. The Circus is waiting for further instructions, twenty miles away. They avoided attention by disguising their train in a shipment yard."

"Good," Arianne said. "I'm glad they're safe."

Blue frowned. "Then what's wrong?"

Lova hesitated, glancing toward the door and the small trickle of light shining through the crack. She slowly sighed. "I thought Rhino and Treena broke up," her voice was carefully quiet.

Arianne and Blue exchanged a look of surprise. Wordlessly, Arianne pulled the Cheetah into her side and hugged her. The twins hadn't been heard from in well over a year—no one could've assumed anything about their relationships. Arianne cursed herself for never asking Rhino.

She'd been so caught up in her own inner turmoil—and the war waging around her—to consider her oldest friend's emotions. Though she'd become a stellar warrior, she realized she'd left no space for being a good friend.

"It's not your fault," Arianne finally said. "Treena's never been good at relaying information." She gestured to the shack around them to prove her point.

"I feel terrible." Lova looked stricken. "I would never want to take him from her, but I can't help but feel—"

"Jealous?" Blue interrupted with a chuckle. "Someone mark the calendar: today is the day the purest of us has fallen."

Arianne couldn't help but smirk. "She's not wrong. You *were* the best of us, Lova. Now, this whole team is just a bunch of ingrates."

Lova squirmed. "No! That's not what I meant! I would never—"

"*Jealous,*" Blue hissed.

"Ari," Lova pleaded. "Order her to *be quiet.*"

Having way too much fun, Blue's smile stretched from ear to ear. "She can't do that. That would be a gross overstep of power."

Lova groaned, her clawed hands raking through her hair as she buried her face in her arms.

Another knock sounded on the door, and Topher walked in. He winced. "Hey, am I interrupting girls' night?"

"No!" Lova responded, quickly sitting up straight.

He hung on the doorframe, slightly uplifted eyes examining each female cramped in the painfully small space. "Okay," he trailed off. Then he smiled, pulling off his backpack to display a horde of various packaged Japanese candies and snacks. "Can I join? I know I'm supposed to bunk with Rhino, but I'm not interested in third-wheeling. I come bearing offerings."

"Holy shit, where did you get these?" Blue ravenously stole the bag, yanking out a bottle filled with milky-white liquid. "I haven't had Calpis since I was a little girl! Did you happen to grab the mango flavor?"

Arianne raised a hesitant finger. "I'm sorry, did you just say *cow piss?*"

"C-A-L-P-I-S," Blue spelled out slowly, looking about ready to smack Arianne upside the head. "It's a sweet milk-based drink, Birdbrain."

Ignoring the sarcastic outburst, Topher fished through his bag and proudly produced a similar bottle filled with yellow-orange liquid. He wagged the bottle before Blue, and she lunged for it. He giggled, pulling it away at the last second. "You need to be nice to me for a week. Can you manage that?"

Blue groaned, lowered her head, and extended both hands in submission. The other two laughed. Most dangerous warriors in the world, indeed.

The group dug into Topher's bag like raccoons who'd discovered a fresh garbage bin to tear apart. After a day of traveling and a stressful mission, the four *Feras* were nearly ravenous. Few things were more dangerous than a group of mutants who hadn't eaten in over five hours. Usually, they terrorized a local buffet after a mission, but they couldn't afford it with the targets on their backs.

Arianne dug her chip-dust-covered hands into another salty-sweet bag of snacks, chewing so fast she could barely breathe. She couldn't read Japanese, so she hardly knew what she shoveled in her mouth, but it was damn good.

Somewhere between gasps for air, she asked, "Topher, where did you get these?"

He raised his backpack, the trusty, never-ending well of supplies he refused to let out of sight. Usually, his collection of explosives and projectiles was nestled in there, but for the moment, it was still half-stocked with food. "You know me," he said. "Always come prepared. There was a mini-mart near where we staked out the theater. I grabbed some food in case we found ourselves in this situation."

"How did you buy them?" Lova asked, face covered in suspicious orange chip dust.

"Blue gave me one of her account cards for emergencies." He smiled.

Blue choked on her drink. "That card was a *fake*. The purchase bounces after ten minutes, so you can't be tracked." She curled up, evil cackles coming out of her in unattractive snorts. "I didn't think you would actually *use* it. Oh, my Ancestors, that just made my night."

Topher stared at her, mortified. The bag of fruit-flavored candies fell from his hands.

"You robbed a convenience store!" Blue cried, tears rolling down her cheeks.

Looking down at her pile of snack wrappers, Lova looked like she was about to throw up. Topher wasn't far behind.

It was clearly up to Arianne to be the voice of reason. But the currents of a deep-bellied cackle fought to break free, and the harder she tried to suppress it, the more it grew. Against her best efforts, it exploded out of her.

Holy cow, it felt good. She fell into Blue, the two practically crying at Lova and Topher's faces. They needed to lean on each other for support lest they fall over in heaps of giggles, caught up in the pure absurdity of it.

They were the Ivory Court, a division of elite warriors who'd committed more war crimes than should be physically possible. And they were worried about stealing snacks from a store.

"My great Deputy," Blue said, trying to sound serious through her giggles. She held out her wrists in surrender. "What do you decree to be my punishment?"

Arianne's cheeks puffed out, holding back another snicker. Some droplets of spit flew out. Trying to look professional, she sat up straighter and deepened her voice. "Blue Krait," she began. Lova and Topher giggled behind her. "I sentence you to death by Rhino hugs!"

Lova began to chant Rhino's name, fists banging on the wooden floor in a synchronous rhythm, and Topher joined in.

Blue collapsed on her side. "No!"

"You leave me no choice." Arianne lifted her chin. "A leader must punish her subjects."

"Rhino, Rhino, Rhino!" a fifth voice joined in.

They all turned. The brute himself stood in the doorway, almost too large to fit through. His face was alight, but when he realized the rest of them had stopped, he frowned. "I thought you guys were summoning me."

Lova composed herself first, folding her hands neatly on her crossed legs, smiling innocently. "Sorry, we didn't mean to bother you guys."

"I punished Blue to death by one of your hugs," Arianne explained, snorting again at how ridiculous it sounded.

To her surprise, Rhino didn't immediately join in. His silver eyes were low, the last of his excitement fading with each passing second. "Maybe tomorrow."

The humor in the room evaporated. Arianne moved to stand. "Where's Treena?"

He slumped. "She went out to patrol the area. If we were followed, they wouldn't be looking for her."

"Is everything all right?" Topher asked.

"Apparently, a year of no contact was supposed to be my sign we weren't together anymore." The large male lowered his head. "I don't really want to talk about it. Can I join you guys?"

Despite the room being packed to the brim, they all squeezed closer together, making just enough space for Rhino to sit down. Topher offered him a selection of their contraband goods, and slowly, the mood lightened again. They talked about dancing at the Valhan and how, when they returned home, it would be cold enough for Selvia's legendary hot chocolate. War was brutal, but gazing at her team, Arianne realized one good thing had come of it: it brought people together. She'd never felt so close to others in her life. It was healing.

As the snacks dwindled and exhaustion crept up on the merry band of mutants, they slowly fell asleep, passing out cuddled together, using spare limbs and shoulders as pillows. The crowded room, filled with bodies, was warm against the night chill. Surrounded by the people she trusted more than anyone, Arianne dozed off against Rhino's shoulder without a care in the world.

It was the best sleep she'd had since before the Siege of Oslo.

Chapter 20

Arianne

Early the following day, Treena returned to the hideaway to report that things had quieted down from the night before. Rhino notably didn't greet her, but if his distance bothered her, she didn't show it. As the Ivory Court slowly stirred from their cramped sleeping positions, with a healthy dose of stiff limbs and groaning, Treena was already all business.

"The Jins have a meeting for us scheduled this morning at ten hundred hours," Treena instructed, still monitoring the boarded-up windows. "I brought street clothes. We'll walk two blocks to a rendezvous point where a jet from the Okazaki estate will pick us up. From there, you'll have an hour to get ready." She scrunched up her nose. "Consider showers—you all reek."

Blue's mother, Jin Emiko, was from the Okazaki family, Tokyo's reigning Elites. While Jin Shi, the head of the Jin family, reigned over Shanghai, they had kept an estate in Tokyo so Emiko could remain close to her family. Emiko's sister currently overlooked Tokyo. All of that added up to one crucial fact: the Okazaki estate, just on the oceanside outside of Tokyo, was the safest place for a team of Selvians in Asia.

But it would be no easy road. Asian politics were fragile, and they couldn't compromise their alliance with the Jins or the Okazakis. The Jins had a transportation monopoly, while the Okazakis were one of the largest steel exporters in the world. If Selvia and their allies had any hope of succeeding, they needed jets and weapons.

Blue was notedly quiet for the short jet ride to the estate, Topher and Lova refusing to leave her side the whole flight. Arianne was thankful for her team's support on that front. While Arianne wished she could support her amica, she was slowly losing the capacity to feel anything. The closer they got to the estate, the more Arianne's Deputy persona took over. When they landed, she felt nothing beyond determination and calculation.

Colla had joined them at the rendezvous point. He'd looked almost unrecognizable with his hair tied beneath a cap, civilian jeans, and a casual black sweatshirt. Had she not known him to be one of the most powerful *Feras* in the world, she might've convinced herself he was just another Pangaean on his way to morning coffee.

"I don't understand why Keston was there," the Lion's voice was deep and rumbling in consideration. "He always finds a way to be in the wrong place at the wrong time."

"For him, it's the right place at the right time. That feathered *Fera* fuck somehow always finds a way out on top."

Her mind played their interaction over and over. Now, a few hours removed from his insufferable charm, Arianne could look at the situation objectively. However, it was impossible to know how Keston's involvement would impact her mission.

The estate grew larger below as the jet prepared to land—the sight extremely similar to her first time visiting the Jins a year before. Unlike before, when Arianne could sit back and observe, she was responsible for everything. She ground her teeth, a dangerous habit that was certainly wearing on her enamel.

She turned to Colla. "Is the Circus compromised?"

"We've dealt with this before," he responded. "We opened our train cars up for Ward inspection. They found nothing, and we were cleared."

"Good, we might need you guys. Keep them on standby."

She caught his long stare from the corner of her eye. He seemed to be considering something. Finally, he spoke, but in a subdued whisper. "I just got another *major* hit of déjà vu."

"What was it?"

There hadn't been a breakthrough in his memory in months.

He shook his head. "I shouldn't have said anything. You just reminded me of someone... again."

"Leon?"

"I don't know. Forget it."

Arianne looked down, her teeth clenching once more. One of her greatest fears had always been turning into her father. With the strife of war surrounding them, she hadn't thought about her father's influence for months. But the reminder of her close connection to Leon, in personality and coloring, was always jarring. She told herself she'd become whatever was needed to win, including matching Leon in monstrosity.

It still didn't stop the icky feeling she got when people she cared about recognized the similarity.

When the jet landed, they were ushered inside the estate with minimal ceremony. Blue was hesitant to go inside, her eyes wide as she observed her former home for the first time since childhood. Only the combined efforts of Lova and Topher coaxed her up the rock path to the oceanside mansion.

In the hour they were afforded to clean up, Arianne utilized every last minute. She was thankful for the mindless task of getting ready. Not a single thought beyond cleaning and eating the provided food crossed her mind during that hour. It was a nice reprieve. She showered, dried and arranged her hair into a collection of braids and straightened strands, painted her face with Champion's black, and dressed in ceremonial green robes. She placed her golden olive branch crown over her ears to complete her look. The crown was barely on her head before Treena knocked on the door.

Time to go.

With one last look in the mirror, she was proud of the reflection that stared back. She was Phoenix, Deputy of Selvia. She'd finally become someone worth listening to.

Blue was the only team member who didn't attend the meeting. The rest, including Treena and Colla, were seated at the round conference table in the middle of the lush greenhouse meeting room. As she entered, all eyes fell on her, the only sound coming from the bubbling fountain behind the table.

Jin Shi and Jin Emiko stood, both in Western formal attire, and bowed to Arianne. From personal experience, that was one of the most *advantageous* beginnings to one of her negotiations.

"Thank you for hosting us." Arianne returned the bow. "I'm grateful for such an alliance."

Jin Shi smiled as he sat at the head of the table. "You've grown, Phoenix."

"As much as I enjoy exchanges of flattery, war waits for no one."

"As you've shown." He chuckled. "Seeing as you've already made an attempt on Qin."

The passive insult was subtle, but she caught on. *Impulsive*. She did her best to swallow her pride—it left a painful lump in her throat. "Apologies, I hoped to finish my mission without involving the illustrious Jin family."

Blue had hoped for such an outcome, but Arianne would never voice that aloud.

"We want nothing more than to aid in Qin's assassination," Emiko remarked frankly.

Arianne couldn't hide her surprise. "Is that so?"

Interesting.

Jin Shi was more composed than his wife. He calmly steepled his hands. "Hana Lang viewed *Feras* as profit—her prejudice against them was nothing more than business. Qin's hatred for mutants runs perilously deep. To be frank, if Qin becomes Commander, it will mean the end of *Feras* in this region. He intends to reduce mutants to little more than animals. At least slaves are still considered human on this continent. Currently, Qin plays coy with Europe, but I've been in meetings with him: he will join Leon's campaign. The second he can call himself Han Lang is the second he lends his power to the war."

With September nearing its end, the countdown had begun. They had three months until Qin Ascended and Asia's forces turned the tide of the war.

Emiko stared at the table. "I've worked for twenty years to protect *Feras* in this region. We hoped we would have more time with Hana on the throne, but I was wrong."

Arianne felt a sharp pang of guilt. She shivered at the memory of the blinding rage she'd felt when the late Asian Commander attempted to kill Sygrid. The sensation of Hana's life force draining at the edge of her sword was still fresh. She would never regret killing someone who'd threatened Sygrid, but she still felt guilty for giving someone like Qin a direct line to power.

It was only fitting that she needed to clean up the mess she'd made.

"So I was right to attempt to kill him immediately."

Jin Shi approached the subject delicately, like he was juggling balloons with needles. "This is where it becomes...complicated. We couldn't even risk discussing the details until we knew we were all in a secure room. We have a very *narrow* path to success here. Outside of Qin, Sora is the only remaining heir—his half-sister from Hana's second husband. Unlike her brother, Sora has shown compassion for mutants in the region, even going so far as proposing legislation to her mother to give *Feras* a chance at second-class citizenship. It was shot down, of course, but many *Fera* sympathizers took note.

"Sora's relationship with her brother may be strained, but she's loyal to her continent to a fault. If Asia can find any way to blame Selvia for Qin's death, we will accomplish nothing. Sora will join Europe to avenge the slight against her people. The only way to keep Asia out of Europe's war and *Feras* in this region safe is to put Sora on the throne while making Qin's death look like the result of infighting. Qin's threat will be neutralized, Sora will Ascend, and Asia will focus on local politics and deny Leon aid."

A neutral party had to cause Qin's death, much like Hana's. The entire world believed that Alvaro killed the Asian Commander when he went feral. For the sake of Selvia's revolution, it was best that the story remained that way.

Jin Shi was right. There were a dangerous number of suboptimal outcomes. But the outcome they were rapidly approaching was just as grizzly. They needed to thread the needle and risk the fallout of failure if they wanted a chance of avoiding Qin's Ascension.

"So what's our plan?" Arianne finally asked.

Treena stood. "We trigger some infighting." She nodded to the Jins. "For that, we need to go on a field trip."

"This is *not* what I had in mind," Arianne said.

Treena had led the Ivory Court to a nondescript warehouse. Among the endless rows of shipping containers and storage shelves, the rust-haired Shadow guided them to a dark corner where she'd stashed a series of outfits and neon paint. The Selvians stared down at the pile of colorful clothing, none of them moving to grab any.

"This is called rave attire," Treena explained. "Electro music is prevalent in the Tokyo Underground. To blend in, we must dress like we're part of the Underground."

Arianne raised a hand as she frowned at the collection of sparse clothing. "Um, I can't even use all of this fabric here to hide *one* of my wings, Treena."

"That won't be a problem."

Arianne could fill an entire book with how often being caught with wings had been a problem.

After a short silence, Arianne realized her team was waiting for her decision. With an exasperated sigh, she waved at the pile. "Seeing as I'm curious now, we might as well see where this rabbit hole leads."

After months of close quarters, her team was hardly shy around each other. They all changed out of their mutation-concealing ponchos, sweats, and windbreakers and into the sparse party clothes. Arianne opted for a platinum-plated body suit with long sleeves, satisfied that they covered the burn scars running up her forearms. She completed the look with large black wrap-around sunglasses, effectively covering the top half of her face.

Once the team was dressed, Treena went around and painted colorful designs on their skin with glowing neon paint: pink, yellow, and green. When she was done, the Ivory Court looked like they'd just returned from an intense acid trip.

Arianne would know what that felt like.

Treena placed her hands on her hips, covered by a flowing hot pink skirt. "You all look wonderful. It's time for the meeting."

Arianne gave her band of highlighters another once-over. "Sure, we can raise a room's sex appeal by ten points, but who is this meeting with?"

"My brother will be there," was all Treena provided before she turned and guided them deeper into the warehouse.

They stopped at a nondescript shipping container. After ensuring they were alone, Treena knocked on the door seven times. Seven had become a popular number among *Feras*. It represented the seven members of the *Filii Luna*—the first team of mutants who fought for freedom during the Last War. The fact should have been Arianne's first hint.

A panel slid back from the shipping container. A hulking brute on the other side leaned so close to the window that only his mouth and swollen nose were visible. He opened his lips, lined with enough saliva to make her cringe. "Password?"

Treena rolled her eyes. "I *love* to party."

Such a cheeky password should've been her second hint.

The panel slammed shut. There was the distinct sound of creaking deadbolts, and the shipping container door slowly swung open. The brute, a *Fera* who beat Rhino in size, held the door open with an unamused expression. He gestured a meaty hand toward the staircase hidden below the container.

Now Arianne's curiosity was close to bursting.

Treena led the team down the staircase, the quake of heavy bass rumbling closer and closer. Had anyone else been guiding her down a dark staircase inside a creepy warehouse, Arianne might've been crawling out of her skin. But Treena had shown time and time again that she had Selvia's best interests at heart. Arianne might not trust the Shadow with her personal life anymore, but she undoubtedly trusted her with her life.

Two large black curtains hung at the bottom, purple fog leaking beneath them. Treena glanced at the Ivory Court one last time. "Stick with me, and *please* save your questions for the end."

"What are we on, a fucking tour?" Blue hissed.

Treena yanked back the curtains, revealing a world of neon. A dancefloor sprawled before them, packed with hundreds of *Feras*. With blacklights shining overhead, the whites glowed, and the painted neons on clothes, skin, and decor made the club look cast in negative color. Music pounded as bodies of every shape, size, color, and limb count mashed together with electric energy. It felt like the Selvian Valhan, if the Valhan had a cyberpunk makeover.

Every person in that nightclub was a mutant. They moved past her with pride: tails, cloven hooves, horns, feathers, fur, and scales all on display. Nothing was off limits. Nothing was shamed.

"Don't tell me," Arianne gasped.

"Mutant speakeasy," Treena said proudly. "You'd be surprised what happens when a continent declares war on an entire species for two decades. The ones with money start making their own little hideouts where they don't have to, well, hide."

Rhino bounced on the balls of his feet, looking about ready to explode. "Jaya and Haris would love it here."

Arianne wasn't ready for the pang of hurt the comment brought. She inadvertently looked at Treena and caught the Shadow flinch.

"Permission to dance?" Rhino asked.

Lova jumped in excitement. "Yes! One dance?"

Arianne wanted nothing more than to forget about her troubles for a few beautiful songs and dance in a nightclub surrounded by mutants. She could feel it now, the pull of the blood-pumping house music. If she closed her eyes, she was back at Shipwreck, dancing with her classmates after finals season.

Her eyes snapped open. No. She was Phoenix, Deputy of Selvia. She was there to work.

"We're on a business trip, not a vacation," Arianne replied, needing to convince herself more than the others. With a scowl, she pushed past a particularly belligerent female with a third breast—she didn't want to think about what mutation caused that. "Treena, take us to our meeting."

Treena retook the lead, pushing them through the crowd toward the VIP booths beyond. A thick fog coated the atmosphere, making the lights refract in strange patterns in the air. But, much like the music, the lights were dimmed enough for *Fera* senses. A human might think the lights were too dim and the music too quiet, but for a mutant, the club was the perfect amount of sensory overload for a night out.

The owner must have been a particularly thorough *Fera*. That observation should have been her third hint.

Treena paused before another set of curtains. On the right, the private booth had a window overlooking the dancefloor, but the platform's angle made it hard to discern who lingered inside. Arianne straightened her shoulders in preparation.

Whoever Treena had brought them to was powerful, someone they needed as an ally if they stood a chance at toppling the Asian Commandership from the inside. Arianne nodded for Treena to open the curtain, ready for what could be the most important negotiation of her life.

The first thing she noticed were abs accented in purple paint. The paint tracked down to his black techwear pants lined with purple. A fur jacket rested over his sculpted shoulders. Earrings of shining silver hung from his ears, matching the crown resting on his black, wavy hair. And his wings, dark and shining in purple glitter, rested behind his throne in a stunning display of unholy beauty.

There was only one way to describe him: King.

"Why, hello, Princess. Welcome back to the Underground. We *certainly* missed you."

Chapter 21

Keston

Keston had been notified that an operative from Selvia would meet him that night. He had no idea it would be Arianne until they'd come to blows the night before. Fortunately, he'd had twenty-four hours to prepare.

Looking at her in that skin-tight platinum one-piece, he immediately knew he still wasn't prepared in the slightest. There she was, looking like her head was about to explode, nose scrunched up in rage. Same old Arianne. God, he'd missed her.

And three...two...one...

"*Keston, I'm going to fucking kill you.*"

Right on time. Same old Arianne, indeed. He couldn't suppress his smile.

He rested his head casually in his hand. "That cute little threat's getting old."

Blue Krait fell back into the white leather cushions of a lounge chair, crossing her legs. "My night just got far more interesting. Thanks for the show, Treena."

Arianne glared at her.

"I'm gonna throttle him," Rhino rumbled, balling up his fists.

Lova moved to stop him but halted, thinking better of it. Keston watched the team of *Feras*, the famous Ivory Court. If Rhino wanted to try his luck against the best gambler in town, Keston would let him. For that reason, he'd made sure to be sober for the meeting.

Rhino charged, and Arianne sidestepped with a smirk, content to unleash her meathead. Keston tracked the attack, waiting for the last second to spring upward. It was comically easy to vault over Rhino's head and land behind him. Barreling into the throne, his momentum made it impossible to turn around in time. Keston took his chance, kicking low and taking out the brute's powerful legs.

Had Keston been a slower *Fera*, Rhino would've evaded his assault. But few were faster than Keston now. Rhino managed a skull-crushing backhand, but Keston casually ducked the attack and sent him tumbling. The entire room shook when Rhino's muscled body hit the floor.

"Anyone else want to pick a fight with me?" Keston turned to his guests. "There's a line, but I'll get to you eventually. No one can ever say I don't have good customer service."

"All right, you've had your fun. Time to stop fighting each other."

Tyrell entered the lounge. At first, no one in the Ivory Court recognized him. Keston didn't blame them.

Arianne slackened. Even Blue looked surprised. Tyrell removed his brown wig and prosthetic nose to stand next to his sister, the pair once more looking like twins. It was satisfying to watch the surprise on the Selvians' faces. At least Keston wasn't the only one who'd been thoroughly fooled.

"Hey, guys." Tyrell waved. "It's been a while. Sorry for the secrets." He made eye contact with Arianne and flinched. "Again."

"Explain. And then explain why I didn't know," Arianne commanded coolly.

That expression on her face was a new one. Keston was used to seeing her simmer, a female seconds away from an explosion. The Arianne standing there now was collected. Still furious, but as cold and terrifying as an ice-covered mountain.

It was infinitely more intimidating. Her time under Strix's influence was showing.

"There is a reason why the Master of Shadows reports directly to the Ductor: it keeps dangerous secrets in a closely protected circle," Treena began. "When my brother and I became Shadows, we reported to Ringtail, who reported directly to Cervi." She nodded toward Keston. "When Cervi got word of a new powerhouse rising in Paris, she implemented a deep-cover mission."

"I took on the identity of Joshua and got close to Keston by joining his band," Tyrell continued. "With my echolocation abilities, I could inform my sister without any digital or paper trail. Selvia had eyes and ears on Keston and Pandora: Europe's most powerful agents."

Discomfort pricked Keston. "Kind of talking about me like I'm not right here, buddy."

"Good." Arianne glared at him. "I enjoy pretending you're not here."

Ouch.

Naturally, he fell back on his lovely Blackjack tendencies, blowing her a kiss. "Too bad I'm too important to ignore." He held up the phone Strix had given him in Mexico City nine months ago. "Aren't you all wondering why I'm here?"

Arianne rolled her head toward him. "Let me think. You got bored, so you're doing what you do best and changing sides? What does this make you now? Triple—no, quadruple agent?"

He pocketed the phone, saving his sob story for later. He glanced at the twins. "Let's just say I'm not interested in being the bad guy anymore—"

"Good for you," Arianne interrupted.

"Can I talk, please?" he barked, the first sign of his annoyance breaking through. He got it. He deserved her spite. But he was trying to help end a *war*. "Listen, whether or not you like me is not my problem. I don't care if you trust my motives or any of that bullshit—I've done enough to get myself killed ten times over these past few months, so there's no turning back. Trust that."

Blue's eyes flickered between the twins and him, and realization dawned on her angular face. "You're Strix's inside agent." A collective gasp passed through the Ivory Court. "You're the one who's been feeding intel about European troop movements and city defenses."

Keston clapped like they were children. "Now you're catching on."

"As I said, Shadows report directly to the Selvian Ductor," Treena said. "That's why Strix had no idea of our mission until she became Ductor—or why you had no idea, Arianne." She pointed to Keston. "Strix approached him directly for an opportunity to help us. When he decided to help, Tyrell broke his cover as Joshua to Keston and became the middleman relaying Keston's intel to me. I then sent the information to Moon Warren."

Keston looked down, feeling Arianne's oppressive stare. He still remembered hiding the phone Strix had given him in Mexico City, terrified of powering it on. Terrified that he was already too far gone. But his mother, Celine, had been a Selvian, and he refused to sully her legacy further. If there was still a chance he could do good, he damn well owed it to himself and his family to try.

And Genevieve had made it apparent she didn't need his protection; his allegiances weren't bound to Europe anymore.

"I don't expect forgiveness," he said, looking directly at Arianne. "I just got sick of digging a deeper hole."

Her mouth was a hard line. "Good for you. Sorry if it takes me a while to believe this is genuine."

It took all his experience as an emotionless Underground kingpin to keep his expression neutral.

"Keston," Tyrell said, pulling him from his self-hatred. "Explain your plan."

Shaking his head, Keston cleared the lingering effects of extended exposure to Arianne's ire. "Right. Leon sent me to Asia to get close to Qin and his allies. In taming the Underground, we hoped to have more leverage over Asian royalty. But controlling the Underground also grants the Selvians more power. I know Qin's movements, I have his trust, and, most importantly, I know his weaknesses. The Underground is something powerful enough to tear Qin apart before he Ascends, but it's a much larger beast here than it is in Europe."

Blue was playing with one of her daggers, and she smiled, showing fangs. "You want to weaponize the Underground."

Keston righted the throne Rhino had knocked over and sat down, folding his hands together. "Cartel is the reigning Underground organization in Europe. There are a few smaller factions, but everyone knows who's in charge. Asia is a different story: a larger continent, more money, and a more established slave trade. In nine months, I've used Cartel's resources to get a piece of the Underground pie, but hardly twenty percent. I've knocked out most of the smaller groups, but three large factions remain.

"From what my Jokers found, these factions do not play well together. If we can pit them against each other—and Qin—we can take him out, put Sora on the throne, and cause enough infighting that Asia couldn't hope to interfere with Europe's war. And thanks to the obscurity of the Underground, we can do all of this from the shadows. The world will never know Selvia was involved."

"You want us to work with Cartel?" Arianne asked.

Keston grinned. "Well, Princess, it would be *my* Cartel. We run things a little differently now."

Glazing at the Ivory Court, Keston noted that other Champions shared Arianne's expression of unease. Their leader took stock of her team and then shook her head. "We prefer to do things independently, thank you very much."

"Ah, yes, swinging your sword and asking questions later," Keston crooned. "How well did that work for you last night?"

"Well, if you hadn't gotten in the way—"

"You don't get it," Keston interrupted, getting far too much joy out of her stunned flinch. "This isn't a soldier's job. You can't just go in and kill Qin, just like you can't just go and kill Leon. You kill Leon, and someone equally bad takes his place. The same will happen with Qin *unless* you can kill him without it leading back to you. And that's not a soldier's mission."

"And what kind of mission is it then?" Arianne demanded, crossing her toned arms.

"A backstabber's mission." He sat back in his chair, satisfied. "I'll admit, I hardly have as much expertise on the battlefield as you do, but this isn't a battle. This is politics. Secrets. Criminals. Face it, you need a guide, and I'm the only one qualified to get you through the muck."

She rolled her eyes but stayed silent.

"What's the matter, Princess? Angry you're in my territory now?"

Blatantly turning away from him, she addressed Treena and Tyrell. "What do we need to do?"

But Keston was having none of her disrespect, not when they'd come to *his* home turf. He stood up and stepped in front of the twins, forcing Arianne to look at him again. "Sorry, can't get rid of me that easily." He jerked a thumb to the twins. "They're great at getting information, not politics. Now, where was I? Right. We were covering all the hornets' nests we need to bash like piñatas if we want to win this thing."

Blue raised a hand, eyes bored. "You can just get me into Qin's palace. I'll just poison him again."

"Again?" Topher, who'd been notably quiet for the whole conversation, chipped in.

Blue blanched. "Meaning, it seems like I do it a lot. What's one more time?"

"It doesn't erase the fact that we can't directly kill him," Treena objected. "Selvia or any of their allies cannot be involved."

Keston nodded. "If you want to guarantee Asia stays out of this, we need to give them too many things to worry about on their own continent: like an Underground turf war."

"What's this about a hornet's nest?" Lova said.

"Right," Keston said. "As I've mentioned, Cartel now holds about twenty percent of the Underground in Asia. Three other major organizations hold slices of that pie."

Raising his wristwatch, Keston swiped a presentation onto a projection television across the room. A map of Tokyo appeared, divided into four distinct color regions. He may hate his father with all his guts, but the man's talent for presentation graphics had worn off on him.

"Tokyo is the Underground's playground with plenty of money, an established infrastructure, and separate from the mainland. All major kingpins hold power here." He pointed to the orange regions, which were significantly outmatched. "Orange is me, Cartel. As you can see, I've had far less success taking over Asia than Europe."

He nodded to the glowing green, red, and blue regions. "These guys are our targets. I made it easy. Red regions are owned by the Ronin: a syndicate of vigilantes and blades-for-hire. Pretty unorthodox when it comes to criminal organizations. They own about fifteen percent. Green is the Gwisin: a female-led organization specializing in sex work and pleasure houses. They hold about twenty-five percent. And last, in royal blue for royal pain in my ass, is Empress. They dominate with a whopping forty percent of control. Fucking assholes—feel free to take a lighter to their entire organization, torch them, and dance on the ashes."

"No love lost there," Arianne muttered.

"They've been assholes since my time with Ace," Keston explained. "We dealt with them mostly for *Fera* trade from Asia. Ace hated them. I hate them. Taking them down will be personal."

It surprised him that Ace hadn't attempted to take Empress down when she was in power.

Arianne analyzed the map with the sophistication of a general. He wondered what nine months of war had done to her. He'd only heard reports here and there of Phoenix's victories. It was hard to separate the female he'd loved from the demon in the news reports. He caught himself staring at her, at how she tilted her head when considering the demarcated regions. It was surreal that her little tics had never changed, even after so much time. She bit her lip, and he both hated and loved how his eyes lingered there, remembering how it tasted. When Arianne looked up, he had to shake his head to clear his ever-worsening thoughts.

Twenty-four hours were not enough time to prepare him for working with her. He'd always considered the possibility when he became Strix's informant, but he needed to remind himself he didn't defect to the Selvians for Arianne. Even if seeing the winged female was a perk, he knew he needed to find a way to keep his expectations in check.

Arianne hated him. He would do anything for her forgiveness, but he was a betting male, and as a betting male, he knew his odds were not good. Only heartbreak waited for him if he let himself get his hopes up—more heartbreak than he was already experiencing from staring at Arianne *alive*.

He'd mourned her for so long...

"Hey, that fifty-yard stare might work with the ladies, but you missed my question," Arianne deadpanned.

He hoped his smirk was believable. "Is it working on you?"

She glared at him. Rhino looked two seconds away from attempting to murder him again.

"It's like the two of them share three brain cells, and they're all competing for last place," Blue muttered. She stood up and wiped invisible dirt off her leather pants. "Let me speed this up for all of us." She pointed to Arianne. "Go figure out if your hatred is a kink, or if you're going to kill him and get it over with." She turned to Keston, and he was caught dreading whatever cutting comment she'd reserved for him. "And you: none of us like you, so drop the asshole act and either be a damn professional, or try to fuck Arianne and get rejected already."

He wondered if curling up in a hole and dying was a viable career option.

Arianne crossed her arms. "This is why you're my second," she said proudly. She lifted her chin, gesturing for her team to prepare to leave. "We'll wait for word from the twins on our next move. Until then, we're done here."

Keston moved to object, but caught himself. There was nothing else he could say. Blue was right: he wasn't a friend and hardly an ally. If he wanted to help protect *Feras* and be a part of something good, he needed to stay professional. And professionals didn't beg someone who still wanted him dead to stick around for something as trivial as conversation.

Even if he found himself searching for excuses for Arianne to stay in that room for just a minute longer.

He needed to get high, if only so the image of Arianne's disdain in his direction wouldn't completely gut him for the next three hours. Luckily, Cindy was in easy supply in a *Fera* speakeasy.

Chapter 22

Keston

In his penthouse overlooking downtown Tokyo, Keston floated in that sweet spot between a mellow high and exhaustion. In those moments, he felt closest to his old self: not plagued by the events of the past two years. Just a body drifting around in the comfort of his home.

Granted, nowhere had genuinely felt like home since Greece.

The desire to write returned to him in that state. Performing was a great outlet, but creating new music evaded him. Writing was hard when despair made getting out of bed seem impossible.

Roaming in the nighttime gloom, he kept his shades open to see the city's glittering lights sparkling below. Grabbing his notebook, Keston sat at his desk facing the cityscape and lit a candle. The scent of dragon fruit and kiwi wafted around him, and the flame's orange glow softened the harsh shadows of the room. Ever since Greece, he'd loved candles. His sister always had a fruit-scented candle burning when she practiced her music.

Slowly, the words to a new song bled onto the page in night-black ink,

Do I seem lost?
The mirror haunts me.
Looking into it exacts a cost.
The reflection is hard to see,
What stares back is me, but glossed.
The real me is no longer free,
My soul feels covered in frost.

Keston looked at the page covered in his scrawl and began singing the haunting melody. The tune came naturally. His mother's musical instincts within him always knew the best way to put his words to song. His pen touched the page to write another verse, but paused, leaving a large black dot bleeding into the paper. He felt it then, a shift in the air. Even with Cindy's fading effects still shielding his senses, he knew he was no longer alone. He straightened. He didn't need to turn to know who'd joined him.

His Jokers were excellent security, but they'd never be a match for her. It also helped that he'd left his window unlocked.

"You were always a talented singer."

Keston's breath caught in his throat. "Until I used my voice to hurt people."

After Oslo, he continued to perform, but he never sang. His voice was reserved for private moments, where even a whisper couldn't hurt anyone. There were still nights when he'd wake up to the sound of his audience screaming in pain. He hated how Pandora used his voice as a weapon. He hated how he hadn't told her no.

Arianne was silent, silhouetted by moonlight. Hidden by a cloak and her mask, she looked more like a ghost than the hallucination that'd haunted him for the year after her supposed death. He might've believed she was a shadow if she hadn't spoken. She just watched him, and he couldn't tell if that stare carried malice or curiosity.

Maybe both.

"You know why I'm here."

Not a ghost, then. A reaper.

Keston stood, hating the distance between them. He wanted nothing more than to shoot across his room and pull her into a hug. He'd always been able to read her. He always knew when she was hurting. And the coldness he felt just then...he knew she was drowning in pain. He wished he could fix it, even though he was at the epicenter of most of it.

"You don't trust me," Keston said.

Her face was unreadable behind the mask. "Can you blame me?"

"No."

"What are you doing here?"

"In Tokyo? Well, besides a healthy dose of drugs, I'm actually doing my job—if you would believe it."

Her eyes narrowed. "You know what I mean. What are you doing *here*, helping *us*?"

Strix's phone felt like a weight in his pocket. He wanted to tell Arianne everything right then. About his Selvian mother, loved by the legendary Strix. About how he was tired of being the villain. How, he'd never belonged anywhere, but speaking to Strix, he'd felt a familiar pull. The same pull he'd always felt in nature. How could he explain to Arianne that he could feel Selvia in his blood? There was a reason why *The Song of the Feras* had always called to him.

But with that painful distance between them, Keston knew she wouldn't listen to that nonsense. Arianne was a female hurt by the world—hurt by *him*. Something told him she wouldn't trust emotions, not anymore. Logic would be the only thing keeping her sword from his throat that night.

He fell back on what he knew: insufferable and unaffected. With a shrug, he tried his best to look nonchalant. "I could ask you the same question. Why did Strix send her frontline trump card when she has a horde of loyal warriors she could send halfway across the world instead?"

Arianne took an aggressive step forward. "I asked you first."

"How old are you, five?"

Another step. "You haven't answered my question."

Keston's secondary feathers stood on edge with the warnings of a fight, a reaction similar to that of a cat's hackles. He tensed, gesturing to his curled fists. "Does every conversation between us have to end up like this?"

Her hand crept toward the baton resting on her hip. Keston knew she could extend it into a molten blade that could slice him in two with half a thought. "I found my people, Keston, and I'll do everything in my power to protect them. If I cannot trust you, if you are of no use to me, I will do what I must to keep them safe."

He couldn't help the sorrow in his tone. "Is that all I am to you? An obstacle you're prepared to cut down?"

"You chose to become that."

Keston flinched. He lowered his head, hoping the darkness of the room would shield the tears prickling in his eyes. "Why did you come here tonight, Arianne? Is it to remind me how much you hate me? Trust me, I got the message, so you can see yourself out." He turned to lean on his indigo walnut desk for support, the weight of pushing her away cutting deeper than expected. "I have plenty of hate for myself. I don't need yours on top of it."

The resounding silence made him lift his head. She'd removed her mask, face ivory pale in the moonlight shining through the window. Her eyes were hard as she stared at the ground. He watched her gloved fists clench and unclench. She opened her lips to speak, shook her head, and looked back down.

"I don't know why I came," she finally admitted. "I think I told myself I'd kill you. But I couldn't get myself to do it...*again*."

He heard the disgust in her voice—disgust in him, but mostly disgust in her weakness. Part of him still wished she would do it and get all the pain over with. But she couldn't. That *had* to mean something.

He decided to take a risk. "I know why I left the window unlocked."

Their eyes met. He heard the moment her breath caught in her throat. Was he wrong to believe—if only for a second—there was more than hate there?

"I wanted to see you," he said, extending the emotional olive branch.

To his dismay, Arianne stepped back. A chill ran through him as her moment of warmth receded like the summer winds giving way to autumn gusts. She didn't meet his eyes. "You should've thought about that before you chose your side."

Keston threw out his arms. "What do you want me to say? That I fucked up? Because I'll say it: I fucked up, Arianne. I had no idea Josephina was your mother, but I never should've kept my involvement in her death from you. For that, I'm genuinely sorry." He took a deep breath, knowing his next words could start another world war. "But you're not guilt-free either. You lied to me about your heritage."

Tears welled in Arianne's eyes. "You're blaming me for this?"

And there they were, back to square one: saying *anything* to out-insult the other, just like in the Darwin Zone. It was disheartening to see them return to that state, but he didn't care.

"I'm saying I gave every ounce of myself to you: every insecurity, hope, dream, and fear. I laid myself bare for you. When I said '*together,*' I meant it." Keston was surprised at the pain lacing his words. "And when you said it back, I thought you meant it, too."

"I did." Arianne's voice was so small he almost missed those two critical words.

"Then why didn't you tell me who you were?" His voice cracked. "Why did you let me believe you *died*? I mourned you for a year, Arianne. My partner in crime, the person I shared the skies with, my *Princess*—"

"*Stop,*" she growled.

"No."

"I said stop." When she glared at him, she looked every ounce the Commander she was born to be.

But he'd never been good at listening to Commanders, so he continued. "No. That wasn't fair. I loved you, and you chose a burning building over me. I understand we had our problems, but commitment means *commitment*—thick and thin. You didn't break my heart, you shattered it and danced on the fragments."

"And how do you think seeing you working for my *father* felt?" Arianne spat. "After everything I showed you—after you kissed the scars they gave me—you still turn and help them?" She hugged herself. "And then the things you did for them," she trailed off, eyes growing distant.

That familiar self-disgust returned. He flexed his Frankenstein body, allowing the cybernetic implants in his eyes to track the heat radiating off his modified muscles. "I'm not proud of what they turned me into," he said slowly. "But you have to see it from my perspective. You were dead. Genevieve was all I had left. And then they offered me revenge on Ace. I *had* to cling to that, or I had nothing."

Arianne shook her head, refusing to hear a second of his reasoning. He couldn't blame her. Tears glinted on her cheeks. She extended her wings behind her, ready to fly away from her emotions—again.

"It's not that easy, Keston. I can't just snap my fingers and make everything *better*. People are dead because of you—people I love, people I was supposed to protect. I don't just want to hate you. I *need* to hate you."

"I don't want to be the bad guy anymore, Princess."

"You don't get to make that call." Arianne's eyes were puffy with tears when her head whipped up to glare at him.

He gestured around him. "I'm trying my best. I know I've made mistakes, but I'm working to fix as many of them as possible. I want to wake up one day and be proud of what I see in the mirror. I'm tired of Blackjack. I'm tired of lesser evils. I don't want to keep falling asleep, terrified that the person who wakes up the next day won't be me. Every night, I fear Blackjack will take my place like he did in Cartel. I don't want to go back to that. I *can't*."

Why was he rambling? Maybe it was because Arianne was the only one who'd seen through the Blackjack mask to the broken boy underneath. Maybe he desperately needed someone to promise him he wasn't too far gone.

"It's not my job to fix your guilty conscience." Arianne frowned, turning to leave. "I tried that once, and all it got me was a dead mother and a broken heart."

Keston's throat constricted like an allergic reaction as he watched her leave. Every fiber and feather in his body begged him to follow, but he felt stuck in the mud. He reached for her, desperate for even an ounce of the female he'd once loved. "I know you like games," he called. "Play one more with me."

She stopped, wings shielding her face.

"A wager," he offered. "I deliver Qin to you, and you go to dinner with me. A normal dinner, no weapons allowed. And you have to act like you're enjoying yourself." He snapped his finger as his smile grew. "And every time I save your life, you owe me a kiss."

Arianne turned just enough for him to see a smirk behind her golden brown feathers. "And if you fail? If you betray me?"

"You have my permission to kill me."

"Oh, Pangaea Boy, if you cross me again, I won't need your permission."

Chapter 23

Andre

After months of administrative tasks, it was good to have blood on his sword again.

The haze of battle crashed around him. Andre breathed it in like the sweet smoke of a cigar. It felt good to move his body, to use the skills he'd been honing in the training barracks. And while he hated to admit it, he'd missed fighting with Pandora at his side.

They'd operated on missions for years before Leonueva fell. Guarding her back gave him a strange sense of nostalgia.

The bridge shook below him. Andre looked down from the stretch of the Artery to the combined might of the Spanish forces, Peregrine Pacific, and Bubblegum Battalion. Angry waters splashed hundreds of meters down. From the dangerous cracks in the asphalt, they were one good explosion from falling into the Mediterranean Sea.

Africa advanced with vigor. Old Morocco was visible over the crest of the road, less than a kilometer away. Leon was right: the Africans had been planning a forward assault for months. Good thing Andre had a stellar counter-attack. Instead of waiting for Africa to barrel across the Artery, hoping the assault wouldn't come, he would take the offensive.

And send an operative over to the other side in the chaos to steal information.

Pandora fended off a group of African Wards with a searing blast from her arm. "Jaya is still ten minutes out!"

"Timer set!" Andre said, starting a countdown on his watch.

It seemed like having a timeline only increased the intensity of the assault. A small horde broke through the Bubblegum Battalion line, surging forward like one of the waves below. The Peregrine Pacific flocked around Andre, and he joined them in the counterattack.

Taking advantage of his long legs, Andre leaped over the Wards' bodies and skewered one of Africa's *Fera* warriors. The male was dressed in a red and yellow patterned tactical suit, looking like a mix of tribal leathers and the classic pattern of an African Ward. Andre hardly paid the male any mind as his blood bubbled out around his blade.

Nine minutes.

It became apparent that the most recent influx of attackers was only composed of *Feras*. The black and red armor was gradually replaced with yellow and red tactical suits. Andre's forces began to lose ground against the oppressive might of the *Feras*. Only the Bubblegum Battalion and the *Feras* in the Peregrine Pacific could withstand the pressure.

Andre's Spanish forces were taking heavy losses.

"We need to hold for six minutes!" Andre called.

His battle cry only bought him a slight forward push.

An electric arrow buzzed past his ear, embedding into the heart of a Puppet at his side. His head whipped around as the pink-wigged automation spasmed and sizzled.

He'd read the battle reports. He knew who that arrow came from.

Andre retreated a few paces to Pandora's side. Her defenses were raised as well, having sensed the rapid death of one of her Puppets.

Prince Khari Sarr stalked forward through the fray. Deep red robes of a Maasai warrior billowed around him, underlaid by black tribal leathers. He looked like royalty, adorned with brass armor and a shining breastplate. While brass was a popular adornment in some African cultures, it was also an excellent conduit.

When Africa declared their allegiance to Selvia, the world learned about the continent's best-kept secret: Prince Khari, Pharaoh of Selvia, was a mutant. And a powerful one at that.

Electricity crackled across the brass lining Khari's knuckles as he notched another charged arrow. Deadly intent shone in his lightning-blue eyes as he aimed. Andre and Pandora prepared themselves.

Four minutes. They only needed to last four minutes.

Khari fired. Andre dodged, and Pandora lunged forward. Her cybernetic arm extended into a blade, and Khari met her with his khopseh. Andre ran to join the fray with his double-bladed sword. Even against two trained warriors, Khari was a formidable force—the perfect mix of speed, strength, and electric offensive power.

And with all her cybernetics, Pandora couldn't afford to get within range of Khari's electric currents.

With his polyester armor, Andre was the most resistant to Khari's attacks. When Pandora managed a stunning blast of plasma to blind him, Andre advanced.

The princes of Africa and Europe locked blades. Andre did his best not to buckle under the force of a full-grown *Fera*. Gritting his teeth, he pushed, every muscle straining. He'd spent his entire life being told he was less than. He wasn't about to let a half-savage prince best him—not after all his hard work.

Khari let out a deep-throated chuckle as he threw Andre off him with a broad outward swing. "Did you think you were a match for me, Prince of Bastards?"

Pandora fired another blast, clipping Khari in the shoulder. Andre lunged forward and managed a deep slice to Khari's inner thigh—that would become concerning soon. Andre jumped away from the retaliation, knowing he had to bide his time. He had to wait for the male to bleed out—even if the effects of such a wound would take longer to appear in a mutant.

Andre grinned at the blood trickling down Khari's leg. "Where's your savage bitch?"

Leon's council had gotten word of Khari's possible engagement to a Selvian warrior—the rumored reason why Khari had convinced his father to fight against Europe.

Khari's smirk returned as he flipped his blade in his hand. "I can't wait for you to meet her," he crooned. "There's something royal about her, almost like she was born to sit on the throne I'm going to steal from you."

Andre laughed. "Not if you can't cross this bridge."

Before Khari could attack, purple hair streaked past Andre's periphery. Jaya ran like the wind, tailed by a dozen African soldiers. Despite the heavy blaster fire at her heels, her face was serene, robotic. Not a single muscle twitched on her face as she swerved around rubble and bodies, and Pandora delivered cover fire. And clenched in the Chameleon's hand was the flash drive they'd started that entire skirmish over.

That flash drive contained the limited communications between Africa and Selvia. For the first time since the war began, Europe would have insight into an enemy who left a minimal digital footprint.

"Well!" Pandora shouted as Jaya blankly handed her the flash drive. "That's our cue!"

And then Pandora blew the bridge to bits.

Hidden charges planted a few meters behind Khari's front line exploded in astonishing blasts of sound and color. It wouldn't stop Africa's advancement into Spain, but would certainly slow them down. Shrapnel flew towards Andre and Khari. The pair exchanged a split second look of astonishment before they dove from the blast.

Andre painfully clapped against the concrete-hard surface of the Mediterranean hundreds of meters below, joined by raining fragments of debris from the bridge. He registered his stomach rising to his throat, white-hot pain, and then dark water pulling him down.

The world faded to black as bubbles engulfed his sinking body.

The sterile white lights of the Palace of Versailles' medical ward burned through his eyelids. Andre's eyes shot open at the distinct sensation of someone changing his bandages. Though movement proved painful, he flinched from his caregiver's hand, still convinced he was in the middle of a battle.

"You're okay," Genevieve reassured him.

She placed his glasses in his hand, and he set them on his nose. His arms barked in protest, but the world returned to brilliant clarity. Genevieve, recognizable by her bright red curls in his periphery, continued to re-wrap a bandage on his arm. He tried to turn his head, but even that felt like icy needles cutting into his skin.

"Try not to move too much. You'll tear your stitches."

Andre did his best to relax his muscles. Genevieve had become a rare friend in the cutthroat environment of Leon's Inner Circle. Granted, she would become his Lady Advisor when he Ascended, so their alliance made sense.

"I'm starting to think working with Pandora is an occupational hazard," Andre groaned.

Genevieve's hands paused. "Pandora's methods were... crude," she admitted. "But, we replayed the battle tape, and she wasn't entirely unjustified. Prince Sarr had you outmatched—the bridge was Africa's only ground route to Western Europe. The blast slowed them down by a few weeks."

Months of serving under her father had done wonders for her English. She spoke without an ounce of an accent. Andre was even ready to admit her vocabulary might be more extensive than his.

He hissed as Genevieve applied salve to a particularly tender section of stitches on his shoulder. "Shouldn't you get a nurse to do this?"

"I've learned a lot this past year," she said. "I know how to patch up a wound."

Andre read between her cryptic words. Most saw Genevieve's cheeks rounded with youth and her innocent freckles and assumed she was simply a bright young girl, yet to be molded by Elite society. But he knew better. She knew more about the politics than she let on. Andre respected that. Anyone who wanted to play Leon's games needed a few cards hidden up their sleeves.

Genevieve was only treating his wound to have an excuse to talk with him.

"What is it?" Andre asked, still staring at the ceiling, thanks to the searing pain in his neck.

"Jaya performed admirably in the battle," Genevieve began. "The intel she received was instrumental. We now know Selvia sent operatives to Asia—they'll likely make a play on Qin before Ascension Day."

"And?"

"Give her a chance to see her sister and Haris."

Andre sat up at that despite the pain. He stiffly turned his neck to face his future Advisor. "And why would I reward Kalinda and Haris for their behavior toward me?"

Genevieve frowned, the look oddly aging her by a decade. "Your power is in Pacifican loyalty. Haris now works in Hera's labs, and Pandora controls Jaya. Wouldn't you want their allegiance so you can have uninterrupted intelligence on the Richards?"

"Pandora can be trusted," he reassured her.

Though he couldn't explain the details of how he'd made a deal with Pandora and Ace, he hoped his engagement to the cyborg would be enough to calm Genevieve's suspicions.

"Do you want to take that chance?"

Andre frowned. "What do you know?"

Genevieve's green eyes darkened. "I know that something is going on in those labs, and I know Jaya and Haris are the only ones who can tell you. I wouldn't want to be blindsided by my fiancé." She pulled a file hidden between her left leg and her wheelchair. "This was in my father's office. I took photos and reprinted them."

Andre gingerly took the manila folder. No one used printed documents anymore unless they really wanted to hide something. It was hard to move his hands with the IV lines and heart rate monitor, but he ignored the annoyance and opened the folder—a small packet rested inside. The images were slightly blurry thanks to the hastily shot photos, but he got the message.

The document read *Project Frenzy*. He flipped through image after image of feral mutants snarling through dog cages, teeth bared and eyes black as night. Subject identification numbers hung from their cages like they were nothing more than lab rats. Andre couldn't help but flinch. Arianne had been kept in cages like those between experiments as a child. It was almost enough for him to put the folder down, but he kept looking.

The last page was the most damning: a grainy map of Asia. Though the photos had lost their color, he could make out the demarcated zones: waterways around major cities. Whatever this Project Frenzy was, it was meant for Asia.

"A contingency plan," Andre realized. "In case Asia doesn't join our alliance."

"But what kind of contingency?" Genevieve pressed. "As Heir Apparent, don't you think you deserve to know?"

Chapter 24

Arianne

"**A**bsolutely not," Arianne objected.

Keston was getting dressed—if it could even be called that, since he was removing more clothes than adding them. His shoulders flexed as he pulled a glittering suspender over an arm, carefully keeping his wing out of the tangle. One of his eyebrows arched upward. "Got any better ideas, Princess?"

She frowned at the glittering silver dress resting on a makeup chair. "I'm not a dancer."

"It's called a disguise for a reason," Keston sang. "Quit pouting and change already. I'm going to check on the others."

He pushed himself out of the dressing room, his large wings almost suffocating the space. Without hundreds of feathers in the way, Blue was finally visible. Bent over her vanity, she carefully painted electric-blue lipstick to match the recently dyed tips of her hair.

Her yellow eyes met Arianne's through the mirror. "I'll admit this could be a good idea."

"You thought crashing a Pangaean Jet with your entire team on it was a good idea."

Blue unscrewed a pre-made venom vial and dipped her stiletto heels in the clear liquid. Since her outfit was hardly more than a sparkling blue hybrid of lingerie and a bikini, there wasn't much space for her small arsenal of blades. Satisfied she'd coated her heels, she straightened. "It still doesn't change that we don't have many options. The Gwinsin pride themselves on security and protecting their clients. We'll get fewer eyes this way—no one gives *Feras* a second look in Asia."

Groaning, Arianne pulled off her cloak, extending her wings in a satisfied stretch. After squeezing into her skintight dress, she quickly added a layer of makeup and silver glitter to her face to match. Far from being as agile as Blue, she opted for silver wedges over six-inch stilettos.

Exiting the dressing room, they were instantly assaulted with the bustle of dozens of *Feras* running back and forth in preparation. Skirts, jewelry, clouds of perfume, lace, and *lots* of glitter floated past as they navigated the fray. The manager stood in the central area, shouting orders to her employees as they filed out of private dressing rooms toward a set of stairs. Arianne had to pause, take a deep breath amidst the chaos, and remind her nervous system she wasn't in the middle of a battle.

"The noise bothers me too."

Arianne whirled, her body primed to attack when she heard Keston's voice. He stood directly behind her, looking oddly sincere as he stretched out a hand holding two earpieces. Unfortunately, those were not the first thing her eyes went to.

As usual, Keston looked stunning.

His dark hair was sprayed with pink highlights, and his eyes were lined with dark paint and gold specks, making the amber impossible to ignore. Matching gold suspenders wrapped around his sculpted shoulders, with his wings on full display. Otherwise, there was only a bow tie around his neck.

Every sinful inch of his torso was on full display. Arianne had to manually close her jaw. *Fuck.*

Keston leaned down, a deadly smirk growing on his face as his head entered her line of sight. "My eyes are up here."

"Did you put *oil* on your stomach?" Arianne asked incredulously. She crossed her arms, fighting a hot blush rising on her cheeks. "You look ridiculous."

"No, I don't." Keston patted her head. "I can still read you like a book."

Rolling her eyes, she snatched the earpieces from his hand and placed them in her ears. The noise immediately dulled to a comfortable volume. Not a second later, Lova's voice came through. "Phoenix? Do they work?"

Lova had remained behind as the liaison between the Ivory Court and the Circus of Artemis. Arianne had also asked her to stay behind because something told her the Cheetah would be blushing too much to be functional. Even though she grew up as a member of the tribes, Lova was modest even by civilized standards. Another glance at Keston reminded her they were going somewhere far from modest.

"Yeah, I hear you loud and clear. All right, connection confirmed. Only use this line for emergencies." Arianne turned back to Keston. "Noise-dulling comms units?"

He nodded with a proud smile. "One of the few helpful things from Hera's labs. After all of her upgrades on me, my hearing became debilitating in environments like this. Those make it bearable—I assumed you might be in the same boat, so I brought an extra pair."

"Upgrades?" she asked, voice notably soft.

He looked down, suddenly shy for a male in nothing but suspenders. "You're no longer Hera's only lab rat. They took me apart and put me back together." A haunted expression overtook his face as he stared at his arms. "Mutated my muscles and bones and added some cybernetics. Even my hair and feathers were darkened by the procedures."

Arianne's eyes immediately went to just below his belt before she could stop herself. "They modified *all* of you?"

"No!" Keston was hilariously defensive. "They didn't touch—at least—I hope they didn't—"

"Good." She winked. "It didn't need any changes."

It was his turn to blush.

"Do I have to chaperone you two?" Blue hissed, stepping in between them. "Yup, been here the whole time. What the fuck did I just watch?"

Stumbling away, Arianne realized with horror how close she'd gotten to Keston. She mumbled something about earpieces in a last-ditch effort to save her pride. Keston provided an equally unconvincing remark about his wingspan.

Topher pushed through the crowd to join them. In a Greek-style toga combined with the Underground's preferred cyberpunk flair, it perfectly displayed his goatlike legs and lean, muscled upper body. His horns, adorned with golden jewelry, curled above sleek black hair tied in a neat braid. With a cleaned-up goatee and slight brushes of eyeliner, the male looked like he'd jumped out of the Greek myth he'd been named after.

Arianne greeted him but found herself looking around. "Where's Rhino?"

"Haven't seen him," Topher said with a hint of concern.

"I sent him back to the Circus," Keston said. "He's too large. Draws too much attention."

And sparkling suspenders and twenty-foot wings didn't?

Arianne's jaw dropped. "This is my team. You can't just order them around!"

Keston leaned in, his expression that particular brand of insufferable that could make her blood boil. "And this is my mission. Sorry, Princess, I'm pulling rank."

"I am Deputy—"

"And I'm not a Selvian, so I couldn't care less." He turned to the group. "But I am your resident Underground tour guide. If we want to infiltrate the Gwinsin leadership, you follow what I say." He swung his head toward Arianne. "Any problem?"

Arianne glared daggers at him. "*Nada.*"

"Okay." Keston clapped his hands together. "This mission has three phases. Step one: blend in. Step two: The Circus attacks, forcing a shutdown. Step three: We follow the employees to the secure quarters in the chaos and infiltrate. I'll attempt to negotiate. But if their boss, Madame Tsing, refuses to cooperate, we'll kill her, and I'll dissolve the Gwinsin into Cartel."

Blue and Topher loyally turned to Arianne for confirmation.

She let out a long sigh. "We'll do what he says."

Keston smiled from ear to ear. "Let's dance."

***

If Arianne closed her eyes, she could've been back at Shipwreck, dancing with her classmates. Club music pounded through her veins, reviving a piece of her that she only allowed out in the Valhan. She grasped that freeing sensation as hard as she could, and her body responded in turn.

Blue's hand found hers, guiding them through the crowd to the main stage, a mischievous smirk growing on her face. The crowd of Gwinsin patrons cheered as the two females stepped onto the stage with a group of other dancers. While Arianne certainly wasn't taking any customers to the private rooms around the dancefloor, she needed to do something to blend in.

Arianne was far from as flexible as Blue, but as the lights flashed and the bass dropped, she felt far more daring. Glitter shot out in sparkling explosions above her as she swayed with Blue around a pole erected on stage. She silently admitted that she might be having a little too much fun on a super-important mission meant to stop a world war. The crowd cheered as she spun around the pole, her wings flaring majestically behind her amid the glittering rain. Straightening, she whipped her hair behind her head and realized there was a particular someone in the crowd utterly hypnotized.

But when she twirled to look in his direction again, he'd refocused on flirting with the table in front of him.

Was she seeing things, or was Keston watching her?

She decided to find out.

Arianne jumped down from the stage with a wave to Blue. The Snake frowned back, currently upside down and spinning around the pole, using every agile bone in her body to her advantage. She hissed at Arianne, speaking every time she spun to face her: "I told you—" Spin. "I'm not—" Another spin. "Third wheeling!"

"Go find Satyr, then!"

A group of businessmen sat around a half-moon couch, a few handles of shared liquor resting in a cooler lined with sparklers. They cheered as Arianne strutted toward them, all in various stages of losing their jackets and ties. Not one complained as she climbed onto the central table, knocking over a few half-empty handles on the way. Then she danced, slowly and methodically, using every bit of beautiful grace she'd trained into herself that past year. The men couldn't take their eyes off her.

But it wasn't those men she cared about.

In a sensual turn, she locked eyes with Keston. His entire face darkened. Her stomach flopped.

Keston didn't break eye contact as he pushed out from between two women. He weaved through the sea of guests like a model—if models were meant to display a *lack* of clothing. Arianne's swaying slowed when she saw where he was headed. At a nearby VIP booth, a woman in a red dress beckoned him over, finger wagging. With one last smirk in Arianne's direction, he turned to the woman and gave her the most sinful lap dance Arianne had ever seen.

She immediately forgot why she was supposed to hate him. His perfect body glided up and down the woman. Arianne wasn't proud of how she documented every single rippling muscle, every delicious flex.

Holy fucking shit, I'm in trouble.

Raising his head from the woman's face, his lips smeared red with her lipstick, he locked eyes with Arianne. Those lips parted into a smile as his eyes narrowed in a challenge. An unholy possessiveness coursed through her.

Game on, motherfucker.

Arianne grabbed the man to her right. He was handsome, with straight black hair, a steel-cut jawline, and a suit that screamed Elite money. Perfect. He happily stood with her, eyes eagerly roving over her wings. She tried her best to hide her disgust at being seen as an exotic vice because, right then, she was using him as much as he was using her. Grabbing the man's tie, she pulled him into a kiss. She let his grip snake around her backside. As his tongue explored her mouth, she looked to the side and took immense pleasure in Keston watching. Every. Last. Second.

Keston looked like someone stranded in the desert, and Arianne was the first oasis in days—and someone else was hogging the last bit of water.

She detached from the man. He grinned at her and held out a five-Unit bill. Arianne leaned forward, taking the tip in her teeth. She turned to wink at Keston, but he was no longer with the woman in the red dress. Slightly annoyed that he'd abandoned their game, she returned to her dance with the businessman. She initiated a twirl, but a different pair of hands received her spin.

"You were tongue fucking him to antagonize me," Keston sang into her ear, his fingers curling around her arms and pulling her away.

"Did it work?"

"You forgot I was your only dance partner," he whispered, his voice low. Possessive.

Arianne turned so that her back was to him, making sure her feathers caressed his neck. She fought hard to ignore the million butterflies that took flight in her stomach as he grabbed her hips and pulled her into him. "I don't remember that being part of the deal," she said, bending over just slightly as she danced.

She didn't miss the curse under his breath.

Keston recovered quickly, grabbing her chin and pulling her back into his chest. He was far from gentle as he turned her head to the side. "Can we add a clause to the contract?"

She didn't respond, not with her words, at least. With a smirk, she danced around him, enjoying his starving, desperate expression as she swayed her hips and traced her fingers across his bare chest. Arianne thought she was the one antagonizing him. She *thought* she was the one in control.

When Keston grabbed her hands and dipped her, never once breaking his paralyzing eye contact, she realized how terrible a miscalculation she'd made. Neither one was in control. And when his thigh moved between her legs, relieving the built-up tension there, she was ready to admit she was in trouble.

International politics were forgotten. Even the name of a specific African prince was wiped entirely from her mind. All she could process was how every part of her body buzzed where they touched, like she'd been struck by lightning.

"What can you give me to incentivize a contract renegotiation?" Arianne said, extremely aware of his hands slowly guiding her hips back and forth over his leg.

Keston's breath was hot on her neck. "I'm afraid that any negotiation would be *terribly* unfair at the moment."

"And why is that?"

He took his time exploring the curves of her body, his hand following everywhere he tracked with his eyes. He bit his lip, still red with someone else's lipstick. "Because, while that dress is killing me, I would give up every fortune to my name for the opportunity to take it off."

Ancestors forgive her. She almost let him rip it off right there.

Their faces were hardly inches apart. It would be as easy as leaning forward. But... Arianne coolly leaned back. "One small problem. I still hate you."

It was getting harder and harder to make herself believe those words.

Keston didn't break eye contact as he unapologetically closed the space between them again. "Well, I hate you for choosing Pacific over me."

Grabbing his arms, she squeezed hard enough to break human bone. "I hate you for being in my father's pocket."

He pushed her into the wall behind them, trapping her between his arms. "I hate you for making me mourn you."

"I hate you for promising 'together,'" she said, glaring at him, even as she made no move to escape.

"I hate you for giving up on our After."

They stared at each other. The mission, pounding music, and strobing lights forgotten. They weren't standing in an Underground club, but in the villa they'd shared during their painfully short season of paradise. And suddenly, the phrase *I hate you* started sounding like another painfully charged three-letter phrase.

Then alarms started to blare, washing the club in nightmare red, and the spell was broken.

Arianne blinked, coming out of a trance. "Time to work for a living."

The disappointment that'd settled in her gut had to be discarded. Quite frankly, she was ashamed. She had a mission to do. People were relying on her—no more distractions.

"Arianne." His voice was close to pleading.

"No, Keston. When I'm on a mission, you call me Phoenix."

If he objected, she had no time to hear him. The dance floor had broken out into chaos. Guests rushed the exit, shoving each other at every opportunity. Arianne cursed herself for not getting more of her father's height. She craned her neck but couldn't see much over the stampede.

Fortunately, Lova was one hell of a teammate. Her voice came through the comms unit. "We're here! I hope you got the message."

"Loud and clear," Arianne replied. "Keep the chaos going, Blitz."

Lova chuckled. "Rhino told me to say that's his specialty."

From the growing thunder of feet and ringing alarms, Arianne was inclined to agree.

Keston grabbed her hand, yanking her toward the steady stream of employees crowding a back staircase held open by a large bouncer. As they approached, she spotted Blue and Topher scanning the crowd with urgent panic.

They converged on the two Selvians, folding into the crowd of employees ushering through the small doorway. No one spoke as they waded through the densely packed bodies and growing panic. Arianne focused on keeping her balance in her wedges as they scaled the stairs from the basement toward the executive offices in the tower above. Most employees dispersed through the lower floors, but Keston didn't slow, guiding them higher and higher up the staircase.

With the disturbance in the nightclub, most security had been routed to contain the break-in on the club level. The *Feras* ran into some Gwinsin agents, but the operatives were so flustered from the invasion that they hardly paid the scantily-clad team any mind. Story after story sped past without incident.

Once the sound of alarms and frantic crowds faded, Keston let them slow, pulling off into an abandoned corridor on the sixtieth floor. His eyes glinted in the darkness, their night vision kicking in. "All right, blueprints of this building point to a false wall on the sixty-fifth floor—that's our target."

Topher, always the most prepared of the group, began pulling out weapons he'd hidden within the folds of his toga. "I don't have much, but I've seen Arianne kill someone with a flip-flop before, so I think this bunch is deadly enough."

Keston elbowed her with a low whistle. "Impressive. I remember when you had that whole 'no killing' hangup."

Pointedly avoiding his gaze, she took the sheathed batons of *Horizon's Edge* from Topher. "I was cornered in a department store in Helsinki."

"I never thought you could fracture someone's arm with a flip-flop," Topher said, snapping out one of his collapsible bows—complete with a half-dozen folding trick arrows.

Arianne smirked at that. "It's all about angles, velocity, and a fuck-ton of adrenaline."

"Remind me not to get on your bad side," Keston said. "Oh, too late."

Blue grabbed a set of throwing stars. "And remind me why you're still here? We can kill this lady ourselves, thanks." She made sure to stick out her forked tongue and hiss the final syllable.

"I haven't met Madame Tsing, but my Underground affiliates have mentioned she can be very agreeable—especially with people she sees as equals," Keston began.

"As agreeable as an Underground kingpin can be," Arianne interjected.

He snapped a finger at her. "Exactly. I'm the only one who can speak her language. You can call me lazy, but I'm not in the mood for a dominance battle against her underlings. The easiest route is getting her cooperation."

Blue and Topher looked to Arianne once more. Pride surged inside her. Keston might be leading the mission, but she still called the shots. Maybe it was how much she enjoyed looking at him, or perhaps dancing had put her in a rare good mood, but she was willing to let Keston stick around a little longer.

"Lead the way, Mr. Tour Guide."

But there was nowhere to lead.

The Gwinsin security detail was long dead on the sixty-fifth floor. Their bodies, clad in polyester armor, were strewn lifeless across the hallway from the stairs. Blood coated the floor.

Arianne whistled, and her teammates fell into a defensive position behind her, prepared for an ambush. Only Keston didn't follow suit. His face was a strange sight as the distress in his expression warred with the bright colors of his makeup. He squatted down next to the closest corpse, the concentration in his eyes showing he was most likely reading something from his ocular implants.

Keston dipped his fingers in the blood below the body, sniffing the already coagulating liquid. "Poisoned bullets," he muttered. "If the gunshot didn't kill them, the toxin did."

"*Feras*?" Arianne asked.

He shook his head, jumping up. "There's only one faction that uses this: Ronin. We need to run. Something tells me Cartel isn't the only organization making a power play tonight."

They ran through the hallway on near-silent feet, passing a dozen more downed guards before reaching a basic grouping of cubicles. At least, the setup had once *seemed* like an office building. The back wall of the cubicles was blown away, revealing an office set in sensual red light beyond.

Madame Tsing's private quarters.

Keston broke into a sprint, Arianne close behind. They jumped through the rubble of the broken wall, landing next to a floor-to-ceiling lava lamp.

Madame Tsing lay dead on the floor.

Standing above her was an assassin in all black, holding a samurai sword. The killer's loose outfit and the fanged demon mask concealing their face hid their identity—and gender—well. Arianne marked her sudden loss of smell. Mist. And behind the masked assailant stood the smoking remnants of the blast they'd used to blow an escape hole into the sky.

A trail of dead bodies, a disguise, *Fera* precautions, and an escape route. The Ronin had sent a professional.

The assassin raised their hand, and Arianne barely noticed that they held another explosive. Blue screamed, running to throw one of her stars, the blade embedding itself into the assassin's arm. One of Topher's arrows fired. Keston lunged to shield Arianne, and they slammed to the floor.

But it was all too late.

The charge dropped, and the assassin jumped out of the opening.

A deafening blast made the building shake like an earthquake. Arianne could only register feathers as Keston fell on top of her, his wings wrapping around her in a protective cocoon. From the lack of gunpowder, she recognized the explosive as a flash-bang, not another bomb.

In the wake of the disorienting blow, Arianne struggled to see or hear straight. It took a few moments to clear her blurring vision and realize who'd collapsed on top of her. Panic squeezed her chest. Keston was unconscious. Upgraded or not, mature mutant or not, he'd just taken the full blow of a flash-bang. Point-blank.

Panic squeezed her chest as she pressed her hands to the motionless male above her. "Keston?" Her voice shook. "Keston? Come on, that was nothing. Wake up." She pressed her hands to his cheeks, giving him a slight shake. "That was nothing, right?"

Hooves clacked above the ringing in her ears. Topher's face was severe as he pulled Keston's body off of her. He extended his hand. Arianne gingerly took it, unable to look away from Keston.

He'd shielded her. There'd been a fraction of a second between detecting the explosive and action, and he'd jumped in front of her like the decision was instinctual. Like there was no other choice to make.

Arianne didn't move, couldn't move. She only stared at Keston lying on the floor, his bare skin a collection of abrasions and speckled blast wounds. His blood stung her nostrils, and her head spun.

Blue ran to the hole blasted into the side of the building, her hair whipping furiously in the wind. "They're gone!" She cursed. "Disappeared into thin air!"

Arianne felt herself sway. She was terribly shaken—in far worse shape than she'd been on a mission in months. Maybe it was her utter failure, maybe it was the flash bang that'd gone off feet from her face. Or maybe it was the winged male unconscious at her feet. Either way, she felt disconnected from her body. Numb. She couldn't look away from Keston's face, strangely peaceful despite being riddled with cuts.

Failure. Failure. *Failure.*

Topher rested a hand on her shoulder, trying to steady her. "Phoenix? Are you okay?" He was concerned. Concerned for a friend or concerned about an outburst—she didn't care to know right then.

Both were possible.

She was far from okay. Success had become her only crutch in a war that'd dominated her soul—her very identity. And she'd just handed her team and her people a catastrophic loss. The Underground was at war when they needed to unite it.

"It's not your fault, Ari," Blue said, sensing her friend's distress.

Arianne shook now, Keston's injured form taking up her entire vision. "I'm Phoenix. City Crusher. The rightful heir of Europe and Deputy of Selvia. Every loss—every setback—is my *fault*. The more we fail, the more people die, the longer this war goes on."

"Arianne." Blue's tone hardened. "You know that's not true. Don't put this pressure on yourself. It'll tear you apart."

Arianne knelt, scooping Keston into her arms. Her wings snapped open, preparing to fly out of the building and rush Keston to emergency care at the Okazaki estate. She turned to face her teammates, then looked down at the male she was supposed to hate but was going to fight like hell to save. "It already has torn me apart—the best I can do now is save as many people as possible."

How else could she describe her terror of turning into her father, paired with how easily she embraced the feeling of his toxic rage and clinical need to succeed? How else could she describe her never-ending desire to protect the male she was determined to kill?

Before Blue could ask more, Arianne dove out of the building.

Chapter 25

Keston

I t turned out the dreams someone had after a flashbang to the face are just as explosive as the thing that took their consciousness in the first place.

Keston was down for the count, but somehow, also distinctly aware of how restless his time bedridden had been. Flashes of Mende had turned to ash. Genevieve's red hair streaming behind her as she ran from him. There were a few fleeting moments of happiness, where he was weightless and soaring above someone with wings of golden brown. Then the bodies. Hundreds of people he'd taken down underneath flashing neon lights as he'd claimed the Underground—one bloody dancefloor after the next.

He could've sworn in the few moments he was partially awake, someone smelling of lavender and cloud-speckled sky sat next to him, their hands squeezed tightly around his. Even asleep, that strange scent laced with something maddeningly familiar had restless dreams subsiding.

Arianne. She'd always smelled like clouds. Before kissing the sky himself, he'd never been able to pin the scent.

"Arianne?" he whispered, slowly opening his eyes.

But she wasn't there. Disappointment poked his chest as he sat up. One thing was apparent: he had no idea where he was. The room was warm, with windows allowing natural sunlight to stream in. Light brown cypress paneling and tasteful green accents of bamboo and fern plants lined the walls. A steady IV drip snaked to the bed and attached to his right arm.

The needle was stuck right above his ace of spades tattoo. He winced involuntarily.

Not long after sitting up, the door to his room opened. Keston was acutely aware of the camera erected above the window to his right. Deep-seated embarrassment settled inside him at the strength of his dismay when Arianne wasn't on the other side of that door.

Things didn't improve once he realized who'd actually decided to visit.

Heir Apparent Zhou Qin strutted inside, his distaste making his already sour face look like he'd chugged an entire vat of lemon concentrate. Keston might've laughed if every inch of his body wasn't throbbing.

"I thought I was dealing with a *professional*," Qin hissed, leaning on his cane. "Instead, I find you lounging in my Lord Advisor's infirmary."

So they were at the Okazaki estate, owned by the Okazaki family but frequented by the Lord Advisor, Jin Shi. But why? Keston had never met that family. Why would they help him? He did his best to hide his confusion in front of Prince Prick.

"Hate to break it to you, buddy, but just because I'm good at making sure missions don't blow up in my face, doesn't mean I'm impervious to things *literally* blowing up in my face."

The Asian prince began to pace, his mouth a hard line. "We're running out of time. If I don't have the Underground under control before I Ascend, I'll be the laughing stock of Pangaea."

Surprise, bud, your intelligence already has you halfway there. But Keston bit back on his retort.

If Qin couldn't control the Underground, he'd become the direct recipient of Leon's ire. Qin would Ascend into a position with enemies on all sides. Precisely Selvia's goals, but Keston kept quiet about that.

Considering his desire to avoid a beating, he needed to play the perfect middleman—as usual. "I went after the Gwinsin first. Imagine my surprise when I walked into the middle of a turf war between them and the Ronin."

Leaning back in his bed, he feigned relaxation, ignoring the strain on his injured wings. Fortunately, they were covered in a robe and a healthy dose of pillows. But his stomach flopped when he realized someone had chosen to hide his *Fera* features.

Fuck. The Jins knew he was a mutant. But why did they go to the lengths they did to hide it? Keston's anxiety grew. Qin wasn't the only one with potential enemies surrounding him.

"I knew I trusted the wrong European," Qin spat.

Keston stiffened. "It's just a minor setback. Now, I know we have other variables to consider when I move Cartel's forces. Not every mission goes to plan—trust me, I would know."

Qin stared out the window, his attitude as cold as their first meeting. That was a common theme with Elites: their favoritism could switch on a dime. The second someone lost their usefulness, they were iced out. Some things never changed, even on different continents.

"It's not just your recent failure," Qin said.

Snapping his fingers, a small squadron of Wards filed into the room. They weren't alone, dragging two cuffed prisoners behind them.

Treena and Tyrell.

The twins were thrown onto the ground, slamming to the floor without their arms to catch them. One of them released a whimper of pain. Keston fought to keep his gaze neutral, apathetic, channeling Blackjack.

"Why are you dragging mutants in here?" Keston said with as much distaste in his voice as possible.

Qin bared his teeth. "My sister caught them snooping around my palace." He pointed to Tyrell. "And this one was in your band. Let me be clear: I don't appreciate spies."

"Where is your dear sister?" Keston smiled. Sora was proving to be interestingly adept at elements far beyond the range of her dancing expertise.

"She was injured during practice," Qin corrected. "Not that you have a right to know the princess's whereabouts."

Keston shook his head, feigning confusion. "Those are not my spies." He gave Tyrell a withering gaze. "As for Joshua, if he's been working behind my back, then I'm more than happy to give him to you to do as you please. Think of it as an apology for a botched mission."

The twins, thankfully, didn't look up. He didn't know if he could bear their expressions, even if they all knew he had no choice but to play along.

Keston's nonchalant response seemed to throw Qin off guard. Either the Heir Apparent was used to more entertaining reactions to his power plays, or he hadn't done business with people who were used to hostage situations.

However much Qin tried to hide it, he wasn't ready to become Commander. His mother must've shielded him, assuming they would have another ten years to train. But Hana Lang was dead, and the power vacuum in the world's most powerful continent had a man unequipped to shoulder the burden.

Qin collected himself, straightening his thin frame. "Well, if they're not your spies, we have another problem on our hands."

"Selvia's Shadows are far-reaching," Keston warned cryptically.

Treena raised her gaze just enough to glare at him, but Keston ignored her. If he was going to lie to Qin's face about his allegiances, the best way to make it believable was to sprinkle in some factual information.

"We have less time than I thought." Qin stroked his chin. "We need the Underground tamed before Selvia's forces sink their claws into my continent."

Too late.

"What do you have in mind?"

Qin paced again, his cane making rhythmic thumping sounds on the hardwood floor. "We need someone more... effective."

Keston blinked at the wound to his ego. For once, his reaction was genuine. He clutched his chest. "I'm the best there is."

"How about the person who trained you?" Qin's smile told Keston he knew exactly what buttons he was pressing.

Ace, the woman who'd enslaved him, branded him, and threatened him with a lifetime chained to her bed. She'd broken him down and rebuilt him as Blackjack. She'd whispered bile into his ear for a decade, turning him into a shadow of his former self. And when he'd finally had the sense to leave, when Arianne had shown him the sun above the underworld, Ace had hunted his family down.

Keston's hands clenched. All his work that past year—all that pain and self-hatred—had been loans on his soul to afford the opportunity to crush Ace. He'd ripped the European Underground to shreds. Ace couldn't come back from that. There was no way she was thriving after everything he'd taken from her. He refused to believe it. He *couldn't* believe it.

"Ace is *gone*," Keston spat, failing to hide his ire. "I am King of the Underground now, not *her*. Cartel is mine. Everything she owned is mine. Do you really want to work with the has-been I replaced?"

There was no way in hell anyone, especially Qin, still believed Ace held something over him. He was King Keston, and she was *nothing*. Keston had made sure of that.

Qin had already walked to the door with a smug grin. "Are you sure about that?" He nodded to Keston's wrist. "From what I see, she still owns you."

Outrage had him speechless even as he covered the brand.

Tyrell and Treena looked back one last time before they were dragged out. A wave of nausea washed over him from the whiplash of emotions—confusion, rage, and now, terror. Qin had the twins. Ace was coming. Keston felt responsible.

As soon as the door closed, a figure dropped from the rafters above. He might've noticed her presence earlier if he hadn't been so disoriented. Luckily, if he couldn't have detected her, neither had Qin or his Wards.

"Lurking, as usual."

"We have a big fucking problem," Arianne said, her mask distorting her voice.

Keston was entering emotional numbness territory. Even her dropping from the ceiling didn't have the effect it typically would. He couldn't look away from where the twins had been pulled away. "Nice to see you, too."

Arianne tapped her earpiece. "Those Wards don't leave the building," she ordered whichever Champion lingered on the other line.

"You attack Qin, and he'll know Selvia is moving against him," Keston reminded her. "You'll play right into Leon's hands."

Arianne whirled. "I don't care. He has two of my Shadows."

"You mean two of your friends. If you attack, you risk their lives, Arianne."

She growled in frustration. Keston didn't break the stare-off, so familiar with that brand of Arianne that he knew all he needed to do was raise his eyebrow. When she saw it, she rolled her eyes with a sigh. Finally, she called off the Ivory Court's strike. The tension in the room dropped from nuclear war to forest fire when the order went through.

"You're tense," Keston said.

"*Tense?*" Arianne squeaked. "You're injured. We just failed a critical mission needed to destabilize Asia. Qin is recruiting Ace. And now the twins are captured. Tense is cramming for a final exam. This is Mariana Trench-level pressure."

"Would a kiss help?"

"Not now."

Keston pouted. "Need I remind you of our deal?"

Arianne pointed at him, all business—it *would* be his least favorite version of her had being a badass warrior not looked so damn hot on her. If she was lecturing him, he didn't hear a word. All he could think about was how her fighting leathers hugged her muscled quads, and how the black paint on her face made her look like a demon he would *very* much invite home.

"You know what? If you have the energy to make insufferable quips, you can attend an emergency meeting. Meet everyone in the conference room in fifteen minutes. And put your damn tongue back in your head!"

"Ace is coming to Asia," Arianne announced, two seconds away from an explosion.

The attention of the room turned to Keston. Spare Blue, who watched the gathering from the far wall, the conference room table was packed with the Ivory Court, the Circus of Artemis, and the Jins. His stomach flopped. Each of them had a reason to hate him. Each of them was looking to him for answers.

Keston cleared his throat. "Our recent setback has made Qin want to consider other options. He's desperate."

Arianne considered. "Ace is the last person we want to interfere with this." Her eyes met his for a moment. "Desperate people are easy to manipulate. Ace already succeeded in manipulating one—more competent—Heir Apparent. This will be a walk in the park for her."

Colla's claws dug into the table, leaving bright white marks in the polished wood, which earned him a side eye from Jin Shi. The male sighed and retracted them. "We might need to call Strix."

"No." Arianne barked. "I can handle this." Her shoulders tensed as she gripped the table's edge. "Ace has bested me twice. It's time to show her I'm not some naive girl anymore."

That room was one nasty comment away from a civil war.

"Control of the Underground isn't the only problem," Jin Shi said. "We cannot lose sight of the larger issue."

"Controlling the Underground would certainly help," Arianne spat.

"The Underground is only a vessel," Jin Shi countered. "A vessel for the Selvians to destabilize Asia or a vessel for Qin to maintain power. Both sides are vying for the Underground's favor. But *why*? Why are we so terrified of what Qin will do with the Underground and Leon?"

Blue crossed her arms. "Qin hates *Feras*."

Jin Shi and Blue finally made eye contact.

"Precisely." The Lord Advisor smiled at the Snake approvingly. "That understanding must guide our decisions, because that hatred is guiding his. We must think like him from here on out if we want a chance at stopping his Ascension and worldwide war."

Jin Emiko frowned and shared a cautious glance with her husband.

Blue spoke up before the Jins could, pushing off the wall. "You haven't told anyone?"

Emiko's face was shockingly soft as she looked at Blue. "It wasn't our story to tell."

Arianne's frustration cracked, replaced with concern as she joined her friend's side. "Blue? What's wrong?"

Blue took a quivering breath. "I haven't been completely honest with everyone."

Keston felt himself brace. Others around him did the same.

"I never wanted to talk about it, but this is more important than my boundaries right now." Blue's hand moved to rest on the tattoo on her neck as she shuffled nervously. "The truth is, I was a monster long before Hera Richards put that collar on me."

"That's not true," Emiko protested.

Blue's snake eyes were glassy with tears. "My real name is Jin Kayda." She looked up at the Jins. "All my parents ever tried to do was protect me." Like she'd taken a blow, she winced and hugged her stomach. "And I—" Her voice cracked. "I failed them."

Arianne kept her hand on her friend's back. "What happened?"

But Keston had already begun to piece all the grizzly details together.

Blue had to hold Arianne's offered hand with white-knuckled might to continue. "One night at a party, Qin and his twin brother, Khan, cornered me in a room. They claimed I was betrothed to whoever didn't become Commander." She sniffled. "They claimed they wanted a '*test run*'."

His veins filled with ice.

She shook her head. "I was young. I had no idea what they were talking about, but they were the princes, so I followed them without question. Like an idiot."

Arianne's eyes darkened. "You were a *child*."

"I don't remember everything, just that it hurt. I don't know what happened next. It was all a blur. One second, Khan was above me. And the next, he was dead on the ground. My mouth tasted like blood and venom." She hugged herself. "I'd never known about my venom before that point. I-It just came out. I had no idea what happened. I just wanted to stop the pain.

"Then Qin started screaming at me. Honestly, his hysterics are the only sounds I remember. I still see flashes of him running at me, his hand balled in a fist. But he moved too slowly. I think I bit his arm before he could hit me. Then I ran." She buried her head in her hands. "I didn't know what else to do."

"Blue," Topher whimpered.

"You all know the rest. My parents hid me until Ringtail came and brought me to Selvia." Blue managed a tight-lipped smile at Lova and Topher. "And I did my best to forget Asia. You two helped me so much with that. I was happy—" Her eyes lowered, and her lips faltered. "Until Cartel's slave traders captured me in Oslo."

"Cartel?" Keston trailed off, mortified.

It wasn't a stretch to believe Europe's largest Underground organization had facilitated Blue's capture, but to hear that grim reality confirmed made Cartel's atrocities hit so much closer to home.

The conference room table splintered as Arianne's fist thundered down. "I'm going to finish what you started," she rumbled. "No Underground turf war. I already killed one Lang, what's one more?"

"*You* killed Hana Lang?" Keston gaped.

When he saw the unapologetic malice in Arianne's eyes, he knew there was no mistaking it. The world believed Alvaro had killed the late Commander, but that proved to be just another lie of war.

Jin Shi was careful as he broke the table's stunned silence. He gave an amicable glance toward his daughter before continuing, "From what I've been able to discern, Hana never learned of the exact events of my daughter's assault. It's safe to assume that Qin will take the secret to his grave. We faked our daughter's death just in case."

Emiko wrung her hands. "We've always been close to the Lang family. We watched Qin grow up, and his hatred for *Feras* only grew each year. If he teams up with Ace, he'll claim the Underground and bring about a new era of *Fera* oppression. And then he'll set his eyes on Europe. I fear nothing will stop him from crushing your rebellion."

Colla frowned. "The combined might of Europe and Asia could be the end of us. Alvaro is no closer to retaining his memories. Africa and the tribes will not be able to weather that storm alone." He turned back toward Arianne. "We need to talk to Strix."

"That's not your call to make," she growled back. "I'm Deputy."

The Lion smiled sadly at her. "I know, Young One. But I also know you shouldn't shoulder this alone—there's nothing wrong with asking for help."

"Without the twins, there's no guarantee we can contact Selvia without compromising our position," Arianne countered. "If Qin knows Treena and Tyrell are Sevian, and Tyrell was associated with Keston, Qin's people will be on high alert. There's a good chance calls and messages from outside the continent are being monitored. We're alone until we resolve this issue."

Rhino's head hit the table with a thud, a small moan escaping him at the reminder of the captured twins.

Keston considered the ever-worsening predicament surrounding them. He folded his fingers to rest his chin, now covered in a healthy stubble. Slowly, his foot started to tap as he thought. The room was terrifyingly silent, as if everyone was praying someone else would come up with the silver bullet to solve their problems.

Good thing Keston had a thing for perfectly aiming bullets.

"We take the offensive," he announced.

Naturally, Arianne perked up at that. "I'm listening."

"Every time Ace has bested us, it's because we were forced to walk into her games. We know she's coming this time, so let's flip the switch. We'll set up a game for *her* instead. And in the chaos of Underground infighting, we'll have the perfect cover to kill Qin." Keston shared a devious grin with Arianne, lightness filling his chest as he planned another classic, chaotic scheme with her. "We kill Qin and take Ace down all in one blow."

Colla nodded, his golden-blue eyes narrowed as he considered Keston's proposal. "It could work. But it's risky." He gave him a warning look. "And I'm not keen on you leading this, or not telling Strix."

"Are you and Strix fucking or something?" Blue demanded.

Colla's jaw dropped open, but he didn't counter. Lova coughed. Even Rhino paused his bout of melancholy to look up.

"We don't have time to unpack *that*." Arianne crossed her arms. "We need a plan—preferably one that doesn't put half of us in the hospital."

Knowing their track record—and where he'd just woken up—that was a logical request.

Standing, Keston walked around to the head of the table and held out his hand for Arianne to shake. He smirked. "Desperate times call for desperate measures. I think I recall you telling me something similar once."

She worked her jaw, looking down at the conference table of Asian Elites, Selvians, and Circusfolk. All looked back at her with varying levels of unease and resignation. This was their best chance, but he knew he was the last person he'd trust in that situation.

That's what made things interesting.

Keston extended his hand further. "You'll have to trust me, Princess."

Arianne let out a long-suffering sigh and shook his offered hand. "I hate it when you say that shit."

Chapter 26

Andre

The *Project Frenzy* files left a pit of internal dread in Andre's stomach as he passed over the images. Somehow, Hera was experimenting on feral *Feras*. Somehow, she intended to force Asia into line. One particular photo was haunting: a young girl, hardly older than ten. She had blonde hair and looked like skin and bones under her white uniform. Her eyes were feral, black as the night sky. Her entire life, stolen, subjected to weeks of madness until she ran herself too ragged to keep going.

She looked like Arianne.

Genevieve was right. Inheritances needed to wait. Andre needed to discover what was happening in those labs. And *soon*. He was interested in ruling a *just* empire, not one based on the horrors formed from Hera's deranged mind.

The conference room doors creaked open on their hinges, a somber note to an already dreadful meeting.

Genevieve led Kalinda and Haris into the room. The latter was cuffed, unable to leave Hera's lab without restraints. Kalinda held Rou, still protected under the guise of being the infant's mother. Despite her growing disdain for Andre, she held his daughter with loving tenderness.

He knew Kalinda well enough—her gentleness with Rou wasn't an act. She'd genuinely fallen for the child in the months she'd pretended to be her mother. A new surge of affection for the woman warmed his heart.

Even if any hope of that affection returning to him was long gone.

"What do you want, Andre?" Haris deadpanned.

He glared at the prince who'd subjected him to a life as Hera's researcher. His eyes were sunken, and his shoulders slumped under an invisible weight.

The Porcupine looked haunted, focusing on something beyond that executive conference room.

Something told Andre that Haris wasn't looking out the floor-to-ceiling windows towards the sprawling image of Paris. No, Haris had seen something. Andre's eyes drifted to the *Project Frenzy* files under his hand. Something told him Haris had every right to look so strung out.

Andre sighed and said the three words he struggled the most to say: "I messed up."

"Then get me out of these cuffs and get us out of here," Haris said.

Andre bristled. "You would so quickly abandon Pangaea?"

Haris rolled his eyes. "So you were testing me?"

Genevieve cleared her throat. "This meeting isn't about returning to Pacific."

It didn't go unnoticed that the young woman had chosen to sit at the head of the rectangular conference table.

Kalinda bounced Rou on her knee, blatantly addressing only Genevieve. "Then why are we here? Paris or Madrid, it doesn't matter—Pangaea is not my home."

"My job isn't to get you home," Genevieve said evenly. "My job, right now, is to moderate. A lot of good can come from the three of you working together."

Haris crossed his arms, refusing to sit down. "I already tried working with Andre." He frowned. "That didn't work out too well for me."

Andre heaved a painful sigh, looking to Genevieve for aid. She only shook her head.

He forced his pride down for one vital moment. Looking to the ceiling above, slightly aglow with soft mood lighting to complement the sunlight trickling in, Andre couldn't look at anyone in the room as he spoke. "As I said: I messed up. I wrongly assumed the Richards would cooperate now that Pandora and I are engaged."

Kalinda scooched her chair to stand. "I don't need to participate in this."

"Yes, you do," Andre barked, slamming his fist on the table. At the room's combined flinch, he quickly took a calming breath. "Yes, you do," he repeated patiently. "Because I can get you a meeting with Jaya."

Kalinda scooched her chair back in.

Haris was less willing to believe it. The male glanced at Kalinda in warning. "He's only being nice so he can bribe Jaya with a visit with you." His blue eyes pierced Andre. "Isn't that right? You want to butter her up, so she'll tell you Pandora's movements."

Andre clenched his teeth. That was *precisely* what he was thinking. But that didn't mean there wasn't a part of him that hoped the meeting would make Kalinda happy.

"Do you want to see Jaya or not?" he pressed.

Neither objected.

He pushed the project files across the table to Haris. "If you want to see your friend, you'll need to work for it. What can you tell me about these files?"

Genevieve watched the exchange, green eyes burning brightly with curiosity. She folded her freckled hands under her chin, content to fade into the background. But Andre kept an eye on her. The Leroy family always found ways to weasel themselves into places they didn't belong—and build crushing intel collections. Something told him Genevieve was turning out to be no different than her relatives.

Haris opened the manila folder and flinched. "I'm an engineer, not a scientist." He gingerly pushed the file away. "I'm not working on that project. But," he said, pupils narrowing to pinpoints. "I hear their screams... every night." He buried his head in his hands. "All night. *Every night.*"

"Can you think of how that project could apply to Asia?" Andre asked. "Have you heard anyone discussing it in the lab?"

Haris didn't raise his head. "I don't know."

"I need you to try—"

"*I don't know!*" Haris cried, baring his teeth. "Stop. Pushing. You don't know what it's like to be stuck in that torture chamber. I block it all out just to stay sane."

"Then what project are you working on?"

Haris only shook his head. "I've stopped asking questions, not like I have a high enough clearance to know anything of substance." His palms dug into his eyes. "I don't want to know—I just know it's *horrible*. There's no *good* application to these designs."

He stood abruptly and marched to the exit, knocking on the door to get the attention of the Ward outside before Andre could object. Haris didn't turn to face the group as the Ward started to usher him out of the room.

"I don't need to see Jaya." Haris's face was shadowed as he looked down. "If Hera knows I care about her, it's one more thing she can hold over me."

"Haris!" Kalinda shouted, her distress making Rou whine. She reached for her friend and said, "Don't push us away."

Haris paused, and the Ward grumbled in annoyance. A half-insane smile painted the Porcupine's lips. "I don't want to push you away, Kal, but I have to. If I don't slow this research down, we're doomed—and the more people Hera knows I love, the more she can force my hand."

Andre motioned for the Ward to wait back outside. Once the door closed again, he walked up to the Pacifican engineer and let him see the genuine concern. "As your Heir Apparent, I have every right to know what is going on in those labs, Haris."

"I thought you didn't care what needed to be done to get your power," Haris seethed. When he craned his neck to look up at Andre, his eyes were flooded with tears. "Hera will give you power, just don't ask how if you want to sleep at night."

Andre didn't hesitate. "I won't become Commander just for the Richards to perform a coup."

He wouldn't marry Pandora and give her more power while her mother built weapons under his nose. But he couldn't become Commander without marrying Pandora—a tricky predicament. His best hope was nipping whatever machinations she and her mother had in the bud.

"How noble of you," Haris spat.

Genevieve finally spoke up, relieving the crackling tension. "Haris." She turned in her chair to stare at the male in all sincerity. "Your efforts are admirable. But you can't stop this alone. Let us help you. You can start by getting anything you can on *Project Frenzy*. Can you do that? And in return, I promise I'll get you a meeting with Jaya that Hera will never know about."

Haris considered for a long moment, his attention darting between Genevieve and Kalinda. Finally, he nodded. "I'll see what I can find." He pointed at Andre. "But I'm not doing this for you."

"—was thinking we could have a Christmas ceremony at Notre Dame. We could have a winter motif with light blue colors that would match the bride's complexion beautifully!"

Andre did his best to keep his eyes open. They were approaching the second hour of wedding planning, and he was ready to jump out of his skin. Well, *planning* wasn't the best word. Andre and Pandora stared at Sensatia's presentation and listened to her media-friendly plans, which were periodically interrupted by Hera.

Since a royal wedding was the one thing Hera had been working toward her entire life, this was one of the few situations in which the Richards matriarch was utterly agreeable. Sensatia chose the venue, flowers, decorations, and even the guest list without issue. Even Pandora successfully made it through that meeting without hospitalizing anyone. In a rare moment, the Richards seemed to align with Andre: they didn't care how the wedding happened, only that it did.

"What does the prince think?" Sensatia's bubbly voice brought his attention back to her presentation. The reporter-turned-royal-media-manager was as enthusiastic as ever as she smiled at him. "This is your wedding, after all."

Pandora swooned, grabbing his hand and squeezing it so tight it hurt. "Yes, *my love,* what do you think?"

Andre frowned at his fiancée. "Whatever ends with you taking my last name before the world works for me."

She rolled her eyes. "That almost sounded romantic."

He shrugged, uncaring about the color of the bridesmaids' dresses or the reception flower arrangements. He just cared that all of Pangaea witnessed their pairing. Only then would he be the unrefuted Heir Apparent of Europe.

A buzzing notification on his watch saved him. Andre's eyes shot down to the message blinking on his wrist. Genevieve. A message from her could only mean one thing: Haris got information. And seeing as Hera and Pandora were scheduled to be in that infernal meeting for another two hours, a meeting about them couldn't happen at a better time.

Andre stood, relieved for an excuse to escape. "I just realized I was double-booked," he remarked with a frown at his watch. "Continue without me. This is more of a woman's thing anyway."

Sensatia crossed her arms. "The groom never participates," she said, groaning. "I should've known."

He made quick work of calling his private jet. The Palace of Versailles and the Leroy Estate at the Chateau de Rambouillet weren't far from one another, but a jet ride reduced the commute to under ten minutes. Andre hardly had time to check some messages from his Wards and communication from Madrid before he landed in the lush gardens of the Leroy Estate. Even so late into autumn, the grass was bright green and well-manicured.

He almost felt bad about landing his jet on the perfect stretch of green. But time was of the essence.

An older valet opened the door, and Andre recognized the man as the Leory's leading servant: Warrane. He bowed. "Your Highness, Lady Leroy is waiting for you in the drawing room."

The first thing Andre noticed when he entered the drawing room was the flash of Jaya's purple hair against a background of maroon. The room was like any other in a classic Elite estate, with a stuffy, velvet feel and finely preserved antique furniture. Jaya stood mannequin-still by the roaring fireplace, purple-green eyes unresponsive even as the prince entered. Genevieve was talking to Haris in a hushed tone at a coffee table filled with pastries and tea. And Kalinda, sunk into the deep back of a luxurious chair, strickenly stared at her robotic sister.

Andre wanted to comfort the woman he loved, but even a touch would be unwelcome. Whatever. He didn't have time for sentiment. They had less than two hours before both Richards had a free schedule to snoop around.

"Let's make this quick," Andre said. "The Richards are only in a meeting until five."

"Make this quick?" Haris demanded as he produced a flash drive. "I risked my neck for this, and you want to rush us?"

Andre's nose wrinkled in annoyance. "I might be a prince, but even I can't control every minute of my subjects' schedules."

Genevieve took the flash drive from Haris. Andre took note of where she placed it in her pocket.

"Stop wasting time frowning at me. Wake my friend up," Haris demanded.

Andre had received a copy of Pandora's remote control for Jaya. It was hardly as complex as the one Pandora kept, but it had the basic mechanisms for emergencies. Wordlessly, the prince raised his remote toward Jaya and shut down the system.

A hush fell over the room as the light on Jaya's black collar flashed. The Chameleon slackened, sinking to the floor. Kalinda pushed out of her chair, lunging to catch her sister with a startled cry. Jaya didn't move for a few tense moments, her skin shifting between gradients of every color. Then, the female's coloring returned to normal, and she inhaled a sharp gasp.

Jaya's eyes were milky as she returned to consciousness. She looked like she was still waking from a midday nap as she looked to Kalinda above her. "*Didi*?" she rasped.

"Jay," Kalinda cried, cupping the Chameleon's face.

Haris whimpered, falling to the floor to join the Bahri sisters.

"What's going on?" Jaya asked, her voice lethargic.

"What do you remember?" Andre asked.

Jaya massaged her temples. "I don't know," she trailed off, still seeming foggy. "I was just on the beach. I was surfing." She looked at the Elite drawing room, brows knit together. "How did I get here? This isn't the Bahamas. This isn't Pacific..."

"You weren't surfing," Kalinda breathed.

"Yes, I was." Jaya shook her head. "I remember checking for high tide this morning—"

"Do you remember *anything* else?" Andre cut her off in frustration.

He was risking everything for that meeting. If Jaya had no intel, he was wasting time.

Her lips parted in thought. The wheels in her head seemed to be spinning painfully slow. "I remember a bridge," she said. She squinted and pointed to Andre. "You were there. There was an explosion, I think."

"That was the stretch of the Artery between Morocco and Spain," he confirmed. "You helped us steal vital African intel."

"No." Jaya's frown deepened. "I wouldn't do that. I wasn't there."

Haris's face screwed up in rage. "It's the control collar. Hera found a way to put you into a simulated dreamscape to make you more susceptible to manipulation. I worked on the modified design."

"Control collar?" Jaya's voice cracked in fright as she raised her hands to her neck. "No." She began to sob, her skin shifting to a deep blue. "*No,* this can't be right."

Kalinda rubbed her sister's back. "Jay, it's going to be okay."

"No, it *won't.*" Jaya's skin and hair turned paper white. She raised her shaking hands to her face. "I've hurt good people!"

Haris cupped her face, tears streaming down his cheeks. "That wasn't you! You didn't have a choice."

Jaya didn't look at him. "But I did it," she whispered.

Andre recalled Blue Krait saying something similar.

"You can fix it," Andre insisted. "All you need to do is remember. Do you recall anything in the labs? Did Pandora say anything to you? Did she force you to go on any secret missions?"

Jaya was close to catatonic now, eyes glazed over and breathing shallow. She slowly shook her head as her eyes welled. "I don't know," she whispered.

"You have to try," Andre barked.

Kalinda lunged in front of him, green eyes furious. "That's enough! Can't you see you're torturing her?"

He should've taken the woman's warning. But Asia's sovereignty was at stake—his throne threatened. This was no time for coddling. No one ever cared about his feelings on their route to power. He needed to follow suit, or he would get trampled. Again. He was playing this game to win this time.

Pushing past Kalinda, Andre shoved down the part of him that flinched at offending the woman he cared about. He reminded himself that Murrays asked for forgiveness, not permission. He descended on Jaya, receiving a shout from Haris as he did. He effortlessly shoved him out of the way. Without her typical confidence, the Chameleon's short stature betrayed her, and it was finally noticeable how small she was.

Jaya hugged herself at his approach, still lost in the confusing fog of her memories to do more than repeat quietly: "I don't know."

"You *must* do better," he growled.

"Hey!" Haris shouted, waving a flash drive. "I got what you wanted. Leave her alone."

Andre turned, took the offered flash drive, and connected it to his wristwatch. The drive's contents projected above his wrist: most files were encrypted, and the decipherable ones were similar to those Genevieve had retrieved earlier that week.

There was only one new piece of information. "The project has exited the laboratory phase," Andre noted. "They're deploying it into the field for broader testing."

We're too late.

Genevieve's fingers thrummed on her wheelchair's armrests. Slowly, she nodded her head. "It's not optimal, but I can get to work on leaking the intel to the press. If there's an uproar in Asia, we can link it to Richards Labs and cause public distrust. It's not a takedown, but it will be a political hit to the Richards."

"That's not good enough," Andre ground out.

A frown came to Genevieve's face, a rare expression of emotion from the typically neutral girl. "This isn't about explosive wins, but slow corrosion. We can use this."

"I agree with Andre," Kalinda breathed. She refused to look at him, like her words of approval were a personal betrayal she was ashamed of.

Andre's heart skipped a beat. He turned to her, his hopes lifting for a moment. Then he saw where she knelt: next to her sister, who'd dropped to the floor and curled her head into her knees. Jaya was sobbing, hardly comforted by Kalinda's soothing touch.

"I won't let the Richards take my sister again," Kalinda said. "We need to take them down now."

"You were supposed to be better." Haris pointed at Andre. "You were supposed to change Pangaea from the inside. Instead, you're just playing their games."

Andre stiffened. "I can't change anything until I'm Commander." He tried to lock gazes with Kalinda. He needed to make her *understand*. "I'm doing all this to get there."

Leaving Pacific, allying with Ace, marrying Pandora, forcing Jaya and Haris to work for Hera... it was all necessary to buy his Ascension.

Haris sat down at Jaya's other side, his nose scrunching up in disgust. "Funny," he muttered. "You seem to be the only one in this room who hasn't sacrificed something. It must be so hard being you."

Andre felt his expression darken. "I don't appreciate your accusations, Pacifican."

Kalinda was the one to respond. Her head snapped up, her expression hard as she frowned at him. "You were supposed to be one of us—a Pacifican fighting for better. I guess I was wrong."

"You were," Andre said flatly. "I am Andre Murray, a Prince of Pangaea. I'm not some discarded democrat from a backwater rebellion."

Even as his heart cracked more at the accusation from the woman who was supposed to love him, he couldn't let any of them see a break in his royal facade.

If they wanted to make an enemy out of him, fine. They'd outlasted their usefulness.

Just then, the doors burst open behind him. Pandora and Hera filed in, their faces alight with glee at the scene playing out before them. The room recoiled as Pandora's cybernetic arm extended into a blaster—the maniacal smile on her face warning everyone she was more than happy to open fire. Jaya whimpered, burying her face into Kalinda's shoulder. Haris rose to his feet, the quills on his head standing on end and ready for attack.

Hera leaned on the doorframe behind her daughter. "Now, what do we have here?"

The decision was easier than Andre would have liked. He locked eyes with Genevieve and was surprised to see her nod.

Steeling his face, he turned on his heel and walked up to Hera's side. He blankly ejected the flash drive from his watch and handed it to the scientist General. "I got word of some rebel activity from Lady Leroy. I apologize for the concern. I wanted to neutralize the situation quietly."

"*What*?" Haris cried.

Kalinda lowered her head to her sister, but neither said anything. The sight should've moved Andre, but he felt nothing. He needed to take the steps required to secure his future power. They would understand one day.

"They were discussing something called *Project Frenzy*," Andre continued, as unaffected as possible. "Does that mean anything to you, General Richards?"

Hera smirked, scanning the files with her cold blue eyes. "It's a contingency plan, that's all," she hummed. "Nothing to concern yourself with, princeling. Asia will be in our fold soon if this project provides the fruit I hoped for."

"I don't remember signing off on such an initiative," Andre said.

"Of course not." Her condescending tone sounded like nails on a chalkboard. "Leon's already approved. It's over your head, so don't worry. I wouldn't want to put stress lines in your forehead before your big day."

Andre glared at the woman, barely controlling his annoyance. "How *considerate* of you."

The scientist General waved to her daughter. "Bring the engineer back to my labs and get Changeling back online."

"Changeling?" Haris protested as Pandora locked a set of handcuffs around his wrists, the bands connecting with that impenetrable stream of blue light. "Her name is *Jaya*."

"We like to give our operatives codenames," Hera said. "Harder for our enemies to know who's coming for them."

"I'm Poltergeist." Pandora grinned as she pulled a squirming Jaya out of her sister's hands. "Now, let's get Changeling back online."

"Jay!" Kalinda screamed.

"*Didi!*" Jaya struggled to reach her sister's hands, but Pandora yanked her back with enough strength to dominate the *Fera*.

"Andre!" Kalinda cried. "Do something. Please!"

He couldn't meet her beautiful green eyes—eyes he knew would crush his resolve the second he saw them.

"Shut up your side whore," Hera warned, "or would you like your fiancé to do it?"

Pandora snickered as she pressed the button on Jaya's remote. The purple-haired female's struggles ceased as she slumped over. Seconds later, she straightened with mannequin stiffness. And then Jaya was gone, her face a blank slate once more—the only sign of her previous emotion evident from the redness in her eyes and moisture on her cheeks.

It was haunting.

Quietly, Andre walked over to Kalinda and pulled her to her feet. He could feel her cutting glare into the side of his head. She was stiff. If her glare was molten hot, her posture was colder than the Russian tundra.

"I see what side you've taken," Kalinda whispered low enough for only him to hear.

There was no question anymore, no hope. In that one phrase, her feelings toward him were clear. She hated him. He did his best to focus on Pandora as she carried Haris out of the drawing room, Jaya—or Changeling—in tow.

Hera gave Andre and Genevieve a proud nod. "Good work today, kids."

He didn't dare say anything until the doors shut behind Hera. "It's no longer about sides," he said, pulling Kalinda closer to him despite her struggles. "It's a race to power. And if I don't win, someone far worse will take my place."

Kalinda wrenched herself out of his grip. "Look in the mirror. There's not much worse than you." She stormed out, uncaring that a squadron of Wards waited for her beyond the doors.

The whirring of the mechanical wheels of Genevieve's chair was the only sign of her approach. She watched the doors close again, worry replacing her steady demeanor. "Burning bridges is preferable to burning cities. Stay the course."

Andre clung to the girl's calming words. If the whole world were against him, he found some strange comfort with her beside him—Genevieve: his Lady Advisor through and through.

Chapter 27

Arianne

"If you told me last year I'd be walking into a festival in matching leotards with you, I would've said you were crazy," Arianne grumbled.

"But I *am* crazy. We both are." Keston smirked and gave her a small push. "Come on, this is going to be fun."

"Fun isn't the objective."

He pouted.

"No, your objective seems centered around putting us in ridiculous outfits," Blue hissed at him, joining Arianne's other side.

"Disguises are one of the best parts of the job," Keston returned with a grin.

"Yeah, when you can fit in them." Rhino glowered, looking particularly uncomfortable in his skintight shorts and vest that looked one arm-raise away from ripping.

The Japanese Autumnal Equinox was in full swing around them. Thousands rushed into downtown to celebrate the peak of autumn with street vendors, parades, music, and pop-up performances. As the sun dipped below the orange-speckled trees, downtown Tokyo burst to life.

Despite the narrowly controlled chaos, Wards and Pangaean soldiers littered the streets, on the hunt to quell disorder before it even considered rearing its ugly head. Unfortunately for the festival's security, the disorder was already ingrained in the crowds, with a thoroughly thought-out plan, and dressed in sparkly circus uniforms.

Colla, in his bright red ringleader's ensemble, led a small group of his circus company through the thickening crowds. His golden red hair was a beacon above the heads of varying shades of black and brown. The male beckoned the Ivory

Court—and Keston—to follow his Circus, pulling the group from their growing bickering.

Arianne waded through the Circus of Artemis performers to join the Lion at the head of the pack. "How long until my team can peel off from yours?"

Colla's blue-gold eyes tracked the thousands of people milling about warily. "Only performers are allowed inside the crowd-control fences in front of the Lang family tower. Security will be tight. We all need to be accounted for during the performance if we don't want to raise an alarm."

"So we'll do some flips, smile for the cameras, and duck into the tower."

"Are you sure Ace will be there?" Colla questioned, eyes filling with concern. "I don't like exposing ourselves based on a hunch."

Arianne glanced back at Keston, who seemed to be talking cordially with Topher. She scrutinized the winged male, waiting for the familiar twinge of distrust to bubble up at the sight. Nothing came. They needed to trust Keston's intel—and him. Seeing as her intuition wasn't flashing her a giant neon warning sign, it was full speed ahead.

Arianne leaned closer to Colla to whisper in a voice quiet enough for only a fellow *Fera* to hear. "Keston's Jokers scoured Europe looking for Ace after Qin threatened to consult her. They found her...landing on a private jet in Tokyo this morning. There's no better cover for an unsanctioned Underground visit than during a festival. She's here."

Colla clapped her on the back, his hand landing on the crest of her wing hidden under her cloak. "I trust you, Young One. Whatever you need, you know I'll provide. I only ask because I care for you, as I do for every *Fera* in my Circus. You're family."

Arianne smiled despite the mission hanging over her. "If only we could choose family." He and Sygrid would be at the top of her list.

"You can," Colla said with a knowing look toward the Ivory Court—and Keston. "I learned this after many years, but as leaders, we must protect our families first. If you must choose between the mission and your family, you know what you must do. You will get another chance on a mission. You don't get another chance with them."

Arianne frowned, her focus returning to the heavily guarded street block and the angular skyscraper built of blue glass and sleek white rising above: Lang Tower. She stared at the top floor of the glacier-like building as if she could see her targets waiting inside. "I'm doing this mission to protect them," she insisted. "We fail, and everyone I love could be as good as dead."

If she didn't kill Qin and didn't stop Asia from joining Europe, they were one step closer to losing the war. One death to prevent millions more that would follow. To add to the desperation, Qin had Treena and Tyrell. Even Arianne, who despised anything related to math in school, could do that simple equation.

"Then, for Europe's sake, the Circus of Artemis better have one *hell* of a performance," Colla said.

Arianne waded to the back of their group, lowering her blue and silver mask over her eyes to blend in. Surrounded by her team, they waited for Colla to communicate with the Wards standing guard at the crowd control perimeter. She watched the exchange, hands clenching in anticipation. If he couldn't get them inside, their plan was over before it began.

Then she felt someone grab her hand, their fingers snaking through her clenched fists to give her a reassuring squeeze. Arianne's rapidly worsening thoughts dissipated when she looked up at Keston, his smile thawing the mission's coldness that'd taken over her heart.

To her surprise, she didn't pull her hand away.

By nightfall, the festival was in full swing. Music played through the streets, the crowd roaring with energy as performance after performance played on the stage in front of the Lang Family Tower. Arianne huddled behind the curtains, watching Lova perform her magic act with Rhino as her subject. The Cheetah's speed made her sleight-of-hand impossible to follow as she performed disappearing acts, changed outfits during flashes of smoke, and threw in acrobatics with Rhino's help.

It was apparent Lova had grown up with a love for performance and had spent her life perfecting her act. She was stunning. The entire crowd was infatuated. Even Arianne couldn't take her eyes off her.

"We're up next." Keston appeared at her side and handed her a trapeze fly bar. "You ready?"

Arianne hesitantly took the bar she would attach to the high-string wires above the stage. "I was literally born for this. Can you keep up?"

He brushed past her as he lowered his mask, which matched hers. "If I recall correctly, I'm pretty good at catching you when you fall."

Arianne didn't have a chance to retort as he stepped onto the stage to the crowd's cheers. She quickly followed, but slowed at the size of the audience. Thousands packed the street, the front row pressing against the barriers to get a better look at the performance. After almost two years of living in the shadows, being a spectacle was a strange feeling.

She didn't entirely hate it.

Keston had already climbed to the elevated platform erected two stories above. People screamed in excitement as he extended his dark wings and jumped, effortlessly looping his legs around the fly bar hanging in the middle of the stage and swinging from his knees.

The electric music grew as Arianne climbed to the opposite platform, anticipation tightening her chest. But the tightness felt good. She enjoyed the rush of being stories above an encapsulated crowd. Clicking her fly bar into the wires, she gave an elated wave to her audience and jumped. Then she swung, building momentum until she reached the top of her arch.

Then she let go with a broad smile as she tucked in her wings and flipped mid-air. She savored the moments of weightlessness, comfortable and confident even as gravity ripped her downward. After a second flip, Keston swung above her and extended his hands, catching her when their trajectories crossed. Her hands tightened around his, the connection effortless, instinctual.

It was like their bodies innately knew where the other would be.

Keston beamed at her as they swung upward. She couldn't help but return the look, feeling as light as the wind carrying them.

The moment ended faster than she would've wished. They swung backward, and Keston let her go. She let her wings catch her, shooting to the opposite platform. She stuck the landing, wings spreading wide behind her as the crowd exploded in applause. Keston swung from his fly bar, legs unhooking as he flipped to catch Arianne's former bar. She was transfixed on him, his muscled body a work of art in that sparkling blue and silver uniform. Confident and beautiful, he let go at the top of the arc and rocketed upward into the air.

The crowd promptly lost their minds.

Arianne shot up after him. They met in a tight spiral, flying closer and closer together until they had to hold each other's backs to keep themselves in sync. They flew higher, eyes locked and breaths combined as their feathers held them in a condensed cocoon, soon too high for most human eyes to see.

But that didn't matter. Something told Arianne they were no longer flying for an audience.

Keston's eyes were alight as he stared at her. He was *so close*. She didn't object when he leaned forward, and their foreheads touched. "We always flew so well together," he whispered.

Arianne exhaled, terrified of how much she wanted him in those painfully enchanting, fleeting seconds.

"Nothing on the ground ever mattered in the sky together," she said, forehead still pressed to his.

She remembered days spent flying over the sea, the problems of their lives fading away as they trained together. When they were in the air, pushing their growing abilities to their limits, they forgot about the world below. They just existed as the purest versions of themselves: avians who loved the skies below their wings... and loved each other.

The world could pull them apart and ground them, but in those fleeting, weightless moments together, nothing else mattered.

It was Keston's turn to take a hitched breath. "Kiss me. When we land, we can pretend it never happened."

"Okay," she breathed. "But only because I owe you."

His arms went around her back, pulling her even closer. Arianne reached up, gripping his face in her shaking hands. Bodies pressed as tightly as possible, they tucked their wings in and let themselves point downwards in a death spiral.

There, rocketing toward the earth, their lips found each other after two painfully long years of searching.

There was no way she could let go. The ground rapidly approached, but neither cared as their careful peck became ravenous. The wind whipped past their ears, and their tongues met with familiarity that even years apart couldn't replace. The only thing Arianne felt was warmth spreading to every nerve in her body.

What should've felt so wrong felt more right than any kiss she'd had since she'd lost him.

She didn't know when the tears started. Maybe it was when she realized the emotions she'd shoved down had never died. Maybe it was when she realized those beautiful emotions could only be felt in fleeting moments like that. Moments that had to come to an end.

The ground was close now. They hardly separated and shot back into the air before their desire turned deadly. With a coordinated loop, the winged mutants regained altitude, flipped, and landed on opposite platforms. They waved and smiled for their thundering audience, but as they locked eyes, their smiles faltered, acknowledging the unacknowledgeable.

Arianne was supposed to pretend nothing happened. She *needed* to pretend nothing happened. But when he looked at her like that...

No. She ripped her eyes away, hastily climbing down the ladder and running backstage. There was a mission to focus on. She couldn't think about him and the traitorous stream of emotions threatening to pierce her heart.

"Ari!" he cried out behind her.

She ducked between some gymnasts, all carrying different props for their act. Among the contortionists and acrobats was Blue, who managed a concerned look in Arianne's direction before being pulled onstage. Arianne ignored it, lowering her head and charging toward the changing tent to get herself in gear for the second phase of her mission.

"Arianne!" Keston's voice was directly behind her. He grabbed her arm, pulling her to a halt. His face was stern. "Stop for one fucking second," he demanded breathlessly.

She couldn't meet his eyes. "I have a mission to prepare for, Kes."

"Not until you *talk* to me."

"There's no talking!" Arianne ripped herself out of his grip, returning to her warpath. "Nothing happened. That was the agreement. I don't have time for this."

His footsteps didn't follow. "Do you seriously want to pretend like nothing happened after *that*? Are you kidding me? I know you felt something. Don't lie to me—or yourself."

Staring hard at the ground, Arianne's fingers flexed and clenched as she fought to bury the exact things Keston was accusing her of. Helping them or not, Keston was fundamentally a Pangaean Elite and an Underground kingpin. They couldn't mean anything to each other. Not to mention that she was *betrothed* as part of a political agreement that kept them in that war.

Emotions couldn't change any of that. They were better off ignored.

"I'm not lying to anyone," Arianne countered. "If anything, I'm the only one being honest." She gestured around at the controlled chaos of the Circus to the crowded streets beyond. "Do you *see* the situation we're in? We're trying to kill the heir to the most powerful continent in the world. You're next in line to an Elite estate, and I'm Deputy to your continent's sworn enemy. There is no way to run this equation and get any outcome you're looking for, Keston!"

He stood, stricken. The hand he'd raised to touch her shoulder fell back to his side. He was silent for a moment, lips parting open and closed. Finally, in the painful silence, he whispered, "Being on different sides never stopped us before."

"There's no *us*. Not anymore."

He laughed humorlessly in her face. "That's a good joke."

Arianne turned on her heel, hating the nauseating mixture of emotions swirling in her gut. "If I were you, I'd lock the fuck in. In case you forgot our deal, we need to kill Qin, or I kill you."

"What if I join Selvia?"

Arianne halted.

"That was the plan—whether you agreed or not. I wanted to honor my mother's legacy and live with people who would accept my gifts," Keston said. "I've been working on the inside for Strix for months. Once my objectives were met, I was going to defect to Selvia. I didn't tell you because I didn't want you to think I was doing it for you."

Arianne stared at the ground, feeling dangerously unsteady. "And you'd give up everything. The riches. The estate. The power."

"You know I never really wanted any of that."

"And Genevieve?"

Keston scoffed. "She makes her own decisions now. She's made it apparent she doesn't need my protection anymore."

Khari was her first thought. They'd yet to officially announce their betrothal. The world was aware the Prince of Africa was betrothed, though no one knew to whom. It was easier to hate Keston—to see him as something unattainable—than to know he was within arms' reach, and she couldn't reach out. Enemy or friend, a relationship was not sustainable.

And while he claimed he was helping Selvia out of the kindness of his heart, could she trust his loyalty if he knew she was promised to someone else? She couldn't break his heart *and* lose their agent on the inside.

Goddamnit.

Before she could speak, Keston's watch buzzed. He hastily answered the call. "Qin, what do I owe the pleasure?" he asked in that insufferable voice he reserved for Blackjack.

"Leroy, where are you?"

Keston stretched, letting an ounce of laziness enter his voice. "If you *must* know, you're interrupting a date." He winked at Arianne. "Now's not a good time. Lovers' spat—you know how it is."

She was two seconds from throttling him.

"Get to the Lang Tower. *Now.*"

"Last I checked, my identification card says I'm a European citizen," Keston sang. "I don't think you can technically order me around, nor do I want to be."

"Keston," Arianne hissed.

Holding up a finger, he muted his call. "This is how you deal with these people," he told her. Unmuting himself, he added. "But if you ask nicely, I'll send my date home. Maybe you'll meet her one day."

One day. Meaning in about half an hour.

"My penthouse. A-S-A-P," Qin said, hanging up.

Keston winced, looking up at Arianne. "I want to finish this conversation."

"You need to go." Her relief at the painful conversation coming to an end warred with an annoying desperation to keep him at her side. She looked away. "We stand a better chance with you on the inside anyway."

"I'm sorry we have to be on opposite sides again, Princess."

"If we succeed, maybe we won't be for much longer," Arianne said, terrified at how genuinely hopeful she sounded.

She didn't know if she could forgive him. She didn't even know how a future together could work. But that didn't erase the fact that she did, in fact, want to see him again. No matter how much that complicated things.

Looking at the distance between them, a softness came to his eyes as he closed the space. "I would like to be on the same side again. I care about—"

"Don't say something you don't mean," Arianne interrupted, unable to hear the rest of that sentence.

"But I *do* care—"

"Don't say something you *can't* mean," she cut him off a second time with a glare.

Keston nodded, resigned. He took a moment to collect himself. When he looked up, he wore his perfect mask of unaffected playboy once more. He smirked. "See you soon, Princess. I wouldn't miss the chaos you cause for the world."

Arianne smiled evilly. "Don't kill Ace before I get up there."

"Deal."

And then he was gone, rushing into the changing tent to change into whatever outfit he'd deemed worthy for a meeting with a future Emperor and former Underground Queen. Arianne watched him disappear before rushing to change herself.

She allowed herself five seconds to reminisce over their shared moment in the sky before focusing on the mission ahead. As she pulled on her battle leathers and strapped her batons to her hips, she imagined Qin bleeding out beneath her blades, and it was just enough to make her forget about the male she so desperately wanted but could never have.

A successful mission would have to suffice. Winning a war had to be enough. Even if something deep in the pit of her stomach told her none of that would matter if Keston wasn't standing by her side at the end of it all.

Chapter 28

Keston

The last time Keston rode an elevator to a Commander's penthouse was in Leonueva. He did his best to hide his unease as each floor passed by with an insanity-inducing *ding*. Based on his experience with that particular brand of scenario, he wasn't keen on repeating it.

But he needed to.

Things would be different. He held the cards that time. He would have backup. And Qin was a far lesser man than Leon. Yet, Keston still couldn't stop his feet from shifting back and forth. Ace would be there, too. Though his power had grown immensely since their last altercation, she always had some sort of wild card.

Keston also didn't know if he could hide his rage when he saw her.

Shaking out his pre-meeting jitters, he jumped on the balls of his feet. "Male the fuck up, dumbass," he muttered to himself. "You've got your former boss and the man you're trying to assassinate in a room. You have your ex-girlfriend ready to back you up. There are two hostages. Basic mission. Nothing you haven't handled before."

The elevator stopped. Keston fixed his suit coat and corresponding cape to ensure his wings were hidden. Adjusting the silver crown on his head—a piece he'd stolen from Ace's collection—he readied himself for one of the best performances of his life.

"Blackjack," came Ace's distinct purr as soon as the elevator doors opened.

His eyes tracked to his former boss. She was seated on an L-shaped leather couch, her back facing floor-to-ceiling windows displaying the night sky over Tokyo. Purple-blue lights lined the corners of the walls and ceiling, casting the lounge in a soft glow. Ace drank a martini in a glowing glass, a cocktail most likely made by the bartender Puppet behind a neon bar in the corner of the room. Had Keston not been two seconds from leaping out of his skin, the soft neon ambiance might've been relaxing.

"Imani." He gave the woman a baleful smile. "I thought we agreed to be on a first-name basis."

The intricate lines of her ace of spades tattoo crinkled with delight. "That was before you attempted to steal my empire from me."

Keston had to fold his hands behind his back to prevent himself from sucker-punching her. "Attempt? You always had a talent for undermining me." He gestured around him. "From what I see, my attempt was extremely successful."

With a knowing sip of her drink, Ace hummed. Keston almost lost his goddamn mind. Same old Ace, same old games. But he would be the one on top that round. He just needed to bide his time.

Even if his time was quickly running out.

"I don't take kindly to being ignored at my own meetings," Qin warned.

Both he and Ace turned to the prince. Qin was seated at the bar, his eyes narrowed as he took a glass from his green-haired Puppet. Keston almost laughed. He'd forgotten about the prince when he'd laid eyes on Ace. It was a funny reminder of how insignificant Qin was without his inheritance. No other Commander would allow themselves to be so forgettable, even without their thrones.

From Ace's red-lipped smirk, she was thinking the same. She licked her lips, probably considering how many hoops she could force the prince to jump through. Honestly, Keston didn't think she'd care if he killed Qin in front of her. If anyone had a low tolerance for incompetence, it was Ace.

"What is this meeting about?" Keston asked flatly. "Need I remind you that you pulled me from an otherwise entertaining evening? Unless you can offer me something to keep my interest, I'll be going."

He needed to seem indifferent, untouchable.

"The Circus has been removed from the block," Blue Krait's voice sounded over his comms unit. "The Court is inside the building."

Let the chaos begin.

"Come now, Blackjack," Ace said in her hauntingly sensual tone. "I can guarantee I'm the most excitement you've gotten all year."

Tell that to the undead princess who'd been haunting every single one of his dirtiest thoughts for the past month.

Keston took a decisive seat on the couch across from Ace. Crossing his legs and stretching his arms across the couch's back, he did his best to look at ease with the situation. Ace had no hold over him anymore—debt, family, or brainwashing. He was the most powerful being in that room. There was no reason why he wouldn't have the upper hand there.

There was no reason why he would ever bow to Ace again.

He let every ounce of gloating satisfaction enter his voice as he blatantly ignored Ace and turned his head to Qin. "Remind me why you invited a washed-up has-been? Last I recalled, I was the poster child of Pangaea *and* the Underground."

Ace laughed. "Funny you think that."

Qin casually sipped his drink. "I've changed plans," he announced, lifting his chin. "I don't need you to take down the other factions, Leroy."

"You only have Cartel in your pocket with your alliance to me," Keston countered, aware his dominance was already slipping. "Sure, the Gwinsin are scattered with the death of their boss, but the Ronin *and* Empress are still at full power. You need my aid if you want any hope of dominating them before the New Year."

Ace cracked her knuckles. "Oh, my sweet Blackjack, you should've continued your apprenticeship with me. There was still so much to teach you." Keston stilled as she sat next to him. A cold shiver radiated through his wings as she ran a knuckle down his cheek, just as she'd often done when he was her pet. "I had so many dreams for you—a shame you only ended up being a pretty face."

He didn't dare react. No. There was no possible way Ace had something over him. He'd checked his bases, scrubbed communications, and security footage across the city. There was no *fucking* way. He refused to believe Ace bested him again. He was Keston Leroy, the apex predator of the Underground.

No one hunted the apex. Right?

"Where do you think I've been this past year?" Ace whispered in his ear. "Did you think you could get rid of me so easily?"

It hadn't been *easy*, but yes.

She snapped her fingers, and Texas Hold'em sauntered into the room.

"I'll admit you've done a good job caring for Cartel. You see, I've outgrown what Cartel can give me, so I decided to give her to someone to maintain." Ace smiled at Tex. "But you can understand I still needed to give you a babysitter while I set my eyes on some more powerful prizes."

Qin snickered from his chair, looking like a boy watching the drama of his favorite television show play out. "Here's where it gets good, Leory." He ordered another drink without taking his eyes off the scene. "You see, it's just business. You've done well, but I've decided to trade up. It helps that I no longer have to deal with your disrespectful attitude."

"Who do you think controls Empress now?" Ace hummed. "Why did you think you could never infiltrate their influence, no matter how hard you tried?" Keston stared forward, hating the familiar feeling of numbness taking over him in her proximity. Ace's whisper brought back painful memories as she leaned into him. "You're good, but the Ace always bests the Jack."

Shit. Every part of him screamed at him to run. He fought to remain expressionless.

He needed to call off the mission. But he knew it was too late. Objectives had already been set in motion. The Selvians might only have this one chance, especially if Qin now had the protection of the most powerful crime syndicate in Asia.

Please, whatever god that will listen, don't tell me I fucked up again.

"Then why invite me?" Keston ground out. "I'm obviously no longer needed."

"Oh dear, don't pout now." Ace frowned. "We still have use for you. Europe wants their playboy back, and I think I'm ready to absorb Cartel back under my control. You still have use, Blackjack, just not in...*management*. Go back to your parties and tabloids, babe. They might be more your speed."

The surging rage inside him was difficult to control. It was next to impossible. It would've been so easy to snap her neck—a human would be too slow even to see the attack coming. He could picture it now: kill Ace, jump over the couch, and do the same to Qin before he even had a chance to scream.

Keston would become the ruler of Empress and Cartel. He'd be the most influential male in the Underground once and for all—a male to be *feared* and respected, even by Leon. And Ace would be dead, dead, *dead*.

But no. He calmed his increasingly reddening vision. If he made a move, he'd ruin his cover and push Sora even closer to an alliance with Europe.

And he couldn't signal the Ivory Court to move until he knew *everything* Ace had on him to make such an ambitious move against him. Trapped, as usual.

"So you've decided?" Keston asked Qin stiffly. "You'll join Europe?"

His performance was terrible. He should've sounded *happier*. After all, his official goal was to bring Asia and Europe together. But even his incredible acting skills couldn't make him sound enthusiastic about an alliance between all three of his enemies.

Qin looked coy as he downed his second drink. "I'm certainly entertaining it. Especially since Ace is so close to solving my Underground problem."

"You see, Keston, I did the thing you couldn't: became the liaison between continents." Ace folded her hands together in satisfaction. He hated how it sounded like she was talking to a child. "And in return for my patriotic efforts, Europe and Asia will give me free rein of their criminal underbellies. I'll be a Commander of my own empire when we're done, all in exchange for brokering world peace."

If world peace meant the global oppression of mutants.

It was Keston's turn to laugh dryly. "You'll both double-cross each other."

"Like you were going to?" Ace questioned. "Come now, when were you going to tell your business associate you were a *Fera*?"

Qin's glass shattered on the ground. The glass shards spilled across the floor. But the prince hardly noticed, too busy spitting in fury. "Excuse me?"

Ace's obsidian eyes sparkled at Keston mockingly. "Oh yes, he's become quite proficient in hiding such an undesirable quality. He almost passes for human, but I can assure you, he is nothing more than a half-born savage underneath. He's lucky he has a drop of Elite blood to hide so much stench."

Keston stood abruptly. "Funny you mention Elite blood—something you have *none* of."

He smiled when her upper lip curled. Just as Ace knew his insecurities, he knew hers. No matter how much wealth and power she amassed, the world only saw her as scum, scum covered in diamonds, but scum all the same. Blood was inescapable in Pangaea.

Outrage contorted Qin's face, an emotion unlike anything Keston had ever seen on him. Standing in a fury, he almost fell over before he grabbed his cane. "Monster!" he cried. "To think I ever entertained an audience with a creature like you. I want him *dead*."

Keston laughed at the man who thought forcing himself on children was acceptable behavior. "I hardly think I'm the monster between the two of us."

Qin's face slackened. "That's right, asshole. I know how you lost your brother."

Somehow, his face reddened further. But this time, terror was mixed in. "I want him dead," he ordered again.

Two Wards by the elevator entrance stepped forward, drawing sharpened katanas. Keston stood and backed toward the window in case things devolved. In his experience, negotiations typically got tense, but they were quickly reaching a point of no return.

Part of him considered signaling the Ivory Court, but he stopped himself. *Not yet.* There was more to uncover.

Ace, returning to her passive calm, tsked. She raised her hand, and Tex trained his shotgun at the Wards. They instantly stopped, eyes turning to their prince for instruction. The room was frozen, waiting for someone to make a move. Naturally, Ace excelled in such situations. Comfortable, she casually shoved her hands deep into the pockets of her jumpsuit.

"Let's calm down." She looked to Qin. "You and I both know Europe wouldn't be too happy to see their star child dead on front-page news."

"I don't care." All decorum had left Qin's body. Only wrath remained. "Asia commands more power than Europe. I'll make them bow."

Ace walked over to him and placed a condescending hand on his shoulder. "Come now, even you aren't that stupid. You may have *slightly* more resources, but do you truly believe you could defeat a veteran Commander such as Leon?"

Reluctantly, Qin settled back in his chair but didn't remove his glare from Keston. Keston prepared to smash his fist through the window—his wings already itched to break free behind his cape. He didn't have long to execute an exit.

But not *yet.* His heart pounded. He could practically taste that there was more to learn.

"Good," Ace cooed with a glance at Keston. "Now that we've established this is *my* meeting, we can continue."

"You were a fool to subject yourself to Ace's games," he spat at Qin. "No version of this situation would've put you on top."

Ace played with a single boxer braid lined with golden ringlets. "Oh, Blackjack, you know me so well. But even I know when to bow to a higher power."

He scoffed. "You can't be serious."

She shrugged. "As we've both seen, Leon is a man you follow, not a man you go against—especially in uncertain times such as these."

She'd joined Leon.

"Qin, I've come up with an exciting proposal that someone such as yourself would jump at the opportunity to sign off on." The queen extended her arms.

"A control mechanism for *Feras* to use as you wish. Punishment, increased labor capability, or good old-fashioned control."

The prince frowned. "I'm listening."

"I heard you had a couple of prisoners who could use a lesson or two," Ace said. "Why don't you bring them out as volunteers?"

Keston stiffened. The twins.

But he didn't dare move. Ace and Qin still believed he was loyal to Europe—it was the only trump card he had left. He couldn't hope to show his hand if he wanted to retain even a fraction of the sway he'd entered that meeting with. Ace might have control of the Underground, but he still held his position as the son of the second-most powerful family in Europe. So, taking an ever-so-slight breath, he fought to keep stoic as his friends were placed at the mercy of his demonic ex-boss.

Two Wards dragged Treena and Tyrell into the lounge. The pair fought against their restraints, spitting and hissing, but it was no use. With cuffs around their wrists and ankles, and blasters trained at their heads, no amount of struggle would help.

"We need to engage," Arianne growled through his comms.

Thanks to his ocular cybernetics, he was broadcasting the entire meeting to the Ivory Court. Arianne was perched outside, one glass window away from providing backup. Rhino should be near the tower's barracks, ready to slow whatever reinforcements would be called. Lova and Topher were on the roof. Blue and Colla hovered in a jet a few blocks from the tower, ready to land if things went south.

An eventuality they were rapidly approaching.

"Not yet," Keston whispered into his comms.

Arianne grumbled but didn't argue. They might have a painfully uncertain relationship status, but even she trusted his ability to navigate those situations.

Ace stared down at the twins with terrifying interest. Her dark purple acrylic claws snapped as she thrummed her fingers together in anticipation. "May I introduce to you the next step in our alliance?"

She reached into a pristine purse, pulling out two masks with gas cylinders attached beneath the chin. She handed the masks to Tex before nodding to the twins. Keston's stomach flipped.

As Tex struggled to attach the masks to the twins' faces, Ace continued. "I understand you wish to kill *Feras* who prove to be too headstrong to be slaves.

It's an unfortunate fact of the industry: you always lose some products to those who refuse to cooperate. But what if you could repurpose it?"

Qin stroked his chin. "I'm listening."

Ace grabbed two black collars and passed them to Tex to attach to the twins next. Keston heard Blue gasp across the comms. "This new product, paired with our newest version of the control collars, is our novel solution. Ten times the strength and no mind to retaliate. I give you the Underground's newest drug: Frenzy!"

Arianne's voice crackled over the comms. "Keston, stop this—"

But her order was cut off. Ace pressed a button in her pocket. The room watched as the gas masks filled with sickly indigo smoke. Keston couldn't stop a startled cry from escaping his throat. Treena and Tyrell collapsed to the floor, the pair writhing in pain.

Six distinct screams assaulted Keston's ears through the comms unit.

The world slowed to a stop as the twins' struggles ceased. Their black collars beeped, a blue light flashing frantically on their necks until it slowed to a single steady green beam. For a moment, nothing happened.

Then, both twins opened their eyes, and only blackness remained.

Chapter 29

Arianne

Treena and Tyrell had gone feral.

Arianne screamed at the broadcast of the room. She almost snapped the tablet in half. The twins were alive, but they were *gone*. Rhino's wails in agony were almost enough to make her fall off the side of the building. The mourning cries of her entire team assaulting her ears were insanity-inducing.

Feral: the living death of mutants. And somehow, Ace had found a way to bottle such a fate into a gas.

"I'm coming in," Arianne growled.

"No! There's nothing you can do for them now—we can't compromise yet," Keston whispered, his voice barely audible over the twins' monstrous snarls.

Arianne knew he was right. Sygrid would agree to hold back—an attack now wouldn't gain anything. It would be emotional, *impulsive*. Arianne struggled against every instinct that told her to move in, knowing they'd lose more than they would gain with the new variables at play.

But still—

Those guttural noises came from her *friends*. Not just operatives. Not just Shadows. Friends. Arianne's breath caught in her throat. She'd spent their last couple of weeks together so caught in her mission that she'd treated them like *objectives*. And now they were gone.

With a screech, her fist careened into the glass next to her. The window to a forgotten bathroom shattered in glittering blue fragments and blood. She felt helpless.

Another loss. Another failure.

"Impressive," Qin's voice cracked Arianne's tantrum. She swallowed her rage, focusing on her newest objective through eyes lined with tears. "This will be a wonderful incentive to keep *Feras* in line."

From the way the video shook, Keston was barely containing his rage. "Incentive?" he squeaked with outrage and horror. "This is beyond alliances and inheritances. This is biochemical warfare. This is against the Constitution. Even Leon won't ally himself with someone who makes something like this—"

Ace's chuckle cut him off. "Honey, who do you think invented this?"

Hera Richards. Arianne's blood went cold.

Leon, her own father, had allowed such an abomination to enter the world. He'd signed off on insanity in a bottle. Frenzy: a terribly fitting name. She thought she understood what kind of monster she'd been born to, but this was far beyond anything in her nightmares. Her *fucking* father allowed this. The blood flowing through her veins allowed this.

"I've heard enough," a new voice came in through the video's audio.

The elevator doors opened again, and Arianne immediately recognized the newcomer: the demon-masked assassin from the Gwinsin attack. The Ronin operative who'd ruined Arianne's mission and killed Madame Tsing. They were there, invading another critical meeting, seemingly well-informed and in control.

What were the Ronin playing?

The Wards turned on the assassin, their blasters poised to shoot. But the Ronin operative was ready, firing two silent shots into their heads before they managed two steps. Tex raised his shotgun, but not before the assassin pointed their gun at him.

A standoff.

Then, the assassin removed their mask, revealing Princess Mori Sora.

Ace gave a low chuckle, gesturing for Tex to drop his gun. "I'm so rarely surprised. What a delight."

"Sora!" Qin bellowed. "How dare you?"

Her face was the picture of abhorrence. "How dare *you*, brother? This is an abomination! The last thing our mother would have stood for would be the defilement of the Constitution."

"You have no right to question Mother's wishes," Qin barked. "I am Heir Apparent. I am the voice of this family. You are nothing but a pretty face to be pawned off to the alliance I deem best. Do you hear me?"

The glare Sora gave him was lethal enough to cut through the broadcast. "I tried so hard to give you the benefit of the doubt. Your Commandership was Mother's will, so I tolerated your idiocy because it was what she wanted. I built the Ronin to clean up the messes you and Mother couldn't. I told myself I'd be happy in the shadows. I told myself Mother saw something I never could."

Qin laughed incredulously. "You'll be arrested for your crimes against the continent. Running your own crime syndicate? You'll be lucky if the world considers you a Lang descendant once I'm done with you."

"I command vigilantes. You let your hatred of *Feras* turn you into a monster I'll never let Asia follow." Sora raised her pistol, adorned with a silencer. "We are not the same."

For the first time, uncertainty played on Qin's face. He raised his hands, finally offering his sister a charming smile. "Come on, Sora, you wouldn't shoot your own brother."

"You're not my brother. Not anymore."

She didn't hesitate. The silencer made the shot almost imperceptible in the video. Qin slumped to the ground. Arianne nearly fell off the building for a second time that mission.

Laughter filled the shocking silence. "What a stunning conclusion, girl," Ace said. "I think we have a bright future ahead of us."

Sora turned. "Future? All I see are the only witnesses to my brother's assassination. No, there's no future for you."

Arianne was moving even before Sora finished. Unlike Qin, she knew Ace wouldn't go down so easily. Unlike Qin, if Ace did go down, she would take the entire room with her, which included Keston.

No thoughts ran through Arianne's head as she burst through the window, the glass exploding around her as she landed in the blood-covered lounge. Keston dove to the ground as she shot over him and landed on the coffee table, her wings surrounding her in avenging fury.

Her entrance was just enough to catch Sora off guard. Ace took her chance in the confusion. Clicking her remote, the gas tanks ejected from the twins' masks. As the smoke radiated throughout the room, Ace and Tex ran, her remote instructing the twins to follow. Sora set off in pursuit, but Arianne wasn't focused on the chase. She was focused on the gas shooting toward them. Toward Keston.

Everything seemed to move in slow motion. Keston was still on the ground, but the gas traveled too fast. Arianne had one desperate idea, a terrible gamble.

She hoped Instinct would protect her. That it would make her resistant to going feral—or at least allow her to come back from the brink. But whatever chance she had against the gas, Keston had *none*.

Arianne didn't have time to acknowledge what drove her desperation. She just couldn't lose him. She wouldn't.

Even if it meant losing herself.

The gas flowed around her wings now. She ripped her mask from her face and lunged at Keston. She didn't know if a moment's exposure was enough to induce insanity, but she couldn't risk it. Snapping the mask in place, she allowed a moment to slump in relief when the air filters activated. The gas was already around them in a thick fog.

"Arianne!" Keston bellowed once he realized what she'd done.

"Go!" Arianne coughed, pushing him toward the window.

The indigo gas tasted like vinegar, and she gagged. She'd been right to protect Keston. They wouldn't have made it out in time. Even then, the toxin pooled outside the broken glass in murky clouds. Arianne made the last few bounding steps toward the window, fighting the disorientating effects of the gas.

And then she tripped, vision blurring. Falling forced her airways to open, and more gas pooled into her system.

"Arianne!" Keston whirled to catch her, his wings unfurling around him. "Oh god. Oh *god*. Tell me you're okay." He helped her up. "You shouldn't have saved me."

"Go, Keston," she pleaded, her head starting to spin.

A primal anger coursed through her, and she shivered to hold the terrible power at bay. Fear gripped her bones. Maybe she'd miscalculated. Maybe she could go feral after all.

"No! I'm not leaving you!" Keston pulled at her arm.

"Go!" she barked, her voice no longer her own.

Whatever was coming, she couldn't hold it back anymore. She didn't want Keston to be at the mercy of *her*.

He grabbed her shoulders and yanked her out of the building. They held each other tightly as Keston opened his wings and rocketed away from the growing gas cloud. But even fresh air wasn't enough. Suddenly, Keston wasn't someone trying to save her; he was someone holding her back, restraining her.

And she refused to be restrained.

Instinct rose to protect her. She welcomed the sensation, giving in to the wild power the rampage promised.

With a bellow, Arianne ripped herself away from his grip. She didn't open her wings before she made impact with the street below. Her body made a crater, uplifting dirt beneath the concrete. But she barely felt anything. Crawling from the crater, the street was in chaos.

But not just from her.

Frenzy's purple cloud engulfed the entire city block: Ace's final distraction to escape. *Feras,* hidden among the crowd, ripped and clawed at the people around them. Blood-curdling screams lit up the night as citizens turned on citizens, humans ripped apart by black-eyed mutants who'd once been their friends and family. Gunshots rang out as Wards and soldiers attempted to control the crowd, but any target they hit only compounded the feral frenzy.

And, in the middle of the chaos, Arianne couldn't resist Instinct's excitement.

A once-beautiful festival devolved into a bloodbath. She cried out, swiping and clawing at any passing body she could get her hands on. Ringing filled her ears. With the violent cacophony of the riot, every nerve ending in her body filled with endless energy.

A feral mutant with fishlike scales lunged at her. Arianne laughed, dodging to the side with little more than a thought. One of her blades was through his neck before the creature could recover. She smiled in delight as the *Fera's* blood squelched and pooled out of the wound. They went still.

The riot's energy grew as the number of humans still alive faded, and the group became more concentrated with feral *Feras*. If Arianne were in her right mind, she might've equated the densely packed blood bath to a dancefloor at a nightclub. But, instead of dancing, they were ripping each other apart, and instead of neon paint, there was only dark maroon blood.

Another excited cry escaped her, her mind almost wholly gone in the clouds of Frenzy around her. Maybe a normal *Fera* only needed to inhale the gas once to go feral, but constantly inhaling it kept Instinct sticking around far longer than she could typically sustain it.

It was incredible.

Distantly, she could've sworn someone called her name. She didn't listen. Arianne wasn't her name, not anymore. She was *Instinct*, and she never wanted to be that weak little female again. Here in the mosh pit of death, she felt more alive and at peace than ever. Here, slashing and cutting and clawing to stay alive, everything made sense.

No pain. No responsibility. No heartbreak. All she felt was the joy of the next kill. It was paradise.

A voice cracked through her craze. "Arianne!"

She recognized that voice and felt pulled to it, even if she couldn't identify why.

A catlike *Fera* knocked her to the ground in her moment of confusion. Bracing her blood-covered hands on the female's shoulders, she fought to keep the female's gnashing fangs from her jugular. She smiled as the cat's black eyes locked with her own, loving the feeling of finally being on the ropes.

"*I dare you,*" Arianne challenged.

The female was thrown off before it could attempt to tear out her neck. And then a winged male stood over her, face shielded by a familiar black mask. Arianne found it strange that his eyes were a shining amber, not black like the others. She didn't attack for a moment as her Frenzy-soaked brain tried to make sense of the new phenomenon.

Who was this male? Why didn't she feel the need to attack him?

He grabbed at her hands. She lashed out that time, but not before he managed to grab hold of her. Wings and legs thrashing, he pressed her to the ground and held her hands to her chest with bone-crushing intensity, pinned between him and the concrete. The feeling of being trapped drove her to another level of insanity.

Images of laboratory cages flashed across her mind. She spat and writhed as the memory of white lab coats holding her down and injecting her with all manner of drugs assaulted her memory. She screamed against the male's grip. She was trapped. She couldn't be trapped. She would never be trapped again.

"Arianne! It's me! I need you to calm down!"

"*No one can trap me!*" she screamed in a voice fueled by Instinct's insanity. "*Not again!* Never *again!*"

The male rammed her on the ground, stunning her for a split second. At that moment, he grabbed another mask from a downed Ward a few feet away and snapped it onto her face. She continued to struggle, but he was strong and held her in an inescapable position.

And, like it or not, the countless injuries she still couldn't feel started to slow her down.

"Come on, Arianne," the male pleaded, amber eyes painfully familiar and filled with an emotion she was too far gone to pinpoint. "Focus on me. Remember me? It's me, your Pangaea Boy. I need Arianne back, please."

She saw images of forests thick with green, following behind someone with curling brown hair. Turquoise waters and a set of dark brown wings carrying a figure screaming with delight above the waves. The roof of a skyscraper at sunset, the silhouette of a winged figure facing the burning orange sky.

"Pangaea... Boy?"

"Yes," he breathed in relief. "There you go. Come on, focus on me. Remember me. Breathe, Ari."

She could see an ancient female with antlers decorated with jewels. "Breathe in, breathe out," the legendary crone instructed beneath an oak tree in the arching walls of a cave. "Focus on your breath. Instinct doesn't control you. You control you."

Arianne's thundering heart started to slow. "Cervi," she whispered, mind slowly clearing.

"There you go."

He sighed again. Keston. Clarity finally returned as filtered air penetrated her Frenzy-filled lungs. Her vision locked on the male above her, ashamed she hadn't recognized him. Keston was bloodied and wounded, but the eyes behind his mask were painted with happiness. She had a moment to look at him in terror. Had she hurt him?

His weight fell off her. "Welcome back."

"Keston," she wheezed, suddenly struggling to stay awake.

As Instinct faded, the pain of her wounds came back faster than she could handle. Each breath was filled with markedly more pain. Her ribs might be broken. Maybe a punctured lung—and that was just her chest, she was too terrified to take stock of the rest of her mangled body.

"You're going to be okay," Keston assured her. But even in her half-conscious state, she could detect the hitch in his tone.

And then the events of her most recent loss of control trickled back. Even as her arms barked in protest, she raised them to her face. Her voice shook when she saw her forearms thoroughly coated in blood. "Oh my god. W-what did I do?"

All she could remember was elation and feral release. The time between the penthouse and that street was a blur. But she knew what that much blood meant.

"Ari, this isn't your fault. You saved me."

She barked in pain, the full effect of her injuries hitting her with agonizing power. "No." Tears welled in her eyes. "I lost control. I lost control *again*."

Keston stroked her hair, which was coated in coagulating blood. "Arianne, look at me. This wasn't you. This was Ace. This was Frenzy."

"No! I keep losing control." She closed her eyes as memories of the riot just minutes before came back in awful detail. She almost threw up at the carnage she'd wrought. "I'm dangerous, Keston."

He scooped her in his arms, and she screamed in pain. He looked equally pained at her shout. "Come on, we need to get you out of here. Asia will be sending their military to stop this."

Arianne managed a look over his shoulder at the riot still burning bright. Without Instinct, she saw the gory mass of feral bodies as what it truly was: horrific. Bodies of the dead lay in piles, dismembered beyond recognition. Cars lay strewn across the street, crushed and burning. And still, hundreds of *Feras* continued to battle each other, the haze of Frenzy doing little to shield the world from the most horrendous sight she'd ever seen.

Even if Arianne had more energy, she was sure her emotions wouldn't be able to process what she'd witnessed.

"Don't look at that," Keston instructed her. "Look at me."

"What are we going to do?"

"Remember rule number one of Pangaea: survive today, deal with the consequences tomorrow." He leaned down and pressed his forehead to hers. "Survive today, Princess. Keep focusing on me. Can you do that?"

"I'm a monster, Keston."

Arianne couldn't take her eyes off the self-feeding massacre. A massacre she'd happily participated in.

Something broke on Keston's masked face. His eyebrows knitted as he looked down. "This war's made monsters of us all. The best we can do is be a monster that does some good."

Arianne raised a shaking hand to his face, wishing she could feel his soft skin and prickly stubble instead of the coldness of the mask. "You're not a monster. Far from it."

The winged male stumbled, almost falling mid-sprint. He took a shaking breath. "I thought that's all you saw me as."

Lowering her eyes, she realized that, while her emotions toward him were complicated, there was one thing that was crystal clear. "You've made mistakes, but how hard you work to correct them tells me one thing: you are better than most people on this planet."

They locked eyes, and Keston slowed his run to a stop. There, standing frozen in time on an empty side street, they stared at each other. Slowly, she raised her blood-covered hands to his mask and pulled it off. For some reason, she *needed* to see his face. It was one she could paint with her eyes closed. Though all his scars she'd traced in bed with her fingers had been removed, his hair two shades darker, and a rough stubble covered the lower half of his face, he looked just like the male she'd fallen for all those years ago.

His face was an open book for her to read. She'd almost forgotten how much she missed that particular book, with words so familiar she could quote them by heart. Keston's lips parted as he wordlessly removed her mask in turn. And then they were looking at each other, truly looking at each other, for quite possibly the first time in their lives: no more secrets, just the ugly truth of their souls on full display.

She thought revealing the darkest pieces of themselves would drive them apart. For a while, it had. But now, as she stared at him, she realized that the lies they'd told had driven them apart, not the truths underneath. Hiding their true selves had been the roadblock to this, this, *this*. And now that there was nothing between them, Arianne couldn't shake the connection she felt, deeper than anything she'd ever felt.

They were just two absolutely broken beings, cursed with more power than they deserved, fighting to leave some semblance of good behind. Two beings willing to risk *everything* for the other. She'd never seen a more perfect reflection of herself in someone in her life.

Her equal. For better or for worse.

And the beautiful thing was, neither of them ran from what they saw.

"Why are you looking at me like that?" Arianne said breathlessly.

"I'm thinking how you couldn't possibly be a monster," he whispered. He closed his eyes and leaned forward to touch her forehead again. She let him, cherishing the warmth. "Because it should be impossible to love a monster this much."

A slight noise escaped her. And suddenly, the pain of her injuries faded to the background. Electricity coursed through her, stinging and jarring, but a strangely welcome sensation. She became intimately aware of every point on her body where Keston touched her. And then, she couldn't ignore all the places on her body where he *wasn't* touching her. It was maddening, yet addictive.

"Phoenix!" Topher's cry came from a block away.

Her heart wrenched. Whatever moment she shared with Keston was fading. It was too soon. She had so much to say... and so much she *couldn't* say.

So she settled on one word. "Stay."

"You know I can't," he responded, pained.

Stay so we can figure this out together. Please.

She didn't know what she wanted. She didn't know if she could ever completely trust Keston again—or if they could ever afford to be on the same side. But she was crazy enough to ask him to throw it all away for whatever emotion was ripping a hole in her chest.

Suddenly, she didn't know if she could bear to stand another goodbye.

"Over here!" Keston responded to Topher's cry. "She's injured, but she's awake!"

Arianne weakly grabbed at his suitcoat, long since ruined with her blood. "Come back with us like you wanted to," she pleaded. "Don't go back to *them*."

"You need me on the inside to sort this out." He seemed to need to convince himself as well. "I'll find you again. I promise."

She ran her hand down his face again, committing the itch of the scruff on her palm to memory. "Don't say that."

Keston's eyes scanned every inch of her. "This is a promise I won't break."

"Don't make promises. They sound too much like goodbyes." She let out a small laugh, unable to remove her hand from his cheek. "You know I hate goodbyes."

"This isn't goodbye."

"It feels like it."

Keston's smile broke. "Now I'm getting déjà vu." He kissed her softly on her forehead. "Let me remind you what I said last time we were forced to part like this: you're my compass, Princess, my true north. Everything I do will always guide me to you."

"Stay," she whispered one last time.

He kissed her lips that time. The kiss was soft and lingering, neither of them wanting to break from the blissful moments of paradise they'd returned to. Because in those fleeting seconds, they were back at their villa with nothing but their After to worry about.

Topher's hooves were frantic. The pair separated before he could arrive. Keston lowered Arianne slowly into Topher's arms, his face pained as their moment—and time together—ended once more.

It felt cold without Keston's touch. She wanted nothing more than to jump back into his arms, but she was too exhausted. Without the adrenaline coursing through her veins at Keston's soft words, her injuries were quickly catching up to her.

"Thank you," Topher breathed. "We'll get her to safety."

"Good." Keston ran his hand over Arianne's hair, his face breaking. "Please take care of her, Satyr."

"Of course," Topher promised. "You're not coming?"

Keston looked back toward the Lang family tower. Red and blue alarms flashed against the glass of the building. Reinforcements had arrived to quell whatever feral mutants were still left alive. He frowned with a regretful sigh. "No, I need to go back and clean this mess up. With everything that's come to light, you'll need someone on the inside."

"Keston Leroy, I command you to stay," Arianne demanded with the last of her energy.

Uncaring if Topher saw, Keston leaned forward and kissed her one last time. He offered a small smile as he stood. "I'm glad I took off your mask. So I could remember Arianne. Not Phoenix. Not the masked vigilante. *Arianne*." He shoved his hands in his pockets, already masking the agony on his face. "And as much as you'd like to pretend you've changed, I can promise you that you're just the same old Arianne to me."

"Selvia could use your skills," Topher said.

"Soon." Keston winked, extending his wings behind him and preparing for takeoff. He offered Arianne one last glance. "Don't forget. I've been guided back to you every time before—now won't be any different."

Keston knelt, letting his majestic, dark brown wings curl around him, then he shot into the air with a thundering boom. As he flew away, Arianne felt a thread she'd never noticed before tighten between them. He faded into the night sky, the thread becoming painfully taught in his absence. It felt like one of her arms had been taken with him—a part of her now missing.

Arianne had lived among other *Feras* long enough to know what that feeling meant. She knew enough to recognize the significance of that interaction, the change it had triggered inside her. A bond had snapped in place, her body making the decision she was consciously too afraid to make.

As her mate flew away from her, Arianne finally let her exhaustion take her, and she passed out in Topher's arms.

Part III

Trojan Horses in Paris

Chapter 30

Arianne

"You should be downstairs celebrating," Sygrid's voice wafted over, as gentle as the breeze.

Arianne turned from the mezzanine railing overlooking the garden courtyard, where a small celebration gathered. Amidst the autumn flowering plants, bamboo, and a trickling stream, representatives of Selvia, Africa, Asia, and even the Circus danced and milled about, but Arianne couldn't drag herself down there.

Her mentor stood between the glass French doors leading deeper into the Okasaki estate, a concerned frown on her lips. Her eyepatch was still startling—a dark spot on her face where a striking orange iris once sat. Sygrid had arrived yesterday, rushing to Tokyo to oversee negotiations with Asia's newest Heir Apparent, Mori Sora, before other, more ambitious world leaders caught wind of it.

"Celebrate what?" Arianne knew she shouldn't sound so bitter. "My team didn't do anything. Sora killed her brother. We just got to watch."

Sygrid walked over, smiling as she moved a stray strand of hair out of her apprentice's face. "The objectives were still met. Qin is gone, and Sora seems a willing ally. That's something to be happy about."

Arianne shifted her head away from the loving touch.

"I should've told you my contact was Keston," she relented. "I didn't want either of you getting your motivations crossed."

"How long has he been feeding you information?"

Sygrid sighed. "Since Mexico City."

The belief that Keston was the enemy had tormented Arianne for ten months. She turned, hoping to distract herself with the party before her thoughts got increasingly traitorous. With the weight of global politics crushing down on her, she couldn't afford to think about *him*—or how he'd left her.

Again.

"And now you've ordered him to crawl back into Leon's lap for more information," Arianne said. "The double life is going to break him, Sygrid."

"I know," she whispered, head low. "But he insisted on returning—and I agreed. This war isn't over until Leon surrenders."

The wave of frustration at her mentor's comment nearly set her off. She did her best to swallow her anger, afraid that something more significant was driving her to lash out against being separated from Keston.

"If this isn't over, why are we celebrating?" Arianne ground out.

"We must celebrate the good when we can, or," she said, pausing to look into Arianne's eyes, "we'll be consumed by the bad."

Arianne ripped herself away, turning to pace up and down the mezzanine. "I'm not consumed by the bad, I'm simply looking at this situation *clearly*."

"So am I, Arianne."

The condescending softness in Sygrid's voice made her fists clench. She took another breath. "You don't know Leon like I do," Arianne warned. "You couldn't possibly see this like I am."

"And what do you see?"

Watching the party for a few moments, her sadness grew. Lova and Topher danced elegantly around the fountain. Blue sat with her parents for the first time in years. Rhino ravaged the concessions, a broad smile on his face. She wanted nothing but to foster her friends' happiness. It hurt so much more to know, deep in her gut, that such happiness was short-lived.

"Leon doesn't stop." Arianne's whole body started to shake. "He wouldn't hinge his entire *Fera*-domination plan on someone as stupid as Qin."

"No one could have predicted Sora would turn on her brother."

"But there was always a chance Asia could turn on Europe—especially with someone as volatile as Qin. Leon expects betrayal from others as a default. He'll have something planned for this outcome." She shook her head. "Don't get me started on Frenzy. Victory over Asia or not, the world just got far more dangerous."

And we lost the twins, Arianne's knees almost buckled at the memory of Treena and Tyrell's blacked-out eyes.

Sygrid took a long breath. "I'm sorry the weight of all this landed on you. You're too young."

"Well, there's no turning back now," Arianne said with a half-crazed laugh. "We need Africa's support. I need people following me if I have to take Leon's place."

The words made her feel cold—trapped. The pressure and the isolation of ruling didn't matter. She was the only one who could step up to the plate. It would be so much easier to tell Sygrid to fuck it all, and beautiful, loving Sygrid would agree. But Arianne could never do that.

Just then, she spotted Khari in the courtyard. He was flanked by his father and a middle-aged woman with short-cropped hair, presumably the African Lady Advisor. As if sensing her stare, Khari turned to look up at her. An unreadable expression flashed on his features, but he raised a bubbling glass in her direction regardless.

Stomach churning, she hated how much she wished it was Keston, not Khari, in that courtyard. She hated the disgust she felt at having to share Khari's bed later that night. Most of all, she hated lying to everyone, including Sygrid, about her genuine feelings. Even if she still didn't know what those feelings were, or if they could ever be pursued.

And it was all her choice.

But stepping away, especially now, would be selfish. People would die if they lost Africa. Europe could re-enter its oppressive regime if they took down Leon and she didn't step up. Her selfishness would lead to mutant suffering.

It was easier to let herself suffer alone.

"How are you two?" Sygrid asked, eyes tracking to Khari.

Arianne shook her head. "I scared him back in Moon Warren. The nightmares are not going away."

I never scared Keston.

"No one would blame you for taking time for yourself—or leaving the engagement," Sygrid said softly.

"*Everyone* would blame me."

Because the damning truth was Commander Sarr was right: this wasn't a fairy tale. A princess married a prince because he had armies. The princess *certainly* didn't marry the snarky bad guy with good hair.

"You might not have a choice," Sygrid warned. "You might not be able to convince the tribes you're mated with Khari."

"And why is that?"

Sygrid pursed her lips regretfully. "You smell different, Arianne."

Heart skipping a beat, Arianne straightened, like doing so would conceal what she'd been in denial about for the past four days. "I don't know what you're talking about." Her voice squeaked, and she winced. "We worked in a close capacity for a couple of weeks, his smell must've rubbed off on me. It'll fade with time."

She couldn't even say his name. Talk about deep-seated denial.

Sygrid's frown said she wasn't buying it. Unfortunately, Arianne wasn't either. She'd tried to logic the powerful draw she felt toward Keston at the end of the mission—how she'd begged him to stay behind. She told herself emotions had been high in the chaos, but even days later, his absence left a sizable hole in her heart, unlike anything she'd felt before.

Arianne refused to even *think* about the cause of that. Thinking gave the desire strength, and she couldn't afford that—not right now.

Her flinch when Sygrid touched her back was involuntary. After months of living on edge, physical contact in her blind spot still made her jumpy. She noticed her mentor's sad smile and returned it. Yes, she was strung out, quite possibly spiraling, but what could be done?

"We have a meeting with Sora and Jin Shi tomorrow, hopefully no more fighting. Hopefully, we can all go home," Sygrid said.

And there, in the comfort of the female she looked up to more than anyone, Arianne let herself be weak. "I would really like that," she sighed and fell into Sygrid's arms.

Looking up, she realized they weren't alone. She pointed to where she'd just seen a flash of sandy red hair. Alvaro Smith had been watching their conversation.

"Um, Sygrid? What's he doing here?"

Alvaro waved, a binder open in his hands with indeterminable contents.

"I told him he needs to check in with me every ten minutes." Sygrid sighed and turned. "You have no idea how often he wanders off. And I thought keeping you alive was hard."

Arianne yawned into a fifth espresso shot at the meeting room concession table. The fancy bigwigs still filed into the conference room, and she didn't care enough to greet any of them. She'd forgone sleep the night before, not trusting her mind to give her *normal fucking dreams* with the amount of stress she was under. She also wasn't ready to talk to Khari—not yet.

So, she'd opted to patrol Tokyo's skies in the late evening hours after the party ended. She'd ridden the cold winter currents, enjoying the twinkling lights until she found herself on the rooftop of one of Tokyo's tallest skyscrapers, watching the sun slowly brighten the sky. In those moments, staring out over the bay, she was painfully aware of the vigil she was keeping: she'd been scanning the skies for *him*.

Each time a bird squawked or a cloud blocked out the moon, she'd whip her head to see if Keston was flying to her. Maybe he was still in the city, maybe he was looking for her too.

Foolish.

Even now, as the soft, natural morning light nearly lulled her back to sleep, Arianne couldn't stop herself from staring at the conference room chair Keston had sat in just days before. She could still picture him there, absently spinning around and pretending he wasn't paying attention—even though he was logging every single detail of that room. Arianne smiled to herself. He was always good at fooling people into thinking he wasn't a threat.

She presumed that the list now included her heart.

"I missed you last night," Khari's voice made her jump up straight, almost spilling her drink.

"Keeping your bed warm is only one of my many duties," she retorted. "I wanted to run reconnaissance. Too many important people in town not to be on guard."

He raised an eyebrow. "Is that why you're wearing Mist?"

She'd put it on just in case Sygrid's observation from the night before was accurate. In a perfect world, nothing happened between her and Keston, and whatever lingering scent he'd left on her would fade. But just in case...

"Sora killed her own brother. Hera invented an anti-*Fera* drug. And we're in foreign territory. You can't be too careful," Arianne said. "Trust no one."

"Hey, about our incident in Moon Warren," Khari began. "I didn't get a chance to tell you, but we were marching on Spain—"

"Not right now," Arianne said. "Look, I'm sorry I hurt you. I'm sorry my dreams aren't under control. But we've got more important business."

They turned to look at the conference room. The indoor greenhouse-themed room was typically cozy, with the round table and plant life providing a bright green softness. But now, as the chairs around the table filled and others pooled into every inch of free-standing space, it began to feel cramped. The nervous buzz of energy was not doing much to help.

"I was going to say my forces marched on Spain while you were gone. I saw Andre," Khari whispered, now aware that at least a dozen eyes were on them.

Arianne stilled. "My brother?"

"How many Andre's do you know?" he retorted, saw her glare, and relented with a sigh. "He was with Pandora and this purple-haired agent with color-changing skin. They all didn't look good—thought you would want to know. Granted, I had a good time kicking their asses, until your insane sister blew up the bridge."

"Jaya." Panic stabbed her gut with a hundred needles. "They had a control collar on her?"

"I barely got a glance before Psychotic Cyborg set off explosives in my face, but I think so."

She felt her expression darken. She quickly downed the rest of her espresso. "So Andre captured Jaya during his Pacific coup. Wonderful. Can you schedule an hour for me to lose my shit later today? I don't have space in my calendar right now."

However complicated her past was with her former best friend, Arianne couldn't bear the idea of Jaya in Pandora's clutches. Unfortunately, such a grizzly update didn't even scratch the top ten list of her problems.

Khari rolled his eyes. "Just because you're my superior and you fuck me, does *not* make me your secretary," he hissed in her ear.

"Hopefully, all our schedules are going to clear up very soon," Commander Kajari Sarr announced as he entered, inadvertently saving his son from an unprofessional elbow to the stomach.

Alvaro filed in behind the African Commander, looking wide-eyed and out of place.

The chaos of the conference room settled down, attention turning to the African and American Commanders. Alvaro caused a slight stir in the Pangaean crowd when he settled with Colla and Sygrid in the mutant faction of the room.

Though the entire room was briefed on Alvaro's state, it was still an obvious shock to see him in person.

Kajari, on the other hand, was pure, undiluted Commander. He wore a light grey Western suit accented with deep red chains, and his hair was tied in a braid down his muscular back. While everyone was focused on Alvaro, Kajari's attention was pointed at only one: Mori Sora.

"Welcome to your promotion, Princess Mori Sora." Kajari dipped his head respectfully. "I respect someone who takes their fate into their own hands."

The air left the room at Sora's withering gaze. "I assure you, Commander Sarr, you will not see me celebrating my brother's death—even if it was at my own hand."

The room stirred in discomfort, and a few more daring leaders leaned toward their allies to share whispers. Arianne noticed Alvaro was nose-deep in the binder she'd seen him carrying the night before, seemingly not paying attention. Arianne squinted and realized, with a hint of entertainment, he was looking at a reference file of the major players in the room—complete with colored photographs.

A bead of sweat appeared on Jin Shi's brow. His words were careful: "The events of the past week are jarring. I implore all parties to withhold strong emotion until all factors have been assessed."

"You expect me to support the death of our Heir Apparent? Commander Lang chose Qin to be her successor. Now you ask us to accept the individual who killed the true Heir?" one Asian Elite protested.

Other Elites took that as their time to throw their retorts into the mix. The room filled with shouts of frustration. Every possible argument from Sora's Underground affiliations to her leniency toward mutants was voiced with unflinching vigor.

Arianne blankly checked her watch. *That went south quickly.*

Arianne closed her eyes, listening to the Elites spit their typical bile. She felt herself stiffening with each protest and accusation, and quickly realized why the meeting had ignited such a visceral reaction in her.

Those screams sounded just like the Pacificans when Arianne was being tried for Bradley Shaw's murder.

When Arianne opened her eyes, she recognized the same fear she'd felt in those moments on Sora's face. The two princesses locked eyes, and Arianne empathized with the weight her fellow heir was carrying: the weight of a continent. A weight she didn't want.

It was enough to make Arianne scream. She barked, voice cracking. The shouting subsided, attention in the room turning to her.

Arianne pushed away from the concession table, shaking in frustration. "None of you know how to listen, do you? You're all squawking just to hear the sound of your voice, and people call me the bird. I understand the situation isn't perfect, but welcome to the real world. Here's the deal: we have *video evidence* of your lovely Qin breaking the Constitution and engaging in biochemical warfare. If you still want that guy as your Commander, you can fuck right out of here, and hopefully my sword doesn't hit you on the way out."

One of the Elites frowned at her, a balding man with a sniveling voice. "And who the hell are you? Care to take the mask off?"

She wished they could all see her deadly smile. "I can guarantee I'm more important than you. As for the mask, I'm keeping it on for your sake."

"Why?" the balding Asian Elite pressed.

Arianne grabbed one of her batons and snapped it out, igniting the Selvian Steel blade. "Because if I take it off, I'll have to kill you."

Negotiations were never her strong suit.

"What my Deputy is trying to say is that Sora was faced with a tough decision: protect her brother or protect the integrity of her continent," Sygrid said, attempting to cool the tension. "Now that we understand what levels Europe is willing to go to, the next steps are fairly simple: we must unite against them."

The same balding Elite laughed at Sygrid. "Sorry, savage, but biochemical warfare is against humans. The Asian legislature says *Homo feras* are not human, so no crimes were committed." He rolled his head toward Sora. "Well, until you murdered your own brother."

Arianne didn't hesitate. She pulled a dagger from her boot and threw it toward the man. The force of her throw had papers flying off the table as it sped past. The impact was powerful enough to knock the Elite's chair backward, the knife embedding itself into his left eye. No one dared move as the Elite hit the floor and his chair tumbled next to him in a loud crash. Arianne simply watched, her arm frozen in the spot where she'd released her blade.

Alvaro frantically flipped through the pages of his binder, took out his pen, and drew a giant ex across the Elite's photograph.

"Sorry, I changed my mind." Arianne chuckled darkly. "Surely only a human could throw a blade like that, right? And if I'm not human, it's not murder."

The room watched her in stunned silence, probably calculating how many more projectiles she'd brought with her. When no one spoke up, Arianne grabbed another blade and pointed it around the table. "Anyone else want to step up and say I'm not human, or can we get back to what's important?"

Sygrid's remaining eye blazed at her in warning. But she found she didn't care. Some idiots deserved to die to prove a point.

Arianne didn't care how much that line of thinking sounded like her father.

Sora smiled at Arianne, "I never liked him anyway."

"Strix is right." Kajari stood once the commotion died down. "Terms should be relatively easy. Africa and Asia make up two-thirds of the Big Three. The two of us combined should be enough to force Europe into a peace treaty."

Jin Shi leaned toward Sora, already her loyal Lord Advisor. "You have many options here, Your Highness. You may agree to lend Africa aid or simply remain neutral. As you know, Europe was seeking your brother's aid. Even denying Leon your forces will force him into an unsavory position. "

Sora considered her Advisor's words, dark eyes staring forward toward Arianne. Slowly, she began to nod her head. "First, Cindy, and now Frenzy. If Europe thinks they can inject experimental drugs into our Underground without repercussions, they would be wrong."

"We cannot do anything until you Ascend," Jin Shi warned Sora.

An Heir Apparent was limited in the scope of their power. They could maintain the status quo, but decisions like troop movements and treaties would be significant enough to be vetoed by the other five Commanders. As it stood, Sora was still ranked beneath the other Commanders and could not make decisions on their level until January.

That reminder sent a chill down the room. They'd hardly hit October. That meant three months of tense stagnation. Three months of Leon's planning.

"Then Africa and the tribal forces will continue to weaken Europe—maybe we can force them into a position that will make them more desperate for negotiation," Kajari concluded. "We'll push our forces toward Paris and attempt to squeeze them. We can afford to be more ambitious as we wait for Mori Sora to Ascend."

Sora pounded her fingers on the table. "It's not that simple. Ace has taken hold of my Underground. For the past seven years, my organization, the Ronin, has worked to clean up the mess. But I no longer have the time to run them, and we can all agree Ace has made Empress a much larger beast than we've ever seen. I need the Underground in check before I weaken myself by opposing Leon."

"My Ivory Court is at your disposal," Sygrid offered. "They can assist you, and in return, you side with the Selvian cause in the peace negotiations."

"The Circus of Artemis will help as well," Colla piped in. "Many of my brothers and sisters were captured and sold by Ace. I know they would like a chance to repay the favor."

Arianne cracked her knuckles in anticipation. Their next mission was set. If her team could uproot Ace, they could end the war before Sora Ascended. The light at the end of the tunnel was so close, all she had to do was go into the darkness for a little longer.

Alvaro closed his binder and stood enthusiastically, hardly aware of what was happening but seemingly willing to die for it anyway.

Sygrid threw her arm out and tugged the American down. "Nope. You're staying with me." Her expression plainly told the room that it wasn't the first time she'd needed to do that.

Arianne looked between Sora and Alvaro, a lump growing in her throat. She could uproot Ace and torch the entire Underground, but that didn't guarantee anything. Their rebellion relied on an undertrained princess and an amnesiac prince to bring two continents to their side. Somehow, that was supposed to intimidate Leon enough to force him into a peace treaty.

Ancestors save them.

Chapter 31

Keston

"What happened?" Leon's voice shook the entire cavern, even if he was only a projection.

In her pool carved out of the rock floor, Ace sat with steam rising around her, covering most of her modesty. She was the picture of calm in her lounge, built into the tunnel systems beneath her favored city of Kyoto. Though built of all rock, the orange lights hidden behind natural cracks and uneven surfaces released a soft glow.

Leon's blue projection simmered with rage, but Ace downed her drink before responding. After a long sigh, she said, "Oh, Leon, you act like the war's lost."

"Someone within my ranks is leaking information to the press," Leon gritted. "The public suspects Richards Labs is behind the feral outbreak in Tokyo. Now there are speculations that my people were involved in Qin's death. This is not what we discussed."

Ace chuckled. "It's not what we discussed, but it is far more interesting."

"This is not another one of your games, Imani," Leon barked. "The war may not be lost, but things are now far more complicated. I'm not a fan of the odds if we lose public favor."

"Please, the Underground has power despite terrible public favor," Ace admonished. "We have power because people fear us. I see no reason why you couldn't wield the same influence."

Leon narrowed his eyes. "I would prefer to maintain my legacy and reputation. All you care about is riches. That's the difference." He paused, collecting his thoughts. "But we're not talking about public opinion. We're talking about your failure." His eyes moved to Keston for the first time. "*Both* of your failures."

Keston folded his hands behind his back to hide how his nails dug into his palms. "I had the situation under control until you sent Ace in to ruin nine months of progress."

"You let yourself get beaten by the Ronin—the same faction run by Asia's new Heir Apparent." Ace scoffed. "Qin was right to lose confidence in you."

"If you didn't use biochemical weapons, Sora wouldn't have turned against us," Keston shot back, uncaring if the Commander who'd signed off on the research to make Frenzy was listening.

Just the mention of that toxic drug had a cold sweat breaking out on his neck. He remembered the sickly indigo gas pooling in the twins' masks, watching them go feral before his eyes. Worst of all, he remembered doing *nothing*. He could've stopped the meeting at any point, but he didn't.

It'd taken Arianne risking her own sanity to save him from that situation.

There was no excuse. He'd frozen. There were so many variables and emotions that he'd shut down, trapped in indecision. Blackjack never had the emotional awareness to let things bother him, but Keston—and his fucking bleeding heart—did. And Ace, knowing all his weaknesses, capitalized on that.

It was all he could do to return to Ace's side and report back to Europe. But it was a necessary evil. He'd lost the twins and the chance at a new life in Selvia with Arianne, but it was all for good reasons.

Hopefully, he only needed to pretend for a few more months. The thought already had him wanting to drown himself in booze.

Leon turned his full attention to him. Keston tried his best to hide all emotion from his face, knowing he'd made a terrible career of keeping things from one of the most powerful men in the world. The look of disappointment from Leon was grating even to someone who'd never craved his praise.

"Biochemical warfare?" the Commander questioned. "I'm sorry, boy, but you added an unnecessary adjective. It's just warfare. We are fighting an enemy and must do everything possible to win."

"But the Constitution—"

"Don't tell me you've grown a conscience," Leon rumbled. "Let me remind you of your stellar track record, Leroy. You didn't care about the rule of law for most of your life, so don't start now. I'll also remind you that the ultimate goal of the Constitution is to keep Pangaea running. If I believe something threatens my Empire, it is my moral right as one of its rulers to take every action necessary to guarantee Pangaea's future. Understood?"

"Who would have thought we would be the good guys?" Ace tittered.

Leon pointed to her. "Get Asia into our folds. I would prefer to do this with as little blood as possible. If Asia refuses, we'll deploy the contingency. I am not a monster; I'll give them one more chance. But if they refuse, it is not my business to pity people who will not accept help."

Contingency? What did that mean?

The towering Commander's form winked out of existence, and the call ended. That was Keston's cue to leave. He marched towards the stairs leading to the upper levels of the estate that Empress occupied.

"Oh, Blackjack." Ace's singing echoed off the cave walls. "Where are you flying off to so quickly?"

He didn't stop. "With all due disrespect, anywhere you're not."

He'd only tolerated entering Ace's home base for that one phone call, and his skin was already crawling. He felt like he was back in Leonueva, a prisoner to Ace's whims. He wanted nothing more of it, so much so that he didn't care to learn how Ace had contacted Leon, or why she'd allied herself to him.

Acting as a double agent was one thing, but even he had a line he refused to cross.

"But Blackjack, we have so much to discuss," Ace cooed. "Your orders are to work with me, are they not?"

Annoyance burned painfully hot in his chest. He might just burn right through his clothes. He hated the way she spoke down to him. He hated that she kept him from the one person he wanted to be near. He *hated* Ace.

"Give me a call if Selvian operatives give you trouble," Keston growled. "Otherwise, leave me the hell alone."

His order was to protect Ace through the negotiations with Asia and the combination of Cartel and Empress. Essentially, Keston was actively cucked. He had to play guard duty while Ace usurped his hard-won Cartel legion.

"Are you not curious about how I took control of Empress?" Ace questioned. "Not even a little bit?"

"Depends." Keston turned to give her an ounce of his ire in a glare. "Are you curious how long it takes me to drown you in that fucking pool?"

Ace stuck out her lower lip. "Aw, Blackjack, I see we've gotten off on the wrong foot. But why? We're even! You ran away from me. I kidnapped your family. You stole Cartel from me. Leon gave it back. Now there's nothing to hate each other for—we have such a great chance for a lucrative business opportunity."

"Pass. Your money doesn't mean shit to me anymore. Daddy's credit card makes me richer than god, so you can take your fortune and shove it."

"There's more to be gained than riches," Ace called as he stormed up the stairs. "Don't worry, Blackjack! You'll come around!"

Ignoring her, he continued up the stairs into her private ground-floor office. He rushed through the traditional Japanese-structured room and the sliding panels leading to the hall.

Texas Hold'em stood guard outside. The Joker brightened when Keston pushed through. "Jack! You're back!" he said excitedly. "I'm so glad I get to work with ya' as friends again."

Without slowing, Keston grabbed the Joker's neck as he passed and threw him through another sliding panel door. It ripped like paper as Tex shot through, screaming the entire way. Keston didn't stop to admire his work, but he did manage a dark laugh. "Call me Jack one more time, and I'll do that from five thousand feet."

As soon as the sky was above him, Keston shot into the air toward his house before another Underground agent bothered him. Spending even thirty minutes in Ace's new compound had him feeling dirty, and he feared a long shower and a *lot* of mind-numbing drugs were needed to cleanse the disgust from his system.

But when he landed in his cottage's backyard, a shower was the last thing on his mind. His feet barely touched the grass before the slightest intake of breath sounded from inside. Fortunately, his Talons' brass knuckles were still on, so it only took a flick of his wrists to extend the purple plasma claws. Slowly, he crept into the house, prepared for the worst but secretly hoping a specific winged female had found him.

He was quickly disappointed.

Sneaking into his living room earned a scream from his guest. She quickly flipped on the light, blinding him momentarily. If the scent didn't give her away, her need for light did.

Arianne could see in the dark.

"Senny, what are you doing here?"

Sensatia Wolfe had taken cover behind one of his couches. Recognizing his voice, she poked her head out. "Keston!" she exclaimed. "Don't sneak up on people with—well—with whatever those are!"

Keston chuckled, feeling delightful levity at the nosy reporter's presence. "For future reference, don't sneak into people's houses."

She stood, adjusting her pencil skirt and blouse before flashing a house key. "I'm not sneaking. Cassius gave this to me."

"And why would my father send you?"

Sensatia fluttered her eyelashes. "He didn't want you to be lonely."

"Okay, and what's the real reason you came?"

Her expression immediately darkened. "Leon wants damage control on the Tokyo incident. And Genevieve," she trailed off, looking around.

"There are no recording devices."

With a tight nod, she continued, "Genevieve believes this isn't the last we've seen of Frenzy. She's also investigating Richards Labs. We know you have the Selvians' ear; we wanted to establish communication with you and the Selvians in case she finds anything."

Keston fell into the couch to his left, suddenly feeling painfully exhausted. "I assume you can't go back to Gen and yell at her for me?"

His sister had gotten annoyingly good at snooping over the past year. He wasn't even surprised she knew about his Selvian connections.

Sensatia frowned. "You know we're doing good work, Keston."

"Gen's a *kid*." He massaged his temples. "I can't let her get herself killed."

"Then help us," Sensatia begged. "You're already working with the Selvians."

He pointed a finger at the reporter. "Not the same. The Selvians are warriors who can protect themselves. They're also not living in the capital of Europe—within Leon's striking range!"

"She's not alone. She has the Pacificans' help. She said you would know them? Haris Cadmilus, Kalinda Bahri, and Jaya Bahri—kind of."

"Kind of?"

"Pandora has Jaya under a mind control apparatus that's some sort of control collar and Simulator combination."

Keston buried his head in his hands, fingernails stressfully scraping down his scalp. "Can I have just *one* fucking day this week?"

He lost Cartel. He lost the twins. He lost Arianne and the home she promised with the Selvians. Frenzy was loose in the world. He was working with Ace. And now Genevieve and Sensatia were actively participating in treason with the help of Arianne's not-so-merry island friends.

Sensatia sat and leaned into his side. "Sounds like you need a drink."

Three hours later and one too many drinks in, Sensatia and Keston leaned over the balcony railing of a Japanese brewery that overlooked the sloping hills of Kyoto. Keston was drunk enough to actually enjoy the traditional architecture and red-orange leaves stretching out below him. With a breath of relief, slumped against the wooden railing, he reveled in the numbness of intoxication.

What should he be worrying about again? Whatever, he would deal with it in the morning.

Keston didn't notice Sensatia had left his side until she reappeared, two glasses of local brew Sapporo in her hands. He gladly took the beer, happy to suspend the inevitable of consciousness a little bit longer.

A soft smile came to her face as she looked out over the village, lit by periodic yellow street lights. "I missed our nights out."

"I needed space," he admitted.

"Space from Europe, or space from me?"

Keston's mind blurred; the subject was a little too complex for his processing power at the moment. "All of the above."

Her shoulder brushed against his. The touch was unexpected and mostly unwanted, but he was too drunk to move. So he stared forward, doing his best not to acknowledge her closeness.

Then she put her hand over his. "I'm sorry I kept secrets. I knew we agreed to be a united front."

Keston squeezed his eyes shut. Another person who'd promised *together* had kept secrets from him. The perfect combination of liquor and recent events had reopened a wound he'd been unaware of.

Even if the feelings weren't the same, a partner of his willingly kept vital information from him.

The stinging in his chest got him to coax his body to scooch away. "We agreed to keep each other company, nothing more. You did nothing wrong. We weren't together."

For some reason, Keston needed to believe that now. If he and Sensatia *had* been together, that felt like a betrayal to Arianne. Sensatia should understand.

The terms of their agreement were that they'd betray each other for another chance with the loves they'd lost.

Well, he'd found his second chance. Even if it was a long shot, he was taking it.

Her hand slid off his with a shaking breath. "You're right." But even she couldn't make her words believable. "I guess... I just thought things had changed."

"We'd both just lost the loves of our lives. I thought we simply wanted to be less lonely."

"Doesn't mean there isn't room to care about someone else after them." Sensatia placed her glass down and spun her wedding band around her finger, eyes lined with tears.

"She's alive," Keston blurted.

Sensatia blinked in shock. "What?"

He shook his head, still in disbelief about Arianne's miraculous survival. "I only found out last December. She was Pacifican, that's where the Citadel Academy T-shirt you asked me about came from. I thought she died during the Drowning of Citadel—I was wrong."

"Who is she?" the reporter asked.

"No," Keston said. "That secret could get you killed."

"I know plenty of those."

Turning to her, he suddenly felt painfully sober. "Not like this one." He looked directly into her blue eyes. "This might be the greatest secret in the world. Leon oversaw her execution personally—it's that level of secret."

Sensatia took a long breath, processing the information. "So that's where you were for those unknown six months," she realized. "With her."

Sadness pierced his drunken haze, and he felt himself wilt. "Those were some of the best months of my life," he admitted. He stared forward, afraid the tears stinging his eyes would start to fall. "We had a seaside villa; my sister lived with us. We were *happy*."

"What happened?"

"Secrets," Keston said, head low. "Too many secrets. And then Pangaea attacked, and we realized we had different priorities."

"How so?"

He laughed. "I chose flight, and she chose fight." He ran his fingers through his lengthening hair. "Then, when I did choose to fight, I chose the wrong side."

"She was in Oslo," Sensatia realized. "You saw her in the battle."

"That's why I had that lovely public anxiety attack. I realized how much I'd thoroughly fucked up."

"And then Genevieve and I started working behind your back. You felt alone."

Keston nodded. "I don't want to be the bad guy either, Senny. At first, I thought I had no choice if I wanted to protect Gen and make something of my life after Pacific fell. After Oslo, I realized I made too many mistakes—possibly too many to come back from." He gritted his teeth. "And then Selvia gave me another option."

"It's all for her, isn't it?"

"I don't think so," he admitted, absently rubbing the scar Arianne had cut across his nose. "She woke me up, but I chose this. Even if I die trying, it feels better than serving those monsters for one more second. It's painful right now, but one day, I'll wake up knowing the life I'm proud of living was my choice—or I'll die trying."

At least, he hoped that was the direction he was heading. He didn't know how much longer he could live that double life without losing himself. Especially without Arianne. Especially without a guarantee that he could fix all the evil he'd caused with his hands.

He recalled those final excruciating moments with her just four days ago. She looked half-dead, moments away from passing out. Yet, despite the pain, she'd reached out to him. *Stay*, she'd begged. He almost buckled over at the memory, wishing he'd listened.

Stay. He was supposed to stay with her. He knew that. But he also knew he'd made too many mistakes—mistakes that needed correcting before he could ever hope to remain by her side. They needed correcting if he ever wanted to live with himself without enough drugs in his system to paralyze a, well, drug-resistant mutant.

Sensatia rocked back on her heels, sucking in a sharp breath. "I'm more of the same," she admitted. "I'm under no delusion that I'll survive this, but at least when I see Sebastian in whatever afterlife exists, he'll be proud of my choices. And if it means I get to see him sooner, even better."

Keston held his drink in the air. "Cheers to our wonderfully depressing lives."

Clinking her glass with his, she chuckled. "Cheers to seeing our soulmates again—in this life or the next."

Chapter 32

Andre

"Ugh, I despise clean-up duty," Pandora groaned as she leaned backward over the arm of her chair.

Andre ignored his fiancée, his attention on the cloudy sky beyond the jet windows. "This isn't clean-up. This is an important executive duty Leon entrusted to me." He felt himself straighten. "He trusts his Heir Apparent to smooth this out."

Pandora scoffed. "If Leon were taking this meeting seriously, he would've come himself. Face it, I only get sent places to blow things to pieces, and here I am."

"You're coming as back-up *if* negotiations fail, not when."

"Jaya, what do you think?" Pandora asked.

Andre turned in surprise, curious why Pandora was crazy enough to let the Pacifican rebel have free will on an outing to a highly charged meeting in Tokyo. He was quickly annoyed when he remembered Pandora's dark humor. Jaya had not been granted free will, but rather sat perfectly still at the back of the jet, purple-green eyes distant and glassy.

Pandora tittered. "Oh, right, you're not conscious. God, I miss Blue Krait. At least with her, I could have a few laughs."

"You're disgusting," Andre muttered, turning back to his window.

The cyborg appeared above his head. Stiffening, he prepared for an attack, only to be surprised when her arms wrapped around his neck in a hug—a hug full of affected affection, but a hug all the same.

"Aw, babe," she gushed. "Only a few more months and I'm yours forever!"

Andre rolled his eyes. On Christmas Day, he would be married to the only living heir of Leon Murray. Necessary, but that didn't disgust him any less. He hated the reminder he was going to be tied down to Pandora Richards; it was part of why he happily took the mission to Tokyo, if only so the reminder of Kalinda didn't follow him for a few days.

Her, Haris, Genevieve... Andre didn't want to think about any of it. He felt terrible for betraying Kalinda and Haris's trust, but he'd been backed against a wall. As for Genevieve, he was starting to suspect she had motives beyond kindness.

Somehow, a meeting with Ace and a semi-hostile Asian princess seemed more appetizing than another day in Paris.

On the helipad of one of Tokyo's skyscrapers, Keston and Sensatia greeted them. Though the winged male seemed right at home against the cutting wind at the top of the tower, the reporter clung tightly to his arm against the extra currents from the jet. Andre and Pandora shared a look of amusement.

But Keston wasn't laughing with them. His amber eyes were on Jaya, a sickly pallor on his face as he beheld her placid expression and ebony black collar. Andre had a split second to wonder what was happening inside the male's head: did he care for Jaya as Arianne's best friend, or was he imagining himself in her shoes?

Pandora looked between the two men. "Why do you two always look so miserable?" She pointed at Sensatia. "Please tell me you have *something* to lighten this dreadful mood."

Sensatia produced her tablet. The device never seemed to leave her hands in Paris, and it was oddly reassuring to see the pattern carry over into Tokyo. She projected an agenda above the tablet. "We have an exciting day ahead of us!"

Andre glowered at the schedule: a sushi lunch with Asian diplomats, an afternoon garden party at Lord Advisor Jin Shi's estate, and a night full of appearances at Tokyo's most elite nightclubs. Collections of different reporters and camera crews were invited to each event.

"It looks more like a media circus," he muttered.

Sensatia never lost her camera-ready smile. "Wars are won and lost in the public eye. We need to show the world that Europe and Asia are on good terms. If Europe's top Elites associate with Asian culture and big celebrities, it'll do wonders for our countries' combined image. It's also good press for your upcoming wedding, so make sure to hold hands in a few photos."

Pandora clapped her on the back, making the smaller woman flinch. "So you want us to eat food and get plastered? I can agree to that."

"I guess it would help smooth over tensions during our meeting with Mori Sora tomorrow if she sees how well we interact with her people," Andre reasoned. He had to agree with the plan, even if the idea of being affectionate with Pandora made his insides churn.

Keston, notably silent, nodded his head but still stole uncomfortable glances toward Jaya.

Considering the group, the day went relatively well. Sushi by the ocean was relaxing, even with cameras trained on their faces at every turn. Andre followed Keston and Sensatia's strangely touchy lead, taking a moment to occasionally hold Pandora's hand, which was as ice cold, or placing a kiss on her cheek, even if he had the urge to gag.

While not technically related, it was hard to erase twenty-five years of believing she was his blood sister. Plus, she was certifiably insane.

The garden party at the Okazaki Estate was understandably tense, but even Pandora was on her best behavior. Jin Shi was polite to the European Elites but only agreed to photos with Keston, claiming he only wanted photos with Asian Elites until tensions settled.

It was an irking reminder that Keston had spent the last nine months in Japan under the name from his father's Saudi heritage: Keston Al-Fayed. Of course, the male who had no interest in being an Elite had two prestigious bloodlines to pull from. Meanwhile, Andre, who wanted nothing but to step into Leon's shoes, had to fight to prove his bastard blood was worth a damn.

As despicable as Ace was, he found he understood her more and more by the day.

Unfortunately, the press tour had gone too well for his group's karma. It should've been obvious the second Pandora and Keston got alcohol into their systems that the evening would take a nosedive. As the sun set and they made it to the second club, Andre was painfully aware that a problem was brewing on his hands.

Sloppy was an understatement.

Sensatia sent the camera crews home as Keston and Pandora devolved into drinking competitions. From the way the saki went down like water, Andre knew he might need to pay to rebuild the nightclub out of the Murrays' personal funds. The only way to explain the desperate race to drink the bar dry was that both cyborg and avian were fighting more than a few demons—perhaps an entire horde.

Keston lay on the bar, Pandora pouring a steady stream of saki into his mouth as a large crowd chanted. Next to Andre, Sensatia watched the scene in horror. "Should we stop them?"

He shook his head, painfully aware that both drunken parties could overpower him even with a blood alcohol percentage twice the legal limit.

With the camera crew gone, there was one terrible way to de-escalate. Andre grabbed his mobile phone, raising it to his ear without taking his eyes off the trainwreck before him. "Hi," he said when the line picked up. "We have a bit of a situation."

Ace chuckled. "I never thought I would hear that sentence in such a monotone. Come on, Daddy. With your life experiences, I thought you'd be more exciting."

"Keston and Pandora are shitfaced."

"Oh, that is exciting. We don't want to miss that, do we? Give me half an hour."

Ace arrived thirty minutes later on the dot, flanked by her loyal second, Tex. The pair looked right at home at the nightclub with their classic Cartel techwear. Ace scanned the scene with a slight smirk on her lips. At that point, Keston was thoroughly entrenched in a game of darts...with Pandora standing unflinchingly in front of a dartboard.

"This is the calmest we've seen them in hours," Sensatia reported.

"Yeah, that's because they're throwing sharp objects at each other," Andre grumbled.

Ace cracked her knuckles. "What do all drunks enjoy?"

Both Andre and Sensatia stared at her blankly, not interested in her riddles or pretending they were friends.

She sighed. "Drunks like games. It's something we know I'm good at." She snapped, clicking her acrylic fingernails. "Let's go clean this up before it becomes another incident we need to take out of the newsreels tomorrow."

Seeing as Ace was the biggest name in the Underground, a fully furnished private room with a view of the club was booked with little more than a look toward the club's greasy manager. One glance at her infamous ace of spades tattoo granted them every accommodation possible: food, handles of liquor, and more drugs than Andre had ever seen—granted, he'd never been much of a partier.

They coaxed Keston and Pandora into the private booth with the most absurd tactic: a promise to play truth or dare along with a platter of Slime, weed, and cocaine.

"Listen," Pandora slurred, her head rolling like it was too heavy for her neck. "This better be quick. I have a meeting with a very pretty dancer in the bathroom in fifteen."

"As your media manager, I'll have to decline that request," Sensatia squeaked. "The last thing we need is a photo of the future First Mother of Europe having sex in a nightclub with someone who *isn't* Andre—honestly, no sex in nightclubs in general, please."

Andre shivered involuntarily at the thought. God, he just wanted to be Heir Apparent—not deal with superhuman drunks.

Keston passively chuckled, his skin notedly glowing a slight green. Great. He wasn't just a mutant powerhouse, but one who was thoroughly cross-faded off Saki and Slime. Hell of a team Andre'd made for himself.

"What's so funny, Birdbrain?" Pandora barked.

The winged male giggled again. "I love it. We're all sitting here pretending we don't actively hate each other's guts. It's hilarious." He almost fell over as he reached for a handle. "And to that I say: let's fucking drink."

Ace had already poured herself a glass. "I couldn't agree more. Now, does everyone know the rules of the game? You pick someone and ask if they would like to tell a truth or do a dare. If they fail to do the activity, they finish their drink."

Andre stiffened. "We're supposed to be sobering them up."

"I agreed to get the chaos out of the spotlight, not stop it." Ace took a sip, grinning ear to ear. "Here, I'll start with something easy: Andre, do you love Roulette?"

The prince glared at her. "Yes, I just don't love her mother."

Keston spat out his drink. "You don't like Kalinda?"

"Oh, you idiot boy," Ace said. "You still don't even know what you don't know."

Keston blew a raspberry. "*Touche*, asshole." He sat back, his eyes rolling as he slurred, "I know things too—"

"Okay, that's enough," Andre said, not keen on Ace spilling the secret that could threaten Kalinda and Rou's safety. "It's my turn now, right?" He looked at Pandora. "Okay, similar question. Did you ever love your siblings? Me or Ari?"

"Siblings?" Sensatia asked softly. "Who's Ari?"

Keston fell to her side, his laughter turning into hiccups. "I'm not the only one in here who's clueless."

Pandora's glowing blue eyes were dead as she stared at Andre. "Pass. Give me a dare."

"That's not fair, you've already done every possible dare in the book," Andre spat.

She shrugged, picking up a bottle of Saki. "Fine, then I'll finish my drink." After finishing the bottle, sitting back up proved to be a herculean effort. Closing one eye, she did her best to point at Sensatia. "All right, I chose the Tabloid Tramp."

Sensatia's ever-present smile faded into a frown. "Thanks."

"I've been called 'Bastard Bitch,' so consider your name a step up," Andre offered.

Keston shrugged. "I don't mind Birdbrain."

"All of you, shut up!" Pandora waved her arms manically. "I have my question. Okay: why are you working with us?"

Sensatia shrugged. "Leon sent me to Tokyo to improve the press on Eurasian relations."

"No," Pandora corrected. "What are you *doing* with us? You're a social climber, a pretty face built for vapid columns about what fancy Elite is banging who. What are you doing with us, covering important stuff that will put ugly little wrinkles on your perfect brow?"

The reporter's mask dropped, not wholly, but Andre clocked the moment her perky personality faded. Sensatia looked to Keston, though the male was too far gone to share any meaningful look back at her.

She took a shaking breath. "I lost my husband, and I uncovered too much dirt looking for him. Leon offered me a choice: this job or my life." She shrugged. "I guess once I pulled the curtain off the shining world of Pangaea's upper class, I couldn't look away and pretend the next fashion trend of the season had any semblance of importance."

Andre finally saw the beautiful reporter for who she truly was. He was amazed when they locked gazes, and she gave him the same look of understanding. Maybe he'd underestimated her. Just like she could've returned to the riches and celebrity, Andre could've remained in Pacific, sitting on a beach and ignoring the world. But they both chose differently.

Maybe he wasn't alone after all.

Sensatia then turned to Keston, her intelligent eyes seeming to connect some concerning information. Her perfectly shaped lips parted, like a thought lingered just behind them, and she debated whether to let it out.

But this was Sensatia Wolfe. She'd made a career out of asking those very questions—no matter how damning.

"I knew Andre was originally considered Pandora's sibling. I didn't know there were more, but you didn't seem surprised when Andre mentioned two. So Keston: Who is Ari?"

The air left the room. All attention snapped to the drunken male; everyone terrified he might reveal too much, but morbidly curious about what he would say. Keston had always been extremely guarded about Arianne—rarely mentioning her and shutting down whenever the subject was broached.

Rumor had it, they'd been lovers. When Andre had almost killed Arianne on that abandoned highway in Madrid, he remembered Keston's heart-wrenching screams. Those hadn't been the wails of a mission partner. Those were the sounds of a broken heart.

Keston's face reflected similar heartbreak as he had that night on Andre's birthday. Slumped in his seat, the bottle rested on his thigh as he stared blankly forward.

"She's my greatest regret." Keston's voice cracked, amber eyes glassy and unfocused.

Sensatia sat back, her eyebrows shooting to her hairline. "You loved her."

Andre expected her to sound jealous. Instead, she seemed stricken. The reporter didn't say more, silenced for a rare moment as her eyes darted back and forth, processing.

From Keston's response, he wouldn't love anyone more than Arianne. And for that, Andre's heart skipped a beat. Arianne's death was one of his greatest regrets as well. But that was in the past, and he was tired of mourning things he couldn't control—it took away from the present.

That was how he would outmatch Keston, who was burdened by past events out of his control. Andre had no such weakness. Not anymore.

Keston let out a long sigh. "I left her to die. I promised her '*together*' and abandoned her to die alone fifteen minutes later." He shook his head, mortification breaking his drunken stupor. "Then, I worked for her executioners. Why did I think anyone could forgive that?"

Pandora waved off his obvious spiral. "Water under a drowned city," she said casually.

Citadel.

Keston raised his head from his hands. "Fuck you for that, by the way."

"My pleasure," the cyborg purred.

Ace leaned back in her chair, her tattooed face bored. "If I'd known this game would get so depressing, I wouldn't have bothered coming out tonight."

Her voice seemed to snap something in Keston. Suddenly focused with terrifying intent, his mouth was a hard line as he yanked his sleeve up to reveal his ace of spades brand.

"I have a question for you," Keston said, staring at Ace through a few stray strands of hair. "Was there any part of you that felt bad? Did any *molecule* in you regret what you turned me, a *child*, into?

She didn't hesitate. "I regret not finishing the job. It hurts to see how close I got to making you the most powerful asset in the Underground, only to see you crumble under something so trivial as emotion."

Keston stood and marched toward Ace, though the walk was hardly intimidating as he stumbled on drunken feet. Stopping directly above her, his scowl could've frozen summer. Andre prepared to jump in case the liquid courage gave Keston *too* much courage, and he slaughtered Ace on the spot.

"I'll give all of you another truth for free." Keston's whisper dripped with venomous loathing. He pointed at Ace. "I promise, when the reaper finally comes for you, it will wear my face."

Pandora let out a low whistle that turned into a laugh. "Shit, Birdbrain. Can I use that later?"

Keston turned away, his face dark. "I'm leaving to see my girlfriend."

"Um, Keston? I'm right here." Sensatia looked around the room nervously. "He must be really far gone."

Keston paused, blinked in confusion, then gave the reporter a look that could only be described as disappointment. "Oh...right."

Ace, hardly phased by a death threat from one of the most powerful mutants in the world, passively stirred her drink with her straw. "Blackjack has a good point, I've seen enough. Time to head home."

Andre moved to help Pandora to her feet, glad for an excuse to finally return to their hotel and get some sleep. Despite some minor objections, he managed to get her to follow Sensatia and Keston, who also struggled to walk in a straight line.

"Prince. Stay." Ace ordered. "Texas Hold'em, make sure we're not disturbed."

Tex walked past with a gloating grin. As the hallway door closed behind him, Andre's blood froze. Alone with Ace. He turned and wasn't excited to see her smirking at him in the neon pink haze.

"I don't recall you being ranked high enough to order me around," Andre said.

"Funny, seeing as I helped get you that rank."

Ace watched him, still as stone. All levity had left the room with Keston and Pandora. Andre was intimately aware he was now alone with the Underground's recrowned apex predator. She'd always carried power, even in her months in hiding, but now there was a different air about her—more unapologetically potent.

Andre clenched his fists. "And for that, you'll get what we agreed on. In time."

Ace absently shook her head. "The game's changed, and so has my price."

"That doesn't work. We had a *deal*. You make me Heir Apparent, and I give you a share of the power when I become Commander—legitimize your industry, scrape your criminal records. I've already convinced Leon to work with you again. I've already deployed my forces to help you win back the Underground. There is nothing more I can give you right now."

"Then you can add my silence to the debt you must repay. Now, prince, how much is the Commandership worth to you?"

Andre shook. "Everything. You know this."

"Worth your sister?"

Bile rose in his throat. He didn't like to think about the horrific image of Citadel Hospital collapsing before him. His knees weakened as his mind forced him to relive the agonizing powerlessness as he watched his sister's demise. Time. They'd never had enough time. He'd thought he'd trained the grief out of him, but there he was, trembling in front of one of the most influential people in the world.

"Arianne's in the past," he ground out. "I'm worried about the future now."

"Is she, though?"

His mouth dried out. "What?" He wasn't proud of the fragility of his voice.

Ace stood, her towering frame walking to the suite balcony to look out over the packed nightclub. Glistening with jewelry, her hands extended across the railing as she exhaled. "I wasn't certain until tonight, but now I *know* what I saw last week in the Lang penthouse."

"What did you see?" he demanded breathlessly.

Ace turned her head just slightly, fingers thrumming on the railing. "A ghost. I still don't know how much Blackjack knows—he might've only found out last week as well."

"Arianne..."

That time, she turned completely. Her face lacked any sign of levity as she lowered her brow to look at him severely. "Phoenix is an interesting Champion name. Do you know what a phoenix is? A legendary winged creature that dies amongst ashes and comes back stronger each time. Sound familiar?"

He had to grip the couch beside him. "No. That cannot be possible."

"I don't know how she's pulled off surviving her death twice, but I know what I saw." Her eyes darted back and forth in consideration. "The moment before I ran, she took her mask off to save *Blackjack*—her supposed enemy. The infamous Phoenix risked her entire mission to save him. It was her, nothing else explains it. Blackjack's behavior tonight confirms it."

"The truth or dare," Andre realized.

"I was hoping the press schedule I suggested to Sensatia got him intoxicated enough to slip up."

He was still too stunned to process the tornado of emotions spinning inside him. "You were just seeing things. The room was in chaos."

No. Arianne couldn't be alive. He'd watched the hospital fall on her. Right?

"And if I wasn't?"

Andre wanted to say he'd run to his sister. His first reaction was to find her and finally make things right. But he stopped himself. If Arianne were alive, it would ruin all his plans. To make matters worse, if his sister was a Selvian Champion, then she was fighting to destroy Pangaea. She was a terrorist who'd ransacked Tokyo, Oslo, and Mexico City. Arianne was once again a weapon primed against the Murray family—different allegiance, same vendetta.

Phoenix was his enemy. And if Phoenix carried Leon *and* Josephina's blood, she had the strongest claim to the European throne. One word from Arianne about their family's infidelity problems, and Andre lost *everything*.

And if Arianne were alive, she would have forced him to mourn a false death *twice*.

"There you go," Ace said as she watched Andre's face darken.

"What is the price of your silence on the rare chance Phoenix is who you say?" the prince rumbled, aware of how quickly he could lose his throne again.

Her broad smile made her look like the Cheshire cat in the hypnotizing neon lights. "If Phoenix *is* Arianne, I want her—Blackjack too."

"Not possible. Blackjack isn't mine to give. He's a Leroy, the future Reigning Elite of Paris."

Ace walked to him, reaching out to hold his chin with a softness he knew too well. "Now, that's not good enough. Answer me this: who's the most powerful person in the world?"

"A Commander."

"No." Ace frowned. "*Think*. Angels walk this earth again, Andre. Two near-heavenly beings are emotionally attached. Simply looking at strength, speed, healing, and martial training statistics puts both of them at the top of the mutant world. Together, nothing can stop them. Leon knew that two years ago. Why do you think he *ruined* them? The most powerful person in the world has just become the one who controls the matched set—a royal flush."

He narrowed his eyes. "And why would I give that to you?"

Her fingers pulled him close, and she kissed him, slowly and tenderly. For some reason, he let her. When she finally pulled away, her smile was the opposite of the heavenly power she coveted. "Because if they're in my hands, they'll never be in Leon's. The more power we withhold from Leon, the more choices you have. If Leon refuses you his Commandership, we could rise to the top together—a new era of rulers, blessed by the angels themselves."

"Just like the kings of old." He shook her hand and kissed her again.

Chapter 33

Keston

K eston woke to the sound of vomiting from the bathroom.

Pandora. He groaned, rolling over in his sheets to cover his ears. The sun hadn't even risen yet. While Cindy's effects had worn off, and his metabolism took care of the hangover, nothing could counteract an abysmal two hours of sleep.

"Go die somewhere else," Keston grumbled into his pillow.

His complaint was answered with a nausea-inducing string of dry heaving.

He managed to close his eyes for a bit longer, but his fitful sleep was soon ruined by the unwelcome arrival of the sun. Keston and Pandora gave half-conscious curses to whoever threw the blackout curtains open, but the two were too exhausted to do much more.

"We leave in fifteen," came Andre's no-nonsense voice.

Was it lack of sleep, or did he sound more irritable than usual?

Pandora raised a cybernetic arm from where she lay in her bed, as if it were a coffin. "Remind me how many sick days we get a year?"

Andre threw her tactical suit and polyester armor plates on the bed. "You used them all after almost dying in Oslo."

"I was a prisoner of war," she wailed. "That doesn't count!"

"We're meeting with the future Commander of Asia to prevent an alliance between Asia and Africa that could wipe Europe off the fucking map," Andre barked. "You're both getting dressed and looking your goddamn best—I don't care if your sweat is pure alcohol."

Keston experimentally licked his arm. He wasn't proud of the results.

Andre slammed the door, leaving the drunkards to pull themselves from their slumber like zombies. Without the hallway's fresh air, Keston gagged at the rancid smell. The entire room reeked of alcohol and vomit, the combined scents doing a number on his sensitive nose.

Now he understood why he'd been quarantined with Pandora.

But he didn't remember returning to their hotel, nor did he recall changing into nightclothes. Keston looked down in mortification at Arianne's blue Citadel Academy t-shirt. Sensatia must have put it on him. But where was she? What happened? He remembered pounding music, bar tops, dancing, and the haze of a private suite lit with a soft neon glow. If he concentrated, hazy snapshots came into focus: blurred dancefloors, a dartboard, and a painfully familiar tattooed face.

He shot up, the sudden movement making him dizzy. "When did we see Ace?"

Pandora tried to roll out of bed and fell face-first on the floor. "Shit. I think I'm still drunk," she said, voice muffled by the carpet.

He ignored her, carefully removing Arianne's t-shirt and folding it neatly on his bed. Once the shirt was safe, he hastily got ready. Seeing as Pandora wouldn't be off the ground any time soon, he had no qualms running into the bathroom in just his boxers.

He showered quickly, careful to keep his wings out of the stream of boiling water—spending an already miserable morning with wet wings squeezed to his back would not be pleasant. His outfit was: flexible dress pants, a stretchy button-up, an armored corset, and a jacket to hide his wings. Presentable enough for a diplomatic meeting, but with enough mobility if diplomacy failed. Tying his hair back and leaving a few strands to frame his face, he was ready for another day of acting.

Somehow, Pandora arrived at the hotel's helipad just as the jet landed, wearing sunglasses and palming a pint of beer. No one dared question her, though Keston did risk a small laugh.

She flipped him off as she boarded.

He realized just how startling it was to see her hangover. Pandora, with her strength and lethality, had never felt human to him. It was shocking to see her with human weaknesses: mutant strength but no mutant metabolism—caught in a terrible in-between. Not quite *Homo fera*, but had certainly left *Homo sapien* behind.

Alone.

Keston didn't have long to consider Pandora's depressing disposition when he saw who waited on the jet: Ace and Tex. He stiffened at the entrance to the pristine lounge, eyes narrowing as she smiled at him in greeting.

"I'll follow the jet. I want to stretch my wings," Keston grumbled, turning to jump off the gangplank, which was already closing for takeoff.

Ace rested her head in her hand. "But we had so much fun last night. Don't you remember?"

"I'm glad I don't."

"Stay, we need to discuss specifics," Andre ordered.

Scanning the rooftop, he noticed Sensatia—the only person in the group he could tolerate—was absent. With a huff, he continued walking. "Any conversation with Ace in the room isn't a discussion, it's her game. I know how to play my part just fine. I don't need to breathe the same oxygen as her."

Ace's gloating chuckle echoed in his ears the whole flight. Even the ripping wind currents couldn't erase the haunting sound.

Mori Sora chose to meet at a small seaside village. Keston supposed he didn't blame her. After her last encounter with Ace, the princess likely wanted to minimize as much risk as possible. Their jet landed on a stretch of sandy beach, the waves of the Pacific Ocean lapping eagerly beneath the wheels. Keston gingerly flew to the seagrass a couple of dozen yards from the water, careful not to ruin his shoes.

He was already antsy; he couldn't deal with wet sand in his shoes, too.

The Europeans approached, greeted by a squadron of unmoving Ronin, all in black ninja attire with cowls over their faces. The Ronin seemed out of place in their dark uniforms in the morning sun. The group parted down the middle, revealing a shorter figure dressed in an identical uniform. They removed their cowl, displaying Sora, ready for combat.

Ace crossed her arms. "These do not look like typical Wards."

Sora's face was hard as stone. "Excuse me if I do not trust men loyal to my brother to meet with a woman who caused a massacre in one of my largest cities."

At the hostility in her tone, her squadron of Underground agents crouched into defensive positions, hands hovering over the hilts of their swords in unison. No Ronin spoke; they stared forward like obsidian statues waiting for their sculptor's orders.

Andre stepped to the front. "Mori Sora, I'm sorry we have to meet under these circumstances." He modeled a perfect prince as he bravely moved between the tense groups. Andre extended a gloved hand. "I am Andre Murray. I hope we can speak as equals and reach an agreement that will put this entire situation behind us."

Sora considered his hand, a scowl growing on her face to match the hardness in her eyes. She didn't move to meet him. Instead, she turned and waved for them to follow her. A feast was already prepared at a restaurant that seemed to be completely cleared out. Scanning the beach, Keston noted the lack of smells, sights, or sounds since landing.

Sora had evacuated the entire village.

Taking her position at the head of the table, Sora gestured to the seats that lined a stunning spread of rice, noodles, dumplings, and fish—lots of fish.

Keston had to fight from drooling as he sat, suddenly painfully aware he hadn't eaten that morning. At his side, Pandora took one look at the fish and gagged. Andre shot her a warning look, but she looked too green in the gills to care. Ace and Tex pointedly sat as far away from Sora as possible.

Andre sat next to Sora, starting his speech before he even pulled his chair in. "Thank you for having us—"

"Let me make one thing clear," Sora cut in. "The only reason I am entertaining a meeting like this is because I was raised to believe in the Constitution. Unlike my brother, I value the strength of Pangaea as a whole. War between continents will only harm our people."

"Exactly," Andre agreed.

She glared at him. "I wasn't finished." Her dark eyes tracked to Ace. "Whether Commander Murray played a role in last week's events is not important right now. But, if we are going to hope for peace, we want her as penance for her crimes against Asia."

Ace pouted. "It was just business, dear."

"*Just business?*" the princess asked shrilly. "Three hundred people: dead. One hundred: wounded. Twenty: missing."

Sweat pooled in Keston's palms. He stared at his half-finished plate, the food he'd eaten settling like a rock in his stomach. Hundreds paid for his mistake. He cursed himself for not acting sooner. He felt responsible for the lives he'd been forced to take in that disaster—and the lives Arianne took in the rampage she'd suffered to protect him.

Andre's shoulders grew stiff. "I'm sorry about what happened, but Imani Azikiwe is not yours to claim. There must be another way Europe can repent for this accident."

"I see no accident. I see the logical escalation to letting chaos run unchecked. Empress and Cartel are scourges, cesspools of crime and decay." Sora's glare locked on Ace like a trained sniper. She dared to point a finger at the crime boss. "She controls them. I created the Ronin to uproot the Underground. Now that I have the power of a Commander, I intend to finish the task."

Ace scoffed. "You ungrateful brat. The Underground existed before I was born, and will be around long after I die. Even this *perfect* empire you imagine will have its trash, and that trash tends to pile up together. At least with me, I keep things in order. Without order, the Underground will fracture into hundreds of factions, constantly at war. I am a necessary evil Leon has learned to appreciate, and you will too—in time."

"You expect me to be grateful for a massacre? For a drug that leaves mutants living in fear?"

"Yes." Ace stood, upper lip curling. "You should be grateful for the control I've granted you over creatures who, left unchecked, will overpower your rule and crash your economy."

Sora, proving Commander's blood coursed through her veins, ignored Ace completely. Turning her head to Andre, her silky black hair shimmered in the sunlight. "You understand you're not in a position to argue with my demands."

That even got Pandora's attention. She'd been slumped in her chair, possibly sleeping behind the protection of her sunglasses, but now she sat up at Sora's barely blunted threat. A small smile of anticipation came to her pale lips—excited for chaos even while violently hungover.

Something seemed to short-circuit in Andre as his trained diplomacy fought with the urge to lash out—something Murray's, even adopted ones, did well. He attempted to fold his hands on the table before speaking with ever-thinning patience. "And what exactly do you mean, Your Highness?"

Sora leaned in, as if she were about to tell her royal counterpart a secret. "You need Asia to fight your war. My brother was bloodthirsty enough to agree without question, but I will not help you. So now you have two options: comply with my requests, and my continent will not interfere, or disobey and add another enemy to your list. A Commander who condones the crimes of the Underground is against the Constitution and is, thus, against me."

The Ronin surrounding the table tensed at their leader's charged words. Keston's wings prickled in warning.

"I do love it when children attempt to make demands," Ace cooed. "It's adorable."

Frowning, Keston remembered Leon's mention of a *contingency*. He scrutinized Ace, recognizing her overconfidence. She was a good bluffer, but Keston knew she rarely needed the trait. If she was looking at her hand and smirking, she had a damn-fucking-good hand.

Andre ground his teeth. "Europe and Asia have been close for decades. Don't let that relationship die with your mother."

"I have no interest in participating in a relationship with a continent that turns a blind eye to biochemical weapons."

"It's a shame," Ace hummed. "We tried to do this civilly."

"I could say the same. Seeing as Europe will not hand you over willingly, I have no choice but to take you by force."

And like those words were the ringing of a dinner bell, the feast quickly became an ambush. A figure rocketed out of the water, droplets raining down from her wings as she blocked out the sun. As Arianne dove toward the table, any hope of diplomacy was shattered.

Chapter 34

Arianne

A ce died *today*.

Shooting into the sky above the water, she watched Khari emerge from the waves they'd both hidden under and charge the beach. Colla's Circus burst from the restaurant. The Ivory Court sprang from their spots hidden amongst the Ronin, all wearing matching black robes and cowls. From Arianne's birds-eye-view, she had a moment to marvel at the ambush and how quickly they surrounded the Europeans.

Europeans, including her siblings. Her brows furrowed, but she forced herself to ignore Andre and Pandora. Crossing them in combat had always been possible, but she still struggled with the sight. Instead of letting her siblings ruin her focus, she targeted her dive bomb toward the one person at the table she *didn't* have mixed feelings about: Ace.

She'd just prepared for a corkscrew that would tear Ace's flesh from her bones when a blur shot to intercept her. The feathered mass moved at blinding speeds, clipping her shoulder. She barked in surprise, forced to shift the angle of her wings to gain altitude and keep her balance.

Finally righted, her attacker rocketed toward her again, dark wings glistening in the late morning sunlight. Keston. Of course, it had to be Keston.

Her stomach lurched when his arm hooked around hers and sent her tumbling through the air. As she flipped, she was ashamed that the feeling of weightlessness wasn't from losing altitude. Her body reveled in Keston's touch, even if the touch had sent her spiraling.

"Get it together, dumbass!"

"What was that?" he called. "I couldn't hear you over the sound of me kicking your ass."

"Keston!" Arianne screamed—as had become their usual script.

Naturally, he laughed. She had to take a moment to remember they were in a very important big-girl fight. He looked like an angel with broad wings flapping behind him, catching the sunlight. And his smile, which had become so rare for either of them, looked like the sun.

"Sorry, Princess. I can't let you down there."

Ignoring him, she utilized her speed to nose-dive to the beach below. Somehow, Pandora's Bubblegum Battalion had arrived. The ambush had devolved into a skirmish, with the Ronin camping out in the restaurant while the Ivory Court and Circus tried to hold their positions behind a sandy bluff. Europe held its own in the middle, but if Arianne could get down there, she could tip the scales—

Keston's shoulder collided with her, sending her spiraling again. She wasn't proud of the screech that left her lungs as she careened into the ocean, unable to capitalize on her speed. Fortunately, her aquatic side instantly kicked in, preventing her from inhaling too much saltwater. Her webbed fingers allowed her to break the surface within seconds. Water surrounded her in sparkling droplets as her wings caught her upward momentum and happily compensated.

He yelped as Arianne slammed into him, hardly expecting her rapid recovery. She locked her arms with his, a move Sygrid had used on her many times in their aerial sparring matches. The extra leverage had him off balance as they flew higher and higher.

"Enough of this bullshit!" Arianne screamed. "We need Ace. Why are you stopping us?"

She'd come a long way from believing Keston was evil, but she could still be pissed at him. He might have his secret objectives with Sygrid, but now he was getting in the way of her mission, and Arianne had zero tolerance for failure.

As they continued upward, Arianne was reminded of a painfully similar scenario from their trapeze act—an act she hadn't stopped thinking about. Keston didn't fight her, accepting the embrace. From the strain on his face, she feared he was thinking of the same thing.

"You guys need to retreat. Right now," he finally said, amber eyes going to the beach in concern.

Pushing away from him, she looked down at the battle. It'd reached a standstill. No one dared attempt to penetrate the circle of Puppets around the Europeans, each primed with plasma blasters and their backsides protected. Even if someone was lucky enough to break the line of automatons, Andre, Tex, and Ace were ready to strike them down.

Pandora lounged in her chair, boots propped on the table. She nursed a cocktail, complete with an umbrella on the rim, looking unbothered in her sunglasses. But her lack of engagement was hardly reassuring.

They would risk very high losses if they attempted to break the Bubblegum blockade. But that was a chance all parties had agreed to take for a shot at three of Europe's largest assets.

Arianne shook her head, her gaze returning to Keston. "It's not going to happen," she snarled. "This is our best chance. Ace needs to die for what she did."

They could also take the others as prisoners, which would give them the edge in negotiations they needed to win.

Keston didn't budge.

"I get you need to keep your cover. You can pretend to go down," she insisted, even if she hated the idea of him returning to Europe.

"That's not it. Ace is too calm. Leon didn't even care enough about the negotiations to come himself. They have something. I can't let Asia declare war on Europe until I *know* what they've planned."

That familiar heat of frustration burst to life in her gut. Ace ruined lives, profited off pain. Andre betrayed Pacific, returning to Leon after *everything* he'd learned. And Pandora was, well, she was Pandora, and that was reason enough.

"I don't care," Arianne spat.

He flew toward her and arrested her in a locking hold. She was crazy enough to let him, still disarmed by his closeness. Finally, high enough to escape the cloud of Mist coating the beach, she could smell him. His scent drifted around her, intoxicating in its familiar citrus and sandalwood. Fingers gripping her, her eyes rolled for a moment as she fought the way her heart began to pound. Suddenly, the ambush below was a hazy memory—a thought left trapped at the back of her head.

Keston shook her lightly. "Leon mentioned a contingency. I have no idea what he meant, but it can't be good. If Asia pledges to Africa and the tribes too soon, we might worsen the fallout."

The wind buffeted her ears as they separated and hovered a thousand feet above the beach, too high for anyone to hear them. God, she hated leadership. If they killed Ace and took prisoners, it would send an obvious message about which side

Asia was on, dooming them to whatever alleged contingency Leon had planned. But if they retreated, they would lose a rare opportunity to hit critical targets.

What was worse? How much weight did she put on Leon's ability to plan for multiple outcomes and wreak havoc?

A lot of fucking weight.

"Okay, how do we do this?"

Keston looked delighted. "We do what I do best: pretend. I'm going to chase you out. Follow my lead."

She crossed her arms. "That's just going to make you look good."

"A bonus." He beckoned her. "Apologies in advance, I'm going to have to make this believable. Make sure to make the landing look convincing."

"Did I ever tell you how much I hate you?"

"All the time, Princess. Don't stop, I'm starting to enjoy it." He yanked her in and started falling.

There was no time to retort. Nearing the beach, Keston twisted to throw her. She braced, anticipating the release and resulting full-body bruise she'd wake up with tomorrow. As soon as the weightlessness hit her, she extended her wings just enough to slow her fall, but not enough to prevent a believable crash-landing.

The earth shook as Arianne slammed on the beach, sand exploding around her. Her unhealed arm took some of the recoil, even though she'd aimed to land on the opposite side. She'd have to get the bone reset later. Her team's shouts barely registered as she fought to right herself, crawling out of the crater she'd made.

Rhino's powerful arms looped around her shoulders and pulled her behind what remained of the bluff.

"Phoenix, are you okay?" Topher asked, already reaching into his first-aid supplies.

Arianne winced, body screaming in pain. "It looked worse than it was. We need to retreat."

Colla knelt at her side. "You stay here, we'll finish the mission."

"No!" she ordered through gritted teeth. "Keston gave me intel in the air. He believes Europe has a hidden play. Asia can't declare war, and capturing the Heir Apparent is certainly a way to start one."

Spitting on the ground, Khari's frustration manifested in crackling electricity around his arms. "I'm not listening to anything a doublecrosser says."

Arianne ignored her fiancé, pointing to Lova. "You're the only one fast enough to get to Sora. Tell her to retreat, *now*."

Lova zipped off without a word.

There was a sharp drop in blaster fire in their direction. She fought her body's complaints to inch her head around the bluff. The Europeans retreated down the beach with the humans still in the middle of their circle of Puppets. Keston hovered over them, primed to intercept any pursuers.

With a shaking breath, she slid down the sand. Moments later, the rapid thunder of dozens of feet ran across the beach toward her. She had a moment to collect her thoughts as Sora and her Ronin rounded the dune, flanked by Lova.

Sora threw her hands out in frustration. "What the hell happened?"

"Europe has something up their sleeves," Arianne said, shaking her head. "Keston warned me in the air: Europe doesn't care if you join them. They're hiding something big."

"Ace's actions harmed hundreds of my citizens," Sora protested. "I need more than just speculation to let her get away."

Arianne called on all of Sygrid's diplomacy lessons to keep herself from screaming at Sora. "Justice can wait. Asia needs to keep Europe in negotiations for as long as it takes for Keston to learn more about Leon's contingency."

Sora clenched her fists. "I want Ace to pay."

"Then get in line. That motherfucker *sold* me. You don't see me throwing away diplomatic strategy to get revenge, at least, not anymore." Arianne scanned the Ronin, Ivory Court, and Circus before taking a long-suffering breath. "Ace is the type of scum that always finds a way to slither out of consequences. We cannot throw everything away just to chase her."

With a patient smile, Colla rested his clawed hand on her knee. "Then, what do you propose we do, Young One?"

Staring at the sky, she wished to see Keston's shadow above, circling lower and lower before he joined them. He would be able to explain everything. But most of all, she just wanted him at her side. As politics got increasingly complicated, all she craved was the reassuring feeling of his hand in hers.

"Selvia will publicly take the blame for the ambush," Arianne decided. "Sora will apologize for the escalated tensions and deny a connection to the tribes. If we do this right, Asia will be as much the victim of the ambush as Europe. Then we pray Leon buys it long enough for us to get answers."

"It could work," Colla said. "You could use the attack to feign a reassessment of your allegiances. Leon might not buy it completely, but it might be enough to keep him from activating this supposed contingency for a little longer."

Sora pointed in warning. "We had a deal: Ace for Asia's troops. This delay had better be worth it."

Arianne scowled, respecting the bluntness but still chafing at the disrespect. "I made this decision for your people," she said lowly. "Leon already has the Selvians on his hit list, so I was trying to keep you from joining us."

"You forget Asia has the largest military in Pangaea."

"And yet, Leon doesn't seem to care. That should *scare* you."

"And is the deadly Phoenix scared of Commander Murray?"

Forcing herself off the ground, Arianne stood above Sora and cast the shorter princess into shadow. She felt her upper lip curl. "I'm *terrified* of him," she admitted. "And you should be too."

Sora turned to the Ronin, shouting a few orders in Japanese before returning to the *Feras*. "You'd better hope you're right about this," she warned one last time before marching in the opposite direction down the beach.

Sora wasn't the only heir frustrated with Arianne's decision. Khari watched the Ronin leave with thinly veiled frustration, his arms lined with black Champion paint, crossed and tense. "You better not be mixing emotions with the mission, Phoenix."

Arianne bared her sharpened canines at her betrothed and rival. "You're hardly the one to be making comments on that subject. As I recall, you helped your mentor perform a coup because he'd raised you like his son."

A dangerous hush fell over the group.

His light blue eyes slowly tracked to Arianne, the ire in his gaze warning of an impending storm. "Funny how I'm still here, fighting for *your* mentor, selling *my* body in an agreement that means I can never love someone else. Did I miss anything, *my love*?"

Her fists clenched. "I'm in the same agreement as you."

Leaning in, electricity sparked between his clenched teeth. "And yet you're up dancing in the sky with your ex-boyfriend—swapping stories, plotting plans."

"Jealous?" she snarled.

Khari grabbed the front of her leathers, pulling her close. Their noses almost touched over their glares. Arianne could smell the sea salt on him, along with the confusing mix of emotions that shifted his scent in a thousand directions. Anger, frustration, exhaustion—there were more, but even her nose wasn't sophisticated enough to recognize them.

"Classic Arianne: gets to do whatever she wants and gets no consequences," Khari bared his teeth.

"Classic Khari: is an asshole to everyone, then gets disappointed when no one wants to be his friend."

"I'll challenge you for Deputy, and then we won't need the engagement."

Arianne laughed in his face. "And you'll lose with—" She turned to count the Ivory Court and Circus. "Twenty witnesses when I drop you from two thousand feet."

Deciding that it was time to intervene, Blue stepped between the warring heirs, her face one of classic boredom. "Okay, let's save the dominance battle for later. You've both been cheating on each other. We have bigger fish than the two of you to fry."

Arianne heeded her friend's words and took two healthy steps away from the male she was two seconds away from slaughtering. But she didn't take her eyes off him as she snarled, "Europe's using biochemical weapons. If your dad still needs an engagement to stay in this alliance, we have bigger problems than who we're sleeping with."

Khari took a lunging step forward, but Topher and Rhino held him back. "What the hell does that mean?"

"It means if your dad is only fighting in this war to gain me as a bride and not because Europe is actively breaking the Constitution, then we might as well add him to my kill list because his values are just as fucked as Leon's."

Khari roared, hardly subdued by the males holding him back. He surged forward with an accusatory finger, sparking with electricity. "My father risked everything to give me the best chances possible. He sent me to the tribes so I'd have a chance at a normal life! He remarried after my mom died to have other heirs, so I was never forced to leave Selvia if that's not what I wanted. He's fighting this war—risking his continent's resources—to protect *me*."

"Everyone, stand down," Colla interjected, his deep voice calming like rumbling thunder on a summer night. He extended his clawed hands toward both feuding heirs. "Tensions are high. Now is not the time to turn on our allies. Arianne is right: we should not start a war between Europe and Asia without all the facts. Khari, we are not questioning your father's intentions, but if neither of you is happy, then maybe it's time to reassess this engagement."

"We all know the engagement isn't just for an army," Khari heaved. "It's for amnesty. If Selvia's leadership and African royalty are connected, both factions can legally protect the other in the event of a loss."

Arianne sighed, feeling her frustration fade. "I know," she admitted. Colla was right. Her emotions had gotten the best of her. Again.

"Then we have no issue." Colla looked between them. "Right?"

The bitterly betrothed both nodded.

"Okay." Colla took a calming breath. "Then let's discuss the next steps. Pharaoh, return to Egypt and update your father's inner circle on today's events. The Circus and Ivory Court will remain in Japan on standby. Any problems?"

Feeling like she was being scolded by her dean back at the academy, Arianne could only nod with the rest of her team.

"Is now an inappropriate time to recommend we stop for lunch?" Rhino asked, pointing to the abandoned feast. "It would be a shame to let it all go to waste."

Khari didn't remain in Tokyo longer than it took to shower, pack his things, and board a jet back to Africa. He and Arianne hardly managed two words in the hour they'd been in their shared suite at the Okazaki estate since the mission. While she wasn't happy with how they left things, she was relieved to be alone in her bed again.

Nights with Khari the past week had been tense and uncomfortable.

Arianne's *condition*, which she was still hesitant to acknowledge, made even sleeping next to him difficult. When he touched her, her body's rejection was far more intense. An activity that'd once been a mutually enjoyable experience for them now felt grating and impossible to withstand. She'd tried her best to pretend, but something told her part of Khari's frustration with her at the beach had come from her unmistakable lack of enthusiasm in bed.

Khari just *wasn't* Keston. She'd always known that, but now something inside her screamed that sentiment whenever he touched her skin. It was maddening trying to hide such deep-rooted rejection. At least she was alone for the time being.

Carefully rolling onto the bed, her right arm throbbed from resetting the bone for the second time in two weeks. She held the cast above her face to inspect how her fingers swelled and conceded she needed to rest. Granted, being thrown to the ground from hundreds of feet up—even if it was an act—hadn't helped her already tumultuous healing process.

Thanks to her injuries and a stressful afternoon preventing a war between Asia and Europe, it didn't take long for her to pass out.

She burst awake to the sound of her window curtains shifting. The sun had set, and the room was now cast in silver moonlight. The scent of the ocean hit her. A window had been opened. But she *never* opened her window when she slept.

Without hesitation, Arianne rolled off her bed, grabbed the knife on her nightstand, and threw the blade at the shadow creeping in. Ducking behind her bed, she braced for a return assault. All she got was a very familiar yelp of surprise, one that almost broke her eardrums and likely alerted the entire estate.

She lifted her head just enough for her eyes to glare at Keston from over her bed. "You really have to get those sonic screams under control."

"Are you going to apologize for almost skewering me?" He yanked the dagger out of the wall where the blade had caught the fabric of his jacket. "This is a brand new windbreaker, by the way."

"That depends. Did you come to apologize for ruining my mission? I took a lot of fire for covering your ass."

Even the sight of him had her heart pounding. She purposefully remained behind her bed, needing the physical barrier between them. She could barely think straight. All she wanted was to touch him, but she held back. With such a tense political situation, she couldn't afford to blur the lines any further.

Keston dug into his jacket pocket. "Don't worry, I brought a present. It's not flowers, but I think you'll like it." He tossed over a flash drive. "I can't stay long; your brother thinks I'm on a night patrol. Sensatia Wolfe gave me that drive. It has all the information she's gathered on Project Frenzy. Maybe your people will find something we couldn't."

A twinge of jealousy crept into Arianne. Sensatia Wolfe was the reporter who was often photographed at Keston's side. Were they working together behind the scenes as well?

She frowned as she considered the drive. "How much does the reporter know?" *Come on, give me a reason to kill the bitch.*

Keston sucked in a breath, and she tensed—his tell when he was hiding something. His words were careful. "I didn't tell her anything. She's working with my sister. They've been operating within Leon's Inner Circle on the surface. Behind the scenes, they've been hunting down and spreading information."

"Does she know about me?"

"No," Keston shot out quickly, but then corrected with a wince. "Senny is smart. She knows how to dig up things that do not want to be found. She knows I had a relationship with someone important, that someone is still alive, but nothing more."

"Senny?" She shouldn't have been surprised; her and Keston's relationship had been well-documented across Europe. But that didn't dull the sting. "And news flash: she knows too damn much. She needs to go."

"She's fighting the good fight, Ari."

"I don't care."

Keston opened his mouth to retort but quickly stopped, a devious smirk spreading across his lips. "You're jealous," he sang, stepping away from the window and toward her bed.

She inched away from him, terrified of what she'd do if he got too close. "No, I'm not," she shot back too defensively. "I'm explaining fundamental espionage rules: if someone is pretending to be dead, you don't tell people about it!"

"Look at you: your face is getting red." His shit-eating grin only broadened as he waltzed around the bed, hands held mockingly behind his back.

"No, it's not!" Her retort was shameful. She crawled onto her bed, attempting to maintain the distance he kept trying to close. "Hey, don't you have somewhere to be? You gave me the drive." She gestured to the window. "Now shoo."

But he just crawled onto the bed after her, which only made her heart leap directly into her throat. The urge to kiss those smirking lips became overpowering.

"Come on," Keston pouted. "You don't see me complaining about the other person I smell in here. Though I should."

Khari

"Political negotiations."

He inched even closer, and she'd reached the headboard. Above her now, his hands braced over her head, Arianne's eyes widened. She resisted every urge to tear off his jacket and witness the muscles working underneath to hold himself up.

Keston was in her *bed*.

"We can call this 'political negotiations' too," he whispered. "Think of this as part of my incentive to keep bringing you information."

Before she could reject, Keston kissed her.

As much as she would've liked to believe a part of her resisted him, she'd be lying. She arched upward to deepen the kiss, her body bursting to life. So many emotions crossed her mind, bringing tears to her eyes. After the Frenzy incident in downtown Tokyo, she didn't know when she would see him again. And then, earlier on the beach, she hadn't let herself believe they could be anything while he was still working for Leon.

But there he was, kissing her as passionately as she remembered. He'd come *back*. She let herself embrace it, for as long as they had. In those fleeting moments, she didn't let herself think about everything unanswered between them. Right then, she simply focused on how amazing it felt to let go.

Keston groaned against her lips, never breaking their kiss as he scooped her up and shifted her into his lap. Positioning herself above his hips, her hands now freely roamed through his long, curling hair like she'd done countless times before. His hands found the sensitive feathers closest to her back, and she gasped in shivering pleasure as he touched her in ways only another avian would know how. Eyes rolling back, she reveled in his corresponding low laugh against her neck.

She placed her own kisses down his stubbled cheek, over his sharp jaw, and down his neck. It was warm and tasted like salt, and her heart fluttered at his sigh. Hands wrapping around her back, he pulled her closer as her kisses deepened. She couldn't get enough, *taste* enough, of him. The feeling of his touch was like rediscovering an old addiction—it made her wonder how she'd ever gone so long without him.

"If you asked me to stay right now, I wouldn't be strong enough to say no," Keston breathed as his lips found hers again.

Before Arianne could respond with her damning plea, the overhead lights in the room flashed on. Both mutants, running on night vision, screamed in unison at the burst of light and jumped away from each other.

Blue watched the scene, hand on the light switch, and a serpentine smile on her face. "All right, time to break this up."

Arianne whirled on her. "Excuse the *hell* out of me, but do I ever walk in on you and your guests?"

Blue shrugged. "The invite was always there."

"Not the point," Arianne snarled.

"Sorry, Blue. I'm not interested in a third at the moment," Keston said, propped up on an elbow. "Maybe we can revisit the prospect later."

Blue's yellow eyes gave him an assessing once-over. "You're not my type." She turned her attention back to Arianne, making the Deputy—her superior—wilt. "You're aware his voice woke the entire estate? It was all I could do to reroute everyone in the building away from this room so they didn't hear the two of you being hormonal dumbasses."

Arianne fluttered her eyelashes. "I take it back, you're the best."

"Listen, do whatever you want. I'm not going to get in the way of whatever messed-up situation the two of you seem to be getting off on. But do it in neutral space, not my parents' estate, goddammit."

Keston was no longer listening. He'd begun absently playing with Arianne's hair, eyes half closed as he smiled at her. The longer she spoke to Blue, the more distracted she got with his unyielding gaze. She struggled to focus as Blue lectured on about the diplomatic issues of one of Leon's Inner Circle members sleeping at a Selvian stronghold.

Only every third word registered, her tunnel vision seeing only Keston as she dared to inch closer to him. He smiled, slowly doing the same.

"Hey." Blue flickered the bedroom lights on and off. "Focus! I'm not above making both of you take a venom nap."

Holding Arianne's chin in one hand and waving Blue off with the other, Keston said, "Hey, I totally understand where you're coming from. Can you give us, like, two minutes?"

"You need to go," she said flatly, pointing at Arianne. "I'm doing this for you."

Those words were like ice water to the face. Arianne blinked, snapping out of her daze. Like ripping sap out of her feathers, she jumped off the bed before she could chicken out. Painful or not, it needed to be done. Keston watched her go, his face betraying the hurt he felt at her rapid change in emotion. Though it was instantly colder without his touch, she forced herself to retreat further.

Blue was right. Too much was at stake. Sora and Khari were already questioning her decision-making, and she couldn't look conflicted now.

"Arianne?"

Arianne couldn't look at him. "She's right. I'm a leader. I must set a good example. The tribe comes first, especially now."

If her suspicions were true, and somehow her body had chosen Keston as her mate, then she'd set herself up for a tough road. But both Cavalier and Sygrid had lived their adult lives without their mates. It wasn't desirable, but it was doable. And to protect the people she cared about, she would do it.

He looked to Blue desperately. "Give us one minute. In one minute, I'll be gone, please." He caught himself and rolled his eyes. "And before you say anything, yes, I last longer than a minute."

Eyes darting between them, Blue slowly nodded. "One minute, Birdbrain. Then I'm back in here, and you and I both know you don't want another dose of my venom."

Keston nodded, and Blue cautiously stepped outside, closing the door behind her.

Arianne's breath caught as he ran to her, taking her hands in his. "Do you remember our deal? I help you get Qin, and you humor me with a date. A *normal* date, like back in Greece."

"Keston—"

"No take-backs, you owe me," Keston interrupted with a crooked smile.

She couldn't look him in the eyes. "We're just going to keep getting hurt if this keeps up."

"I thought you hated goodbyes."

"I do, but—"

His nose nudged her. "Well then, stop saying goodbye. We always find each other. Why keep fighting it? No matter how unlikely the odds are or how long it takes, we always find a way. Leonueva, Porto Cheli, Citadel, Oslo, and now Tokyo. And when we say goodbye in Tokyo, we'll find each other somewhere else. So why not enjoy being in the same city for as long as it lasts?"

Because it's only going to hurt more when we have to return to reality.

But she couldn't get herself to say those words out loud.

Keston's eyes were beautiful as he looked down at her with more hope than she'd seen from him in years. "One date," he pleaded. "You can choose the venue. It doesn't matter to me as long as we're together."

"Okay," Arianne relented, unable to resist the chance to see him again.

Even if it meant saying goodbye would hurt so much more that time.

"You can find me in Kyoto. I have a private property there on the outskirts of the town, miles away from Ace." He listed an address, and Arianne quickly committed it to memory. "I'll see you in one week, right after Andre and Pandora are scheduled to return home. How does six o'clock sound?"

She couldn't hide her excited smile. "I'll make sure to wear a dress."

His lips pressed softly against hers. She closed her eyes, savoring every stolen second. She felt him pull away, but refused to move, pretending he was still right there with her. When she opened her eyes, he was gone, disappearing into the shadows he'd called home since long before they'd met.

Chapter 35

Andre

When Leon returned from the battlefront, it should've been obvious it wasn't for a break. There was only one reason why the great Commander of Europe had removed himself from his passionate Spartan leadership.

After his return from Tokyo, Andre had relished in one day of peace within the Palace of Versailles. Pandora had disappeared to whatever Parisian loft she'd called home, and Hera was overseeing her Puppets on the front lines. For a few lovely hours, he'd been alone in the ancient halls of his future palace. He'd savored the quiet: taking his time roaming the long corridors and familiarizing himself with the place he'd been told for twenty-five years was his birthright.

Most of his life had been spent in Leonueva, where he rarely visited the original capital, and he was determined to make the palace as comfortable as the Murray Monument once was to him. While the Murray name was no longer his by default, he was certain he'd worked hard enough to earn the honor. In some ways, earning the position was more satisfying than having the legacy placed in his lap.

But the peace of his most recent successes was short-lived with his father's arrival.

The front doors of the palace burst open. Leon stormed in, clad in his military uniform of shining badges, a flowing half-cape, and pristinely shined boots. Most would assume that his perfectly kept uniform meant he'd been watching the war from behind the front's fortified barricades, but his sword told a different story.

His broadsword, *Lion's Fang,* was an infamous heirloom passed down from Murray to Murray. Since it'd been promised to Andre as a child, he'd coveted the finely crafted leather hilt and glinting light blue steel. He would marvel at the craftsmanship whenever he visited Leon's private study. Even Arianne hadn't gotten the honor of holding the blade like Andre had. *Lion's Fang* was the mark of a Murray.

The sword's blade was created with lightweight and porous steel crafted using methods forgotten during the Great Disaster. The pores collected the blood it spilled, allowing it to display in a collection column in the middle. With each life taken, the sword grew redder. It was equal parts spectacle and warning: what every true Murray aspired to be.

Lion's Fang's inner column was shining crimson red.

The wielder of that sword walked toward Andre now, eyes dark and face determined. Had he not grown up idolizing such a man, Andre may have wilted. A *lesser* man would have wilted, but he refused to believe himself a lesser man any longer. He was the Heir Apparent, the man destined to carry *Lion's Fang* in Leon's wake. It was good to remember his status. So he stood straighter as Leon approached, ready to steer his boat through his father's impending storm, confident in his sails.

He offered a slight bow. "Father, you return."

Cassius Leroy had informed him an hour before the Commander's landing in Paris. Leon had returned to conduct an investigation. The vagueness of the message didn't bode well for the palace—or his father's mood. Andre only hoped he wasn't somehow on the receiving end of Leon's rage.

Tokyo hadn't gone perfectly, but the unsanctioned attack by Selvian forces had forced Sora to reconsider her stance in the war. Though not a success, it was far from the failure he'd walked into Tokyo expecting.

Leon stopped before Andre, his scared face menacing when combined with *Lion's Fang* strapped across his back. "Where is Pandora?"

The first comment that came to Andre's head was something along the lines of mentioning the revolving door of women and booze passing through her riverside loft apartment. But he bit back on the retort. Anything weakening Pandora in Leon's eyes weakened Andre now.

"She received your message. She's most likely on her way."

Cassius appeared, his sides heaving. Most people struggled to keep up with Leon's long strides, and the short-statured Parsian was no different. The Lord Advisor tapped his wrist watch, and a map of Paris appeared, including a turquoise dot shining next to the Seine River. "She's still at her apartment, Your Majesty."

Leon huffed. Andre stared at the location, the scar on his wrist throbbing. Had they put a tracker on Pandora? When? After she'd returned from Pacific or before? He stilled. Did he have another tracker he didn't know about?

"Andre, tell your fiancé to be in my study in fifteen minutes," Leon said, turning away. "I need a briefing on her previous mission in New York."

"New York?" Andre questioned.

New York was a wasteland, and from what he'd heard, Pandora's mission there had been cut and dry: a massacre that'd started the war with the tribes. What else was there to review?

Leon paused, turning his head just enough for Andre to see his scarred eye. "Was I not speaking English?"

A cold sweat broke out on Andre's back, and he quickly pulled up Pandora's contact information and called her. Cassius fumbled after Leon with similar urgency. It seemed everyone in the Inner Circle knew what to do when the Commander was in one of his moods: move your ass.

Pandora knew that rule, but she'd become less inclined to heed it in the past year. "*What*," the cyborg barked when the call connected. "We're not married yet, so I don't need you monitoring my every move."

"Leon's back."

"Yeah, I got Cassy's message. What I didn't get is why it's my problem."

Even though she couldn't see it, Andre rolled his eyes. "Leon wants you in his office in fifteen—make it fourteen since you took so long to pick up."

Her exhausted sigh was concerningly soft. "Who does he want me to kill?"

"He wants an old mission briefing. New York."

"The report is filed. Cassy will have it in one of his fancy color-coded folders."

"*Pandora*," Andre hissed.

"Oh." There was the distinct sound of shuffling on the other line. He heard a zipper sliding and a door closing. "Leaving now."

Pandora and Andre had never been the best siblings—they were even worse as a couple—but that was one understanding they always held dear. She didn't typically listen to Andre, but that particular tone meant Leon was in a mood neither wanted to ignore.

Even Pandora respected it. After Arianne left them, they were all they had. It was an unfortunate alliance, but valuable in extreme times.

Andre repeatedly eyed his watch until the doors to the corridor flew open. Pandora sprinted up the stairs with a minute to spare. Her feet still smoked, indicating she'd used her rocket boots to fly the distance to the palace. Andre waited at the top of the steps, the timer on his watch ticking down the remaining seconds. He fell into step with her as they walked the remaining meters to Leon's private office together.

Leon paced before the window of his study, a set of rooms he'd combined and modernized. Most would scold the modernization of European history, but Leon had repeatedly shown that he didn't care about scandalized Elites. Unlike most rooms in the palace, the study was spacious. The walls were white instead of the ancient-looking yellow, which brightened the open space. Andre enjoyed the feel; it reminded him of the Murray Monument.

As the prince and princess entered, Leon's eyes flashed. "I shouldn't be kept waiting."

Pandora frowned at the sleek floor before his glass desk, her eyes going to the scuff marks his newly waxed boots had left. "Yes, waiting seems to increase the risk of you wearing tracks into your floor."

Andre stiffened, convinced she had a death wish at that point.

"I don't have time for your attitude." He reached onto his desk, producing a familiar silver headband. "I need to access your memory from the Librarians' stronghold in New York. The Simulator should show me what I need."

Seated on a white loveseat, Cassius nodded eagerly.

Glowing eyes growing wide, she accepted the headband from her father. "It's not a pleasant video," she warned.

Was Andre crazy, or did she seem wary? Was she hiding something? Or was she afraid of reliving the destruction she'd wrought? He watched her carefully as she placed the headband across her temples. If she didn't want to see what she'd left behind, did he?

The room shifted, the bricks of a dark underground tunnel rushing past as Pandora and her Bubblegum Battalion ran. The room moving around him while he remained stationary was a strange feeling, especially when accompanied by the echoes of boots on concrete. It was enough to give him vertigo.

Then light washed in up ahead. That's when the screaming started. And blood, lots of blood. The Bubblegum Battalion took the lead, rushing ahead in a swarm of white polyester armor and flashes of pink hair. Caught completely off guard, the Librarians were helpless to stop the assault.

Their shocked looks quickly gave way to fear. Few reacted quickly enough to fight back. The ones who tried to retaliate hardly knew how. The most terrifying detail was how *normal* the Librarians looked. They donned simple jeans and t-shirts, carried books and plants, and wore gardening gloves and glasses. From the reports, Andre had expected a militaristic rebel faction, not regular civilians.

"Jesus," he whispered.

Even Cassius seemed stricken by the video. "We don't need to see this part," he ordered tensely. "Fast-forward to the facility sweep after the targets were neutralized and the Selvians retreated."

The video glitched, shifting to a cavernous space with a hole in the ceiling leading to a library above. But the main focus was what hung from the first-person perspective of Pandora's hand: an antlered head, severed from its body. Bile rose in Andre's throat. He'd never seen the former Selvian Ductor, but the whole world had heard the Legends enough times to recognize Cervi's famous ivory antlers.

His hand went to the chair at his side for support, invisible with the vision playing around him. It wasn't regret that he felt—Cervi was a terrorist, the leader of the Selvian War, who deserved to pay for her crimes—but he was shocked to feel the weight of the scene. That was the moment that'd started a war. Anyone would feel the pressure of such an event if they saw every silver-haired detail.

Pandora lowered her head and summoned her Battalion. Together, they moved throughout the Librarian stronghold, conducting a routine search. Spare a few holdouts, the initial assault had wiped out the entire Librarian population. The holdouts didn't survive much longer: Pandora didn't enjoy taking prisoners.

The video's subject moved to Keston. He was crying on the ground, his sister clutched to his chest. Genevieve was limp, her eyes closed. Tears streamed down Keston's face, leaving trails in the blood splattered across his cheeks. When the male looked up, his bloodshot eyes were distant and glassy. He hardly acknowledged Pandora as she passed, his head dipping back down to bury itself in Genevieve's wild curls.

Andre's heart constricted. He knew that distant look too well—he'd felt it when he'd watched the hospital fall on Arianne. It was the face of a brother willing to do anything to protect his sister.

Leon was unmoved. His only reaction came when Genevieve appeared, his brows furrowing. "Your report said Keston found his sister in an infirmary? Did you investigate?"

Pandora shrugged. "Not much to find. Keston killed the doctor who'd put Genevieve in the coma. But I couldn't find any known anesthesia drug or anything on her brain scans to indicate a reason for the condition we found her in."

"Show me," Leon ordered.

The walls blurred as Pandora scanned the hallway up to the infirmary. The glass doors were broken and bloody, a few stray feathers indicating who'd desperately slammed his way inside. Only one observation table and an ancient-looking computer monitor were housed there. Sparse medical equipment was left discarded on the ground. The luminescent light above the table flickered, casting the crime scene in a light worthy of a horror movie.

Motionless on the floor, blood pooled from two gunshots to the doctor's head. His eyes stared emptily at a silver tray next to the observation table. Pandora seemed to follow the doctor's line of sight, and she investigated the tray. Her cybernetic arm picked up a syringe, spinning it to observe the empty vial.

"We searched the lab," Pandora said. "There was no indication of what was in that vial. Like I said: the medicine cabinet had no answers. Any intravenous medication I found was either not opened or would not induce the effects we observed in Genevieve."

"Toxicology reports came back negative as well," Cassius reported.

Leon sat on the edge of his desk, chin resting on his knuckles as he watched his daughter's memory. He'd been strangely still as the video scanned the lab, his face intensely focused.

As the video turned to leave the infirmary, Leon stood, seeming calmer than before. "That's enough," he said easily. "I've seen everything I need."

Pandora removed the headband, restoring the room to pristine white. "What?"

"I can't believe I missed such a critical detail," he rumbled.

Cassius sat ramrod straight, his green eyes staring forward in horror. "Your Majesty, I don't understand what my daughter has to do with this—"

"I don't suspect you would," Leon cut his Lord Advisor off. "You and Pandora are dismissed. Andre, come with me."

Following Leon to Hera Richard's lab in the palace's eastern wing, Andre didn't dare speak. In the late afternoon, the laboratory was packed with white-hooded scientists and engineers. Even without Hera's presence, the three stories of equipment, offices, and holding cells were a bustle of organized chaos. Monitors, test stands, chemical cabinets, and machines he couldn't even begin to name surrounded him in neatly-kept aisles. If Hera's brilliance and manpower didn't explain her lightspeed research, her organization certainly did.

Richards Labs was a tightly run machine.

"Dismissed for routine inspections," Leon's voice boomed. "The lab is closed until tomorrow."

The ant colony of researchers stopped instantly, all heads turning toward the god who'd just graced them with his presence. Some researchers actually knelt. Others watched wide-eyed from where their heads poked out from the balcony above. Leon frowned at the hundred scientists, unmoving. They quickly got the message. They scattered, closing down test stations, cleaning up chemicals, and returning research subjects to the holding room.

Haris Cadmilus was one of the researchers who ran past, recognizable because his quilled hair made it impossible to don the infamous lab coat hood. The Porcupine rushed past Andre, sharing one charged glance before disappearing. Even Haris, with all the courage he'd shown the past year, wasn't brave enough to stand in Leon's presence for longer than a breath.

In ten minutes, the entire laboratory was eerily empty.

In the silence, Andre finally risked the question, "Now what?"

If Leon was looking for information, he didn't need to clear out the entire lab. The Commander came and went as he pleased, and, seeing the reverence the researchers held for him, they would hand over any information he asked for.

Hands folded behind him, Leon walked to the back of the lab. He patiently pulled out a rolling chair from a researcher's blueprint-cluttered desk and took a seat. The rolling chair bounced under the Commander's weight, and Andre found the movement oddly humanizing. Unfortunately, there was nothing human in Leon's preternatural stillness.

"We wait," Leon said, gesturing to a seat behind him.

Andre didn't speak again. He sat down, crossing his long legs underneath the desk. And he waited. They sat until the lab's motion-sensing lights turned off, leaving them lit only by the sparse lights on the machines that were left running. Then they waited longer. At that point, Andre was too scared to ask what they were waiting for. He looked down at his watch, noting it was now past six. His stomach grumbled.

And right when Andre was about to jump out of his skin for sitting in silence for so long, the laboratory doors opened. Leon didn't move, watching from the darkness in the back of the lab as one figure rolled into the room. Suddenly, Andre knew what they were doing: staking out.

For Genevieve.

The girl pressed the switch near the lab's entrance, turning off the motion-sensing lights. Andre perked up. Whatever she'd come to do, she didn't want to draw attention.

Everyone knew Hera didn't have cameras in her labs—no one wanted evidence of what went on getting out. The only videos that came from those labs were from specific experiments, and those recordings were hidden behind so many clearances that even Andre had trouble accessing them.

Leon analyzed her, still as a lion watching its prey move closer and closer into its striking range. The anticipation on the Commander's face said he was ready to pounce, but still he waited.

Andre looked between them, wondering what the Commander wanted from her. His father's intentions were definitely far from good. But Genevieve had become like a friend to him in those past months. What could possibly be wrong?

Genevieve logged into a computer. Her freckled face reflected the screen's slightly green glow as miles of encryptions and code streamed across. The girl's fingers furiously flew across the keyboard, moving with a mechanical efficiency that rivaled the device she was hacking into.

Hacking.

Since when did Genevieve, a teenage girl studying economics, know how to hack through military-grade firewalls? Since when did she need to?

He looked to his father for confirmation, but Leon was transfixed. Watching the girl work, a look of excited interest bloomed on his face. Andre frowned, realizing he hadn't seen that expression since the days of Arianne's experimentation. He'd learned to dread it.

Genevieve's work was finished with the distinct sound of her finger pressing down on the *Enter* key. She turned the computer off, removed her wristwatch, and smashed it to pieces on the keyboard. Next, she grabbed an alcohol sanitizing bottle and dumped the contents out across the shattered watch and keyboard: erasing her fingerprints.

Andre bristled. She'd been so kind to him, had made him believe she was on his side, helping him secure his position with gentle nudging and information. But sneaking into his palace's labs and destroying evidence pointed to far more sinister allegiances. Genevieve had never helped him. She'd been helping herself.

But why?

Reaching to his side, Leon drew a blaster from his hip. Andre gaped, but didn't have time to protest before the shot went off. The plasma illuminated the room as it rocketed toward Genevieve–

–And continued past her head to hit the light switch near the door.

The room burst into light, illuminating the predators in wait.

Genevieve's initial fright faded faster than expected in a teenage girl. After just one reactionary flinch, the girl straightened and turned to the gunman, who could've killed her, with more composure than some of his best-trained Wards.

When she frowned, her expression was oddly reminiscent of Leon. "I knew my time was limited when I heard you were returning to Paris."

Leon holstered his blaster and sat back in his chair, looking uncharacteristically relaxed. "I'm surprised you didn't attempt to escape."

"I'm merely a bishop in this game. My sacrifice is worth it if it means the other pieces can get closer to the king."

"That's where you're wrong." Leon chuckled darkly. "The knowledge we carry makes us grandmasters, not pieces on the board."

"Yet, here I am playing." The girl smiled. "And the play I just made wouldn't have happened if I ran. I may be out of time, but so are you once this information gets out there."

The Lion of Europe stood, taking his time to reach the lamb, who didn't even attempt to run from his fangs. "Oh, I remember my first year on the Serum," he hummed, clearly delighting in her continued defiance. "The world opens to you in the brightest technicolor. The knowledge at your fingertips is unlike anything you were ever able to *conceive* as a mere mortal. The power goes to your head quickly."

Her face was strangely serene. "So you figured it out."

"I'm offended you thought I wouldn't catch on."

"The Serum?" Andre whispered. As the pieces fell into place, he looked to Genevieve. "In New York? How? Why?"

The betrayal hit him harder than expected. All that time, Genevieve had been like a confidant—an apprentice. He thought he was teaching *her* about royal life, and in return, she gave him level-headed guidance as a third party. He thought they'd developed a friendship as future Commander and Lady Advisor. But she'd had the Serum running through her veins the entire time, her whispers in his ears so quiet he hadn't even realized they'd been orders.

Andre glowered and reached for his double-bladed sword. He would kill her for this. He was slowly learning that the only good Leroy was a dead Leroy.

"Go ahead," Genevieve said. "I made peace with this outcome when I calculated its likelihood."

Leon's laughter was deep and rumbling. He held his hand out, stopping Andre mid-stride. His sword stopped in the air with trained stillness, ready for the order.

"You think you're so smart," Leon continued. "You're smarter than you ever dreamed, so you fail to dream more. You fail to consider that there is more to unlock." He leaned forward and tipped her chin up with a finger. "You forget I'm you plus a quarter century of experience, girl. Good try, though."

"Your dirtiest secrets are leaked. The history of Pangaea—the true history—I carry is already spreading. It will all destroy what little hold you have on the world." She narrowed her green eyes in his grip. "The world will hate you, and everything your Commandership stands for. There is no winning now."

"You would have to unearth the depths of hell to dig up all my secrets. As for your threats, they make my life easier: I no longer have to play nice. In a way, I should thank you for saving me the trouble of bending to popular opinion." He shrugged. "It would have been nice to have their love, but Ace was right. I'll do just fine with their fear."

"No one will fight for you now," Genevieve snarled.

"Maybe not for patriotism, but I have a few ideas," Leon countered. His smile was devoid of humor as he tapped her forehead. "And something tells me you'll give me a couple more. The Commanders always speculated there was a version of the Serum that held the secrets from before the Last War, and now those secrets are at my fingertips."

A gasp of terror escaped Genevieve's lips, eyes growing wide.

"Checkmate," Leon said. "But I must credit you for playing a good game. You almost had me duped, almost got away as the mole in my palace. Alas, you are not me, girl. I suspect you even calculated I would kill you before I could think to use the gold mine in your brain, but you forgot one crucial detail."

Her upper lip curled. "My calculations have always been perfect."

"You forgot I let you win every chess game we played," the Commander said, and the temperature in the room seemed to drop twenty degrees. "You're brilliant, Genevieve, but you're not me. I'm sorry your rebel friends have to pay for you to learn that little lesson."

Her freckled face paled.

Leon snapped his fingers at Andre. "Take her to the isolation tank—I find the Simulator works best when the subject has no external stimuli."

Picking her up out of her wheelchair, an ounce of the young girl hidden behind the Serum finally surfaced. She gripped his arms with cold fingers, eyes darting with terror. "Andre," she breathed. "Andre, you have to stop this. He can't—"

"I'm tired of everyone lying to me, manipulating me," he growled to her. The betrayal he felt at her lies came through in his voice. "All I wanted was to lead, to do a good job. And I thought you wanted that for me too—I thought you were different."

She struggled in his hold. "I do want what's best for you. But you have to see that you won't lead anything good. Not like this."

"I'm not listening to you anymore."

"*Kill me*," the girl wailed.

But Andre had stopped listening. Everyone tried to control him. Everyone thought he was the idiot in the room, lying to him and playing with his emotions. Well, he was done. If Genevieve was Leon's key to winning that war, so be it. Screw promises and morality; those hadn't gotten him anything but manipulation. He would help Leon win that war, and then he would inherit the highest power in the world.

No one would look down on him then.

Despite Genevieve's struggles, she was relatively easy to carry. The isolation chamber was a coffin-shaped structure with a foam and mesh mattress. Dropping her on the mattress, he forced her arms and legs into the stability straps. She was screaming blood-curdling cries now, but he didn't listen. He'd gone numb. This is what he had to do.

"Andre! Andre! Kill me! Kill me *now*! *Please kill me now!*"

He didn't respond as he lowered the hood of the isolation chamber and pressed the button that released the coma-inducing fog. The ringing in his ears only faded when Genevieve's screams were silenced.

Leon appeared behind him, his arm wrapping proudly around Andre's lean shoulders. "Good job, son. I cannot wait to see what secrets she's holding, secrets that will win us the world for our future generations to inherit. With all the knowledge of Before and now, the Murrays no longer need to stop at just one continent. With this, we can rule it all, as the forefathers intended: one *true* nation connected under one all-knowing Commander. No more war, no more division, just a peaceful planet."

"And I'll be by your side?" Andre asked, lost in a trance as he stared at the isolation cradle.

Leon squeezed his son's shoulder. "I can think of nothing better."

Chapter 36

Keston

A set of tribal clothes resting on the balcony outside his bedroom caught his attention. Keston slid the door open and looked up and down the road outside his Kyoto home, but there were no signs of who'd dropped them off. With a curious raise of his brow, he retreated inside and inspected the clothes. A message fell out:

Pangaea Boy,

Seeing as you're famous now, we'll need to have our date away from prying eyes. You said you wanted to become a part of the tribes? Here's your chance to try it out. Put the clothes on and fly five minutes north of here—you'll see fires, you can't miss it.

Princess

PS. The belt is not a corset, do NOT call it that. People will get offended.

He smiled at Arianne's familiar scrawl. He'd gotten used to seeing her messages left around their villa, from notes about going to the store to death threats if he touched her leftovers. A pang tightened around his chest. It was strange that even after years, the mundane things were what he remembered—and missed—the most.

"What's that?"

Turning, Sensatia leaned against the doorframe in a bathrobe. While Andre and Pandora had returned to Europe, the reporter had remained behind to filter the news coming out of the region. Keston typically appreciated her company, but at the moment, he hated how exposed he felt under her observant eyes.

He pocketed Arianne's note. "There's a tribe in the area. I asked one of the Selvian representatives for these clothes. I want to do some outreach and didn't think techwear would be welcome."

"Do you want me to come? Part of my job description is diplomatic relations."

"Some tribes don't take well to Pangaeans," Keston said. "It's best if I go alone, just to be safe."

He hated lying to her, but not enough to stop. Like an addict looking for his next hit, he looked out the window again, half expecting Arianne to be hovering there in wait. It was shameful to be lying to one of his few friends, but Arianne would always be the exception.

Sensatia frowned. "What happened on the beach last week? Sure, I got the official Murray mission briefing, but," she said, stepping fully into his room, blue eyes assessing him too closely, "I know it wasn't the whole story."

"Selvians attacked the peace talk. I'm assuming they were afraid of Europe and Asia making a deal."

"The whole world might buy that, but I don't. You're in communication with the Selvians. Unless you signed off on it, there shouldn't have been an attack." Then she paused, eyes widening. "You *did* stop the fight. That's why the Selvians retreated when they had the advantage."

Keston nodded. "I'm sorry. I'm trying to keep as much information as need-to-know as possible to stop the bleeding in case either of us gets caught."

At least, that was a partial truth. He mostly didn't want her guessing he'd met with his former lover-turned-Selvian. Even if that was exactly what happened—and would continue to happen. Arianne's note burned in his pocket.

It felt like cheating. But why? Sensatia and him had never been *exclusive*... that was evident from how often he woke up with others in bed after a night out together.

Still, hiding Arianne felt like a betrayal, maybe in more ways than one. He told himself he needed to hide her for all of their sakes, but deep down, he knew he was more terrified of the emotional fallout.

There was no denying the sadness on Sensatia's beautiful face. "Enjoy every minute with her. I'm happy one of us got to get our person back."

She closed the door on her way out. Keston wished he didn't have super hearing when her muffled cries emanated from two rooms down.

As Arianne instructed, he put on the tribal clothes and reminded himself not to call the belt that held up the harem pants a corset—even if that's what it *was*. Keston looked at himself in the mirror as he adjusted the corset that stretched from the mid-waist pants down to his chest, admiring the comfort of the flowing fabrics. He completed the outfit with the open-chested vest, admiring how the design gave him ample space for his wings.

With the eye for fashion he'd gained over the past few years, he'd noticed that tribal wear was meant to be functional for both living in nature *and* adjustable. The loose fabrics and multiple-piece outfits were designed to fit *Feras* of all body types. Wings, cloven hooves, extra arms, and fins could all be easily accommodated with crop tops, loose pants, and tunics.

Out of his entire—very extensive—wardrobe, this outfit might have been his favorite.

It only took a few minutes of flying north to see fires lighting up the forest below. The autumn forest reds and burning yellow of the sunset mixed with the fires, setting the world ablaze.

It was a fitting setting to meet with a phoenix.

He spotted Arianne waiting below, wings outstretched behind her. Just seeing her erased every sadness in his mind from his conversation with Sensatia. That should've made him feel bad, but anticipation clouded all else.

After two whole years, they had a chance to simply be just Keston and Arianne. He wondered if it would feel the same. The thought both excited and scared him. What if they'd grown apart? What if all the emotions rising in his stomach were just remnants of memories?

His spiraling thoughts almost threw off his landing. He stumbled, coming to a running stop on the stone walkway Arianne was waiting on, his stomach going to his throat as he quickly righted himself. The most powerful male in Europe, and he couldn't even stick a simple landing. He huffed.

"And here I thought I taught you better than that," Arianne chided.

For once, no snide remark came to him. His mind was blank as he took her in. Arianne looked so much like how he remembered... and yet *not*.

The same open smile graced her lips, the one that she made when she expected an exchange of jabs with him. Those familiar golden brown waves fell over her shoulders, lining her face in a way he knew made her feel beautiful. The only difference in her hairstyle was a few stray braids and a white feather tied behind her right ear—Strix's feather.

But the Arianne before him had left the girl from the island rebellion long behind. She stood taller, carrying herself with more confidence than she had while living in the shadow of her father. She was a warrior revered around the world, a leader to her people, and the power radiating from her reminded anyone who looked at her. And her clothes: long gone were the cargo shorts and t-shirts, what she wore now resembled a fae creature from long-ago fantasy.

Forest green skirts fell from her upper hips. The central piece of her skirt, which hung from her navel to between her legs, was adorned with a stag embroidered in golden string—the symbol of the Selvians, and to some extent, all the tribes. The top of her outfit was a green cropped halter-top bodice with matching golden stitchwork. The bodice ended a few inches above her skirts, exposing dense abdominal muscle. Wrappings covered her arms up to her elbows, and golden jewelry hung from her wrists. And around her forehead was a golden olive branch crown, marking her as a tribal Deputy.

"What?" Arianne asked.

Keston shook his head. "You're beautiful. Please don't let anyone tell you differently."

She hummed and started walking. "Don't worry, they don't."

Gaping at her, he smiled and immediately followed her like the lost puppy he'd resigned to be that night. Most famous Elite in Europe, richer than the kings of old, and deadlier than most pagan gods, yet hopelessly following Arianne around. Honestly, he didn't even blame himself. Anyone with a view of her butt in those skirts would be doing the exact same.

He understood what had been going through the heads of ancient emperors when they chose to go to war over one woman. Keston was ready to do the same—he technically already had.

Jogging up to her side, he leaned into her like he was about to tell her some highly secret intel. "So, miss fancy Deputy, what date do you have planned for us?"

Arianne's hand interlaced with his, and warmth radiated through his body at the touch. She gracefully turned on her tiptoes and rose toward his lips, only to stop an agonizing breath away. Her smirk told him she knew she was taunting him. "I asked you to stay, now I'm going to convince you why."

His eyes closed, leaning closer to her. "Let's just say I'm extremely impressionable right now."

She pulled his hand, leading him down the stone path toward the fires he could see lighting up the darkening sky ahead. The trees hung over them, casting them in the growing shadows of night. For once, Keston didn't recognize the shadows as the ones Ace and the Underground called home. These were different, friendlier. While most would stare into the dense forest surrounding them and feel a sense of fear, he only felt comfort. Nature always had that effect on him. He'd forgotten about that until he'd traveled through the Darwin Zone with Arianne.

That was when he'd been woken up from his brainwashing.

They walked over an arching bridge into the tribal village. Keston had to stop at the bottom of the bridge to stare at the sight in awe. The village melded with the forest, becoming an extension of the streams and trees growing around them. Orange lanterns hung from walkways connecting houses built into the canopies of trees, illuminating the darkening evening and lighting the way for hundreds of tribespeople. So deep in the forest, Keston wouldn't have believed such complex communities would be impossible, but here they were, watching a city spawn from the greenery.

A couple of children ran past, playing tag. One of the children jumped high enough to land in the walkway connecting the trees above. The child's friend shouted in frustration as she took off down the planks. Keston couldn't help but smile. He'd never seen *children* so happily expressing their abilities.

For his entire life, any *Fera* he met had been a *Fera* hiding in fear.

"That's why we're fighting so hard," Arianne said, watching the children run. "So our children can be free like them, not hide like we were forced to."

"Our children?" Keston asked, his stomach flopping involuntarily.

Blushing, she quickly guided him away from the village entrance. "You know...Like, the next generation."

"Right."

Dreaming such things would only hurt him more. The moments he had here were fleeting. He couldn't hope for more. He needed to be happy with what they had. Yet, as he looked back at the children chasing each other across the walkway, he couldn't drop the seed of thought in his mind once it was planted. For a fleeting moment, he imagined those two children with down-covered wings streaming behind them, and his heart skipped a beat. Was dreaming so bad? Just a year ago, holding Arianne's hand seemed like an impossibility. Was something more than running and fighting possible?

She led him to a large overhang with seating and a burning hearth near the back. "I haven't had a moment to dream since I lost you," he said quietly.

And there, looking at the village full of people like him, living happily and free, he felt a spark he hadn't felt since Greece.

Arianne slowed, her eyes fixing on a point beyond the dining area. "I don't remember the last time I dreamed. Awake or asleep."

"Ari—"

"This is supposed to be a normal date," Arianne said, stopping him. When she turned back to him, whatever emotion had been displayed on her face had been carefully hidden. "Let's forget about everything else, okay?"

"Okay, Princess."

He let her pull him toward a table and mats where rice and curry waited in steaming bowls. Cayenne and chili stung his nose as he sat, but the sting was quickly accompanied by a sweetness that made his mouth water.

He sighed. "This smells incredible."

The haze that had crossed over Arianne faded as she sat on the ground and readied a set of chopsticks. "There are perks to being the Selvian Deputy—that includes asking for favors from other tribes. Welcome to the Onsen Tribe, the proud new owners of one I-O-U from Phoenix."

Looking around as they ate, he took in everything going on around him: tables of painted Champions eating while they swapped stories, a dedicated chef rolling dough by the hearth for dumplings, and a small band near the far side of the overhang playing upbeat music. The tribe felt like a deep breath after spending too long underwater, its vitality burning as brightly as the fires that illuminated the village. Though Keston had never spent a night in a tribal village, and had only worn their clothes for the first time, he felt like he was home.

These were his mother's people. These were *his* people.

He hadn't noticed Arianne was watching him until she said, "What are you thinking about?"

Keston blinked, suddenly worried he'd offended her. "Sorry, it's just strange to step into a world I've never been to, and yet feel like it's already home."

"I know what you mean." She smiled. "You don't have to apologize. You look happy. Never apologize for that." She looked down at her half-finished bowl of rice. "People like us don't get many chances to be happy."

"I don't deserve to be happy." The admission came out before he could stop it.

The familiar wave of loathing he typically drowned with Cindy and whatever other vice he could get his hands on rose inside him. He didn't deserve any part of this. He didn't deserve to defile his mother's heritage with his presence. He didn't deserve to feel safe in a home full of mutants who'd been directly impacted by his work with Leon. Most of all, he didn't deserve the person sitting across from him. Not her kindness, forgiveness, or love.

"Hey." Arianne sighed as she reached across the table to squeeze his hand. "Don't do that. I know that face."

Poking at his food, he no longer felt hungry. "What am I doing?" he whispered to himself, the blanket of depression smothering him in its darkness. "I-I shouldn't be here."

He stood up abruptly to leave.

Flinching, he remembered the Siege of Oslo. He'd knocked down a tower, crushing tribespeople. He'd stood on a stage and used his voice—his mother's voice—to harm innocent civilians. He'd cleaved his way across Europe, drowning Cartel strongholds in blood. He'd sanctioned a massacre that resulted in the death of Selvia's leader. And most recently, he'd paved the way for Ace, both as Blackjack and Keston, and allowed her to grow her slave-trading empire.

Evil. Evil. Evil.

Why did he think he could come there? Why did he think he belonged after everything he'd done? His legs weakened, the world swaying.

Arms wrapped around him, sending warmth throughout his body. His panic burned away, and the world slowed. When his mind cleared enough to process anything outside his cloud of loathing, he managed to look down. Arianne squeezed herself tightly to his chest, her ear pressed to his heart. Her breathing came out in deep, steady breaths, as if attempting to guide his manic lungs to slow. Only when she heard his heart stop hammering did she look up, gray eyes wide with concern.

"Arianne," he breathed, embarrassed.

Her eyes were closed, listening to his heart. "Breathe in, breathe out."

"I'm sorry."

"Stop apologizing. Just breathe."

He listened, falling into her embrace. Breathing with her, he let the soft rise and fall of her chest guide him. With each exhale, clarity returned. He was suddenly aware that it wasn't the first anxiety attack she'd dealt with. The reminder that he'd abandoned her to fight her battles alone for two years almost sent him spiraling.

"Your heartbeat is rising. Breathe."

"I'm so sorry, Princess," he said, burying his face in her neck.

Her breath hitched, and to his dismay, she stepped away. She didn't look at him. "Come on, I have more things to show you."

"Arianne—"

Tugging him along, they moved from the dining area and toward a torchlit path through dense forest. "We're having a happy night, remember? We're forgetting about everything else."

Keston nodded, willing himself to fall back into the magic of the night. The morning would come in time, but right then, he could pretend it never would.

The trees parted at the end of the torchlit path, revealing a place he'd only seen in visions. Staring at the half dozen fires stretching into the star-flecked night sky, his breath left him. Five smaller flames circled the large pyre residing in the middle, the heat and light of the blaze rivaling the sun. A male dressed in bright blue stood on the platform before the blaze, directing a lively band through music that felt like it was pumping blood through his veins. Dancing around the fires were hundreds of tribespeople. Some moved with a single partner, others moved in organized dance numbers, and others simply embraced the chaos.

Keston swayed, almost brushing off the scene before him as another vision. His mother's voice came into his mind as she sang *The Song of the Feras*. As the memory of her voice mixed with the sight, something deep in his soul connected.

His mother always said those who truly heard *The Song of the Feras* were transported elsewhere when they listened. Keston realized he was always sent there. He'd seen that place a thousand times. He'd just never known it existed.

Arianne was once again his compass, guiding him home.

"Welcome to the Valhan," she said, pulling him into the fray of music and swaying bodies. "The lifeblood of every tribe."

Closing his eyes, the music filled his veins with the familiar ache of seeing an old friend after too long apart. The touch of music on his soul was freeing. He felt more like himself than he had in months living under his father.

When he opened his eyes, Arianne's hands waited for him. "Let's just pretend for the night. Just two people dancing together, okay?"

He considered her offer, scared to say yes but equally unwilling to say no. In another life, they could have simply been two people allowed to navigate their feelings amid the flames of their home, rather than fighting the world and each other. He hoped that in some universe, some version of them got that chance.

For one night, they could pretend everything mounting against them didn't matter.

But deep down, despite the games, Keston knew one thing: "If I take your hand right now, it won't just be for one night, Princess. It will be for life."

Every bird of prey mated for life. He suspected he would be no different.

Arianne didn't waver. "Then take my hand, Selvia Boy. We'll figure out the rest."

Chapter 37

Keston

He gladly joined her.

The world became as close to heaven as someone like him deserved as he let himself draw her close. Arianne guided him through the common tribal dances, helping him move with the crowd during popular choruses. There was something beautiful about moving with a group, of feeling in sync with the others around him. He didn't have to speak their language or know their names, but for a few minutes, he shared everything that mattered: connection and *life*.

The Lyre led the Valhan into a slower song, and people coupled off to sway to the melody. Months of working with the twins allowed him to translate the tale. It was a classic Legend told in the tribes about love and loss: Heron and Koi.

The story chronicled a Ductor named Heron, named for his long white hair and tall stature, and an aquatic Healer with orange hair named Koi. When a battle left Heron mortally wounded, Koi nursed him back to health. Heron fell for Koi, and once he healed, he would linger by her pond in the early mornings before his duties. Late at night, he would return to her, bringing gifts from the day. There, they would talk until the moon hung high in the sky.

One day, the rival tribe that had wounded Heron arrived with a proposition: the battle between their peoples would end if he could find a mate. A mating bond would show Heron could find respect and equality in an enemy, paving a way to the end of their feud. Heron refused, insisting he could only love Koi. But Koi begged him to try. In her mind, only two outcomes could come of the proposition: Heron would find a mate and end the feud, or he would prove his love for her.

Heron left for the rival tribe, determined to end the war between their peoples. He returned a year later with a mate. In the joyous end of the war and lost in admiration of his mate, Heron forgot Koi. But things continued to worsen. The rival tribe followed their promise and ended their war, but not without punishment. Heron discovered his mate had played him, refusing to love him in return.

In saving his tribe from further conflict, Heron was forced to suffer imprisonment not of the body but of the soul. He returned to his tribe, forced to pine over a love who would never return his feelings.

And Koi patiently waited by his side.

"Do you love me?" Koi would ask Heron every night when the moon rose.

For twenty years, Heron answered, "I want nothing more, but I cannot."

Heron continued to meet Koi every night, hoping his mating bond had faded, but left disappointed each time. They had a son together, Heron refusing to let Koi lose out on the life they'd planned because of another tribe's tricks. Though he couldn't get himself to enjoy lying with Koi, he loved her and never strayed.

Then, one night, when their son was grown, Koi asked Heron the same question she asked of him every night: "Do you love me?"

And when Heron turned to her, the fading bond that had kept him away finally disappeared. He touched her, and when he did, an emotion he hadn't felt in twenty years surged inside him. "For the rest of my life, and not a day less."

The song ended. Keston didn't notice how close he held Arianne until the music stopped. Looking down at her, he hoped she wouldn't move away from their soft swaying without the song to guide them. "What a sad story."

Arianne kept her head pressed against his chest. "It's no sadder than the stories we're familiar with." She didn't look up. "Heron and Koi taught us that the greatest punishment is cutting someone off from their chance at love. It's a prison sentence of unknown length and unknown limits. We honor the connection as sacred. Many fear to love because of it."

"Why," he asked as they continued to sway.

Her face was cryptically unreadable. "Because there's no greater pain than having an incomplete mating bond. There's nothing worse than connecting to someone who will not connect back."

A deep sense of dread washed over him, shaking him to his bones. Keston tried to hide it.

Fighting the hole the story of Heron and Koi left in his chest, Keston pulled her into a spin. "I can think of one thing worse."

Arianne twirled, her skirts flowing with her feathers in a beautiful display of gold and green. "What is it?"

He pulled her close again. "Connecting and being forced apart."

She stared up at him, eyes wide and lips parting. She didn't respond, arrested in his hold. He knew then that she knew exactly what he was saying. He knew they both recognized the danger of that night. But he couldn't stop himself. From the way she looped her arms around his neck, he knew she couldn't either.

They were flying straight for disaster, but couldn't get themselves to stop. Classic.

"I have one more thing to show you," Arianne said, voice shaking.

"Show me," he whispered, finding it harder and harder to move his face from her neck. The heat of her skin was just below his lips. Her lips...he was slowly losing the ability to think of anything else.

Leading him down another torch-lit path away from the Valhan, the music faded, replaced by the rustling of bamboo leaves. His body buzzed with energy when he realized for the first time that night they were completely alone. They arrived at a grove, and Keston picked up on the distinct sound of water splashing against rocks. Rounding a set of well-groomed trees, he found a steaming hot spring cast in the orange glow of torchlight. The large pool was lined with stones, with a small waterfall leading to a stream that flowed back toward the Onsen Tribe camp.

Keston gazed at the hot spring, the humidity coming off the water a welcome sensation in the mid-autumn chill.

"Onsen means *hot spring* in Japanese," Arianne said. "This tribe is known for them. I asked for a private spring. No one will bother us."

At the distinct sound of rustling clothes, he turned, and Arianne stood undressed. His entire body shook with barely controlled desire. She looked just like she did in every dream he'd been blessed with in their time apart. For a moment, he didn't trust the vision in front of him, too terrified that another one of his drug-induced hallucinations was tricking him.

Because if he let himself believe this was real, only to find out he was wrong again, he didn't know if his heart could handle it.

As she walked toward the spring, a classic smirk appeared on her face. She dragged a finger over his exposed chest, beckoning him while stepping down into the water. "Are you going to join me?"

Keston almost dove in after her, clothes and all, but he paused mid-step. There would be no stopping him if he got in the water. The rocky walls of the spring became both a physical and emotional threshold to him. Stay on the shore and keep the lines between them solid, or dive in.

"Do you want me to join you?" he replied, voice shaking more than he wished.

As if sensing the weight of his question, Arianne didn't turn to face him, keeping her scarred back to him. He could see every detail her father had slashed on her: the ugliness of her past mixed with the heavenly majesty of her wings warred in sharp contrast to make a breathtaking mosaic. Her skin turned gray in the water, making the golds and browns in her wings and hair pop against the light blue-gray. He remembered when she'd been ashamed to show him that side of her—the side that proved she'd left humanity behind—and he remembered loving her more for it.

Love. Did he still love her? Would he allow himself to love her? Had too much happened?

Arianne turned her head just slightly, her face shadowed by the flickering torchlight. "When I lost my mother and my home, I needed someone to blame."

"I'm sorry."

"Stop apologizing," Arianne hissed. "I wasn't finished."

She raised her webbed hands above the water, analyzing them. That was the first time Keston had seen her without gloves or wrappings. He realized how scarred her hands and forearms were. They were not just simple scratches from years of combat wounds like Keston had before he went under Hera's knife; they were burn scars.

Scars from when she was left to die in that crumbling hospital.

"But I am sorry," Keston gritted, his heart aching as more emotion filled his chest. "I lied to you, I took your mother from you, and then I left you." He ripped his eyes from the water, knowing he shouldn't even consider joining her after what he'd done. "I will say I'm sorry every day for the rest of my life, and it still won't be enough."

"If you didn't pull the trigger, someone else would've."

"I still abandoned you."

Arianne shook her head. "You had to choose between death with someone who hated you or life with a sister who needed you. There was only one choice, yet I blamed you for making it."

"Arianne—"

"I lied about who I was, I was spiraling long before you shot my mother, and I lost my home thanks to my decisions, not yours." She turned to him now, tears falling down her face. "I was so caught up in my own apathy, I couldn't own up to the damage it caused. So I blamed the one person left in my life who actually *cared*—who hadn't left yet."

Keston wasn't moving, but he felt like he'd stumbled. He was still upright, but it felt like he'd tripped and rolled his ankle on the way down to falling in the mud. Out of nowhere, the world was spinning around him, his stomach flopping, and then all he could feel was pain.

His hands clenched and unclenched, his eyes burned, and his emotions flooded. "One *year* spent believing you were dead," he whispered. "Two *years* spent waking up and reaching for someone who wasn't there."

"I know."

Keston's lips quivered. "Did you wake up reaching for me?"

He was terrified of hearing her answer. He couldn't figure out which one would be more painful to hear.

"Almost every day."

Two years wasted. Two years of unnecessary pain.

He sank to his knees.

"We both made mistakes." Arianne's voice was uneven. "We both lied to each other. I'm sorry if it's too much to repair. I-I don't know if we can repair it, but I can't stop myself from trying."

Keston stared at the steam rising from the hot springs, knowing his eyes were not burning from the heat. He didn't know what to do with the ache in his heart. It was a dizzying mixture of disgust and desire. One part of him wanted to be angry—that'd certainly become his default. The other part wanted to throw the past behind him and run to the female in front of him, damning the consequences. Both options would leave him in a world of hurt.

But only one of those choices gave him a chance for happiness in the end. And he quickly realized he'd known his answer all along. His After was standing in front of him, and he'd always known he would do whatever was needed to get it. Even if the chance of that After coming to fruition was slim.

For the first time in his life, Keston was willing to make a gamble with the odds stacked against him.

He sighed, and in that breath, he let go of every piece of frustration and resentment he had weighing on his soul. In that breath, he forgave her as she'd forgiven him. Though only air, it felt like a thousand pounds removed from his heart.

And then he made his decision. "We'll repair it just like we do everything from now on: together."

No more turning back. It was Arianne, or it was no one.

Keston dove into the spring, and she turned to greet him. Then they were kissing, their hands desperately roving over their shoulders, backs, wings, and hips. Keston sighed against her lips, fighting to pull her as close to him as possible. Arianne complied and wrapped her legs around his waist. He smiled as he held her in his arms, her body always instinctively knew what to do when she was with him.

Her hands shook as she ran her fingers through his hair. "I missed you," she said between kisses.

"I'm right here."

"No," she protested breathlessly. "I missed having you at my side." She cupped his face, punctuating each word with a kiss: "My. Perfect. Other. Half."

The words were more intoxicating than any liquor. Keston groaned, needing her more than ever. He carried her to the back of the spring where a waterfall fed fresh water into the pond, kissing her every step of the way.

Pressing her against the rock face, water cascaded down his back and gave him a thrilling sensation with its chill. "I'm hardly perfect, Princess."

Arianne laughed, and the sound was the most beautiful and joyous thing he'd heard in years. "We're perfect together because we're the same kind of imperfect."

He leaned back for a moment, just long enough to take her in. His eyes scanned over her gray skin and gills, admiring the way her soaked hair stuck to her face. And then he landed on her eyes. For the first time since finding her alive, the eyes that stared back at him were unequivocally Arianne's. Not Phoenix. *Arianne.*

The world might believe Phoenix was a demon. Those who knew Arianne might even believe the old her had died with Citadel. But looking at her right there, Keston knew the female he'd loved was still the same at her core—even if he was the only one who could bring it out anymore.

He believed she was the only one who saw the real him anymore, either. It made their connection all the more special.

"Still the same Arianne."

She paused, her eyes going down. "I don't know what I am anymore, Kes."

"You're impulsive, violent, opinionated, and a little annoying." He nudged her with his nose. "But you're loyal, brave, and unapologetic. Sure, you can be a dumpster fire, but no one does it better than you."

She gave him a playful shove. "And you're still an asshole."

Keston leaned closer, pinning her to the wall. "What I'm trying to say is: you're still the person I fell hopelessly in love with two years ago."

There. He said it. The one word he'd been terrified of two years ago. But now, after everything, he wasn't scared anymore.

Arianne blinked, something made all the more adorable with her large, rounded eyes. Her lips parted, and for a moment, Keston feared that somehow, while naked and pinned by him, she would reject his emotions.

"Y-you were in love with me?"

"'Were'? I never stopped."

She looked ethereal with droplets of water falling from her eyelashes and the gray in her eyes reflecting the moonlight above. For a few charged moments, they simply stared at each other, their breathing thick and ragged. Wordlessly, she placed a hand on his chest, directly over his heart, her palm warm despite the night air.

Then she smiled, it was a strangely beautiful mix of longing and affection. She whispered, "I love you, too. I'm sorry I had to come back from the dead to find the courage to say it, but I love you, my amazing other half."

And then nothing held him back.

Cupping her face like he needed to guarantee there was no more running, he kissed her again. Arianne was right there, she wasn't going anywhere, and he needed a firm hold on her to remind his nerves every second she wasn't a figment of his imagination. Real. Arianne was real. The emotions he felt for her were real. And the bond they shared was *real*.

There was no questioning any of that anymore.

As Keston refamiliarized himself with all of her muscled curves, her shaking hands got to work removing the soaked remnants of his clothes. She struggled with the vest around his wings, and with a provocative laugh, she grabbed two fistfuls of the material and ripped it clean off. Something primal triggered in him, and he surged forward, pressing her to the rock wall with as much force as possible. Arianne, the only being in the world who could take his strength without breaking, simply took his pressure as a delightful challenge.

Resisting his force and adding to the charged power between them, they fought back and forth, their kissing and touches growing in intensity. He'd had to be delicate with his human partners in the past year, but he found with each delightful test of his power that Arianne held her own. A human would have been crushed by then, but they were just getting started.

Kissing her neck, right in the spot he knew she couldn't resist, he almost lost all rational thought as she let out a shaking breath against his ear. A smirk came to his lips as he removed one hand from her hip and moved downward, determined to hear more than just her breathing. She stiffened as he reached inside, and to his delight, she squeaked, her hands clawing into his backside.

As he worked his fingers, exactly how he remembered she loved, he was amazed at how much pleasuring her was still muscle memory. It felt familiar, like coming home. Their bodies remembered each other.

They were not strangers starting from scratch. They were two connected souls finding each other again.

As he brought her closer and closer to completion, Arianne sighed his name, driving him increasingly insane with each syllable. Her hands found the soft feathers on the inside of his wings, and she started to explore. Keston lost focus for a moment, his eyes rolling back at the sensation of his lover's fingers running through his wings once more. He almost let her finish him with just that touch.

Almost.

"We're focusing on you right now," he rumbled, pinning her hands above her head with his free hand.

Arianne's eyes were leaden with desire. "But I want to participate."

"Then finish and scream for me, Princess."

She complied.

And with that amazing sound of her pleasure, the sleeping part inside him—the part that allowed him to feel joy and excitement—awoke. The restraints of Blackjack snapped once more, and it was everything he never knew he'd lost. As Arianne trembled above his leg, he couldn't wait a second longer. He was half-convinced he'd gone feral as he pulled and clawed at his belt and pants, desperate for the pairing he'd gone without for two whole fucking years.

But right before he took that final step, when they were tangled together without anything between them but water and air, he stopped. He collected his ragged breaths and leaned his forehead into Arianne's, their eyes connecting for a sobering moment. This was the final step; they both felt it in the heaviness in the air. If they did this, there would be no turning back. No matter what allegiance, no matter who survived the upcoming war, they were signing up for all the love and pain that came next.

Together was an amazing and terrifying thing.

"I'm yours," Keston said.

"I would say 'until death do us part,' but we've already made it past that point."

"Let's say 'to heaven together or bust,' then."

"Let's go with bust." She winked, reaching a hand downward.

Rolling his eyes, he kissed her. "I love the way you think."

Keston grabbed her shoulders and thrust himself inside her. Arianne cried out as they connected, her wings wrapping around him and her hands gripping his face with a desperation he knew too well. They kissed as he moved, his body effortlessly pinning her against the wall at the perfect angle that made them both sigh with pleasure.

He didn't know how long they remained in that spring. He lost himself in the feeling of her, the muscles on her back, the softness of her feathers, the tangles of her hair. Neither could get enough. Neither could stop.

And Arianne burned just as brightly at his side.

She was beautiful, warm, deadly, and life-giving, just like the fires she wielded with her blades. She was everything he remembered and more. She was, without a doubt, the only love he would accept in that lifetime or the next.

His equal. His mirror.

They finally fell asleep next to the spring, warmed by the steam rising from the water and spare blankets. Arianne curled into his chest, like she always had, and tucked her wings in tight so they rested flesh to each other. Keston wrapped his body around her, needing to touch as much of her as possible. Even as she drifted to sleep in his arms, he couldn't force himself to join her.

Not yet.

After losing her time and time again, he wanted to savor every fleeting moment with her. So as she slept, he brushed her hair and kissed the scars arcing over her shoulders. And when he studied her face, a powerful feeling hit him with the strength of a hurricane blast.

Keston blinked, almost falling back at the force of the emotion. The sensation squeezed his heart at the sight of Arianne, and as the tightness eased up, it was replaced by a full-body warmth unlike he'd ever felt before. Suddenly, her scent was all he noticed, the sound of her breathing the only thing his ears were calibrated to, and every nerve begged to feel the brush of her skin.

Though he didn't know what the sensation was, he pulled her closer to him, and it was enough to ease the newly burning desire in his heart. He fell asleep with his head buried into her neck, knowing only one thing for certain: he would tear down anything that kept him from holding her like that again for the rest of his life.

There was no longer any other possibility. It was Keston and Arianne, or it was death.

Chapter 38
Arianne

Arianne woke to the sound of screaming.

She stirred in Keston's arms, the desire to remain entangled in his warmth quickly dissipating as the distress pierced her ears. She crawled out from under his protective wing and frantically shook him awake, her adrenaline rising.

"Keston," she hissed.

He tried to pull her back into his arms. "Five more minutes."

Damn it, the bounty hunter with a laundry list of war crimes looked adorable. "We have a situation."

One amber eye opened. "What kind?" Any levity in his voice faded when he registered the screams. He jumped up, hastily pulling on a set of spare joggers and a cotton shirt next to the spring. "What's going on?"

Arianne was already throwing on the fighting leathers she'd packed. Suited up, she grabbed her bag and batons, and prepared to sprint into the village.

"Um, Ari?" Keston's voice was wary.

Turning, her stomach dropped when she saw where he pointed. A large purple cloud rose into the sky miles away. Kyoto. Dread made her insides recoil. "That's a cloud of Frenzy."

"Winds are heading this way," Keston warned, extending his wings.

"We need to get the tribe moving! We can't risk the cloud making it this far."

The winged *Feras* nodded to each other and took off down the path toward the heart of the Onsen Tribe village. They were met with chaos. Arianne slowed and tried to take stock of the situation, tried to find the tribe's Ductor in the stampede. No luck.

"Hey!" she screamed in Tribal Latin, trying to draw some attention. "Hey, listen to me! You need to move away from that cloud!"

It was no use. The village was in disarray.

Keston stepped to her side, spreading his wings behind him to generate an air wave strong enough to send a blast of wind through the village. "Hey!" he bellowed, his sonic voice bringing the chaos to a halt.

Arianne squeezed his hand in thanks before looking at the people around her. "Get whatever you can carry and continue north," she ordered, then pointed to the faint purple cloud rising higher into the sky to the south. "Do not let that cloud reach you. Understood?"

She didn't wait for further confirmation. Reaching into her bag, she frantically pulled out her Ward's mask and the spare she'd packed—she always kept a spare since Frenzy arrived on the Underground scene—and handed it to Keston. They took off back toward Kyoto.

"What's happening?" Keston asked, his voice coming in through her mask's audio as they flew at a desperate pace toward the purple cloud.

Arianne didn't take her eyes from the upward spiral of Frenzy as it climbed higher and higher into the atmosphere. Tears filled her vision. "I don't know, but we need to stop it."

"I'm sending a warning message to the Okasaki Estate. We'll keep other *Feras* out of this until we investigate."

They reached Kyoto, and Arianne's heart shattered. The small city was shrouded in Frenzy, the drug coating the streets and the air above in a dense fog. An agonized squeak escaped her as they dropped from the sky, landing in the cloud and the hellscape barely concealed below.

She heard the screams and feral growls more than saw anything. Smoke pooled around her in suffocating intensity, her eyes struggling to see beyond purple, purple, *purple*. The snarls of feral mutants surrounded her, but with the mask filtering her breathing and the smoke blocking her eyes, she had no senses to rely on. It was maddening. Her head swiveled around her, blind. She flapped her wings in a desperate attempt to see *anything*, but more Frenzy drifted into the cleared space.

Keston landed next to her, his eyes glinting with a strange light as he scanned the area. "My heat vision isn't detecting anything in our immediate area."

"I can't handle this," Arianne whimpered, sagging into his shoulder. Her tears fell freely now.

She couldn't. After months on the front line, she thought she was numb to it all. Even after the outbreak of Frenzy in downtown Tokyo, she thought she saw the worst of it. But here they were, an entire city was drowned in Frenzy, leaving the thousands of occupants subject to—

A shadow shot past in the mist, just feet away from them. Arianne ignited her twin batons and handed Keston one of the simmering blades. They stood back to back as the figures darting past grew in number, their mist-shrouded bodies getting closer and closer. Growling and the gnashing of teeth shot past. She knew what had her scent, and she knew she had to kill them before they killed her.

Even if, just an hour ago, those feral enemies had been simple citizens waking up to another simple morning.

With a blood-curdling screech, a feral male dove out of the mist. Arianne had a fraction of a second to react, dropping to the ground. Keston's heat-vision prepared him for the assault, and he reached over her and slashed, cutting the feral male in half.

"That's our window, fucking book it!" he screamed.

Arianne pushed herself up and followed after him, her spine prickling at the sound of claws scraping on the pavement and several howls of frustration. She reached into her bag and grabbed her bottle of Mist, dousing herself before tossing the spray to Keston. Hopefully, it would be enough to keep them invisible long enough to investigate.

"This can't be another accident," Keston huffed as they ran.

"The whole city is covered."

"It's quieter than expected."

Recognizing a doorway to her right, she kicked it in, grabbed Keston's shirt, and pulled him into the house with her. As they entered, they fell into a familiar pattern: he scanned right, she scanned left, both searching for an ambush. They operated without a word, used to one too many life-or-death situations together. When the ground floor was clear, they advanced upstairs.

The smoke in the house wasn't as dense, but they were still in a slight haze. Arianne feared that even a slight haze was enough to turn a mutant feral. Reaching the main bedroom, she had to hold back a scream. Keston followed behind her, took one look at the sight, and gagged.

The room was a bloodbath. The remnants of what could've been a woman covered the bed. Blood was splattered everywhere. A flashback of Carol, the female servant from Ace's Leonueva branch, came to Arianne's mind. Carol had been dismembered just like that: neck bit out, stomach torn to pieces, and intestines splayed like unwound rope. The window beyond the bed was shattered. Dripping blood tinted the shards red, signifying where the creature had escaped to continue its rampage.

Everything was quiet for one reason: they'd arrived too late. Any living human was long gone or deep in hiding. Only feral monsters roamed the streets now, on the hunt to satisfy their insanity.

Arianne's fist careened through the wall with a cry of rage. But even with her growing tidal wave of anger, all she could do was sob. It was too much, too much. Somehow, this was her fault. Somehow, she could've stopped this annihilation.

"Arianne…" A haunting wariness hung off Keston's words. "Arianne, it's coming through the ventilation ducts."

She wiped her tears to see where he pointed. Purple smoke pooled out of the vents and snaked venomously through the room, curling around furniture in agonizing silence.

Keston doubled over, looking ready to throw up. "Ace's been hiding out in Kyoto. She could've been leaking Frenzy into the town's air systems for months. I should've noticed *something*."

"This is Leon's contingency plan: poison Asia town by town until they comply."

He fell at her side, making her cry more when she saw tears welling in his eyes, the irises shining with a beauty a moment like that didn't deserve. Wordlessly, Arianne held his masked face and wiped a tear away with her thumb. He leaned into her touch, his whole body shaking. She clung to him, needing his touch amidst the overwhelming pain surrounding them in clouds. He pulled her in tight, his hand palming her back and gripping her to him as closely as possible. They remained there for a while, sobs making their shoulders shake.

The failure was isolating. The only thing making the beginning of the end bearable was that she wasn't standing against it alone.

"What do we do?" she wept into his shoulder. "We lost, Kes. We lost."

He stroked her hair, which was in as much disarray as her heart. "We haven't lost yet. I refuse to believe that."

"I hate him," Arianne growled. "I'm going to *kill him*."

A switch flipped inside her. It was almost instant. Every breath she took from then on would simmer like hellfire. She would burn with that hatred until her father melted beneath her flames. Leon was her beginning, and he would be her end, but she would take him with her. This wasn't about winning anymore. This was about mutually assured destruction.

"Give me a month," Keston pleaded, trying to break through her growing fury. "I *will* find a solution. Please wait for me. Get your people out of Japan and wait for my word."

The words barely registered. "I'm going to kill him."

Holding her at arm's length, he shook her softly. "No. Come on, Arianne, don't do this. Don't give up yet. I can still fix this."

"Look around you, Keston. You were a fool to think you could beat Ace and Leon in their games."

His face broke. "I needed to try. Please have hope." He shook her again. "Arianne, please."

She wasn't looking at him. "I shouldn't have gotten distracted."

"We had no control over this."

"I can't afford more distractions right now." She ripped herself away from his grip. The movement broke her heart, but the world needed her to be untouchable, not emotional. Keston left her vulnerable—she couldn't allow that, not with the tides of the war shifting so rapidly. "I'll get my people out."

"Don't shut me out right now," Keston demanded, standing with her. "Not when we know what we mean to each other."

Arianne moved toward the shattered window, unfurling her wings for takeoff. "I need to be whole right now. I can't be conflicted or torn. I need to focus on my people, and you need to focus on finding *something* that could give us a chance."

Even the act of moving away from him felt impossible, which further convinced her that it had to be done.

"We promised together, Ari." Keston reached toward her.

Arianne allowed herself to take his hand, allowed herself a brief moment of humanity. "Together," she promised. "But not yet. The world needs us apart right now."

His face softened as he loosened his grip. "One month, Ari. Please give me one month, and I won't say goodbye again."

"One month, Selvia Boy. I'll prepare my forces. You'd better have a plan."

Chapter 39

Keston

The entire palace shook as Keston landed on the roof. He cherished the building-wide quake through his boots. Everyone inside should fear his rage. He might still be their puppet, but he was tired of letting them believe he couldn't break the strings.

Someone would answer for Kyoto.

Thousands were dead. It wasn't an accident like Tokyo. It was planned, plotted, and executed with chilling efficiency. No explanation would suffice, yet he desperately needed to know *why*. The memory of Arianne's agonized wails as she cried into his shoulder steeled his resolve.

Please give me one month.

Keston winced against his promise. Walking into the palace from the rooftop entrance, he feared that no matter how much rage rested in his heart, there may not be a way to stop the oncoming avalanche.

He threw himself down three steps at a time. No Wards stopped him; anyone who worked closely with the Inner Circle never did when he was on a warpath. And as if he was summoned, Cassius appeared out of the shadows below the staircase, bearded face strangely serene despite his natural disaster for a son coming his way.

"I don't want to hear a word from you," Keston warned in French, storming toward Leon's office.

"I wouldn't advise what you're about to do," Cassius said mildly.

He didn't slow. On the flight over, Keston had considered tamping down his reaction, but had decided against it. Sure, it would be uncharacteristic to pretend he didn't care. But really, there was no way he could sit back and say nothing anymore. He refused to be a coward.

"I'm glad you're advising someone. Because it seems like you neglected to advise Leon on the moral pitfalls of a fucking massacre."

"Genevieve is in Leon's custody," Cassius said simply.

Keston halted, his heart wrenching. He gripped his chest, suddenly terrified he was having a heart attack. "What?" he choked out. "What did you say?"

"She was the mole."

Pinching the bridge of his nose, he turned away, uncertain what reaction to display on his face. He'd known Genevieve was leaking information for months, but how much did his father know? Did Cassius suspect Keston was involved?

He went for a mixture of shock and frustration. "I knew she was hiding things from me." He clenched his fists, allowing an ounce of genuine emotion through. "I worked so hard to protect her...for nothing."

Failure. At every turn, he was met with failure. The walls suddenly seemed to close in on him. The losses were stacking up and burying him alive. If he wanted any chance of seeing the sky again, he needed to keep digging and pray for a solution.

"They're in the lab," his father continued before shifting to depart. "I suggest you calm down and meet me there."

Keston stared at the carpet, focusing on the intricate floral designs swirling across the ground as he fought to collect his breath. The stress almost made him pass out. One feather out of place and he not only lost his life, but doomed a rebellion that relied on him.

He'd failed the Selvians, his home. He'd failed Arianne, his heart.

Hera's labs comprised one entire palace wing, the multiple stories affording space for every terrible thing she could imagine. The sterile floors and the antiseptic scent in the air had Keston tensing, his body associating the sensory inputs with being torn apart and sewn back together. He entered cautiously, his overwhelming discomfort making him unbearably nauseous.

The lights were dim, but the Inner Circle was easily recognizable: Hera, Pandora, Andre, Sensatia, Cassius, and Leon. Standing behind the group with placid green eyes was Jaya, her black collar more vibrant than her purple hair.

Mori Sora's flickering projection cast blue light on Leon, who dwarfed her. For the first time, genuine uncertainty reflected in her sharp eyes. Not just uncertain, but utterly stricken. It was the rite of passage for someone who chose to defy

Leon. Like all who'd come before her, Sora was facing the moment she realized Leon had her utterly outmaneuvered.

"I'm glad we've come to an understanding," he purred, his scarred face deceivingly cordial.

Sora's mouth was a hard line. "I never hope to understand you."

Leon lifted his chin. "Hence why you've lost. Don't look so sour, Your Highness. You have the makings of a great Commander in you. Once I've aligned you to my goals, you'll be a critical piece in my new Pangaea."

"Is that supposed to be a compliment?"

"Take it however you want." Leon shrugged. "What matters is that you comply. As you've seen, I've planted Frenzy in strategic places throughout your continent: near water reservoirs, ventilation—trust me, the list goes on. All you need to know is that I've selectively placed these *time bombs* in places that will hurt, my dear. You can agree to work with me now, or I'll unleash Frenzy on your continent. You'll watch as we weaken your cities, economy, and military. Then, I'll take Asia by force."

Sora physically stumbled. Confident or not, the young princess had just been given the political equivalent of an ejection of poison directly to the jugular...and the only person holding the antidote was asking for her soul in exchange.

"And my brother wanted to join you willingly." Her upper lip curled. "I'm glad I killed him."

"So am I," Leon said, laughing. "His idiocy was easy to manipulate—something I believe your late mother valued so she could control him even after retirement—but such stupidity gets old quickly. I enjoy sharper minds in my company."

"And if I comply?" Sora's voice shook.

Leon spread his hands out in a peaceful gesture. "Frenzy has a half-life of two years. That's more than enough time to win this war. Cooperate, help me reset Pangaea, and your Frenzy problem will, quite literally, disappear."

"Reset Pangaea?"

"Yes. With Asia and Europe's resources, North America stagnant, and Africa weakening itself, we have a simple path to victory. We will unite, take out the African and tribal threat, then set our sights on Australia and the Americas. Our founders were onto the right idea, but they didn't get it *quite* right. I'm here to correct that."

"By putting yourself in charge," Sora deadpanned.

"Think about it: no more war, expedited decision-making, and a balanced economy without borders. A world united. A *true* Pangaea."

"And what of *Feras*?"

"What about them?" Leon said, turning his head just enough to display his scars. "Our society was created with a specific range of human capabilities in mind. I stand for uniting a balanced society. Mutants threaten that balance; they threaten my hard work. They will be handled accordingly."

Keston's blood chilled. What did he mean by accordingly? Sora's eyes seemed to ask the same question.

Satisfied, Leon crossed his arms. "The logistics do not matter now. What matters is your cooperation. I recommend that you take the deal for the sake of the innocent humans of your continent."

Sora stared at a place beyond the recording device, likely to her own inner circle. Keston imagined her Lord Advisor, Jin Shi, watching in thinly veiled horror. They'd all witnessed the terror Frenzy wrought and felt the pressure of the hidden threat. There was no choice, but the world wouldn't see it that way.

There was only one choice, but I blamed you for making it. Arianne's words from two nights ago came back to him. Sora faced the same terrible predicament: she didn't have a choice, but the world would blame her for making it. She was bowing to a tyrant, agreeing to lend her forces to aid in the death of innocents and those fighting for good.

But millions more would suffer Kyoto's terrible fate if she said no.

So Keston found himself forgiving Sora, even as she became the enemy that tipped the scales of the most critical war in generations.

Her eyes were wet as she bowed. "Asia is with you."

The room was silent as the weight of the Heir Apparent's words landed in full force. The war had obviously shifted into Leon's favor the moment Kyoto fell, but now, the outcome was damningly official. Keston wondered whether the pressure could be felt everywhere, whether his allies in Selvia could sense the moment their fate was sealed.

And somehow, he'd promised to find a way to fix everything in thirty minuscule days.

"Good." Leon smiled at his newest subject. "I'll see you at my son's wedding. It'll be a perfect day to announce our alliance—a union of the next generation: in blood and borders."

The call dropped with no response.

Leon then turned to his audience, blue eyes landing on Keston, freezing the male with their hoarfrost. "There's the bird who was throwing a temper tantrum on my roof."

Keston stilled. No matter how much he practiced, maneuvering through Leon's mental games never got easier. With a losing hand, as usual, he kept his mouth shut. He caught Sensatia's sideward glance, her eyes wide in warning. That's when he noticed her hands were bound behind her back.

He cursed internally.

Leon placed his hand on a cradle to his right; the lid closed, obscuring the contents inside. That's when his wedding band glinted in the low light. For some reason, the sight was enraging. Leon's actions would abhor Josephina, yet he continued to dishonor her legacy by wearing the mark of their former love. The ring wrongly made it seem like Josephina had supported this nightmare.

Arianne would be even more furious than she already was.

Reaching out to Arianne with his thoughts, Keston hoped she wasn't currently losing herself to her hatred. He hoped someone in Selvia was keeping her heart from freezing over when he couldn't. *Don't give up yet, Princess.* Because if Arianne, the most determined being he'd ever met, gave up, what hope did anyone else have?

The idea of touching her mind despite being miles apart brought him a warmth he hadn't imagined.

"Do you know what your sister is, Keston?" Leon said.

The winged male blinked, like his cybernetics had short-circuited at the question. He weighed his words heavily before speaking. "I suspected she was hiding something. Unfortunately, my love for her put her in my blind spot."

For a while, that had been the truth. Maybe a half-truth would be enough to convince Leon.

The Commander inclined his head, satisfied enough with the answer. "Your sister is what the rebels call a Scion. The Legends speak of the Librarians: a race of Great Disaster survivors who carried the secrets of the war through the generations, keeping the original rebellion against the infant Pangaea alive. The Scion was the chosen recipient of the Librarians' knowledge, specially selected to have a place of influence within Pangaea to sow chaos when the time for rebellion returned."

Pandora scoffed. "Legends are children's stories, and then they make great plot devices for porn when you're an adult."

Leon ignored her vulgarity, as had become a talent of his. He closed his eyes, probably praying for patience. "And yet, you found the Librarians and beheaded Cervi: two Legends in one day. It is not a stretch to believe other Legends are true."

The disbelief Keston expressed wasn't a lie. "My sister? She's eighteen, not some torch bearer of Legend."

But even as he spoke, he lost confidence. Genevieve had changed drastically since New York. Was it so crazy to believe something had happened to her? He eyed the people in the lab around him, careful not to clue anyone in on his emotions until he was certain they wouldn't spell death for himself or his sister.

Good lord, he needed a drink.

"The Librarians gave her their version of the Serum. I've confirmed it." Leon looked at the cradle under his hand, and Keston realized, with growing horror, that his sister rested inside. There was an uncanny softness in the Commander's face. "The knowledge she carries changes everything. I once fought based on moral principles, but now, with the true events of the Great Disaster explained to me, I know without a doubt that my mission is the right one."

Though he'd always been confident, something had shifted in his words. This was no longer about ambition. It was a holy war. Leon believed he was doing the work of his forefathers, that his work was righteous, an absolute moral good.

Genevieve, what did you show him? Keston pleaded as he stared at the sensory deprivation cradle. His eyes burned, wishing he'd been modified with laser vision. He could cut her from her prison and fly far, far away.

"But Genevieve wasn't working alone." Leon's voice dropped an octave.

Sensatia squeaked. Keston couldn't stop himself from whipping his gaze to her. She was disheveled. Her typically pin-straight hair was frizzy and kinked, like she'd slept on it at a wrong angle. Her blue pantsuit was wrinkled and dusty, the fine-pressed fabric torn beyond repair. While the gloom made them hard to recognize at first, her exposed skin was covered in bruises.

Heart breaking for his friend, they shared a long, pained look. Keston had seen her two nights ago... when he'd run off to see Arianne and left her in tears. Though he would never regret that one, potentially last, night of peace with the love of his life, it still ached to feel like he abandoned Sensatia.

"Ace was so kind as to bring her to us when she evacuated from Kyoto," Leon said as he ran a knuckle down Sensatia's face. "I can't say I'm surprised, but I am disappointed." She tried to rip away as he held her chin with a frown. "I hate wasting talent, especially talent so beautiful."

The elastic band of Keston's emotions finally stretched too far. He couldn't pretend everything was fine anymore. Sensatia, his only *friend* in that eighth ring of hell, had her neck in the jaws of the Lion of Europe.

He lunged forward. "G-Genevieve manipulated her," he insisted, voice cracking. "Sensatia has sway over public opinion. She's a celebrity, that's irreplaceable. I'll keep her in line, I promise."

He feared he was making too many promises he couldn't keep.

Pandora chuckled. "Careful, Dad, this is starting to look very familiar."

The lab shifted, suddenly looking like the hospital room in Citadel, and Keston nearly sank to his knees. All the same people were there, only Sensatia replaced Arianne. His heart thundered, and the pounding of blood drowned out his ears. *Not again.*

"This does look familiar," Leon said, considering Sensatia again. "But I'm not thinking about the fun we had in Pacific." The Commander's smile was not human. "I'm thinking of something that offers a little more *insurance*."

Keston could practically hear the sound of the bullet. The kickback of the pistol in his hand. The splatter of Josephina's blood. All like it'd occurred just yesterday.

"Senny," Keston pleaded, body shaking. "Tell them you'll cooperate. Tell them it's a misunderstanding."

Tears streamed down her cheeks. She shook her head slowly, genuine sadness in her eyes. "Come on, Kes. We both know there's enough dirt on me to fill an op-ed."

No. His breathing began to come out in ragged gasps.

Hera, who'd been watching the meeting from her laboratory desk, stood and walked to Keston's side. She snidely handed him a pistol. "'Best aim in Europe,' right?" The ghostly scientist smirked. "This is familiar. Let's end it on the first try this time."

The pistol felt exactly as it had when he'd taken Josephina's life. He'd just repented for that sin, and now he was doing it all over again. Had anything changed, or had he fooled himself into believing he'd found freedom? No, he was just a hamster running on a continuous wheel. He'd never been free. He'd arrived right back where he'd started that day at the top of the Murray Monument.

"You know the drill," Leon said. "You have too many connections to the traitors in this building. Your sister was hacking into my data systems. Your girlfriend was leaking the information to the public. I want insurance. Prove you're still my reaper, and I won't harm a feather on your pretty head."

His vision blurred. He barely heard his father's voice from somewhere in the room. "This isn't just about loyalty, son. This is about legacy. Protect the Leroy legacy."

Keston wanted to turn and fire a bullet into Cassius's skull, but he couldn't move. Once again, he didn't have a choice, but he would blame himself for making it. His father was wrong. This was about loyalty, just not to the Leroys, the Murrays, or even Pangaea. This was about loyalty to the dream of a better future.

Genevieve was right: he needed to be the villain for a little longer. He would never forgive himself. But this wasn't about him.

The same resignation rested in Sensatia's eyes. She subtly nodded, and Keston couldn't help but see Josephina standing there. The former First Mother of Europe had given him the same look. Neither Sensatia nor Josephina blamed him. They'd already accepted their punishments.

"Hold me before I go," Sensatia breathed. "Please."

Keston stumbled over to her, the woman he'd once believed was nothing more than a conceited celebrity, now making his heart ache with her altruism. He pulled her into a hug. Sensatia was a brilliant woman who'd loved and lost, and then taken that loss and turned herself into a hero. Like Josephina, she wasn't a warrior, but she'd proven that power didn't always come from fists.

She'd been the one to teach him how devastating a well-crafted façade could be in a world of sin and superpowers.

"Senny," he whimpered. "Senny, I'm so sorry."

Her breathing became panicked, but her words remained collected. "I'm happy it's you."

"I'm sorry." He was sobbing now, holding her as tightly as possible to savor their last moments together.

He hoped the hug calmed her. He hoped she didn't feel alone. She'd felt alone for so long. But, even facing the end, Sensatia didn't care about herself—there was always a job to do. Keston felt the subtle touch of her hand slipping into his jacket, where she knew he kept a secret pocket. A weight landed there, and then she withdrew her hand, finally returning his embrace.

"Don't be sorry." She sighed and separated from him. Closing her eyes, she took one step back, removed her wedding band, and held it to her heart. "I get to see Sebastian now," she said through quivering lips.

Keston could barely hold the pistol level, but he forced himself to focus as he lined up the shot. He would make sure it was quick and painless. It was the last thing he could offer.

"Thank you for being my friend." Keston stared down the blurred barrel.

In her final moment alive, Sensatia looked unapologetically like the ambitious reporter who'd won the hearts of Europe. She looked death in the face and winked. "Do me a favor: play my broadcasts where everyone can see. I put too much work into them to be forgotten so soon."

"That's a promise I can keep, Senny."

And then he fired.

The minutes following her death went by in a blur. Her body hit the ground, but Keston didn't hear. He didn't acknowledge Pandora's comment on the swift death. Cassius clapped him proudly on the back, but he barely felt the touch.

Andre's voice swam through the haze. "Congratulations, you're officially the Best Man at my wedding."

Keston didn't even have the heart to shout at him.

And then the room emptied, and he was left with the body of the only friend he had in Pangaea. He fell to his knees, pulling Sensatia into his arms as he wailed into her neck. Two years at his side, two years of trusting each other amidst the blurred lines of family politics and news cycles. She'd not only taught him how to navigate the pristine realm of the Elites, she'd taught him to dominate. In a world he wanted no part of, she'd been the only bright spot.

Another light snuffed out too soon.

When Keston's eyes stung and his nose burned, he finally remembered his pocket. Uncaring if his hands were coated in blood, Keston frantically reached into his jacket and carefully pulled out the contents his friend had snuck inside. And despite his misery, a kernel of hope shone its way through.

In his hand was a flash drive and Arianne's golden angel necklace. As those sapphire eyes glinted at him, he realized Sensatia might've just bought them one last chance.

Clasping the necklace around his neck, he welcomed the familiar weight of the angel. And as he weighed the golden pendant in his hand, a piece of Arianne, he felt her resolve fill him with its invigorating fire. The odds might be astrological, but that had never stopped Arianne before. So, it wouldn't stop him.

With the flash drive clasped in his hand, Keston prepared for the greatest act of treason in his life. Sensatia gave her life for this opportunity.

Victory or death. It was desperate, but desperate was all he had left.

Chapter 40

Andre

"**C**heers to the groom, and shout out to me, who's not a man and *far* from the best, but here I am: the Best Man!"

The bachelor party, filled with dozens of people Andre had never cared to know, screamed excitedly at Keston's toast. The winged male, who never left his quarters sober nowadays, raised his sparkling glass of champagne, almost falling over in the process. The crowd surged to catch him in a mosh pit, cheering as he finished the glass. The music blasted, and the celebration raged on, the bachelor they were supposedly celebrating forgotten.

Andre's own champagne glass hung passively in his hand. He was never the life of the party at the top of his celebrity, but a year away from the social scene had ruined his relevance. Especially compared to star-boy Keston Leroy.

"It's not even a real marriage," Andre grumbled, tossing back his drink with a scowl. "Why did I expect a real party?"

Why did he care about the party anyway? He was the Heir Apparent of Europe, the next in line to one of the most powerful positions in the world. Popularity and a cool set of party tricks hardly mattered in the grand scheme of world domination. His wedding on Christmas Day would be the culmination of everything he'd ever wanted: respect, recognition, and a line to the throne promised to him for twenty-five years.

Yet, Andre couldn't shake his jealousy as it sat like sticky sap in his lungs, making his chest heavy. The emotion had become familiar in the past year, and he almost welcomed it like a friend. At least there was *something* at this party he was familiar with.

He turned from the main gathering room into a less crowded hallway. Keston had hosted the celebration at his Great Aunt's palace in Muscat, a city on the Arabian Peninsula. The Al Fayeds were the reigning Elite family of the seaside city, living in the spacious Al Alam Palace. Keston likely enjoyed any debauchery he could get away with outside the shadow of Leon and Cassius's influence. For the time being, the Arabian Peninsula was a part of the Asian continent. Considering the peninsula's strategic position between the three continents, Andre assumed ownership would soon transfer to Leon in the coming year.

While Europe's palaces felt suffocating with all their artwork and fine carpets, Al Alam Palace felt more open and breathable. The marble floor and walls were accompanied by sparse pops of color where the architects had added designs into the stone.

Wandering alone, Andre finally had enough peace to think. He didn't know how Keston, a mutant, bore the noise. Even rooms away, the faint pounding of bass assaulted his ears. Keston liked to pretend he was heartless and cold like the rest of the Inner Circle, but Andre knew the truth: the male was an empathetic bleeding heart underneath all the scar tissue the Underground had slashed there.

Unlike the rest of them, Keston was taught to care about trivial things like empathy and family. The only empathy that mattered was what could be broadcast to the masses, and family only mattered to maintain power.

Naturally, Keston couldn't stomach the *harsher* sides of leadership—he simply wasn't raised to do so. Andre presumed he could understand, at least to a degree, why the winged male needed to numb it all.

Outside of his feelings for his mother and grandparents, Andre had grown up numb to everything. And look where that lack of emotion got him. Now all he saw were objectives, and he felt so much better for it.

To complete his coldness, he had one last task before his wedding. He was thankful to be outside Leon's borders for it.

Kalinda sat alone in her assigned quarters, her sleek dark hair highlighted orange by the candlelight. She didn't react when Andre stepped inside. Staring forward, shadows hung off the harsh lines on her face. Andre's servants had informed him she hardly ate anymore.

"You won't even acknowledge me?" He frowned, the last of his feelings for the woman poking through his apathy with a sting.

Her dull eyes looked through him instead of at him. "You've brought me to a party to celebrate your marriage to another woman, the very woman who has my sister enslaved." She looked back toward the windows—windows he'd ensured were locked and bulletproof. "I have no more words for you."

Andre said nothing. He simply stepped to the side, holding the door open.

They stared at each other for what could've been eternity. Kalinda looked like an exotic pet who'd never seen grass outside her cage: uncertain of the new world before her, and terrified of a catch. But Andre didn't move. He simply held the door.

For a moment there, he'd believed they'd loved each other. Maybe they'd loved versions of each other, vague imaginings of what the other could be. Neither had been interested in the other's vision.

And that wasn't a crime, so there was no longer a reason to hold her prisoner. At least, that was his logical reasoning. Deep down, part of him—a part he needed to silence if he was to become the ruler he'd been born to be—knew it hurt too much to have unrequited feelings. He might care about her, but he wouldn't give up his destiny for her. He couldn't.

Keeping her around would only be a weakness, a gradual collection of minor abrasions that would eventually shatter. But he couldn't kill her either. He needed to let her go. It was the only way his future would remain *whole*.

Kalinda stood slowly, as if afraid any noise would snap him out of whatever trance he was in and he would change his mind. As she approached the doorway, her green eyes were so wide and beautiful—no, he couldn't think that anymore. Her eyes were just wide, scared. Scared of him—no, he wasn't supposed to care how she felt.

For a fleeting moment, he feared she wouldn't say a thing. Maybe that would be better—

"I hope you're happy." She waited until she was outside his arm's reach to speak. "I hope this life is everything you've dreamed of."

Andre didn't look at her. "This isn't about dreams. This is about being who I was born to be."

"Funny, because you left the only people who loved you for who you truly were. You turned into something else to fit in—ugly and contorted. You can pretend I didn't know the real you, but I did."

That struck one of the few nerves he had left. He puffed out his chest. "I am Prince Andre Murray, Heir Apparent of Europe. This is all I have ever been, and all I ever hope to be."

Kalinda didn't flinch from him. "What would these people do if you were just Andre?"

His fists clenched. "That will never happen."

Genevieve's manipulation was out of the picture, he was marrying his greatest rival, Ace was chasing a ghost story, and Leon, despite his claims, was mortal. In the past nine months, Andre had kept his enemies close, making deals and contingencies with each.

No matter how the story played out, he would never be *just* Andre again. He stiffened at the reminder of his isolation and insignificance while in Pacific. He would never feel that way again.

Tears welled in Kalinda's eyes now, some strange look of longing coming to her face. "I loved you, Andre. That wasn't fake. I *know* you're in there somewhere. When you find him again, come find me."

For some reason, those words enraged him. "I loved you when I believed I was insignificant. I've outgrown that belief, so I've outgrown you. I have no interest in seeing that version of me again."

That time, she didn't respond. She took off down the hallway like she'd been nothing more than a courtesan walking past his door.

"Sounds like you need a drink, man."

Andre jumped. Keston leaned heavily on the wall behind him. Looking minutes away from passing out, his eyes rolled just slightly as he slurred his words. Yet, even plastered, Keston had managed to sneak up on him. Andre wasn't sure if that was a testament to the winged male's stealth or a painful reminder that he was a human in a world of gods.

Once he received Serum, that would all change. People would respect him. People would *revere* him.

"I have some reports I should get to." The prince frowned. "Enjoy your party."

Keston was toying with his cape, and Andre wondered if he'd even heard. With a huff of annoyance, he moved to brush past the drunkard, not in the mood for more conversation. The palace's library, with its beautiful marble columns, called to him.

Keston's hand was surprisingly steady as he stopped Andre. "Come on, I know you want me as your Best Man as much as you want Pandora as your wife, but here we are. And the Best Man code requires me to get you shitfaced."

For some reason, Andre relented. He needed at least one drink before he retired for the night.

In a private lounge connected to Keston's bedchambers, a skylight offered a view of the night sky with a fountain bubbling underneath. There were no stools at the bar, but a table rested beside the fountain where Andre gladly took a seat.

He was suddenly exhausted.

Keston took a place behind the small wet bar, hands expertly mixing drinks in a shaker. Neither hesitant ally said a word as Keston worked, both intimately aware they had every reason to hate the other. Yet, as the minutes passed, he found he saw things differently.

Both were unfortunate sons of the Pacific rebellion. Both mourned Arianne. Both had impure commoner blood running in their veins. Both needed to wear well-sculpted masks to survive in Leon's Inner Circle. Not so different.

Keston covered the rims of two cocktail glasses with a fine powder that could've been sugar or salt. For the first time in their tense existence, Andre was urged to ask him, "What are you still doing here?"

Keston didn't look up from his work. "No drinking while flying. I'm grounded until I'm sober."

"You know what I mean."

Amber eyes flashed upward. For a split second, Andre saw a glimpse of the feared demon of the Underground that the world whispered about. But as soon as the expression arose, it was expertly hidden behind placid drunkenness.

Was Keston more sober than he let on? Or was Andre's question significant enough to pull an ounce of sobriety out of an ocean of drunken thoughts? He gave the male credit. Though not raised in Europe's Elite halls, Keston was an expert at keeping people guessing.

"Ah," he said, pouring the drinks. "I see. Arianne gone. Genevieve imprisoned. Sensatia executed. All logic points to me cutting my losses and disappearing. It's not like anything is holding me back anymore."

"From what I've seen from you, logic isn't your strong suit."

Keston chuckled. "I may have increased senses, but that doesn't mean I got a boost in common sense, unfortunately."

"Question still stands," Andre deadpanned, accepting the drink. He took a sip, shocked at the cocktail's impressive mixology and the sweet taste of the rim.

Keston slid into the other chair, quickly downed his drink, and let his head roll back to look at the skylight. "I have a very specific skill set." He twirled his empty glass in his hand passively. "So I'm here because I'm doing what I do best. I'm not proud of it, but I've tried running from what I am, and that didn't get me anything but grief."

Andre took another sip, blinking as the alcohol started making his limbs prickle. "And what are you, Lord Leroy?"

Those haunting amber eyes flashed again, and intelligence lingered there—intelligence the male expertly liked to hide behind drugs, alcohol, and copious amounts of sass.

The grin the fallen angel gave was far from reassuring. "Depends on who you ask. I've heard backstabber, double crosser, and manipulator. All works just fine."

Andre's lips suddenly felt numb, like he'd drunk far more than the cocktail and two drinks he'd had earlier. He pointed at the winged male, a little levity coursing through his system, making him laugh. "I guess you're in the right line of business, then."

If he were sober, he might've placed more significance on the golden chain he saw poking out from Keston's collared shirt.

Keston eyed the prince finishing his drink. "I think there's one term that sums it up well, though."

"And what's that?" Andre said, swaying.

Beautiful and frightening, Keston was like a demon straight from the depths of hell as he stood. Colors and lights distorted around him, bringing the male into sharp focus. Vision blurring, suddenly it felt like Andre was surrounded by a dozen clones of the Underground urchin. He was smothered, cornered by dark hair and devious smiles of inhumanly white teeth. Then the clones closed in on him, their voices combining and surrounding him as they spoke one last maddening sentence.

"I'm the villain," the voices echoed.

Andre's head hit the table with a thud.

Chapter 41

Arianne

From her hidden corner by the hallway stairs, Arianne watched her brother leave the party, fighting the part of her that told her to follow him. It'd been hard to determine what she would feel when seeing him again for the first time in years. The conflict within her was unexpected. She wished she could hug him. She wished she could kill him. Trapped between the two, she could do nothing but analyze Andre as he walked away.

Arianne lifted her face veil and took a quick drag from her vaporizer. A determined calm settled over her, and she closed her eyes. The emotions fighting to come to the surface *had* to be pushed down. The mission couldn't afford her sentimentality, just trained precision.

It'd been a painfully long month of pushing down the heartbreak and longing: both for the family she never had and the love she couldn't chase. With a shaking breath, she took another sharp inhale of the vaporizer before tucking it into the folds of her embroidered dress. If there was enough fabric to hide her wings, there was enough to conceal the crutch she'd become reliant on those past weeks.

"He's on the move," Arianne reported in Tribal Latin into her comms unit.

So far removed from any power center in Europe or Asia, they'd determined that communications units were a necessary evil on such a critical mission.

"I gave Booty Call the signal," Blue reported from inside the main ballroom. "He'll pursue."

Arianne slapped her forehead, suddenly regretting the decision to bring comms. "Give him a better codename, *please*."

Blue snickered. "You took Birdbrain."

"Can we keep communication on this channel to what's *relevant?*" Khari hissed.

There was a painful amount of feedback as Blue shot back, "The only person not relevant here is *you.* Have fun squatting in the sand."

Arianne sighed. Her fiancé had a point. She hated having to bring Khari on the mission, but his forces were the only ones with experience navigating the desert terrain around the city. If things went south, Khari and his African mutant squadron would get them out alive. Sure, they weren't dealing with Paris-level security, but they were still invading a party with the Heir Apparent and future Lord Advisor in attendance. There was no way a jet would escape that airspace.

But they needed to be there. It was the only place they could coordinate an information swap with Keston: right under Pangaea's noses. And... they needed Andre. Arianne still wasn't a fan of that part of the plan, but objectives were objectives.

"Important question," Rhino's voice crackled through the comms, speaking English since European partiers surrounded him. "Is it unprofessional to eat right now? The party refreshment table is empty, and I'm just sitting here..."

"He already ate half the table," Lova deadpanned.

"Can confirm," Topher said.

Rhino sputtered, "Satyr? Y-you can see me?"

"That's the point of being the eyeball," Topher said with a long-suffering sigh. "I'm hidden, but I can see everything."

"How this team accomplishes anything is beyond me," Khari grumbled.

That's when Keston walked out of the ballroom. Arianne stiffened, the bickering in her communications unit forgotten. Her heart began to pound. Every fiber of her being begged her to run to him. One month. Four weeks. Thirty-one days. Each moment agony.

Her mate.

He was right there, but she didn't pursue him. She couldn't. Her hand clawed into the marble column behind her, quite literally holding herself back. Logic was quickly fading. Her mutant genetics screamed at her to see him now, now, *now.* No matter how much she told herself she'd see him in approximately twenty minutes, her body didn't want to take that chance.

He snuck away in the direction Andre had disappeared, striking in a dark purple throbe embroidered with golden trim and a matching golden cape. The traditional Middle Eastern clothing with modern Pangaean flair was a new yet fitting look for him, highlighting his Saudi heritage that she rarely saw beyond the tan skin and curling hair. Though Jaya might take after a chameleon in abilities, Keston was the true chameleon: blending handsomely into whatever culture he was thrown into—Underground King, European celebrity, Asian courtesan, son of Selvia, and Middle Eastern prince.

But there was also something off about his gait. Arianne squinted. Was he *drunk*? She shook her head, forcing herself not to follow him. Sure, she'd heard of Cindy and its effect on *Feras*—she suspected Cindy had been the dust Keston had blown in her face in Tokyo. But she never thought he'd use it. Especially now.

Approximately ten seconds later, Blue crept out of the ballroom, the Shadow naturally passing like a ghost behind Keston. It was interesting to see her in action. In a dark blue kaftan and matching veil, the Snake looked like a simple partygoer looking for a private room. But no human would notice her near-silent footfalls in her padded slippers. No human would notice she wore a thick coat of Mist.

Their entire team was.

Barely acknowledging Arianne, Blue only flashed a quick hand signal before disappearing. If things went according to plan, she would return and bring Arianne to Andre and Keston.

Waiting for her to return was excruciating. Arianne couldn't even pace, lest she attract too much attention from the Wards guarding the ballroom doors. At present, the Wards passively observed the foot traffic as guests arrived, used the bathroom, or disappeared into the palace gardens. Leaning on the columns by the staircase, she looked like a guest simply getting air and remained relatively unnoticed.

"Booty Call is ready," Blue reported. "It's go time, Birdbrain."

"Rhino, stop eating. I need you outside," Arianne said.

Moments later, the silver-haired male appeared, his bulky frame one head above the small crowd of guests exiting with him. Rhino wore a gray throbe, the outfit's tightness doing little to make him look smaller. Fortunately, most guests were too inebriated to pay the brute any mind as he waded through them.

The month since Japan had changed Rhino almost as much as Arianne. His silver eyes, which had once sparkled like diamonds, were dull like jewelry left to tarnish. He seemed older, more restrained.

Losing Treena and Tyrell had shifted something integral inside him. Her old friend was strong in many ways, but there was still a point when tragedy weighed too much, even for the strongest mutant she'd ever met.

"Are you okay?" Rhino asked, reading his friend like a book.

She was going to see her brother and Keston. Just to say goodbye to both again. She was falling apart, but she *needed* to succeed.

Arianne frowned. "I have to be."

Without another word, he pulled her into a hug. Arianne didn't know how much she needed it until his meaty arms squeezed together the cracked pieces of herself. "One day at a time, Ari," he whispered. "We take this one day at a time."

Right. She needed to focus on that mission. Nothing else mattered. All she needed to worry about was the next step. Any more thought into what came next would crush her.

"I love you, Rhino," Arianne whispered into his chest.

She didn't say it enough.

He squeezed her tighter. "I know your brother is in the other room, but don't forget your *real* brother is right here."

"Never."

And with that, she took one last deep breath of his familiar scent and marched toward the beginning of their desperate Hail Mary.

Blue met her halfway to Keston's quarters, her dark blue veil covering everything but her eyes, which had been disguised with brown contacts. They fell into step together, locking arms to look like another set of courtesans wandering the palace. They passed other guests, but the crowd thinned as they ventured further from the ballroom toward the narrower halls of the residential quarters.

They stopped in front of a deep red wooden door, the frame standing well over nine feet tall. Blue knocked twice before letting herself in, holding the door open for Arianne. Taking a deep breath to collect herself and turn off her comms unit, she followed. Something told her she didn't want the conversation recorded—even by her closest friends.

Andre was sedated, face down on the floor. At the wet bar, Keston watched the prince as he stressfully downed a cocktail with shaking hands. Up close, his visage was striking. His eyes were sunken, his typically sun-warmed skin was pallid, and an untamed scruff dominated his face. Keston looked like a frayed rope two yanks away from snapping.

Arianne almost reached for her vaporizer but stopped herself.

"Keston," she breathed, lunging toward him. She reached for his face, and he leaned into her touch, closing his eyes. She caught the pungent stench of liquor. "Keston, what happened?"

"Reunion later," Blue said behind her. "We're in enemy territory, Phoenix."

Right.

Arianne pulled away. Such a simple movement was harder than she thought possible.

Some animation returned to Keston, but he still looked shaken as he stared at Andre. "He'll be out for at least an hour. Let's get this over with." He reached behind the bar and produced a probe ending in a large needle. "Genevieve's instructions were specific: this needs to go into his—" He grimaced "—anal canal."

Both he and Blue looked at Arianne, and she recoiled. "I'm not doing it, he's my brother. That crosses some sort of line."

"Ancestors forgive me, I'll fucking do it." Blue surged forward and stole the device, placing a vial from her kafta pocket in the injector.

The vial carried a microchip engineered by scientists under Jin Shi's command. Once the chip was completed, Jin Shi found a way to get it to Blue. Sora might've bowed to Leon, but that didn't mean her forces were loyal to him.

As much as Arianne hated being in the dark on such a critical plan, Keston's encrypted instructions to organize that meeting could only be so detailed. Without Treena and Tyrell, communication with Selvia had taken a painful hit.

Blue continued to mumble to herself as she unbuckled Andre's belt. "I've seen what you two are capable of, but *now* you decide things have gone too far?"

Keston wordlessly placed a pair of latex gloves on the floor beside Andre's head.

At the distinct sound of Blue ripping her brother's pants down, Arianne turned away. She'd seen several terrible things in her life, but she wasn't keen on watching her best friend shove things up her brother's rectum—especially if the scene gave her a bonus view of other things a sister should never see.

Keston was also averting his gaze. "Make sure to inject the device into the tissue, we don't want him to, um—"

"Shit it out?" Blue hissed. "If you have so many suggestions, how about you do it?"

"Pass," Keston said blankly, taking another drink.

The silence was painful. Arianne hated how she could hear everything Blue was doing behind her. Finally, she heard the sound of Andre's pants sliding back on. She turned in relief, happy that the first step was over. Blue, on the other hand, looked absolutely mortified as she threw the probe on the floor and yanked off her gloves.

Her dark hair was frayed as she stared down at Andre. "I have images I never wanted in my brain." She placed her hands on her hips and glared at Keston. "This plan better work."

Leaning heavily on the wet bar, his eyes fixed on Andre. "I wouldn't have asked you to do a non-consensual prostate exam unless I was certain." He curled a stray strand of long hair behind his ear. "Genevieve was certain this was the only way."

His voice hitched on his sister's name. Arianne's stomach lurched. In the sparse information Keston was able to relay before the mission, one detail concerned Genevieve's capture. Knowing all his hard work to protect his sister had ultimately been for nothing, Arianne had the urge to comfort him.

Blue was still frowning at Andre. "Why not just kidnap him? Use him for leverage?"

"Genevieve explains her plan on this." Keston held up a flash drive. "I'll follow the objectives she set out for me. You just have to follow her instructions to the letter, and there's a chance we take Paris."

Handing Arianne the flash drive, she frowned at the blood caked on the protective plastic. She exchanged a charged look with Keston when she realized he was also focusing on the red stain.

He shook his head, and the fog in his eyes visibly cleared. "Andre does not hold sway over Leon. We wouldn't get much leverage by taking him hostage. This is about buying time, not winning negotiations now. With Asia joining Europe once Sora Ascends, we only have until the New Year to gain as much ground as possible."

Arianne felt her frown deepen. That past month, she'd had countless discussions with Sygrid, Colla, and Kajari about that very subject. This war was no longer about minimizing impact; it was about winning at all costs. And winning meant conquering. Winning meant securing as much power as possible to establish a solid base before Asia joined the war.

It was a terrible position, but it was their only option.

"We need to weaken Europe as much as possible, which means taking Paris, not hostages," Arianne agreed. "It means forcing Europe out of its stronghold and putting it on uneven footing before they combine with Asia." Arianne handed the flash drive to Blue. "Get this to Ringtail. Take the Ivory Court and rendezvous with Pharaoh and his team to retreat. I'll follow behind you."

With one last glance between Arianne and Keston, Blue nodded tersely and snuck out.

And then they were alone.

For a few painful moments, they simply stared at each other: just two desperate, broken people hanging on to one last desperate, broken plan.

Arianne cracked a smile that likely didn't reach her eyes. "Why do we always find ourselves in this situation?"

Keston shook his head and started mixing another drink. "I'm starting to think it's us." He laughed dryly. "We cause chaos when we're together. And now we're causing World War Four."

"This is not our fault."

With a long sip of his drink, Keston shook his head. "After we crash a royal wedding, it'll be seen that way."

Growing warm at the thought of everything her father had taken from her, Arianne clenched her fists. "We can't just sit around and wait for Leon to take over the world. I told you I would do anything to win, including this."

Arianne started to shake. Instinct's comforting claws began to curl around her anxiety. She hastily took out her vaporizer and took a long drag. As soon as the smoke filled her lungs, she felt Instinct's influence fade.

"You're smoking Frenzy."

It was a statement, not a question. She heard the mortification in his tone. It was enough to make her wince.

"Africa was researching the drug," she explained, squeezing the vaporizer in her hand. "A diluted dose helps me siphon off the pressure of Instinct—almost like I'm passively burning its energy without completely losing control. I'm constantly simmering instead of building up heat and exploding."

Keston approached her. He rested his hand on her forearm and slowly pushed the vaporizer from her face. "Who else knows about this?"

"No one." She felt her eyes burn, and she lowered her head in shame. "It's the only way I can stay sane anymore, Keston."

And that was the painful truth. The low dose helped her unleash Instinct's energy at a steady and controlled rate, but it also meant Instinct was always slightly turned on. Once she figured out the correct dose of Frenzy, she'd felt more in control than she had in months, maybe years. No overwhelming dread, anger, longing, or mourning. Just objectives. Just the next step.

The only side effects were an inability to sleep while the drug was still in her system and a nasty caloric intake increase due to setting her metabolism into overdrive.

Keston exhaled. "I understand wanting to turn it all off." He was silent for a moment, and then, "They made me kill Senny." His breath hitched. "They have Gen in a coma, trapped in a lightless chamber like a casket. I hate suppressing my abilities with Cindy, but I can't stop. Being sober means thinking. Arianne, when you *hear* what my sister knows—about our past, about everything—there's no going back. So much death, and it's all repeating itself."

It broke her to look into his glassy, miserable eyes and know there was nothing she could do to help.

She knew how he felt. Thinking led to pain, and pain made her weak, and people couldn't afford for her to be weak. The world needed Phoenix, not Arianne, if they wanted any chance at surviving the upcoming months. Just like they needed Blackjack, not Keston, to do the dirty work for that final chance.

Keston might be the last person in the world who needed Arianne, not Phoenix.

She buried her face in his chest. "None of this is our fault, Keston," she reassured him. "But it is our responsibility to fix it. I'm so sorry the weight was put on us. I really am."

As she'd promised Sygrid months ago, Keston was breaking. Arianne wasn't far behind him.

"I know you're engaged to Khari," he whispered. "Gen detailed the political incentives in her recording. I don't blame you, but—" His voice caught again "—it *hurts*."

Arianne stopped breathing.

"I'm sorry I didn't tell you."

What a lame response.

Her hands bunched up the fabric of Keston's cape, clawing for the touch of his wings she knew too well. Slowly, she found more words. They came out in unsure whispers, "I guess I just assumed we already knew we could only promise each other that one night. I only love you, yet I can't have you, and I didn't want to think about it then. I'm a coward. I'm sorry."

Voicing that painful reality almost made her knees buckle. All logic pointed to Khari: she'd spent more time with him, they had less history to recover from, and their alliance had already bought them countless victories. But despite all that, there was only one being in the world she wanted.

"I love you," Keston said, the words like air under her wings.

"We'll take Paris," Arianne reassured him. "And you'll come home with us to Moon Warren. We'll celebrate the victory in the Valhan and dance together until our legs fall off."

He leaned his forehead into hers, hands gripping her hips and pulling her closer. "Promise me we'll be together when this war ends, even if it's a lie, Princess."

"I promise," she whispered.

It was the best lie she'd ever told.

Chapter 42

Arianne

North America had arrived.

A Pangaean jet with jade markings landed next to Africa's in the clearing outside Moon Warren. Hidden in what remained of the underbrush in the late fall, Arianne watched Miguel Smith and his father exit, the pair clad in more leather and denim than fashionably possible. With Alvaro's memory gone, Miguel was the Heir Apparent marked to Ascend in January. He was barely twenty. Arianne wasn't the only young royal forced into leadership that year. She would almost feel bad for the young prince if she weren't suspicious of his presence.

North America had been understandably cagey after Alvaro's ruined Ascension Ceremony, even if Selvia's efforts had been in good faith. And until Miguel Ascended, North America couldn't offer aid. So what was the point of them being there?

Arianne retreated deeper into the woods as Commander Sarr greeted the Americans. She didn't want to interact with any brand of Pangaean royalty until absolutely necessary—yes, she was aware she was stuck with herself, unfortunately.

Before Sygrid called her to do draining things like being diplomatic or welcoming, Arianne went for a run. As her body finished maturing and her use of Frenzy increased, she found she had more energy than she could expend on most days. A long run through the brisk December air would help clear her mind.

An hour later, breathless and skin warm from exercise, she jogged back into Moon Warren. Sygrid converged on her immediately. "Get changed into something more—" She paused and analyzed Arianne's sweat-covered training clothes. "Presentable. We have guests."

"Well aware, why do you think I disappeared?" Arianne said with a smirk.

"*Arianne.*" Taking a deep breath like she was preparing for a lecture, Sygrid just deflated. Her face softened as she closed the space between them and squeezed Arianne's shoulders. "I'm sorry, I know this is overwhelming."

Arianne looked away, ashamed that tears of exhaustion and stress were already pooling in her eyes. "You think?"

Sygrid squeezed her tighter. "Get dressed, and after we can have hot chocolate in my quarters, okay?"

After changing into something more fitting of her position, Arianne flew directly to Dara Cave. The rushing waterfall outside the caves was comforting as she crossed the river and followed the torch-lit tunnels into the heart of the mountain. She paused momentarily at the entrance, offering a respectful bow to the antlers. She hoped Cervi's ghost would be there to keep her emotions in check.

Every leading player in their alliance stood inside the cave, all waiting patiently near the underground pond surrounding Selvia's Dara. The large oak tree had just lost all its leaves to the early stages of winter, the vast branches barren and skeletal underneath the gray December sunlight sprinkling through the natural skylight above. Arianne found it was fitting that it looked so barren and inert.

The group of leaders surrounded Sygrid in a crescent shape, who stood with her back to the underground pond. Arianne gave a quick flutter and landed at her mentor's side: Ductor and Deputy, a united front.

Sygrid pounded her ivory staff on the rocky ground, the deep thrum echoing across the cave. "It's time we begin," she announced.

Breaking from Luna and Ursa—Selvia's Senior Champions—Ringtail produced a projection simulator they'd confiscated from their raids in Oslo. He inserted the smuggled blood-covered flash drive into the side of the device. He looked distraught as he navigated the file. "This will not be easy to hear," he warned. "But we must listen regardless."

Sygrid's reassuring hand landed in the space between Arianne's wings, delivering warmth against the chill of dread. The recording began, and a projected image of Genevieve appeared. Though only her flickering blue upper body was visible and her projection was two times larger, Genevieve's presence made it feel like she was seated in the cave with them. Arianne took a moment to study the severe look on her face, and she was taken back to a time not too long ago when it'd been filled with nothing but joy and wonder.

Did Genevieve miss their days spent together in Greece, or did such mortal desires no longer concern her?

Genevieve's opening words were grave. "I'm recording this because we have officially hit the point of no return. At the time of this recording, Europe has unleashed Frenzy on Asia, putting the continent—and our best chance at success—in a headlock."

Images glitched in and out of view around her. Gasps passed through the group. They watched as lab reports, videos of feral test subjects, and documentation of the Kyoto disaster flashed in the recording. Bile rose in Arianne's throat. She'd seen the horrors of a city drowned in Frenzy first hand, but reliving the video evidence was just as revolting.

Genevieve continued gravely, "Come the New Year, Leon will have control of Asia's forces. We have limited time to secure as much territory as possible. At the moment, Tribal forces have dominated the north, and African troops have trickled in through Portugal and Spain in the south. While attacking Paris is a stretch, we are as prepared for the assault as we can hope. Taking the capital will not win the war, but it will weaken Europe enough that we may just survive the combining of Europe and Asia's might—we must gamble on this.

"We will take heavy losses. We will have to play cards we would have otherwise hoped to withhold. I will not detail the chances for success because, unfortunately, this is our best bet. By this point, you may assume the best day for the attack would be Christmas Day: Andre and Pandora's wedding. If things have gone to plan so far, my brother would have secured a microchip within Andre, which will activate a signal similar to the ones Wards have in their masks, known as the *'Friendly Fire Protocol.'* More details on this in my video titled: *'Friendly Fire Microchip.'* This signal is how Hera's Puppet army knows not to attack their allies. With it, we will have an advantage within a five-mile radius: all Puppets will be effectively inert."

Ringtail paused the recording, Genevieve's likeness freezing mid-frame and hanging midair like a specter. His tail swished back and forth. "The Ivory Court successfully inserted the microchip into the prince, so the first part of this plan is complete."

"How did you do this?" Kajari questioned with a frown.

"Must you know everything?" Blue spat.

Leaning toward his father, Khari whispered something in his ear. The African Commander grimaced and smartly asked no further questions.

Ringtail continued Genevieve's video.

"A more in-depth breakdown of this assault can be found in my alphabetically categorized mission plans in the folder on this drive called *Operation Paris*. But what's essential in this summary video is not how we will win, but why we must win. For those not in attendance in New York City, I will provide a recap before delving into the details that were unfortunately forgotten by time.

"The Great Disaster was not a world-ending event, but a human-ending event. During the Before, *Feras* lived at population densities similar to those of today. Scientists of the time developed an equation that calculated a value known as the *Precipice Coefficient*. This value was the tipping point of humanity: the point where mutant spawn rate outpaced human spawn rate, marking the beginning of the end of the human race. The world reached this point Before, and humans faced the likelihood of their extinction within three generations.

"I'll spare the specifics, but a group known as *Protecting All Nations from the Greater Adversaries of Evolutionarily Advanced*—PANGAEA—grew in power. Their message was simple: mutants had to disappear if the human race wanted to continue. Oppression started as it usually does, slowly. At first, legislation was put in place that criminalized *Fera* reproduction, but naturally, hatred and fear made things spiral out of control. The most outspoken of mutant groups was the *Filii Luna*, taking their name from Artemis, the goddess of beasts. This is where Legend remains relatively accurate: the *Filii Luna* were led by Angel and her mate, Cervi. Things escalated as the world's support divided between PANGAEA and the *Filii Luna*. The Last War followed. Finally, after years of warfare, the world was on the brink of economic and social collapse. This is when the two sides' leaders decided on a ceasefire to discuss a truce in New York City."

Arianne stifled a gasp, remembering the newspaper she'd discovered in the abandoned city a year before. The front page image had been of Angel, Selvia's progenitor, charging up the steps of the New York courtroom with her beautiful golden wings streaming behind her. Reporters and cameras had surrounded the warrior, but she'd been walking alone. Arianne had a chilling feeling about what happened next.

"Angel met the six Commanders of PANGAEA alone. She did this as a distraction. She and Cervi knew something they couldn't admit to the world: they'd lost in the most colossal way. The only chance they had was going into hiding.

Angel sacrificed herself as a distraction, a martyr who gave a small group of *Feras* the chance to hide and keep the truth alive. This was because the true Great Disaster *ended* the Last War... it completed halving the population after the war had already ravaged billions. But PANGAEA's founders wanted to blame the population reduction on an environmental disaster, rather than on what they actually did—hence the obscurity surrounding an event known as 'The Great Disaster.'

"History claims the city was nuked, but that was simply to hide the evidence. In reality, a great battle ensued right in the heart of New York City. Angel died protecting a group of insurgent scientists that would one day be called the Librarians. The battle was a loss from the start, but it allowed the *Filli Luna* and the first members of the Tribes to disappear into the forests around the world, places as far away from population centers as possible. This was because of PANGAEA's true endgame: genocide."

A ripple of horror passed around the group. Ringtail paused the recording again as he took a collected breath. "This is going to be difficult, but please listen intently until the end."

Arianne took a shallow breath, remembering Keston's warning about what they would hear on the drive. Ringtail's similar warning only compounded her dread.

The recording played.

"PANGAEA developed a gaseous toxin that directly targeted *Fera* anatomy. Much like scientists today are rediscovering, the Serum reacts directly with the *Fera* mutation in the brain. The scientists of the Last War simply took it a step further. They made a Serum derivative that killed mutants and erased memories in humans.

"These gas clouds were disbursed from every population center around the world. And in one move, PANGAEA killed ninety-five percent of the *Fera* population and rewrote history for the survivors. The six Commanders from the war took over their respective continents and took the details of their horrific acts to the grave, starting the world over. Spare the small populations of tribes-people and the Librarians, the whole world now believed they'd been citizens of a supercontinent known as Pangaea for the past three centuries. Cervi was forced to corroborate this story to quell any ill-fated rebellions. As generations passed, Cervi selectively hid this history until the world approached the *Precipice Coefficient* once more.

"This is no longer a war about rights or personal grievances. This is a war against erasure. The Serum was created so we would never repeat history, but this history was collectively forgotten. Now we are rocketing down the same path as our ancestors. If we don't correct the course now, we are doomed to repeat this same cycle."

Ringtail barely had time to pause the recording before outrage sent the meeting into chaos. Some tribal representatives were crying. Others were screaming. Even Kajari looked stricken. Arianne looked down at her hands, which had begun to shake uncontrollably. Her ancestor had billions of mutant lives on his hands. She could practically feel all that death and pain, like a curse passed down from generation to generation. In those moments of horror, she managed to look toward Khari: the only other person in that room who could relate to her utter disgust.

Two mutant descendants of the people who'd almost culled the world of their kind less than two hundred years ago. It was unthinkable.

"Were their deaths quick?" Lova's small question pierced the miserable sounds of weeping and rage.

Ringtail didn't look her in the eye. "I've found there are some questions we don't want answered."

Staring at the ground, Arianne focused on each emotion she felt at the truths of her family's past. The words came to her easier than she could have hoped. "You heard her," she said to no one in particular. "We're winning because we don't have a fucking choice anymore. We're winning because someone needs to avenge what they took from us." She raised her head and pointed a shaking finger toward Kajari. "No more alliance bullshit. No more half measures. It's all or nothing. We work together, and we win, or we die trying."

To her amazement, the African Commander nodded his head. "For penance to what my ancestors have done, you have my undivided support."

Then he turned to Sygrid, touched his hand to his forehead, and knelt in the most humble of Selvian gestures. Sygrid straightened, the hardness on her face softening as she nodded in recognition. And then, like a wave washing to shore, the rest of the leaders knelt before the Selvian Ductor. Arianne, in shock, realized they were bowing to her as well.

And for the first time, the reverence didn't feel foreign. She might hate having leadership thrust on her, but now she understood that she owed it to everyone who'd died before her. In her, she carried the sins of an empire and the sacrifices of martyrs. In her, she carried the ingredients necessary to break them out of the deadly cycle they were almost doomed to repeat.

In her reflection, she almost missed Ringtail continuing the video.

Genevieve's stoic yet mindful speech penetrated the atmosphere of determination and fear that had surrounded them:

"Now that we know what we're fighting for, it's time to take the city. Our assault will have three prongs: Palace invasion, distraction, and the main assault. Included on this drive are the aerial defense shutdown codes. An advance team will invade the Palace and turn off Paris's aerial defense system to give our main assault a chance to invade the city. The distraction will come from Arianne. She must step forward as Heir. To win this battle, we must throw everything at Leon and hope something hits, including weakening his position and distracting his forces with his undead daughter."

Arianne's stomach flopped at that. Keston had warned her in his sparse communication with Selvia over the past month, but she still hadn't adjusted to that reality. If she was ready or not, it didn't matter anymore. She needed to do it.

Genevieve's knowing smile was unnerving. "I bet you're wondering why I asked Sensatia to contact North America. Well, that's because they have the best air force in Pangaea, and I know more about Serum-induced amnesia than anyone on the planet. Removing this specific brand of amnesia requires a natural trigger. The Serum resets the brain to deliver new information. Unfortunately, in *Feras*, this mechanism is interrupted and can result in side effects from memory loss, ferality, or death—depending on severity. If the *Fera* recipient survives, we must find the natural trigger to finish the incomplete Serum reset. If things have gone to plan, I can assume Miguel Smith is with us. I think he will do the trick. And with that, I wish you all luck."

The video winked out.

Arianne looked up to see Colla's eyes boring into hers. *A natural trigger*. Her mouth dried out as she returned the Lion's gaze. Could that solution fix his memories? Was the Serum truly behind Colla's missing twenty-five years? The pair said nothing as Alvaro was ushered into the cave, his trusty binder already opened to study the profiles of each person waiting for him.

Miguel turned to his uncle, tears lining his eyes at the sight of his relative and mentor. Arianne bit her lip as the prince ran to hug his uncle and was met with confusion. Alvaro hardly moved. A collective sigh of disappointment washed through the group as the Commander and his heir separated without ceremony.

"*Tio.*" Miguel frowned at his uncle. "*Recuérdame.*"

A desperate plea: *Remember me.*

Alvaro blinked. A stillness fell over the group at the shift in the air. He blinked again. No one dared to breathe too loudly. And then he collapsed, his binder crashing to the ground next to him. Miguel braced to catch him and, with the help of his father, lowered the unconscious body to the ground. Alvaro seized, his hands shooting to his temples as he curled in on himself. Eyes squeezed shut, he fought the shakes with a horrible cry.

The entire room could only watch, unsure of what to do.

Colla's clawed hand went to Arianne's shoulder. Without taking her eyes from Alvaro, she squeezed it in reassurance. Everyone in that cave was desperate to see Alvaro—Denzel Smith—return to them, but Colla held an even stronger stake: if Alvaro could be brought back, maybe there was hope for him as well.

No one knew for sure what could trigger Colla's memories, but Arianne had a sinking feeling Leon might be at the top of that list.

And then Alvaro stilled. With a long, heaving gasp, his eyes opened. Arianne didn't move, terrified that even the slightest noise might disrupt whatever was happening. The Commander palmed the ground and pushed himself up. His forearm shook as he braced himself, chest heaving and drool trailing from his lips onto the rocky ground.

Alvaro's voice came out in a strangled rasp. "M-Miguel." He was still breathing too heavily to look up.

Colla's claws dug into Arianne's shoulder.

"*Felicitaciones.*" Miguel knelt and helped his uncle with tears misting his face. "Welcome back."

Sygrid's hand went to her mouth, swiveling to the Dara Tree in amazement. "The Ancestors finally gifted us with a victory." She held Cervi's staff in the air, which received a collection of excited shouts from the Selvians around her.

For the first time in over nine months, Alvaro gave one of his classic smarmy grins. Despite looking sickly pale and leaning heavily on his nephew, his smile radiated energy. "I think I recall hearing that you need an air force." He pulled Miguel into his side as he let out a cackle. "Let's show Europe and Asia what happens when you invite Americans into a World War. Commander Smith reporting for duty."

Chapter 43

Andre

"I know what I saw," Ace growled.

Andre frowned at the fireplace, leaning into its warmth as a December chill gripped his private foyer. The Palace of Versailles was majestic, but even the most advanced heating technologies could not defeat ancient walls. The prince watched the flames crackle below him, wishing he could return to the days when he would sit in front of the fireplace in the Murray Monument while his mother told stories of Tribal Legends.

Those days were long gone. Now he was at war with those Legends, and his mother's homeland was occupied by African forces.

He took a long sip of the cabernet Ace had poured for him, focusing on the hint of cherry wood in the smooth vintage. He had to give the Cartel boss credit: she knew how to select her wines. The pair didn't have much in common outside their sexual chemistry and daughter, but he could acknowledge they had similar tastes when it came to the finer qualities of life.

Rou babbled behind him, pulling him from the trance the licking flames had put him in. On the loveseat by the fire, Rou fussed with Ace's low-cut dress, looking for another feeding. Ace hardly paid the baby any mind as she glared at Andre with her obsidian eyes. He groaned inwardly, knowing her well enough to know she wasn't dropping the subject any time soon.

But he wasn't *interested* in Ace's conspiracies. In two days, he would be married to Pandora, and everything would be perfect. He would be the undisputed heir. He would fall into his rightful place at Leon's side.

Leon had promised him that.

He rested his arm on the mantle, wanting to show Ace he was comfortable and in control. She didn't hold the cards anymore—he did. He lazily shifted his attention to the Underground queen. "What you're describing is impossible."

"It's not impossible. You're just in denial. You're scared."

"Did you forget Madrid?" He scoffed, shaking his head. "I *handled* Arianne then, and I'll handle her now. I'm not scared of her." He corrected himself. "That's even *if* she's alive, which is an utter impossibility."

Ace lowered Rou to the floor, finally tiring of the baby's constant attempts for milk. Even with a baby on her hip, Ace was one of the most intimidating humans Andre had ever met. Somehow, she made lowering Rou onto a light pink blanket with an assortment of toys a terrifying spectacle. If Andre were a lesser man, the never-ending eye contact from under those thick lashes would have him running for the hills.

Wielding the room's silence like a weapon, she took her sweet time to readjust in her seat before speaking. "Do you have any idea why I'm still around?" She took a sip of wine. "Do you know how hard it was to crawl from nothing to where I am today?" She scoffed in disgust, looking away. "Of course you don't. Even as the bastard you are, you were handed everything on a silver platter."

"No—"

Ace wagged a finger, stopping him. "Don't try me. What little fight you needed to do for your power was orchestrated by me. Without me, without my planning, you'd still be wasting away on that backwater island. Remember that before you start thinking you can throw me away."

"What you're implying is impossible."

"Don't mistake what's truly impossible with what you simply don't want to believe is possible. I asked if you knew how I made it this far. That's how. Those who win consider every possibility—no matter how improbable or undesirable—without bias. They have plans for every contingency."

Andre rolled his eyes. "I tolerate these lectures from my father. I will not tolerate them from you."

"Do you want to be Commander?"

"What a ridiculous question."

Annoyance prickled in his chest at her attempt to control him again. He was no longer willing to tolerate her manipulations. Everyone in his life manipulated him. He'd seen it with Genevieve, Leon, and even Kalinda. Everyone wanted to bend him to their whims, wielding what they believed he desired: companionship, leadership, love…

Ace raised an eyebrow. "You don't act like you want it. All I see is a boy who wants the trophy for his bookshelf but doesn't want to put in the effort to shine it."

A smile came to her full lips, and she looked away like a schoolgirl trying to suppress laughter in front of a teacher. But they both knew she was far beyond things like embarrassment or the suppression of emotion. Ace was being condescending to him, the *prince*. That made his blood start to boil.

"I've dedicated my entire life to this. How dare you—"

"Yet, when I warn you of the one person who could threaten your Ascension, you would rather live in denial than deal with the problem." Ace's smile widened, happy with the reaction she'd stirred in him.

But Andre didn't care. He'd made a deal with her months ago: aid in exchange for Rou receiving royal status and Ace obtaining a spot in his Inner Circle. But she decided she wanted to keep changing the rules. She wanted him to work behind Leon's back, she wanted him to give her Keston and a ghost story, she wanted Andre to make her his queen. More, more, *more*. Whatever Andre gave her was never enough.

Now Ace was willing to pull on the stitches of his greatest wound—losing his mother and sister—to weaken him enough to cooperate further.

Enough. Andre was done. But he wouldn't say that. No, he was happy to give Ace a taste of her own medicine.

"Fine." He offered his glass. "Tell me what you need. I'll ensure you get front row seats to deal with our lovebirds. If you're right, you'll get your *royal flush*. If you're wrong, this is the last I'll hear of this. Understood?"

Satisfied, she finished her glass and stood, sauntering over to Andre. She was beautiful and toxic like a venomous snake as she approached him and trailed an acrylic nail down his chest. "You were always my favorite," she sighed into his ear. "And when I have the matched set, we can rule the world that Leon wins for us."

"You have a deal, Mistress."

Andre let her kiss him and started unbuttoning his uniform. He waited as the Underground Queen dropped lower and unfastened his belt, deriving a deep sense of pleasure at the sight of her on her knees before him. She thought she was manipulating him, but for the first time in their relationship, he was holding all the cards.

That thought was almost more arousing than what Ace was currently doing with her tongue.

He had to grip the fireplace mantle as the thrill of victory mixed with pleasure, their combined forces stronger than the bottle of wine he'd just finished. His eyes rolled back at Ace's touch, and he grabbed her hair, craving a physical representation of the control he felt over every aspect of his life.

Close, he was so close.

In two days, he would be Heir Apparent, and the entire world would be at his fingertips.

He wondered if Leon always felt this good. Andre was ready to live the rest of his life feeling that way.

And as Ace brought him to completion, he knew he'd tear down anyone who tried to take that feeling from him. He glanced at the fire as the last convulsions of pleasure passed through him, watching the flames dance with a smile. Andre wouldn't just tear down those who tried to take his birthright from him. He would reduce them to ash.

Even if one of those enemies claimed to be reborn from the ashes, he'd make sure she didn't rise again—sister or not.

Chapter 44

Arianne

R ed and black looked foreign on her.

Arianne never thought she would wear Pangaean colors. She stared in the mirror, transfixed by her reflection. She looked like a true Murray. Never once did she think she deserved to look like that, even as the blood coursed through her veins, even as she conquered more of Europe than any of her predecessors since the progenitor of their Commander line.

Despite her surprise, there was no denying that the look suited her.

Leona Murray.

She never wanted that name. But if the day went as planned, that could be her future. Straightening the jacket, cut to accommodate her wings, she tried to feel at home with her new reality. The world was about to find out who she truly was. After a lifetime of living in the shadows behind closed laboratories, hidden rebellions, and face masks, the world was about to see *her*.

Not an experiment. Not a runaway. Not even Champion. An *Heir*.

Sygrid appeared in the reflection, her hands curling around the armor on Arianne's shoulders. The Selvian Ductor regarded her apprentice with her remaining orange eye, a strange expression on her face. Arianne had to avert her gaze as tears started to well.

There was no guarantee either of them would return. And if Arianne did succeed, there was no guarantee the version of her standing in that room would return—a Commander might fly back in her place.

"You're ready," Sygrid whispered.

Arianne tightened her jaw. "I have no other choice."

"I know you didn't want this."

Sygrid squeezed her shoulders again with a frown, and Arianne was hit with a painful reminder of Josephina. The ghost of her mother practically stood next to Sygrid: both mothers looking at her with those mixed expressions of sorrow and *pride*.

"You've become a strong leader right under my nose." Sygrid's lips wobbled. "So dedicated to your people. So *strong*. The world will follow you. I have no doubt."

I don't want the world to follow me. I don't want to lose myself as my father did.

But that couldn't be said out loud. Sygrid couldn't hear how much Arianne had already lost herself. She was fading. She could already feel it. With how much of herself she'd already bartered to that war, announcing her desire for the throne would erase the last part that was still *her*.

It hurt, like ripping off a limb and throwing it to the wolves chasing her down just to slow their pursuit. But such a strategy only worked for so long. Eventually, she'd be consumed—the only thing all that pain had bought was time.

If she had to lose herself for the people she loved to win, she would do it. It wasn't the slot in life she'd ever wanted for herself, but it was better than dying in that laboratory all those years ago.

Shit life she'd been born into. Yet, as she'd told Keston, this wasn't her fault, but it was her damn responsibility. She would win at all costs, and then she'd deal with collecting what remained of her after.

Sygrid made sure to meet her eyes that time. "Just say the word, and I will hide you forever, Arianne." The determination on her face was nothing shy of the Legendary female who'd lived in the world as the Silent Death: uncompromising, protecting. "The world could end around us, and I would protect you until there is no air under my wings or in my lungs. Do you hear me?"

"I know." Arianne's voice cracked.

They both knew there was no choice. That made her love Sygrid even more. Because she would do it, even if it cost them the war, she would hide her until mushroom clouds consumed them.

It just made Arianne want to protect all of it even more.

A strangled noise escaped Sygrid, and she spun Arianne around into a crushing hug. Tears fell freely down her face as Sygrid wrapped them in a protective blanket of white feathers. For a few fleeting moments, they were safe from the outside world, just Ductor and Deputy, mentor and Tyro, mother and daughter holding each other. Arianne's tears turned to sobs in Sygrid's hold.

"I'm scared."

Sygrid palmed the back of Arianne's braided head to her breast. "Cervi and Genevieve put their trust in you. I believe in you. You've become greater than I ever was. There's only one being in the world who can do this. Trust that."

Arianne sniffled. "I'm not scared of fighting." Her voice caught as she wrapped her arms under Sygrid's shoulders and squeezed. It took a few moments to work up the courage to continue. "I'm scared of losing myself."

"Arianne—"

She pulled away far enough to look her mentor in the eye. "If I lose myself, kill me. *Please*."

Instinct was like a clawing possession at the back of her mind, the thrill of battle too hard to resist. The darkness crept closer with every moment, the pull to become as detached as her father getting worse by the day. It would be so easy to surrender to it all, and when she did, she didn't want to know what she would become.

All she knew was that such an existence was not something she wanted.

Sygrid was crying now. Her hand shook as she wiped a tear from Arianne's cheek. "That's it. You're not going. We can call off the attack. We can win another day."

"You and I both know this is our best chance. Losing me is a small price to pay to protect millions from genocide."

"You have people who love you for *you,* Arianne. Focus on that." Their foreheads touched. "Your conflict is one I know well. I dedicated myself to war—made it my god. My mate and child became second to the next death I could offer as a sacrament. It was agony when I woke from the battle haze and saw what I had lost. I will not let you live in the same regret I had for twenty years."

Closing her eyes, Ariannge fought to let those words penetrate her numbness. It was no use. Her decision was made. The thing was, she didn't intend to survive long enough to regret any of it.

She breathed in Sygrid's familiar scent of bonfires and evergreen, savoring what could be their last moments together. "I love you, Mom," she whispered.

Somehow, their embrace grew tighter. "I love you, little Fledgling."

And just like that, the final moment of weakness Arianne allowed for herself was gone. With one last breath, she stepped away from Sygrid and marched out of the tent before her tears could ruin any more of her war paint.

In the chilly overcast morning, the war camp was bursting with the controlled chaos of a battle on the horizon. The Selvians and North Americans were in London, the closest rebellion-controlled major city to Paris. If everything went to plan, North America's air force would deploy from London while Africa's limited air forces would shoot up from Spain to pinch the capital.

The camp's chaos had her heart rate rising. The looming battle and charged conversation she'd just left had her itching, on edge. She felt a growing urge to punch a tree—a warning of Instinct's growing temptation. But she couldn't give in, not yet.

Looking around, Arianne pulled out her Frenzy vaporizer and took a quick drag. The unpleasant urge to call on Instinct faded. She felt herself sag with the relief at the emotionless calm and boost of energy that washed over her.

As she tucked the vaporizer away, she spotted Colla leaning on a gnarled oak tree, waiting for her. From the frown on the bearded male's face, he could most likely detect the distress in Arianne's scent—she probably wasn't shielding her expression well either. Hopefully, he hadn't seen her Frenzy pen.

"I'll take good care of them, I promise," Colla said as he approached.

He was joining the Ivory Court to infiltrate the Palace of Versailles. After Rhino and Arianne, Colla was the best pilot they had, and his leadership skills made him a natural selection in her absence.

"I have no doubt," Arianne said, already incapable of injecting any emotion into her words.

"Do you want to see your team?"

"No need. They've been briefed."

Colla stopped walking. "They're your friends, Arianne."

That stung for a moment. She shoved it down. After her conversation with Sygrid, she couldn't afford to have more people distracting her focus. Topher's steady presence, Lova's sunshine smiles, Rhino's deep-bellied laughter, Blue's sarcastic humor—

"I danced with them in the Valhan last night. We had our time."

Arianne brushed off the urge to run to her team, hug them, and bask in their combined glow until her last moments in that camp.

"Arianne?"

"Yeah?"

Colla's bearded face swept into a smile. "Merry Christmas." He extended a necklace to her, one made of a collection of pointed teeth hanging from a sturdy black string. He pointed at his sharpened canines. "Something to remember me by when we're separated. A reminder to never stop bearing your fangs."

Holding up the necklace, her hard-fought numbness cracked for a second time that morning. Her lips parted as he gently took it back and clasped it around her neck. It was almost short enough to be a choker, and she marveled at the familiar feel.

It'd been so long since she'd worn a necklace.

"Did I get a smile out of you?" the Lion hummed, leaning over with a knowing smirk. "Yup! I can see those canines. Look, I put shark and lion teeth on it. Little bit of you and a little bit of me."

"Colla..."

The large male chuckled and opened his long arms. "I'll take a hug for payment."

She fell into the Lion. "I love it."

And that's when his planned ambush sprang into action. Holding her down, Rhino, Topher, Lova, and Blue rushed in and enveloped her in a hug. Wings pressed uncomfortably into her back, and she was squeezed with the strength of five mutants.

"Flying off without a goodbye?" Topher challenged.

"Classic," Blue piped in.

Rhino picked up the entire group, including a very concerned Colla. "We're in this together. All the way."

Arianne relented, melting into her friends' embrace. "I'll see you guys in Phase Two. Stay alive until then."

"We're the *fucking* Ivory Court," Lova exclaimed. She giggled at the group's combined surprise, an innocent smile coming to her face. "What I'm saying is: if we can't do this, no one can."

Arianne caught sight of Sygrid stepping out of her tent. The Selvian Ductor managed a small grin before her expression turned severe. She held up one finger: one hour until the wedding.

It was time to fly.

Separating from her friends, Arianne gave them all one last loving look before she extended her wings and prepared for takeoff. She might be slowly losing herself, but she'd never felt more genuinely *Arianne* as she hit them with her best devilish smirk and announced, "Let's go save the world, motherfuckers."

Chapter 45

Keston

The wedding was beautiful. Keston almost felt bad about ruining it.

In the heart of Paris, Notre Dame was a spectacle, decorated with Christmas garlands, lights, and a small fortune in flowers covering every inch of the cathedral. In true Pangaean fashion, red dominated the decorations from the poinsettias to the velvet bows on every pew. False snow fell from the rafters above, coating the aisles and seats in fine white powder. If Keston had seen the scene as a child, he would've believed it was a Christmas miracle.

Growing up, his family had always tried their best to cut down a tree and decorate their small cabin. The choir's soft Christmas music almost brought him back to his living room, where he'd sung ancient carols with his mother while his father played the piano. Then he caught his father's eye, and any fond memory was quickly squashed.

Emmanuel was dead. Now the sight of his father's face haunted him: the source of some of his best memories... and a reminder of who'd taken such a wonderful life from him. Cassius betrayed his family, burying his town and wife. Cassius approved of his own son's mutilation and experimentation. Cassius stood by and applauded Leon as he unleashed Frenzy on the world.

Concentrating on his father, Keston let his rage grow, channeling his focus. He would need every ounce of bitterness to carry him through the next few hours.

It all ends here, Father.

Keston was done being complicit. He was done aiding in any more of the Inner Circle's evil. Come that evening, life or death, Keston would no longer bow to their tyranny.

In a way, that wedding also represented a new union for Keston. A union with the light, a promise to protect at any cost. It felt good.

"This might be the first time I've seen you sober."

He jumped, turning to face Sora. It didn't go unnoticed how she'd chosen to wear a deep green pantsuit—*Selvian* green. The Jins had not joined her either. She'd arrived in the belly of the beast alone, protecting her loyal followers.

Keston ducked his head toward the future Asian Commander. "I think we can all agree this day is too important for me to be fucked up."

That earned a smirk. "The Best Man: on his best behavior. I never thought I would see the day."

"I didn't think I would see you here." *You shouldn't be here.*

If Sora recognized the message, she didn't let off. The princess turned and looked at the people rapidly filling the cathedral. The royal wedding, even without Africa and North America, was already proving to be the event of the year. The pews were crowded with the world's most influential people. Keston caught sight of his Great Aunt and her family from the Middle East. He managed a furtive wave, knowing he'd caused a mess in their palace a few weeks prior but already too close to breaking down to deal with an apology.

Seeing how he'd orchestrated the wedding crash of the century, he also saw no use in apologizing to his family yet. There was about to be much more to repent for—he might as well group everything up in one go.

He was efficient like that.

"I didn't have a choice," Sora whispered, continuing to survey the audience decorated in the finest jewels and fur coats. "I think you can understand. We're controlled by the same master now. I think I can finally consider you a friend, Leroy."

Keston could've sworn it was disgust on her face—he'd looked the same way the first few months he'd been forced to grace Elite gatherings. It was a look of annoyance, a look that saw below the glittering surface to the copious greed and hypocrisy underneath. He then remembered that, until a few months ago, Sora was much like him: an outsider pushed to the front lines. Sure, she'd been royalty, but the sickly sweet politics had never been her responsibility.

Much like Keston, Sora was more comfortable with the grit and grime of the Underground. The criminal underbelly of Pangaea might've lacked much of the Elite charm, but there was something authentic—unapologetic—about it. People of the Underground, though just as despicable, were nothing but their genuine selves. Here, among the wealthiest fraction of the world, any authenticity was hidden beneath layers of fine fabrics and plastic smiles.

Sensatia, someone he'd once believed was a product of such a world, had seen through the glamour better than most. Then she'd wielded her control over it like a Champion did their Selvian Steel blade. A pang struck his heart, and he found himself wishing he were as intoxicated as Sora had expected.

Only a few more hours and you're done with this life.

A few more hours, and he could live a life that didn't make him want to numb it all.

Authenticity. Genuine intentions. Keston didn't know how much he valued those things until he'd been forced to live with their utter absence for two years of his life. No wonder he'd fallen so deeply in love with Arianne. She was nothing but her authentic self. She was a lot to handle, but no one could ever say she was anything but genuine. She stuck to her beliefs and *refused* to let anyone corrupt her vision.

Something told Keston the people around him could use a lesson in that particular subject.

"Your Highness," he said, grabbing Sora's arm before she could walk away. The princess glared at him, but it quickly faded when she saw his urgency. "I would sit near the exit if you want to avoid the crowds at the end," he offered in a barely imperceptible whisper.

Sora blinked one. Twice. Then she inclined her head, looking every inch like her mother, and said, "Good luck, Keston Leroy."

He would need it.

But he didn't have a choice. *Feras* around the world didn't have a choice. This was no longer just about a Commander who wanted to conquer the world. It was about sin so horrible it rippled across generations. They'd already seen the consequence of failure once. They couldn't afford for history to repeat itself.

Once more, Keston glared at his father. Leon stood next to him, looking about ready to burst with pride. The next generation of Murrays would be crowned today, the inheritors of Earth itself if he got his way. This wasn't just a wedding; it was a declaration to the world, a showcase of the next phase of Pangaea.

A Murray's Pangaea.

The Commander and his Lord Advisor paid no one any mind, seated to the right of the stage and away from the rest of the guests. Keston preferred it that way. He feared that if he had to exchange more than a few pleasantries with them, he'd give away every ounce of his vile hatred and ruin the entire plan. Keston was spared as Leon stood and proceeded to the back of the church, preparing to take his victory stroll down the aisle with his cyborg daughter.

Let them think they'd won. It would only make their surprise all the sweeter.

"I think you're supposed to be taking up your position at the altar," Ace's familiar purr sent shivers up his spine.

Even now, that voice took him back to the casinos beneath Leonueva. Her phantom touch haunted his mind even then, working to pull him away, to bring Blackjack back. He squared his jaw and stood taller.

Smirking as he turned, his eyes went to Roulette on the woman's hip. "I didn't think you'd be so keen to marry off your baby-daddy." He winked. "Though I'm glad you found someone to fuck you after all those years of me rejecting you."

Ace's deep purple lips gave a tight smile that didn't reach her eyes. She didn't break eye contact as she adjusted a bow in her daughter's wispy hair. "We can both agree her father is a level up from you."

Keston openly laughed in her face.

Though her infamous tattoo was covered with makeup, the look she gave him reminded him of the years he'd spent as her pet. The laughter died in his throat. The Underground Queen gave him another once over. "Careful how you talk to me, Blackjack. If you're content to make an enemy out of me, I will remind you why my name is Ace, and yours is Jack. In any game we play, the ace always beats the jack."

His upper lip curled. "Your favorite suit might be spades, but I'm willing to bet hearts will give you a run for your money."

"A lot of confidence for someone who lost their wildcard."

Even standing so close to her, he couldn't smell anything thanks to the thick coat of Mist—the entire room was covered in it. Keston stared into Ace's dark eyes, searching and wondering if anything human remained outside her games and ambition. The master and former slave held the charged gaze, both daring the other to shatter the thin veil of pleasantries preventing them from ripping each other to shreds.

Ace raised a finely tweezed eyebrow. "What would your lovely Arianne think if she could see you today? Back on the same team as me? Working for her father?"

Keston didn't break eye contact. "Something tells me she'd tear this entire cathedral to the ground.

"A shame, that would have been a spectacle."

He was already walking away.

Most of the audience was already in their seats. He pushed past a couple of stragglers, focused on reaching the grand altar at the head of the cathedral. A reporter's camera flashed, stunning him for a moment, but he ignored the paparazzi and kept going. It would only be a few minutes now.

The choir disappeared to the side of the church, exposing the altar and the stunning array of flower garlands on display. True to Sensatia's flawless party planning, she'd arranged an event that was equal parts elegant and stunning: not too gaudy, but detailed enough to display the Elites' vast wealth and power.

The thought of Sensatia brought another sharp stab of guilt. Keston almost stumbled as he climbed the altar. Catching himself, his hand snagged the golden angel pendant that'd been exposed from his collar. He squeezed the pendant and took a breath. The warm metal in his hand reminded him of Sensatia's sacrifice. He would make sure her loss was worth it. It was the only penance he could afford.

The pastor greeted Keston with a nod. Keston blinked and gave the man's white robes a once-over, realizing he'd never seen a religious leader in his life. He knew some faint remnants of religion still existed, especially in landmarks like Notre Dame, but he wondered how much the position resembled what it had been Before. Did the pastor believe in the dead religion that'd inspired the chapel's creation, or was he simply playing a part?

The organ began to play, ethereal and all-encompassing. The very building became its own instrument as the air vibrated with the deep sound waves. Keston's breath caught at the sheer majesty of the sound. All guests stood as the doors to the back of the cathedral opened, and the groom strode through.

Prince Andre Murray looked every inch like the title he'd fought so hard to earn. For that minor detail, Keston had to give him credit. Andre's black uniform with shining gold buttons and red trim was perfectly tailored to his lean body, making him look like a Greek statue: human, but as close to divinity as possible. Untouchable, cold, and sturdy. Billowing behind him was a cape of deep Pangaean red, matching the carpet his perfectly waxed boots marched down.

While Andre hadn't been born with the blood of a prince, he certainly knew how to walk like one.

Andre arrived next to Keston's side. Keston was going to comment, but quickly realized Andre wasn't paying him any mind. He stared out at the crowd, his face emotionless and body rigid. Keston huffed and took a step back. If Andre wanted to ignore his Best Man, it was no skin off his neck.

Ace walked down the aisle next, guiding a barely walking Roulette as they scattered white petals across the ground. Keston watched the pair with thinly veiled disgust. He never thought he'd see the day where *Ace*—of all people—would attend a wedding, let alone be the one throwing petals around. He tugged at his red bowtie, aware he might be dead and living in his special brand of hell. Maybe that explosion back in Tokyo had actually killed him.

The organ music swelled, and the crowd turned to the doors again. Pandora strolled into the chapel, arm linked with Leon. The sound of applause melded with the organ, drowning out Keston's sensitive ears. For those uninitiated with the horrors the two had concocted, the moment looked straight out of a fairy tale: a princess in a bright white ball gown and the king dressed in regal regalia—obsidian and ruby-jeweled crown and all.

Pandora had added extensions to her bleach blonde hair, and the strands fell in perfect waves down her back. A diamond crown and a veil stretching the length of the church trailed behind her, the lacework pattern of lions and swords more intricate than anything Keston had ever seen. Her dress had a high neck and fitted sleeves that complemented her muscled shoulders, hiding the vast array of cybernetics around her chest. The tight bodice extended into a collection of billowing skirts below her hips, the dress's circumference almost taking up the entire aisle.

In the cyborg bride's hands was a bouquet of poinsettias. Most applauded the beauty of the flowers, but Keston could only see the red. It made her hands look drenched in blood.

Pandora almost looked in love with Andre as the prince took her hand from Leon and guided her to the altar. Keston knew the truth: she was in love with what the union would give her. The pair clasped both hands before the pastor and smiled at each other. Keston ground his teeth, wondering if everyone else in the room could *feel* how lifeless those smiles really were.

Fortunately, Keston was spared from witnessing one more second of that wedding from hell.

A shadow appeared through the stained glass windows behind the altar, growing larger and larger until it blocked all light. The audience barely had a chance to start screaming before the stunning glasswork shattered in a crash that sounded more beautiful than any note the organ had played that day.

With shards falling around her like the deadliest of rains, the winged warrior landed in the middle of Notre Dame. Wings bloodied from the glass, she looked every inch like the unholy angel she'd become. The warrior of death and reincarnation stood and bowed like the screams of her victims were thunderous applause. Her face, painted in black and cast in a euphoric smile, was the stuff of nightmares. Her uniform, almost identical to Andre's, was the mark of what she'd landed in that church to become.

Conqueror. Avenger. Heir.

Princess Arianne Murray stood from her crouch, her golden brown wings extending behind her in all their infernal might. Her cold, gray eyes examined her subjects in disgust. "You'd think I would be invited to my own brother's wedding. You can imagine my disappointment." She turned toward the altar and gave a mocking bow. "Is this the part where I object?"

Chapter 46

Arianne

Arianne might hold the world record for recklessness, but it was safe to say she would break all her personal bests that day.

She wasn't certain how the return of the rightful heir to the continent would go, but screaming followed by silence was certainly not what she had in mind. She'd anticipated a *lot* more screaming. Maybe applause? Sadly, stunned silence made sense, though nowhere near as satisfying.

The entire church looked like a movie on pause—something should certainly be happening, but instead, everything was unnaturally still. Even Keston, doing his best to look as surprised as Andre next to him, didn't dare move. The tension was killing her. She wished someone would shoot at her. Pandora looked two seconds away from attempting it. At least then she wouldn't be stuck waiting.

As Genevieve had predicted, Arianne's arrival was *quite* the distraction. Her existence put Europe's leaders in a stalemate. If Pandora or Andre attacked her, they revealed their hidden martial talents. If Leon ordered the execution of a legitimate heir, he could face consequences under the Constitution and other Commanders—if he still cared about the repercussions of that. But even the potential consequence of killing an heir in front of an audience would give him pause.

That's all she needed: stall enough major players for as long as possible while her allies worked to shut off Paris's defenses.

Every eye in the room went to Leon, waiting for their leader to make a move before even breathing out of turn. Anticipation made Arianne shake as she locked eyes with her father for the first time in two years. The last time she looked into those eyes, he was tearing her heart to shreds as he prepared to drop a building on her.

The thinly veiled outrage on Leon's face was almost enough to make up for what he'd done to her. Almost. Arianne was sure the only way to truly feel any ounce of closure would be if she dropped that cathedral on him in return.

She just might.

Leon stood slowly, a baleful half-smile coming to his face as he daringly walked closer to his daughter. "Didn't I have you killed?" he asked passively.

That was the worst response she could have heard. Arianne's insides boiled at the emotionless simplification he put to the most agonizing day of her life. It made her sound like just another task, another successful mission he hardly thought about. One simple sentence reduced her pain to nothing. From the look of satisfaction on his face, he knew exactly what he was doing.

"Considering you fucked that up twice, I'd add killing me to the list of things you're not good at. Right under being a father," she spat as she flicked her wrists down, extending the two blades of *Horizon's Edge* and igniting the steel.

Leon placed his hands in his pockets. "A short list, really."

Arianne looked back at the crowd. "In case you're wondering if we're related. That comeback was better than a DNA test."

The Commander stared down his only legitimate heir with amusement. She wanted to wipe that expression off his face with the sharp edge of her blade. But she couldn't move. Not yet. She needed to hold the audience's attention for as long as possible. Still, the urge to attack was getting harder and harder to ignore.

Behind Leon, Keston caught her eye. He subtly shook his head: the only support he could give in those moments. They both knew it was only a matter of time until his cover was blown, but like Arianne, he was buying as much time as possible.

"So tell me," Leon rumbled, walking around a frozen Andre and Pandora. He considered the two half-heirs with a mild interest. "What was your plan today, Phoenix? Stop the royal wedding? Attempt to cause political turmoil? Get some of Europe on your side? Civil war?" He tsked condescendingly. "I have to say, desperate never looks good on a Murray. You'll have to do better if you want to claim that last name, Little Beast."

Leon's cutting name for her hurt more than she'd anticipated. Arianne fought back the flinch at the memories that name invoked. She'd grown from the girl who'd first attacked Leon in the Murray Monument. She was in control. She would prove she could stand toe to toe with her father, no matter how hard he tried to knock her off balance.

But then she realized: Leon was far too calm. Arianne's inner emotional turmoil came from someone. And that someone's scourge of a daughter had just reincarnated before his eyes for a second time. And instead of losing his mind, Leon was exchanging insults. Even a stoic like Sygrid would struggle to keep her composure.

Something was wrong.

Arianne took a daring step forward. "Desperate is marrying two half-heirs because you know your line of inheritance is utterly fucked without me."

Her father smiled, and Arianne wanted to rip his head off. "Have any heirs I haven't heard of?" He jerked his thumb back toward Keston. "Let me guess the father."

Keston coughed.

Screw stalling. She knew one very satisfying way to get everything over with.

Arianne gave Leon's smile right back to him. "You know what? I should have done this years ago."

She drew her blade, ignited it, and thrust it straight into Leon's skull.

"Arianne!" Keston lunged, eyes wild in panic. "No!"

The crowd started screaming again.

But no blood fell.

Then the world started to glitch. The image before Arianne pixilated and fractioned into varying colors. Arianne's breath caught as her vision split, doubled, repeated, and blurred. It was like trying to watch a television after thoroughly cracking the screen. She stumbled back, crashing into one of the pews. The Elites promptly cleared the bench, their shouts of terror drowning out her ears as they made a break toward the exit.

But Arianne didn't watch the stampede of Elites. She watched her father.

Even with her sword lodged through his eye, Leon's smile remained. Then his facade glitched, revealing the world behind him. His face faded, replaced by a Puppet, its cybernetics sparking with the blade through its faceplate. As the Puppet collapsed, so did the rest of the illusion.

Arianne stood alone with Keston in an empty church as the remaining Elites cleared out behind her. Keston's jaw hung open in utter shock. Still standing next to the Puppet that had once been Andre, he didn't move. The only thing that proved he wasn't frozen like the rest of the projection was his eyes: frantically darting back and forth, fighting to make sense of everything.

Looking at the remote at her hip, Arianne's blood turned to ice. If Andre wasn't there, that meant she had no protection against however many Puppets were in that building and the surrounding streets...

She only prayed Andre was still in Paris, or both sides of their assault would be overrun.

Slow clapping echoed through the church. Arianne turned.

Ace stood from her seat two rows from the front, the only wedding guest who hadn't been scared away from Arianne's assassination attempt. Her daughter pixelated away in her hands—another illusion. A smug grin painted the Underground Queen's face as she continued to applaud with her newly empty hands. She stepped out into the aisle and extended her arms in welcome.

"Oh, Arianne. I wish you weren't so predictable."

Chapter 47

Andre

A ndre had never seen his father so pale.

The projection call dropped, leaving the conference room in deafening silence. Leon stared at the ground, bright blue eyes wide. If Andre hadn't known his father, he might've described the Commander as scared. Even Pandora, who stood next to Andre just as their projections had in the cathedral, shook with uncontrolled emotion.

"Your Majesty," Cassius Leroy's hesitant voice broke the shocked silence. "We need your orders."

The clock on the wall behind Andre was louder than a grenade. The relentless *tik-tok, tik-tok, tik-tok* threatened to drive him insane. Their fears had come to fruition: Selvia had enough intel to risk an attack. That contingency had been planned for—expected, even. Yet, Selvia still found a way to surprise them. The shock from that day's events rested in the unexpected, the unspeakable. In fact, no one in the room dared to voice their new reality out loud.

Arianne was *alive*. Andre hadn't believed Ace's suspicions because they were illogical—he'd warned no one for that very reason. Warning meant there was a chance it could happen, and he'd been convinced it wouldn't. But as he stared at the live feed of Notre Dame, he knew his supposed logic had only been denial. He'd been too scared to face reality, a reality he'd known deep down would leave a hole in his gut.

Leon's right eye twitched. For a moment, Andre wondered if the man before him was another projection and the real Leon was already continents away. But the moment of stasis passed, looking like nothing more than a glitch in his seamless confidence. Leon took a deep breath, as if resetting a computer in his brain, and the typical unflinching Commander returned.

He marched toward the exit to the conference room they'd commandeered in the Palace of Versailles. "You saw the wedding," he announced, pushing the doors open. "The rebel forces sent a distraction. They're most likely targeting here next. To your posts."

Cassius ran to catch up. "Sir, what are we going to do about..." He trailed off with a flinch when he saw Leon's expression.

"About what, Lord Leroy?" the Commander demanded. "About the rebel operative that just landed in Notre Dame? Nothing. We have the security systems of Paris's air defenses to protect. That is priority one now."

"Yes, sir."

Andre fell behind the group, his attention going back to the conference room. Curiosity pulled him to continue watching the cathedral livestream. As he'd promised Ace, she got a shot at Keston and Arianne. He wondered what Ace would do with her opportunity at her Lovebird royal flush. He wondered how quickly Keston would turn on Pangaea now that his precious Arianne had returned.

Most of all, he wondered if Ace could survive them. Time would tell.

Andre stood still, waiting until he locked every bit of sentimentality behind iron walls. Certain he was under control, he waited to feel something stir inside of him, but nothing came. Staring at the open conference room door, he waited for some tidal wave of anger, grief, or even love to rise to the surface, but he was utterly numb.

Arianne was a scourge who'd broken his heart one too many times, and now she was actively vying for the Commandership he'd worked his entire life to obtain. She was no longer dead or alive, sister or stranger. She was just another hurdle he would surmount.

Pandora tugged on his arm. "Come on, love. The honeymoon has to wait. We have a laboratory to protect."

Right. His wedding. The laboratory.

With allied tribal and African forces rising against them, Leon had always intended their wedding to be a way to lure the rebels out. The spectacle the world knew as the royal wedding was nothing but an afterthought. Andre and Pandora had been legally married two nights prior. He looked at his wife as she insistently tugged on his arm. Once again, he searched for even an ounce of compassion or love for the woman he was linked to for the rest of his life, but felt nothing.

The apathy was an advantage. To survive the upcoming battle and protect the laboratory, he was thankful for no distractions. Duty, ambition, and fury were the only things he allowed himself to feel now.

Or ever.

How dare savages attempt to take what was rightfully his? Andre had been unrefuted Heir Apparent for two days, and someone was already trying to take it away from him. It was unacceptable. They would all burn—including the firebird herself.

Leon waited with Cassius outside Hera's three-story laboratory. The Peregrine Pacific stood loyally behind them, draped in a deep purple representing the melding of their alliances: blue for Pacific and red for Pangaea. Spare the Peregrine Pacific; the wing was mostly empty. Most scientists and engineers had been evacuated to their Alpine military base, save a few stragglers to maintain security and critical systems. The likelihood of a tribal attack had been high enough to warrant precautions, but someone like Leon would never condescend to a complete evacuation. That showed too much respect to an enemy he barely deemed human.

Besides, Andre knew his father enjoyed getting his sword bloodied.

Leon unsheathed *Lion's Fang,* whatever uncertainty he'd shown in the conference room long gone. "Hera and her associates are wiping this lab as we speak—a protocol we wanted to avoid unless necessary. We need thirty minutes to complete the data transfer to our Alpine stronghold. This is top priority."

Pandora rolled her cybernetic arm shoulder, the fibrous metal glinting in the sterile laboratory light. "What about the air defense codes?"

Hera's laboratory was the center of technology in Paris. It made the most tactical sense to keep control in that lab. With Paris's sheer size, it was common knowledge that the air defenses were the city's best option against potential attack.

Until recently, the location of the defense control and the specs for how the system was run were closely kept secrets. Thanks to Genevieve and Sensatia's combined efforts, those two critical elements were now compromised. Even Hera's best scientists couldn't completely re-code an entire defense system in mere weeks.

If the Tribal-African forces reached the systems, they could disarm them, opening up Paris to aerial attack. But that was *if* advanced operative forces could make it that far into the city unscathed.

Unfortunately, Selva had already proven they shouldn't be underestimated that day.

Leon glowered. "We know we're compromised. Our main priority is holding for thirty minutes." He held up his wrist. "Synchronize your watches. The countdown starts now. If we find ourselves at a disadvantage and cannot hold after those thirty minutes are up, we evacuate. Understood?"

"Yes, sir!"

Leon and Cassius turned to move down the hall, taking ten of the Peregrine Pacific with them. "We will prepare the escape jet," Leon continued. "We'll keep your evacuation route open, should you need it."

Andre felt his stomach drop as he watched him disappear. It made logical sense for Leon to remain away from combat unless necessary, but a part of him had looked forward to fighting by his father's side. They'd trained together his entire life. Andre knew Leon's fighting style and powerful tenacity better than most, and he craved a chance to join such a warrior in a fight that truly mattered.

"We won't need to evacuate." Pandora smiled, eyes glowing red. A squadron of twenty pink-haired Puppets marched from their charging ports at the back of the lab. The Bubblegum Battalion whirred in efficient unison as they surrounded the prince, princess, and remaining dozen Pacificans in a protective circle. "Failure is unacceptable. Especially now that our lovely sister is back."

Andre scanned his wife for any sign of her volatile insanity. Arianne always had a way of bringing out the worst in Pandora, but right then, the cyborg almost seemed tranquil. Maybe Pandora had come to the same realization as Andre: if they wanted to retain everything they'd fought for, they couldn't afford to focus on emotion.

Maybe there was love for her inside him after all. Not a romantic love—he'd conceded it never would be—but a love he'd argue was just as powerful. It was the love of understanding, the love of knowing that it'd been them against the world for their entire lives.

Arianne had always been on a pedestal above them. Not anymore. Andre and Pandora would weather any storm their sister sent their way. They were the future Commander and First Mother of Europe. It was time the world treated them with the respect they deserved.

From the far corner of the lab, Jaya appeared, followed by Treena and Tyrell. All three mutants had the glassed-over look in their eyes, courtesy of their control collars. As the Inner Circle had learned from Ace's demonstration, the control collars granted different advantages over feral subjects versus sane ones.

Control over Jaya was more refined, perfect for specific orders and tactical missions. With the twins' ferality, however, granted unmatched strength. The price was a loss of control and longevity. Even now, the control collars barely restrained the twins, who were almost zombielike as they twitched and growled. On multiple occasions, they looked prepared to strike, only to be stopped at the last second.

But that wasn't what was most haunting about the feral twins.

Feral subjects lacked the basic desires of their sane counterparts. This included the urge to sleep, eat, or practice hygiene. Most feral mutants died within days of their transformation: their energy expenditure, compounded with their injuries, killed them relatively quickly. With the control collars, Hera found a way to keep the creatures alive longer, but that didn't completely counteract their bodies' deterioration. Ferality pushed a mutant's body to its max, but without the want to eat or sleep, the collars could only slow the rot so much.

The twins were emaciated, practically corpses. Their skin was almost gray, already taking on the pallor of the dead. Their rusty hair had been shaved down to their skulls to feign some level of cleanliness. Inky veins originated at their black eyes and spiderwebbed across their faces and necks, the corruption creeping like tar across their bodies. Andre had watched in horror as those veins spread with every passing day. He wondered if the blackness would completely consume them, or if they'd be graced with death before that happened.

The circle of Puppets opened to let Jaya and the twins in, who took their position with the Peregrine Pacific. Jaya brandished a semiautomatic rifle, and the twins curled their hands like claws. The defensive circle closed around them once more, protecting the prince and princess at the epicenter.

Europe was ready for attack.

"I, Andre Murray, take you, Pandora Richards, to be my wife," Andre repeated the phrase that'd tasted like bile in his mouth just nights before. Now the words felt like a prayer of protection.

Pandora's grin was far from romantic. "To have and to hold—" She snapped her cybernetic arm, and the metal extended into a sharp blade. "Weapons, plenty of weapons."

"From this day forward," Andre continued.

"For better or for worse... a *lot* worse."

He smirked. "For all the riches and never poorer."

"In all the sickness in the world. Maybe some health peppered in there."

Andre and Pandora Murray drew their weapons just as the palace alarms started to blare. Now the real countdown began. Fifteen minutes, they needed to fight for fifteen minutes. The alarms were insistent, red flashing lights and wailing sirens warning of the enemy closing in. A bead of sweat trickled down his back as he watched the countdown, the seconds seemingly lasting minutes.

Any moment now.

Andre held his double-bladed sword in a lateral line out in front of him, a Ward ready to begin his watch. "Until the deaths of our enemies do us part."

A figure sauntered out of the shadows, followed by four others. The heels immediately gave their serpentine guest away. He should've known: if anyone could break into the capital of Europe unscathed, it would be her.

Blue Krait and her squadron of *Feras* stopped twenty paces away. The Snake's blue-painted lips curled into a smile as she placed a hand on her hip. In her other hand, she waved a remote back and forth. "It is my great pleasure to accept your surrender on behalf of the Ivory Court."

Before Andre or Pandora could react, Blue pressed a button on the remote, and every Puppet in the Bubblegum Battalion lost the red glow in their eyes. With one unified thud, two-thirds of their defensive force tilted face-first and hit the ground—a deadly squadron, twenty strong, now just unanimated husks.

But that wasn't the most detrimental turn of events.

Three distinct chirps sounded behind Andre. He tensed, recognizing the sound. Whatever signal had just turned off the Puppets had also deactivated the control collars

Chapter 48

Keston

"Oh, Arianne, I wish you weren't so predictable."

Ace's mocking voice surrounded Keston in a cloud of insecurity. He recognized that tone. Once again, Ace was a million steps ahead. They were so far behind he didn't even know if it was worth trying to catch up.

Arianne stiffly turned, her feathers fluffing up like the hackles on a cat. "Tell me where Andre is, and I'll make sure your death is quick."

Ace laughed. But before Arianne could lunge, she disappeared. Then dozens of Aces sprang up around the church, their projected forms surrounding them in a circle. His head shot back and forth between Arianne and Ace, his brain malfunctioning.

For two years, he'd been nothing more than an actor. Now he had no idea what part to play. Was Ace working with Leon? Was she betraying him? Protecting Arianne could blow his cover. But he couldn't stand by and let Ace destroy her. Was there still an advantage to maintaining his guise of loyalty?

Frozen in indecision, Keston could only watch the scene before him. Arianne screamed in outrage and attacked Ace after Ace, growing in fury every time she cut down a doppelganger, and the image pixelated out of existence. The room echoed with Ace's rich laughter. Arianne's sides heaved, more in frustration than exhaustion. The Underground Queen was taunting them: Arianne's specific weakness.

When the sixth Ace disappeared under her simmering blade, Arianne let out a guttural scream, "*Ace!*"

Keston glanced at the small army of Aces slowly spawning and crowding the cathedral. He grit his teeth as dozens of obsidian eyes landed on him, each cutting him down with condescending entertainment.

He wanted to kill her. How could he manipulate the variables to get close enough to try?

Then he realized. He needed Blackjack one last time.

Arianne, despite her frustration, seemed to settle enough to make calculations of her own. She glanced at him, and a silent agreement passed between them.

She turned and pointed her left blade at Keston, her animosity so believable that for a moment he feared she somehow believed he'd betrayed her. Her upper lip curled as she growled at him, "And what about you? Do I need to kill you, too?"

To ensure they were on the same page, he briefly touched his collarbone where her angel necklace rested under his tuxedo. She gave him a faint nod, and he prayed she'd read him correctly.

Keston shoved his hands into his pockets and smirked. "I thought it was you who saved me back in Tokyo," he drawled. "I should thank you. Too bad I have this lovely heartbreak policy: you break my heart and," he said, sliding on the brass knuckles of his *Talons*, "I crush yours."

"Careful, Blackjack." Ace's hum surrounded him as all her projections spoke in unison. "We could use her."

"Fuck this," Arianne spat. "I have an invasion to finish."

Without another word, she opened her wings and shot toward the windows she'd broken through. Keston was almost relieved. That was until he heard Ace's mocking laughter. He didn't get a chance to cry out before Arianne slammed into a solid wall. The Simulator had fooled them into thinking the window was there. Their reality must've been subtly rotating without their notice, preparing for the very high chance the caged birds might flee.

Expecting glass instead of concrete, Arianne wasn't braced for the crippling impact. She cried out and crashed to the floor.

As Arianne fought to pick herself up, the room began to spin. Faster and faster, the images swirled around until Keston could hardly stand with the vertigo. Windows swept past walls. The floor became the ceiling. Shadows and sunlight blended until he couldn't make out anything aside from the hands in front of his face. He could see everything, but he was blind. Overwhelmed, he braced his hands on his knees to keep himself from falling.

The only constant throughout it all was Ace—her dozens of bodies merged into one as the room's spinning slowed. And when the simulation around him stabilized again, only one of her remained. Directly before him, her arms gestured to display a grassy meadow around them. Keston recognized the mountains rolling in the distance: Mende.

Ace now wore her favorite ensemble of black techwear joggers, a white muscle tee, and a techwear leather jacket. Her signature tattoo and boxer braids had returned, replacing the bun and heavy makeup. This version of his boss was only a projection. Still, Keston knew this was how she wanted to present herself for her victory lap: an unapologetic Underground urchin, not some wannabe Elite.

He wondered how long Ace had been manipulating Europe in order to steal Leon's two prized weapons.

"You didn't think I'd let you two go that easily, did you?" Ace pouted.

Keston blinked, fighting to remind his brain that what his eyes saw was not the whole story. The bright green grass and clear blue skies were a lie. He was in Paris, in Notre Dame Cathedral. But the more he looked around, the more disoriented he felt.

The exit was behind him, right? No, he'd been turned around. The exit was in front of him now. But how far? Ten feet? But there were pews in the way. And Puppets. Would invisible targets shoot him if he made a run for it?

They were left with only one option: play Ace's game.

"You never wanted to work with Leon," Keston gritted.

Ace shrugged. "In combat, it's advantageous to remain nimble on your feet, ready to make adjustments at any time. I didn't know what I wanted. I was willing to play along until the best route to success presented itself. Whether that means working with Leon or betraying him."

"And you've decided to cash in."

"The Crusade for humanity is here," Ace said as if that explained everything. "It's time to build our bunkers with as much power as we can carry. The world is about to tear itself to shreds, and I intend to survive the fallout. That might make me a cockroach, but at least I'll be alive."

"Keston!" Arianne's disembodied voice echoed around him, but her screams were quickly suppressed.

He lurched, head whipping around in a desperate attempt to locate her or orient himself. But it was no use. A perfect combination of Mist and the Simulation left his senses completely useless. He couldn't risk any movement.

It was like a giant game of poker. He knew his hand, but he didn't know his opponents', and he certainly didn't know how successful his hand would be until more was revealed. Yet, he had no choice but to go all in.

"And let me guess, you're trying to recruit Arianne and me onto your all-star team?"

Ace considered for a moment, tapping her chin like she was solving an equation in her head. "Two advanced superhumans with powers blessed by the heavens. One valued as a world-changing weapon since birth, strong enough to maintain a Commander's obsession for decades. The other was modified to be her replacement, her equal in every way. It's obvious: Leon understands the power a mutant of your caliber can carry. Naturally, I took notice. And naturally, two are better than one, and I certainly don't want to let one stay in enemy hands. So, I'll take the matched set."

"You had me for ten years." Keston clenched his fists. "You never recognized my power, not like that."

Her knowing smile was devastating. "Your blood was a bargaining chip I couldn't lose. But politics have changed, and your blood is no longer my problem." She walked up to him and tracked her hand across his back like she'd done countless times growing up. "Do you know the easiest way to lose power over someone?"

He stilled. "You take their soul away."

"Sure." Ace shrugged. "That works for *humans*. But you're not human. I would argue you and Arianne left humanity behind the day you razed Leonueva and got a taste of how much *more* you could be."

Keston ignored her attempt to stare directly into his soul, looking beyond her as he deadpanned, "What's the answer to your stupid question? I'm dying to know."

Ace petted his hair like he was just another purebred dog in her menagerie, studying him with a look that could almost be called affection. She leaned forward to whisper in his ear, "The easiest way to lose power over someone is letting them surpass you. My beautiful Blackjack, I was your sunrise and sunset when you were just a human. But," she said, lifting his cape just high enough to reveal the tips of his feathers, "if I ever let you realize the angel you were born to be, I would've been powerless. So I suppressed you. I got a competent bounty hunter, a bargaining chip, and the guarantee that an avenging angel could never be used against me. Sometimes, never using power is preferable to allowing the power to get into the wrong hands."

To hear the words out loud, so explicitly, made all his pain and misery *real*. Keston shook, staring at the ground, mortified. Ace hadn't just enslaved and brainwashed him, she'd suppressed an integral part of his biology. In every way that counted, she'd controlled him. He wanted to throw up. Like a jack-o'-lantern, Ace had dug out his guts and replaced everything natural with a candle that only glowed for her.

The visceral acknowledgement of the husk he'd become underneath was numbing. He didn't know how to feel. He didn't trust whether he *could* feel. Had he been lying to himself the whole time? Had there been a Keston to return to, or was Keston long dead?

Once a jack-o'-lantern was carved, there was no putting the pumpkin back together.

Was finding himself after all that evil even possible? He'd thought he'd changed in Greece, but it had been so easy to fall back into death and betrayal after he lost Arianne. Maybe Keston was nothing more than another role he'd played. For a short time, he'd even fooled himself.

Keston might be dead. Maybe Ace was right. He would always just be Blackjack. The boy from the meadow they stood in was long dead.

Ace's fingers curled around his shoulders. "But now the power's been unleashed. Pandora's Box opened. I'm amazed at what you've become. Just think what we could do together. You won't fall into Leon's hands if you work with me. You would break the cycle."

He almost fell for the trance, but caught himself before he tripped over her words like he'd done countless times before. She'd nearly made him give up. But no. Keston was *real*. He would fight every day to prove it if he needed to. Freeing himself, he pushed Ace away. He'd likely just shoved a Puppet with her image simulated over it, but he hoped the gesture got his point across.

"I refuse to be a slave anymore," Keston said lowly. "Not to you. Not to Cassius. Not to Leon."

He didn't care if those words damned him. They felt fucking good.

A sneer slowly overtook her serene kindness. "Oh, look at you. You think you're so righteous. Let me remind you of the past you're so quick to brush under the rug."

Keston spat on the ground. "The past doesn't matter."

I'm Keston Celineson. I write my own destiny now.

Ace paced around him in a slow, predatory circle. "You claim Keston is better than Blackjack? Then, let's look into what you've done with your emotional freedom. Do you know why I made you numb? To protect you. You lost your home. You ran away from your family. Caught between the bloodlines of rebellion and savagery. I wanted to save the little boy I rescued off the streets from the pain that would have torn him to shreds. I was looking out for you, Blackjack."

"Lies." Keston squeezed his eyes shut, refusing to let even an ounce of her poison into his veins.

"Be honest with yourself, how has that new conscience been working out for you?" she asked, still circling. "Because what I see is a miserable bleeding heart. You're unraveling at the seams. Drinking." She poked him. "Drugs." Another poke. "Public panic attacks."

Poke. Poke. *Poke.* Each poke struck home with increasing intensity until the last jab felt like a bullet piercing his skin. But he didn't respond. He could only stare at the ground as the ugly truth bled out of her dizzying lies.

A lie always holds truth. Ace had been the one to teach him that lesson.

"When you were my Blackjack, you were solid, perfect. You came and went without a care in the world. My Jokers worshipped you. You felt nothing. You may not have been happy, but you were certainly not this shell of a person."

Keston swayed. Maybe she was right.

And then came the damning whisper, "I can take that pain away again. You and Arianne could step away from all this right now. You could be together. No more royal politics. No more fighting in a war you won't survive. No more 'lesser evils.' You could leave it all behind. Isn't that what you wanted when you ran away to Greece?"

As she spoke, the scene changed. He recognized the beach before the Simulator completed the scene. He turned to the villa he'd bought with Arianne, signed with the name *Keston Ortiz*. Tears misted his eyes as he stared at the house he hadn't returned to since he'd heard of Arianne's passing. His mouth wobbled as he took in the stamped concrete patio and that one upper-story window that never closed properly.

His home. His After.

"I'll let you keep the house." Ace shrugged. "I'm thinking of our relationship as something more pro bono this time. You two lovebirds would be loyal to me, I'd send you on the missions I need, and when you're between jobs, you have that cushy little life you've been dreaming of."

They could walk away right now. No war. Guaranteed survival. Ace couldn't possibly make them do anything worse than what they'd been doing. They were falling apart, torn to bits by the requirements of their roles, and here was a chance to stop that.

Working with Ace, he would either be numb or happy. Both options were preferable to the hell he was living in now. He'd been working so hard to be the hero, but he'd failed at every turn. Even the attack on Paris hadn't gone to plan. Maybe he wasn't meant to be the hero. Maybe it was better to cut his losses now.

Ace watched him consider her offer with eagerness. She seemed to hang onto every shift in his facial expression, from his brow furrowing to a hand raking through his hair.

"You're right," Keston began. "I don't know who I am deep down. Pangaean or Selvian. Good or bad. I might never find the real me because of what you did to me. And that *sucks*. I wish for that pain to go away every day."

He smiled passively at her, placing both hands on her cheeks. He held her there for a moment, and for someone watching on the outside, the gesture could've been sweet. That was, until Keston's angelic smile turned into the picture of wrath.

"But there's one thing I *do* know about myself: I keep my promises. I promised Arianne I would help her win this war, and I promised you that your reaper would be wearing my face."

With one synchronous push, he crushed the Puppet with Ace's image. The metal crumpled in his hands as he pressed harder and harder, compacting the automation's head like a soda can. Only when he felt the Puppet's body go limp in his arms, and he heard Ace's shouts of annoyance, did he drop the lifeless husk on the ground with a shuddering thud.

Ace reappeared ten feet away, outrage plain on her tattooed face. "Fine," she spat. "I'd prefer not to use control collars, so here's one last test for your newly minted perseverance: I'll show you what you'll have to endure if you stay in this war. Let's see how many times you need to watch Arianne die before you fall in line. Be careful, or you might just kill the real one—again."

Before he could reply, Ace disappeared, and twenty Ariannes appeared around him. Each one was a different reincarnation from various eras of her life. Surfing wetsuit, Pacific uniform, hiking boots, khakis, techwear, bathing suits, dresses, and Selvian robes.

Keston had loved every version.

He didn't know if he could watch Arianne's death again. But he had to. Nineteen of them were Puppets he needed to kill to escape. Only one of those Ariannes was *his;* he refused to leave her behind. Never again.

Unlike his training sessions, if he got hit in that simulation, he would bleed. He smiled at the challenge.

Extending his *Talons*, Keston braced himself. With a collective scream, the Ariannes charged. Some paired off and fought each other, almost a poetic representation of the war he knew she struggled with daily: two versions of herself warring for dominance. In a move almost equally poetic as fighting herself, four Ariannes peeled off from the group and converged on him. It seemed that, even when in love, they were destined to fight each other.

I always find you, Arianne. What's one more time?

Chapter 49

Arianne

One moment, Arianne was pinned to the floor by three invisible Puppets, spitting and kicking to break free. The next, at some point between her abysmal crash landing and her even more abysmal attempt to bite off one of her assailant's metallic fingers, she was let go.

She screamed as her adrenaline surged, uncaring how she escaped, just happy to capitalize. She jumped to retaliate before the Puppets held her down a second time, but stopped mid assault. The room around her flickered, and suddenly the three invisible Puppets that had captured her materialized.

They all looked like her.

Her simulated copies wore outfits from her past, like photographs brought to life. Arianne could see equally painful and beautiful versions of her old self. All the pieces of herself she'd left behind nearly made her cry.

Watching all the girls she'd once been made her realize how cold and distant she'd become. Surrounding her was *her*, but she didn't have a thing in common with what she saw.

She wanted to hug each one, knowing the pain and rejection deep inside them, knowing how close they were to breaking every day. In each doppelganger, she was reminded of every fractured piece of herself she'd rejected to become the Legend she was.

Hundreds of times, she'd convinced herself that she was happy that those Ariannes had been left in the past. It was all necessary to save room for what she'd become. But the longer she stared at the former reflections of herself, she became suddenly unsure.

For some reason, she had the traitorous desire to trade her Champion's paint just to feel a connection to her past selves once more. All around her was *Arianne*. Same face, but it was clear that was where the similarities ended. One Phoenix lost in the sea of Ariannes.

Stumbling back from her reflections, her mouth dried in horror. Surfer Arianne marched forward on bare feet, fist reeling back to strike her. Pacific Officer Arianne sprang from the right and attacked Surfer, the two falling into an ugly brawl on the ground. Too busy watching the fight, Arianne barely had a moment to brace before Experiment Wetsuit Arianne sprinted at her into a shoulder check.

Arianne hit the ground hard, feeling the metallic sting of Wetsuit's strike. She scrambled up, frustrated that she could best the Puppet under normal circumstances. But those were not normal circumstances. Her swords were lost to the simulation, she was surrounded, and she was admittedly psyched out.

"Come on! You hate yourself!" Arianne screamed as she swept the legs out from under Wetsuit. "Beating the shit out of a Puppet with your face should be therapeutic!"

It was strange to see the simulated expression of surprise on Wetsuit as she landed on the ground. It was like looking in a mirror. Arianne didn't waste time waiting for Wetsuit to recover—automations wouldn't lose their wind like a living opponent. Flipping Wetsuit over, Arianne wrapped her legs around the Puppet's midsection. Then she clawed into Wetsuit's neck, ignoring the Simulation's attempt at generating blood, and dug through the mesh of cables and metal for the power cord.

In every fight with Puppets, she'd found cords hidden behind their polyester neck plates that routed power to the computer systems in their heads. Cut the power, cut down the robot. While it looked like she dug through flesh, the hard plastic and wires peeled under her fingers. She found the thick power cord and pulled. Spare a brief electrical zap, Wetsuit went limp in her grasp without further struggle.

Arianne took a moment to lie on the floor and catch her breath under the limp automation. If she pretended for a few seconds, the weight of the Puppet felt like a weighted blanket. She managed a sigh in her brief moment of comfort during an invasion starting World War Four and a battle literally against herself.

Her life had gotten so complicated.

Rolling her head to the side, she spied Pacific Khaki Arianne, hair tied back in a bun and boots shining like she'd spent all evening polishing them. Arianne's fingers almost throbbed at the memory of all the routine scrubbing. With a smile, she pushed the automation off her and rushed at Khaki. She needed someone to blame for her current shit life; Khaki would work perfectly.

If that dumbass version of herself had just been happy and remained on the *damn* island, none of this bullshit would be happening.

"Hey, you!" Arianne screamed. The Puppet barely turned as Arianne jumped and rocketed a flying kick through its head. "Time to knock some sense into that thick skull of yours!"

Her momentum carried her through. She landed behind Khaki and watched the robot wearing her face correct itself. Khaki attacked with her feet, proving the Simulation had pulled information about her fighting style. Raising her right shin to counter, it felt like fighting a clone. But she was faster than the automation.

Khaki leaned back and kicked high, but Arianne was ready, rolling beneath it. She jumped, and in one decisive flip, her wing shot into the back of Khaki's neck and crushed it on impact.

Khaki was down. Which version of herself did she need to have a therapy session with next?

Arianne spotted herself in a sleeveless tank top with a guitar strung across her back. Her heart wrenched. That was the tank top from the bar she'd visited with Genevieve and Keston when they'd performed as the *Fuck Ups*. The sight of that version of her brought up feelings she couldn't process right then.

For that specific reason, she wanted to rip Tank Top to shreds.

Keston beat her to it. Amidst the fray of golden brown wings and braided hair, she hadn't had a visual of him the entire fight. He'd removed his tuxedo jacket and cape, throwing punches in his white button-up with the shirtsleeves hiked up to his forearms. His outfit was torn, but as usual, he somehow made it look fashionable.

That's when Arianne realized her dopplegangers were talking to him.

Tank Top dodged Keston's brass-knuckle punch. "Don't you remember? We were so happy!" she pleaded as she back-stepped another attack. "We could be happy again. We can go back to playing at that bar we loved so much!"

Keston refused to look at her, swinging a powerful right hook. "What was the bar's name, Arianne?"

"The name doesn't matter!"

He didn't reply. He simply snapped his fists down, ignited the purple plasma of his *Talons*, and jabbed upward through Tank Top's jaw.

Arianne got one look at Keston as he pulled his *Talons* out. His face crumpled. It was an expression she didn't ever want to see again. She weakened at the exact expression he must've made when he believed he'd lost her two years ago. With every Puppet he defeated, he was forced to relive that death.

An emotion she couldn't afford to feel fought its way to the surface.

Fortunately, she was spared that breakdown as Keston's face changed. He only watched the Puppet with her face a moment, waiting for her to fade before his amber eyes hardened like the stones. He shook his head and kept moving.

Looking at the bodies surrounding him, Arianne realized he'd already had to take her life ten times. The bodies were left discarded at his feet, bearing her likeness and bleeding out in gory, convoluted detail. Graduation gown, sundresses, tribal tunics, bathing suits...

"Keston, it's me!" the real Arianne cried.

At least, she was the *breathing* Arianne. She wasn't certain which version of her was real anymore. A sinking feeling struck her. Had there ever been a real her? Was there ever a time when she wasn't hiding or suppressing some part of herself?

She shook her head violently. She could have one of her infamous breakdowns later.

"Keston!" she screamed again.

When his attention snapped to her, she realized she'd made a mistake. There was nothing human in the eyes that stared back. The person looking at her didn't see her as his love; she was his mission. And with the past ten Puppets he'd downed, he'd numbed himself to any attachment when looking at her face.

Even if her face was the original copy.

She hadn't been on the receiving end of that side of Keston since before the Darwin Zone. The look he gave her reminded her of the first time they met: an empty shell, a caged animal ready to do whatever it took to survive.

Keston extended his wings and shot at her in a blur. She crossed her forearms in front of her face, bracing for impact. He slammed into her with enough force to rock her to her bones. Digging her feet into the ground as he pushed her, she felt the full force of his momentum through the soles of her feet.

She slid back into rows and rows of invisible church pews. Wooden benches flipped and splintered around them as she redirected Keston's attack. Her limbs burned as invisible debris collided with her, unable to brace without proper vision. He shot past her, tumbling into the hidden obstacles. While the scene on the Grecian beach remained the same to her eyes, the way Keston was thrown left and right confirmed he'd been knocked into the pews.

He stood, his hand seemingly grabbing at air, knuckles turning white. The strain in his arm proved he had a bench in his hand. Those emotionless eyes locked on Arianne, and she realized too late what he was planning. With a flex of his shoulder, he launched the pew. It careened toward her with a terrible whistling sound. Unable to see it, she screamed and hit the deck last second, the bench painfully raking over her wings as it shot over her head.

An Arianne wearing a Christmas sweater dashed at him. His eyes remained locked on the real Arianne as he shot his hand out and caught Christmas Sweater by the neck. He didn't break his gaze when he ignited his *Talons* and stabbed the purple plasma blades through Christmas Sweater's skull. Dropping her to the ground with little thought, his expressionless face was the stuff of nightmares.

"I'm tired of your games, Ace," Keston said, but those were Blackjack's words.

"Keston, it's *me*," Arianne insisted.

He still advanced. "Heard that three times already. You'll need to be more creative."

Preparing to counter his attacks again, she stood. She refused to harm him. She was *done* harming him. "You're not thinking straight. Look at me. It's *me*."

His laugh was crazed. Raking a hand through his hair, he pointed at her with a shaking finger. "Arianne's not even here. Is she? That's *exactly* something you would do. You want to torture me, make me think I might kill her, but the answer is that she isn't even here!"

Arianne slowly backed away as he advanced. A few remaining versions of her battled around them, their cries tricking her body into believing she was the one screaming. With Keston advancing on her with death in his eyes and the surrounding shouts, her entire body shook from sensual and emotional overload.

Another Arianne appeared behind Keston in her navy blue Pacifican military uniform. Hat slightly ajar on the side of her head, her hair fell in golden brown waves over her shoulders. Arianne paled when she realized who that one was: the first version of herself Keston had met. Major Arianne Ortiz. Pacific's spoiled island princess.

His Princess.

"Kill her. We need to go," Major Ortiz ordered, almost sounding bored.

When Keston turned to her, his jaw slackened.

"What did the Simulator make me look like?" Major Ortiz asked, her hands going in front of her face as she feigned confusion.

"You look like the first day I met you," he responded distantly.

Before the Simulation could confuse Keston more, Arianne attacked Major Ortiz. The past and present collided, each doing its best to grapple and swing on the other. And there, locked in Major Ortiz's grip, Arianne realized she felt muscle, not cybernetics, under her fingers.

This doppelganger wasn't a Puppet.

It was Ace.

Ace moved faster than expected. Unlike the other versions of herself, Major Ortiz had her own fighting style: Ace's style. Counters taken straight out of a boxing match matched Arianne's Muay Thai. She kicked out, and Ace kept her muscled arms tight to her body. When Arianne teetered off balance, Ace delivered a barrage of swift punch combos. The minute her defenses opened to attack, she closed them moments later with a speed that could rival a mutant.

It only made sense that the Queen of the Underground could hold her own against a Selvian Champion.

Ace backed up, and Arianne advanced aggressively, only to trip over a discarded pew. That confirmed it: Ace could see outside the Simulator, putting them at a tactical disadvantage. What was hidden behind the illusion? Were there other Puppets lying in wait?

But before Arianne could attack again, someone grabbed her and threw her backward, and she careened into an invisible wall. Drywall rained on her, her body screamed in pain from damage she couldn't see. She barely pulled herself out of the hole in the wall before Keston attacked again.

His *Talons* were out that time, convinced she was just another Puppet and Major Ortiz was the real copy. There was no need to pull his punches anymore.

Arianne ducked under a left-handed swipe that whistled with momentum. "You do that move every time," she quipped. As if to prove her point, she easily sidestepped the right uppercut he always combined with his left swipe. She smirked. "See? It's *me*, Keston!"

The words didn't even register. "Just because you give her attitude, doesn't make me believe it's her. Ace knows my combos too: she taught them to me."

"Don't you get it? She's pitting us against each other!" Arianne jumped away, painfully aware they'd started playing a deadly game of tag. "We're hurting each other. We always do this! We fight and fight until there's blood everywhere, and we never realize we're killing each other until it's too late! It needs to stop. *Please*, Keston."

Whether it was their enemies pulling the strings or their own stupid immaturity, Arianne and Keston always ended up at each other's throats. It had to stop. Because if she'd learned anything over the past few months, it was that they worked better together. They might have had their fun as enemies, but united, they were unstoppable allies.

That was why Ace was trying so hard to get the matching set. It was why she pitted them against each other now: she knew her only chance at winning was if they were too busy fighting each other.

Keston lunged, and Arianne dodged again. Someone needed to break the cycle. Just one year before, she would've never considered putting down her arms against Keston. But now, watching him attack her with bloodshot eyes, she knew she was the only one who could put an end to it all.

She thought she'd forgiven him already, but the act of putting her fists down was the final step on that path. It didn't matter if he kept attacking. She wouldn't raise a hand against someone who deserved nothing but love.

"I forgive you, Keston," Arianne said and dropped her arms.

Stumbling, his relentless barrage of attacks came to a halt for a vital second. "What did you say?" His voice was almost inaudible in disbelief, the words hardly more than a breath.

She could feel it; he was so close to coming back to her.

Pouring every ounce of love she held for him into her voice, she repeated, "I said: *I forgive you.*" To her amazement, the love didn't weaken her voice. It strengthened it. She stood taller. "So keep attacking me. Keep trying to push me away, but I won't budge. Not anymore. Not ever. Together, and this time I mean it."

"How dare you use this against me?" he screamed, his serenity gone almost as quickly as it came.

Arianne jumped away. "Strike me as many times as you need. I will never hurt you again."

The cry that came out of Keston's mouth was closer to that of a beast than any form of human language. Still, it was so loud that her eardrums nearly burst. Arianne barely had a moment to wince before she saw a flash of purple plasma. The *Talons* raked across her arm, delivering gouges so deep her arms forgot to bleed. It was her turn to scream. Then the blood came, the bright red torrents soaking the remnants of her sleeve.

"You know her screams drive me crazy," Keston wailed. "You'll die for making me relive that!"

He attacked again.

Arianne was flagging now. The blow to her arm was on fire and deeper than she was willing to accept. She'd expected Instinct to come to the surface, but its haunting claws didn't scrape against her mind. Then she realized: if Keston was her mate, her body saw him as safe. If Instinct was a protective mechanism, something told her it would never activate against him, not after that bond snapped in place.

He approached, face cast in the purple light of his *Talons*. Then his arm shot out. Arianne used all her concentration to catch his forearms. They strained against each other, plasma dripping burning purple droplets in the space between them. The tips of the *Talons* were inches away from piercing her heart. Shoving all her weight to her back foot, she strained against Keston's steady pushing, knowing she was facing a significant leverage disadvantage.

Feverous pain emanated from her wounded arm—she couldn't keep him at bay much longer.

But she refused to give up just yet. Taking a deep breath, she stared defiantly into Keston's lifeless eyes. "Don't throw away our After again, Selvia Boy."

Keston blinked. And then those cold amber eyes melted, and he *saw* her.

Arianne smiled. "Together?"

Slowly, the haze faded, and the male she loved returned. He leaned close enough to whisper, "See? I always find you. Still the same old Arianne."

Her heart thundered in her chest. She wanted to fall into him, to whimper and cry with relief, but she kept her focus on the *Talons* still burning between them. It wasn't over yet.

"We have to pretend one more time."

Keston nodded. In one swift movement, she let go of his forearms. He gave her a charged look before he swiped down toward her chest. Arianne feigned a scream and collapsed. The *Talons* cut through the open air a breath away from her sternum, just close enough to look like a killing blow.

Through barely open eyelids, Arianne watched from the ground.

"Keston! Are you all right?" Ace, disguised as Major Ortiz, exclaimed. She ran up to examine him, the concern almost as fake as the face displaying it.

Keston grinned down at her. "Better now that I found you."

"I knew you would find me," the demon wearing Arianne's face swooned.

He sheathed his *Talons* with a downward flex of his arms. The plasma disappeared, leaving only the shining knuckles across his fists. He leaned into Major Ortiz's touch, just intimate enough to look genuine. Though the Simulation showed Major Ortiz's face, the hungry expression was undoubtedly Ace's. Blackjack: hers at last.

"Tell me why you love me," Keston whispered, resting his cheek in her hand.

Major Ortiz beamed up at him. "I love your power. The power we could have together."

Keston embraced her. Arianne watched as he moved a hand to Major Ortiz's head, as if he was about to brush her hair back, as he'd done to her countless times. But he stopped at the forehead. His fingers grasped at something hidden there and pulled.

Something snapped. The Simulator headband. As soon as it left Major Ortiz's forehead, the Simulation collapsed around them. The pixels of color looked like heavy rain as they dissipated, washing away the imaginary and rushing in reality. And just as the rest of the room returned, so did Ace. Arianne's facade melted off the Underground Queen until she stood before them in a black techwear jacket and joggers.

Arianne took that as her cue to stand. She savored Ace's brief moment of surprise, taking a gracious bow like an actress at the end of a play.

"Well done." Ace applauded, looking between them with pride. She then touched her earpiece and said, "I've held them for as long as I could. It's time for extraction."

Arianne recognized her brother's gruff voice on the other end of the line. "Extraction? You wanted the Lovebirds, so I gave them to you. They're all yours." Ace's lips parted in mortification as Andre finished, "Careful what you wish for, Mistress."

"*Andre*," she hissed.

"You've attempted to manipulate me one too many times. I hope you like the taste of your own medicine. What? Did you not consider this possibility?" Andre laughed dryly. "Don't worry, Rou will be in good hands."

The call dropped.

In a rare moment of uncertainty, Ace turned to the Lovebirds and raised her hands in surrender. "Well played. I guess I fold."

"I don't think so."

Arianne didn't dare intervene. In fact, she stepped back. Ace had been the source of Keston's misery and torture for most of his life. Whatever Arianne wanted with the Underground Queen took a back seat to his desires.

Keston's eyebrows furrowed, and his upper lip curled in fury. "I've been dreaming about how I would do this."

To Ace's credit, she didn't back away. "Come on, Blackjack, think about this. You intend to commit treason without taking a trump card with you? With me, you have leverage. I trained you better than this. "

"But you trained me just for this." Keston smiled sweetly at her. "Don't you remember, Imani? Jokers don't win until their opponents are dead."

Ace returned the artificial sugar smile. "The ace always beats the jack."

The Cartel kingpin turned to run, but Keston was faster. His left arm snapped out, his fingers wrapping around her neck. Ace's sprint was stopped before her second foot could even leave the ground. Keston yanked her back toward him, her feet lifting off the ground. She kicked wildly, fighting desperately to escape the monster she'd created, but to no avail.

Ace, with all her manipulation, knew when she'd reached the end of the game. Genuine fear flashed on the kingpin's face for the first time since Arianne met that soulless demon two and a half years ago. Ace's fingernails clawed at Keston's arm, the sharpened points digging into his skin. He didn't so much as flinch.

He lifted her until he held her just inches from his face. The movement was effortless, a chilling punctuation of his dominance over the situation. He inhaled deeply, savoring the sound of her gasps for air and the smell of her fear. Even Arianne could smell the reek of horror pooling out of Ace's pores.

It made her toes curl in excitement.

Keston leaned close enough to kiss his former boss. His mouth curled into a hideous smile. "Mark this as the day the Ace of Spades lost to the Jack of Hearts."

Arm moving almost too fast to see, Keston smashed his right fist through Ace's sternum and ripped out her still-beating heart.

Her blood pooled in his palm and cascaded down his forearm. It coated the tattoo she'd branded him with, her death finally canceling out the contract she'd written into his skin a decade before. He dropped Ace's body to the floor with a lifeless thud. And only when her limp body failed to rise, only when it was guaranteed the mistress of trickery wouldn't surprise them one last time, did Keston fall to his knees.

It was over.

Head tilted back, he let out a scream filled with every visceral ounce of grief, hatred, and exhilaration in his soul. Arianne had to cover her ears as all the windows in the church shattered from the sonic cry of victory, loud enough to reach the heavens.

And when he'd screamed his lungs hoarse, the energy of his anger and vengeance collapsed inward, and he with it. Doubled over, he was wracked with gasping sobs that shook his shoulders and wings. Arianne ran to him and wrapped her arms around his shoulders, holding him as he released every vile, confusing emotion he'd felt for his former owner. Keston leaned into her as he cried, laughed, whimpered, and hiccupped. She held him through it all.

Ace was dead, Blackjack with her.

Keston Leroy was free.

Chapter 50

Andre

The control collars were deactivated.

Andre had a split second to register Blue pressing the button and calculate what the corresponding beeps meant before all hell broke loose. The prince dropped. Treena lunged above him, soaring over his head. He was thankful her clawed hands weren't currently cutting up his face. To his relief, she continued forward and barreled into Blue, stunning the operatives.

Jaya was on the ground next to him. Andre turned to her, ready for another attack. To his relief, she still seemed out of it, eyes darting in confusion, unaware of where—or who—she was. Before another enemy could turn on him, he launched himself at Jaya.

Chaos ensued around them. Pandora fought off Tyrell's gnashing teeth while the Peregrine Pacific rushed the Selvian operative team. But as he'd learned in his years of missions, he had to focus on what he could control. In those moments, it was getting Jaya out of the fray. He gripped her half-conscious form in his arms, keeping low to avoid the tangle of bullets, blades, and limbs.

In one quick sprint, they broke out of the worst of the skirmish. She didn't protest. Good, one less opponent to consider. Andre didn't think about the other reason he prioritized getting Jaya out of battle: Kalinda. Even if she was a chapter of his past, he couldn't stomach the thought of her heartbreak if she lost her sister.

If a stray bullet didn't get Jaya, Pandora certainly would once she realized the collar was turned off.

"Andre?" Jaya breathed, blinking back to reality.

He didn't respond. As much as she'd hate him for it, he found a cage for Hera's lab subjects and tossed her inside. He couldn't look her in the eye as he locked it. Jaya started screaming. Andre ran. She would hate him forever. He was okay with that.

The lab was a warzone.

Both feral twins had turned on the Peregrine Pacific and were cutting through their dwindling forces. The Satyr and Cheetah *Feras* had joined the attack, picking off Pacificans with arrows and well-timed melee attacks. Pandora fended off a three-pronged attack from Blue, a towering silver-haired brute, and a third golden-haired male. Collecting his blade off the ground, Andre ran to his wife's aid.

"Ready to clock in?" Pandora shouted, dodging a swing from the brute's hammer.

He intercepted a two-clawed swipe from the golden-haired male. "Dealing with our collar problem!"

"What did you do to the twins?" the silver-haired brute bellowed behind him.

"Friends of yours?" Pandora asked, firing a plasma blast.

The brute barely flinched, his skin smoking but unharmed. Pandora's glowing eyes widened, but she recovered in time to shield herself from a knife thrown by Blue. Going back-to-back, the newlyweds prepared for another three-mutant assault.

"We don't want to hurt you," the male, who Andre realized resembled a Lion, said.

Blue's yellow eyes glinted, and she produced two more daggers. "Speak for yourself."

Glancing at his watch and then up toward the scrambling scientists a floor above, they needed seven more minutes. Talking wasn't his strong suit, but it would waste time.

He adjusted his grip on his blade. "Let's catalog grievances so we know what we're killing each other for."

"I'm just the chaperone." The Lion shrugged.

The brute's upper lip curled as he raised a battle hammer that threatened skull-crushing force. "The twins." His eyes shone. He was crying.

Blue lowered into a crouch, coiled to strike. "I can tolerate you hurting me, but—" She gave an uncharacteristic look of sympathy to the brute at her side. "No one hurts my fucking friends."

Pandora pointed the bladed end of her cybernetic arm at Blue. "Is it wrong that I'm turned on right now?"

In answer, Blue attacked.

Running at the Lion, Andre went to neutralize the male's long-armed reach. To his surprise, the Lion drew a broadsword and intercepted Andre's topside blade. Before his opponent could warm up his new weapon, Andre pulled his topside blade away, spun, and swung at the male's shoulder with his bottom side blade. He was fast, but not fast enough to avoid a well-placed gouge.

"I remember you." The Lion jumped away on graceful feet. "I crashed your birthday party!"

"The circus."

"I hope you liked the act!" The male beamed and attacked again.

But when their blades locked for a second time, Andre was struck with a strange sense of déjà vu. It wasn't from his birthday in Madrid—he'd never gotten a good look at the male behind the lion's mask that day. He narrowed his eyes, wondering if his contacts were failing him. Why did the Lion look so familiar?

Before his confusion cost him the fight, Andre pushed the male off him. The move took more effort than he was proud of; the adult mutant was undoubtedly stronger than him. Luckily, Andre had been training to go toe to toe with super-humans his entire life, whether mutant or cyborg.

"Hold up," the Lion exclaimed as he intercepted a spinning attack. "You gave me a double-take! Do you know me?"

Andre raised a brow. "Have we met before?"

So many of his missions had blended together at that point.

The Lion shrugged. "I'm asking you!"

I'm already trying to kill you, you don't have to piss me off more.

"Do you not know who I am? I'm Andre Murray, Heir Apparent to Leon Murray."

"Perfect." The Lion's smile displayed sharpened canines. "I've been trying to get a meeting with your dad. I think I knew him."

Andre almost failed to parry the next attack. He had to shake his head to clear his shock. He *did* recognize that male. He'd seen him in Caesar's memories years before. Though the Lion had been decades younger, there was no mistaking his sunny smile, clawed hands, and *Murray* coloring.

"Lionel?" he breathed.

The male slackened. "What did you say?"

There was no mistaking it. The male before him was Lionel Murray, Leon's long-dead brother. Which meant one damning thing: *two* threats to his inheritance had emerged in one day.

Judging from Lionel's confusion, the male had no idea who he was. It was likely the dose of Serum he'd taken two decades ago that had turned him feral. At least, the world thought he'd gone feral. But there Lionel was: almost sane, a few pearls short of a necklace, but *mostly* there.

The last thing Andre needed was to remind his uncle who he was.

"Sorry, I need to kill you now."

He didn't get a chance. Pandora grabbed his arm and yanked him through the door. "We need to go!"

Glancing behind him, she'd found a way to stick the feral twins on Blue, Lionel, and the brute. As the three struggled to hold off their former friends, the scientists filed out the side exit, led by Hera.

Pandora sprinted toward her mother, covering her as they rushed into the corridor. Covering their backs, Andre ensured no one pursued them before wrenching the lab doors closed. He barred the door with his double-sided blade, hoping to buy them enough time to escape.

"What happened back there?" Hera demanded, lab coat streaming behind her as she ran. "The Bubblegum Battalion should've held for thirty minutes at least!"

"Something blocked their signal," Pandora reported. "I couldn't connect with the reinforcements either."

Hera cursed. "We lost the collars too, then."

Nodding, a sickly sheen coated Pandora's face at her mother's look of disapproval. A similar brand of nausea rose in Andre's gut when he heard the distinct sound of glass shattering in the lab. It seemed that their final defense, Ace, had lost as well.

The avenging angels had arrived.

Hera registered the same sound. Her icy eyes raked over her daughter and Andre. "I hoped you two enjoyed your wedding. From this day on, the throne you married each other for is no longer guaranteed. Paris is lost."

He almost stumbled. Everything he'd worked for that past year, gone. Reduced to rubble. With one last look over his shoulder, he partially hoped his sister was there to see the hatred in his gaze. He'd sacrificed everything to change the world, to be better than Leon, only for his sister to strip it all from him.

He had nothing if he didn't win now. He wondered for a moment if fading away on the beaches of a forgotten Pacific colony would've been preferable, but shoved that thought down.

All that was left for him was the war. Arianne died, or he did. He made peace with that and let it consume him.

Chapter 51

Keston

The first thing Keston noticed when he landed in the Palace laboratory was the ravaged bodies of the twins.

The Ivory Court and Colla surrounded the feral remnants of their friends, each one too stricken to attack. The rest of the lab was a warzone, but no one paid attention to the downed bodies and Puppets. Everyone's mortified attention was on the twins.

Treena and Tyrell were decomposing—it was the only term he could use to describe them. Their skin hung from emaciated bones riddled with black veins. Yet, no one moved to take them out of their misery.

Arianne landed next to him, and a broken whimper escaped her lips. Keston wordlessly rested a hand on the small of her back, the only support he could give her as they stared at the grizzly scene.

Rhino was the first to step into the circle. He dropped his battle hammer as he extended a hand toward the creature who'd once been known as Treena. In such an exhausted state, she managed a growl as her former partner approached her. Both twins looked like cornered wild animals as they backed toward each other, snarling at the circle slowly closing around them.

"Tree?" Rhino asked as he extended a slow hand out.

The beast nipped at his hand.

Lova wordlessly grabbed Rhino and pulled him behind her. She glared at the twins with a look of dominance strong enough to make the feral creatures step back. She bared her teeth. Watching such a small female protect one of the strongest mutants Keston had ever met was a harrowing sight.

Topher and Blue had their weapons readied, but neither moved.

No one could bring themselves to attack the twins, even at such an advanced state of insanity. Keston told himself that they were monsters now. The humane thing would be to take them out of their misery. But even he couldn't stop seeing who the monsters had been. Treena and Tyrell: two rare friends he'd found in that cold world. A thick heaviness shrouded the room.

Colla raised his broadsword, yellow-blue eyes looking at Arianne. "Just give the order, Phoenix."

Arianne's lips parted as she stared forward. For a few moments, she was silent. Keston felt her lean into his touch for a few seconds before she stepped toward her team. Her gaze flicked to him, and he saw something turn her stormcloud gray eyes to steel.

With a long sigh, she faced her team. "Everyone, back away from the twins."

"We need to take them out of their misery," Keston whispered to her.

Her face hardened. "I know."

That's when he realized her intention. He extended a hand and let it brush down her arm as she walked toward the twins. Pausing just long enough as their hands intertwined, they shared one painful moment of understanding. While Ace's death had freed Keston, these deaths would nail Arianne down to the cross of leadership. She gave him a subtle nod and let go of his hand.

No turning back. A leader made the hard choices. A leader bore the weight of those around her.

The Ivory Court recognized her sacrifice. They all retreated and knelt, heads going down in reverence to grant a moment of privacy. Only Rhino kept his head raised and chest held high.

The twin blades of *Horizon's Edge* snapped, their heat making the air sizzle around them. The twins turned to Arianne, their black eyes glinting at a new threat. She seemed unfazed as the creatures bared their teeth at her. She looked resolute, impartial, like the goddess of justice ready to hand out her sentence. Emotion didn't matter, only the next step.

"Selvia thanks you for your service," Arianne said, walking forward to meet her friends. "Treena and Tyrell, Whisper and Echo, we will honor your sacrifice in our Legends for as long as our Dara holds leaves."

Like her mentor before her, Arianne was cold and efficient as she swung out with both blades and beheaded Treena and Tyrell in one swift movement.

Their heads barely hit the floor before she stood and said, "We have a mission to finish. Get those aerial defenses down now. We mourn our dead after we take the city." A flicker of emotion came to her eyes as she looked at Rhino. "You sit the rest of this out," she said softly.

He didn't respond, face frozen as he stared at the twins' bodies. Colla, Blue, and Topher launched into action. Only Lova hesitated long enough to wrap her tail around Rhino, giving the paralyzed male one last hug before zipping off.

Keston approached Arianne, his bloodied hand reaching out to comfort her. "Ari—"

She brushed his hand away. "Not right now," she said tightly. She didn't look at him as she took out her vaporizer and took a long drag. Purple vapor clouded her mouth and nose when she said, "We have to finish this."

The female who'd held him while he cried just minutes ago was gone. She'd been so careful and loving when he'd killed Ace, knowing how much it would weigh on him. For a few seconds there, as the final beats of his boss's heart thumped in his hand, he'd feared he'd lost himself to his screaming, like a banshee left to wander the earth in endless purgatory. Arianne's touch had been the only thing that had brought him back to reality after ripping Ace's heart out.

Ace... He looked down at his bloodied hands. He expected to feel more from her death. She'd been a monster, but in a way, she'd raised him. For over a decade, she'd been his companion, his support. Losing such a significant staple in his life should make him feel something. Instead, her murder lightened his heart, made him feel *normal* for the first time in years. He felt neutral now.

Keston knew Arianne was just as conflicted about taking the twins' lives. The difference was that their bond had been rooted in genuine love.

"I know we have a mission." He reached out again. "But take a moment. We're only human. Take a moment."

"I can't afford to be human."

When she turned to him, her eyes were black.

"I can help with the aerial defenses," came a voice Keston could've sworn he recognized.

Haris Cadmilus, in a white lab coat, stood next to Blue and a gaunt-looking Jaya. The quilled male's wry grin melted away into a mixture of horror and disbelief when he saw who stood next to Keston.

"Ari?" Haris's voice cracked.

"No," Jaya breathed.

Arianne turned toward her Pacific friends and... nothing. She stared past them numbly, her black eyes fixing on Blue. "Get Haris on the defense systems. We need to start the main assault." She pointed at Keston. "You're with me. Leon and his Inner Circle escaped. We're chasing them down. *Now.* Before our window closes."

He didn't have a chance to reply before she pivoted to storm off.

Haris stepped forward. "Arianne."

Blue had the two-sense to hold the shorter male back.

Coming to a halt, Arianne straightened, the grip on her blades tightening. A hush fell over the group, and Keston had a moment to consider what he would do if she attacked. He braced for that eventuality as she rigidly turned.

"Let's skip the reunion because I don't have the time." Baring her sharpened teeth, fear sparked in Haris's eyes. She marched forward and stopped before her old friends. "Yes, I'm alive. No thanks to you." Arianne jabbed a finger into Jaya's chest. "Yes, I'm leading this assault, which you are currently slowing down." She jabbed a finger into Haris's chest. "Yes, we rescued both of you. No, I will not be elaborating at this time."

"H-how?" Haris breathed.

"Refer back to my comment on *elaboration*," Ariannne hissed through clenched teeth as she leaned in dangerously close to Haris's face.

Jaya had gone as white as a ghost. "We went to your funeral, Ari," she whimpered. "I-I carried your coffin."

For a split second, Arianne's expression softened, and her black eyes faded to gray. Keston recognized the love she felt for her friends there and the grief she felt at losing them. But she quickly shielded everything behind a mask of steel. He couldn't blame her; he didn't know how often he shoved everything down, too overwhelmed to handle it during a mission.

Like it or not, they were in the middle of a battle.

Keston stepped between Arianne and Haris, giving the Pacificans a regretful look. "Now is not a good time," he said delicately.

Haris glared at him. "You have no right—"

"No." Arianne's voice was as uncompromising as the winds in a storm.

Whatever Haris was about to say died in his throat, flinching away from her for a second time.

"Let's get something straight," she said, looking between her former friends. "I'm not Ari. Right now, I am Phoenix: Deputy of Selvia, Champion of the Ivory Court, and rightful Heir of Europe. As we speak, the signal jammer we planted on Andre gets further and further away, making us more susceptible to automation attacks by the second. African and North American forces are waiting on us to lower the defenses, and the longer they wait, the longer my *fucking father* has to formulate a counterattack. I do not have time for your tears, I hardly have time for this conversation, so do your damn job or sit your ass down next to Rhino and shut the fuck up."

It made sense then.

Arianne didn't want to be numb; she *needed* to be numb. The entire world was crumbling around her, and that one mission could keep their rebellion limping along for a few more months. Failure wasn't an option. She had to expose her identity to the world, fight Keston and bring him back from trying to kill her, shoulder his chaos from Ace's death, and then kill her former friends. And now she stared down her two oldest friends, friends she let believe she'd died.

With a brisk nod, Haris sprinted off, Blue darting behind.

Arianne ignored Jaya. Keston kept close, unsure how to help but ready at a moment's notice. He may not be a Selvian and was barely part of their alliance, but he wanted to do what he could. He wanted to carry the impossible burden he knew was resting on the person he loved.

"Satyr and Blitz," Arianne snapped. The warriors fell in line. "Cut the lines on all the Puppets. I don't know when Andre will be out of range, but I don't want surprises."

The Selvian Champions nodded and got to work.

Then Arianne's attention shifted to him again. "Keston. You know we have to go after them."

He nodded. He'd been dreading it since they landed and discovered that Leon's Inner Circle was long gone. A part of him wanted to push back. They'd fought so hard for a reprieve. The idea of going back to Selvia at the end of the day and falling asleep with Arianne in his arms was too enticing. If they did nothing, that ending was almost guaranteed now. Unfortunately, he knew she was right.

They had a chance to cut the snake off at the head. They had to take it.

"Defenses are down!" Blue's announcement was answered with cheers from the Selvians.

"You guys can take a seat now." Khari's voice was loud enough to hear across the team's comms units. "My forces got this covered from here."

For once, his obnoxious voice wasn't unwelcome to Keston's ears. They'd done it; Paris's defenses were down. North America and Africa were inbound. Leon's Inner Circle had retreated. It was only a matter of time now.

"That's our cue," Keston said to Arianne.

He prepared for one last fight. A victory could mean the end of the war. Leon was on his heels; they needed to attack while he was off balance. Another opportunity like that might take years to find.

"Let me come," Jaya said, barely perceptible over the commotion of celebration.

Keston and Arianne turned to the Chameleon. Though her natural coloring had returned, Jaya's skin was still pallid and her hair dull. Dark circles hung under once vibrant fluorite eyes. The culprit of her transformation was obvious: the black collar squeezing her neck.

Blue was the first to protest. "You're free. Don't go back." Her long fingers brushed over her snake tattoo, the remnant of her own collar.

Ignoring her, Jaya continued, determined, "I know the stops the jet is going to take. If they leave France, I'm the only one who can guide you to their stronghold. And—" She looked down. The female who looked back up was unrecognizable to the island officer who'd once adhered to the rule of law like it was oxygen. "If you're going to kill them, I want to help. At least, I want to watch."

As someone once enslaved within his own mind under Ace, Keston could understand her plea. For that reason alone, he didn't object.

"Wait!"

Haris rushed down the lab steps, nearly tripping over his lab coat. Screwdriver in hand, he went straight to Jaya. "You should keep the collar on for disguise, but I won't let them use it on you again." His blue eyes shone with the look someone saved for an abandoned duckling or a three-legged dog. Pulling at the collar, Haris removed a small imperceptible chip and stepped away. "That should do it. The collar will still send an 'on' signal, but the simulation won't take hold."

Jaya gave the Porcupine a broken smile. "Thanks, Haris. I'm sorry you had to see that."

Tears welled in his eyes. "I'm sorry I couldn't save you sooner."

Awkwardly removed by a few steps, Arianne watched her Pacifican friends. Something in the way she folded her arms indicated some level of restraint. Keston knew she wanted to hug them, to throw the awful past behind. But she held back. The chasm between herself and her friends might've grown too deep, and they certainly didn't have time to attempt a hike into its depths now.

"We need to go," she managed regretfully. Her eyes went to Blue. "You're in charge."

Blue nodded solemnly and pulled Arianne into a hug. The pair didn't say anything, just locked eyes for a few charged moments before separating.

Colla stepped forward. Glancing at his necklace around Arianne's neck, he gave her a smile of approval. Keston finally recognized what hung from the black string, usually hidden beneath her jacket: shark and lion teeth. The Lion and Phoenix linked forearms and shared one last meaningful smile before parting.

"See you soon, Young One," Colla said. "Maybe you can get me that meeting with your father."

"Not if I kill him first."

He nodded once. "Then we can both rest easier knowing our pasts are finally buried."

A nice sentiment. Too bad pasts never remained buried, not for long. The past needed to be exorcised, its still-beating heart ripped from its chest. But Keston wouldn't interrupt the one moment that seemed to bring Arianne an ounce of peace that day.

Jets screamed past overhead. All heads whipped up to the ceiling. The presence of those beautiful turquoise exteriors was their sign: the end had come. As the rumbling of more engines filled the sky and mortars shook the city, Keston prepared to fly, extending his wings behind him and shoving his nerves deep down.

Jaya walked up to his side, and he silently scooped her into his arms.

Arianne shot out her wings and hoisted her sword into the air. "I, Phoenix, City Crusher, Princess of Europe, and Deputy of Selvia, claim this city as my own! We will never bow to Leon again. I'll return with his head!"

The Ivory Court screamed back in victory, their weapons going to the sky.

With that final war cry, Arianne rocketed into the air and out the same window they'd crashed through minutes before. Keston followed, launching from the ground and earning a small squeak from Jaya, who clutched his chest tighter. Then he realized: it was his first time carrying someone who couldn't fly in his arms.

He'd be terrified too if he were a thousand feet in the air with nothing but two arms keeping him from falling to his death. He gripped Jaya tighter to his chest, a small courtesy that brought some color back to her terrified face. Not too long ago, he'd been just as frightened of heights until Arianne had trained him to love the sky.

Though unsure why, the thought of his training days with Arianne convinced him to speak. He did his best to be heard over the howling wind. "Arianne's still in there," he promised Jaya. "I've seen it."

She looked distant as she stared out over the city. "We've all been tainted by this. I hope she's still in there because..." She faced Keston with a vulnerability she'd never revealed to him. "Then there's a chance that I'm still there... somewhere."

She averted her eyes and didn't speak again.

He didn't ask what she'd endured during her time as one of Hera's Puppets. His own memories filled in the gap enough to make him feel nauseous.

North American jets shot past them, the pilots inside waving when they recognized the winged *Feras*. Keston felt a genuine smile brighten his features. He was a part of something *good,* and the feeling was quickly becoming addictive. Even Arianne let out a victorious battle cry. Slowing, the pilots saluted before they spun and rocketed back over the city, raining down strategic strikes on Pangaean barracks scattered below.

With a deep breath, the smell of gunpowder filled his lungs. For once, the scent carried a sense of safety. No matter what happened next, Western Europe belonged with the tribes and their allies. Asia could retaliate, Leon could get away, but no one could take away the fact that their little rebellion had become a global superpower. Thanks to the winged female flying in front of him, they stood a chance of stopping history from repeating itself.

He hoped Arianne allowed herself to appreciate all the good work she'd done. He hoped she could see the world was proud of her. Maybe it would be enough to lessen the crushing pressure. Maybe she would see that she didn't owe anything to anyone anymore.

Arianne had given everything to turn the tide of the war. And she was still giving more. It was one drop in the chasm of reasons why he loved her.

They flew until Paris and the din of battle was long forgotten. About halfway there, Keston realized where they were headed: the Chateau de Rambouillet, the Leroy family estate.

For some reason, that didn't sit right with him.

Why escape just to land fifty miles outside of the battle zone? Did they think they could hide in plain sight? Or had they gone somewhere they *knew* Keston would look?

"Cover your ears real quick for me," he instructed Jaya. She gave him a strange look but obliged. "Arianne!" he shouted with his sonic voice.

She turned, her eyebrows knitting in confusion.

Keston signed for her to fly closer, remembering the small language they'd developed during their training days.

"I don't like it."

He instantly knew she'd object. He wasn't disappointed.

"They're *right there*. No armies, no Puppets with Andre's signal blocking, and only one escape jet. We won't get another chance."

Jaya nodded in affirmation. "They'll retreat from here to their base in the Alps and then to Asia. If you want a chance at them, it's now. You two go in hard, I'll pretend to be under their control for an extra surprise."

Keston frowned, betrayed. "I thought you were the one to err on the side of caution."

An ugly expression contorted Jaya's features as she looked at the Chateau in the distance. "They've taken enough from me. If there's a chance to return the favor, I'm taking it." She turned her attention to Arianne, and an understanding passed between the former friends. "I know I cancelled our friendship subscription, but I can see things through your eyes now. I know your hatred as intimately as I once knew your love."

Arianne's eyes revealed nothing. She only managed to nod as the wind pulled strands of hair across her painted face.

That meant only Keston's hesitation remained.

There'd been a similar moment two years ago when he'd faced the same choice. He could remain behind with his safety guaranteed, or he could follow Arianne unflinchingly. He wouldn't make the same mistake twice. He wouldn't wait until it was too late to fight by her side. Not anymore.

"Together," Keston said sincerely.

His family's estate appeared through the trees. Though their escape jet was hidden in its secret hangar beneath the pond, the Inner Circle hadn't attempted to hide within the mansion. Their heat signatures appeared instantly: five bodies in the main foyer.

Four humans and one cyborg were no match for the world's two most powerful beings. Even Leon's hubris had its limits. Hopefully, that limit was about to be tested and surpassed.

He pointed to the arching windows overlooking the rippling pond, and Arianne didn't hesitate, diving in feet first. Keston flew in after her. As he landed, he and Jaya glanced at each other before she returned to her role. With a mighty shove, Jaya separated from Keston and dashed off toward the Inner Circle, eyes dull.

If things went south, they had their mole.

Pandora smiled, stepping past Jaya with a loving brush of the female's purple hair. "Thanks for bringing my favorite pet back to me." She tsked. "Should've taken the collar off."

So they didn't suspect Andre had anything to do with the signal scrambling earlier. Good. He returned Pandora's obnoxious smile.

Surveying the foyer, he snapped his *Talons* from their brass knuckles. Glass littered the ground, and brisk winter wind gripped the room with its chill. Like a flock of geese, the Inner Circle stood in a V formation. Pandora and Andre flanked Leon on either side. Behind them were Hera and Cassius.

Cold as the winter air, Leon's blue eyes raked up and down Arianne's body. "I was supposed to be out of the county by now, but missing a meeting with you face-to-face would have been a shame."

She didn't reply. Not with words, at least. She screamed, jumped into the air, and rocketed toward Leon. Keston froze, ready to witness the death of a god, but it never came. A high-pitched siren shook the room. Arianne fell from the air. Jaya collapsed. Even Keston stumbled for a moment before his ears, evolved to adjust to his own sonic voice, tampered down the noise to an almost bearable level. He stood against the sonic attack even as he was forced to watch Arianne writhe in silent pain.

He smiled grimly, but the feeling was short-lived once he realized the Inner Circle looked unsurprised by his tolerance.

"Come now, boy." Leon folded his arms behind his back. "Did you think we'd unleash you on the world without knowing your strengths and weaknesses? A high-pitched sonic attack is debilitating to most mutants." He gestured to Arianne and Jaya, still writhing on the floor, then to Keston. "Unless a mutant has sonic abilities himself. Naturally, his body would have adaptations."

Hera observed the *Feras* with unbridled interest. "Your kind is genuinely so fascinating."

Keston moved to take a surging step forward, his wings extending behind him—

"I wouldn't do that." Leon inclined his head. "Let's be smart about this."

Ace had said something similar. Look where that had gotten her.

He bared his teeth. "All I see are scared little humans," he growled. "I've already killed one person who's spoken down to me today. Five more shouldn't be a problem."

Cassius shifted next to Leon, putting himself directly in line with his son—a terrible decision on his part. "You've removed a mutual enemy. Good job, son."

"I'm not your son," Keston spat.

He'd wanted to say those four words for years. It felt good to drop the facade.

Leon gave him a warning glare. "Are you sure about that? Would you like to retract that statement? Since you're the son of my closest friend, I will give you one last chance."

His whole body shook with rage now. "No, I think I'll elaborate, actually."

Keston raised his purple glowing *Talons* at the Inner Circle, not just in warning, but in promise. Hatred surged inside him like the electric crescendo of a guitar solo. His blood blasted through his veins like the booming rhythm of bass. The symphony of vile, putrid, toxic emotions played its beautiful melody with every piece of his body, mind, and soul.

If he thought about it, that specific song had been playing from the moment he was ripped away from Arianne in Citadel Island. It was time to pay up, and as Ace had taught him, he would always come to collect.

"Let's make sure my statement is as clear as possible," Keston seethed as he stared down the dripping plasma of his *Talons*. "I hate all of you. I hate what you turned me into. I hate what you forced me to do. Most of all, I hate playing dress up like I'm your show poodle. Every opportunity I got to double-cross you, I fucking *took it*. If I could kill all of you ten times over, I would, but it's biologically impossible. So, I'll settle for sending you all to hell and getting the remaining nine deaths there, to which I'll promptly pleasure myself to the sight of your hellish undead corpses. Then I'll kill you one more time just because I can." He smiled charmingly at Leon. "Have I made myself clear, Your Majesty?"

"Crystal." Even as he smirked, his features darkened. He looked to Cassius. "Unfortunate, but not entirely surprising. Too bad, too. I've tried so hard to be nice, but no one appreciates my efforts. Not Asia, not Genevieve, not Sensatia, and sadly..." His head rolled to freeze Keston with those blue eyes. "Not you."

Cassius gave Keston a look that made him pause. For a fleeting moment, the Lord Advisor looked like a father beholding a beloved son. "I wish things could be different."

Keston frowned. "Same here."

He allowed a moment's sorrow for the remnant of Jaleel still lingering within Cassius. For the life he lost with his *true* father. But the feeling was short-lived. Unfortunately, most of his memories were of Cassius, not Jaleel, so the face he saw before him triggered *vastly* more bad memories than good.

Cassius stole Jaleel from him. So many years lost. So much love soured.

With a thundering cry, Keston shot directly toward his father, *Talons* aimed to cut out his heart like he'd done to Ace an hour before.

He didn't know if his aim struck true. The last thing he remembered was weightlessness, his Talon's primed and targeting his father—

Keston shot up from his dream, drenched in a pool of cold sweat. With a shout, he ripped his sheets off of him, freeing himself from their suffocating tangles. Hyperventilating, he fell backward into the headboard, his sides heaving painfully.

He raked shaking hands through his long brown hair, stopping himself when a curling strand fell in front of his eyes. His breathing slowed to almost nothing, panic setting in. *Brown* hair. He didn't have brown hair, not anymore. Then he saw his arms and recognized the countless collection of small scars he'd earned over the years of working as Blackjack. Hera removed those scars... right?

Someone stirred the covers next to him. He felt her calloused hand land on his inner thigh, the touch sending an electric shock up his spine. She gave his leg a reassuring squeeze. "It's just a dream," she said, still half-asleep. "Come back to bed."

"A-Arianne?"

The hazy background of his dream faded, and he realized he was in his villa in Porto Cheli. Specifically, his shared bedroom with Arianne. He recognized the peaceful white walls accented with light blue paintings and seashells. Even the salty sea breeze wafted through the half-open windows.

Why did he remember a winter breeze?

Arianne rolled over, her wings shifting to fall off the far side of the bed. She was naked, the sheets he'd left hopelessly tangled just barely covering her. One gray eye opened sleepily, the blues and greens of the iris sparkling in the morning sunlight. There was so much love in that peaceful, lazy gaze. The sight broke his heart. For some reason, it felt like he'd gone years without seeing that look.

A slight grin cracked her lips as she reached to caress Keston's face. Her thumb ran affectionately over his lips, and he almost cried at the touch. He *missed* that touch. But why? She always did that, she'd been doing it for months. Still, he felt an ache of longing he couldn't explain.

"Kes," Arianne whispered in that delicate way they saved for moments like those—moments when dreams made them forget where they were. Arianne moved to curl into his side. "It was just another dream. You're not in Pangaea anymore."

Right. Another dream.

He kissed her temple. "I missed you."

She snuggled closer. "I'm right here."

Focusing on the warmth of her touch as she nuzzled her face into his chest, her hand rested above his rapidly beating heart. He inhaled, recognizing the shampoo smell that she'd bought from the artisan market the week before. He reminded himself to push the nightmares away in moments like that, to keep his frazzled mind focused on the present. He anchored himself to Arianne, concentrating on the spectrum of sensations: the feel of her heat, the smell of her hair, the sound of her breathing, and the sight of her body perfectly curled into his.

Slowly, the events of the dream became a haze, blurring and fading to nothing, leaving only remnants of emotion. He didn't know why he felt so angry and desperate, but he didn't want to remember. He forced himself to lean into the fullness in his chest, knowing he was safe in his bed with Arianne. Soon, as his eyes fluttered closed, the echoes of the dream faded away.

There. Back to normal. He was just Keston, the owner of a small seaside villa. He lived with his sister and the love of his life. They'd wake up in a few hours, make breakfast, and maybe go surfing. Just a normal family. Just Keston. That's all he was anymore, and all he wanted to be.

Just a dream. Just a dream. Just a dream.

"I love you, Princess," he whispered, happy his life had finally become better than his dreams. He drifted back to sleep.

Chapter 52

Arianne

Through eyes almost clenched shut in pain, Arianne watched Keston collapse just a few short feet from Cassius's face. Was he shot? Was he dead? She wanted to scream, but her voice was nearly gone. She strained to hold herself up against the oppressive sonic force, but everything appeared foggy and disoriented. Blood trickled out of her ears, leaving its sickly warm trail down her neck. The ringing surrounded her like a cage, holding her down with an oppressive force. Some distant part of her registered that the rest of her body could move, but the noise drowned out any cognition.

Then the sound disappeared. For a moment, she feared she'd gone deaf. Despite that, she collapsed to the ground in relief.

"Are you finally ready to listen?" Leon's voice came in through the relentless ringing in her damaged ears.

She knew she was dangerously off balance when she tried to brace herself and could hardly prop herself on her arms. But she found just enough ire to glare at her father. "If your goal was getting me to listen, deafening me beforehand seems counterintuitive."

He hummed in disappointment. "If only you'd been born human, I would've enjoyed our conversations."

Arianne mimicked the noise. "If only you weren't the toe fungus equivalent of a father." With great effort, she stood. She swayed on her feet but refused to break eye contact. "I guess we're both disappointments."

"Let's remedy that," Leon said, placing his hands in his pockets.

Her nose scrunched in fury. She was the deadliest being on the planet, standing ten feet away from him with death in her eyes, and he had the gall to look comfortable. Like he was untouchable. He'd acted just like that when she was a child. She would make him pay.

"I'm going to give you the same chance I gave the boy," Leon continued with a passive look at Keston's unconscious body. "It's in your best interest to listen, Little Beast."

Arianne stared at Keston, unmoving on the ground. What had they done to him? She didn't linger long on her concern, focusing back on her father. Leon first, then Keston. She couldn't help him until she dealt with her family reunion from hell.

Grip tightening on the dual handles of *Horizon's Edge*, she connected them in one swift movement. "We took your capital, and you've lost access to your resources to the west. North America and Africa have united against you. There is no way even you can spin this in your favor, *Father*."

Leon smirked. "I'm glad you've finally decided to recognize the ichor that runs through your veins. You've stopped running from your last name."

"You never let me believe I was allowed to use it," she said, surprised at the bitterness lacing her words. "So I decided to conquer your continent instead." She grinned. "I'm a Murray *despite* you, not *for* you."

"Pitty." He shook his head. "We could rule together."

Behind him, Pandora and Andre stiffened, sharing a look of concern.

"Your offer is one dead mother and a couple massacres too late," Arianne spat.

Leon glanced at Hera behind him. The scientist General nodded. Turning back to his mutant daughter, his face was all gloating satisfaction. "I tried to break you before to get you to cooperate. I grossly miscalculated your resilience. So this time, I'll appeal to your logic."

"Don't have much of that. Or did you forget I already chose death over any life you could offer me?"

"Well aware," Leon said through tightly clenched teeth.

Pandora growled in frustration. Her cybernetic arm sparked with plasma. "Let me take care of her, Father."

Arianne pouted at a sister she'd once loved. "Come on, sis, you know I'm out of your league."

Pandora roared in fury, but Leon held her back with a hand in the air.

Attention settling on Andre, annoyance finally overpowered Arianne's sadness at the sight of him. She'd been conflicted at Keston's party, but her mind was solidly made up: her brother was a spineless coward. She hated cowards.

"And you," she snarled. "You're just running back to him with your tail between your legs?"

Andre's eyebrows furiously knit together. "The worth of your opinion died when you came back to life."

Arianne shrugged. It seemed the bridge had been burned both ways. Fuck him, then.

"There was a time when you wanted nothing but to be my loyal daughter," Leon said, pulling her attention back to him. "You were perfect. You were to be my companion in rule, my archangel."

She twitched, fighting hard to keep those words from hitting home. Remnants of that awful truth lingered in some of her fractured memories. There were still moments when she felt the ghost of her desire to make Leon proud of her. She despised those parts of herself. She wished she could exorcise them like the demons they were.

"I was a little girl," Arianne growled. "Of *course* I wanted my damn father's love and attention." She pointed *Horizon's Edge* at the Inner Circle. "It's not my fault my father was a speciesist egomaniac with a passion for experimentation and torture."

Even as she said the words out loud, the guilt still ate away at her soul. She'd maimed and killed for that man. She'd worshipped the very ground he walked. It didn't matter that she'd been a child; she still did it. She still felt those emotions over a decade later.

Even then, she felt herself standing straight as a pin, some passive part of her still aching to ensure Leon was impressed by her.

"I'm giving you the offer to come back to my side." He held out a hand. "You told the world you're ready to be a Murray, so stand with your kin."

Looking at his open palm, Arianne felt like a little girl again. Her missing memories pulled at the back of her mind, invisible in their detail but vivid with their corresponding emotion. They urged her to take his hand, whispering hauntingly, reminding her that, once upon a time, all she'd wanted was to see that hand extended her way.

Not a Little Beast anymore, but an equal. His archangel. No fear of losing herself. No more war. Maybe she could truly be herself at his side. Maybe Leon was the only one who could understand her. He certainly was one of the few who had never flinched away—

No. No. *No.*

"I'll maintain my former stance." Arianne leaned forward, bracing for the sonic attack that would try to debilitate her when she charged. She wouldn't fall that time. "You'll have to kill me. I'm consistent like that."

Leon shook his head. "There's no need to kill you anymore. We've developed a...solution for insubordination. How fortunate you didn't die in Pacific." He looked at Hera one last time, then back at Arianne. "So I repeat: join me willingly, Arianne. This is the last kindness I'll extend your way."

"Eat shit."

His angelic features turned demonic. "Then allow me to demonstrate your future."

Arianne reached into her jacket for her Frenzy vaporizer. She cracked the glass container holding the purple gas and inhaled sharply. Instinct happily took over.

But before she could move, Keston rose. Even in Instinct's possession, she halted. He was bonded to a part of her that went much deeper than physical—even Instinct respected that. The winged male stood slowly, his body facing the Inner Circle like he was studying who he'd kill first. The thought made her smile.

Keston and Arianne together: there was nothing more powerful on the planet. Game over.

Then Keston turned, and she realized it wasn't Leon's game that was ending. It was hers.

Two golden eyes stared straight through her, shining like a black hole. There was no expression on his face, only placid subservience. He looked possessed, a husk controlled by an invading poltergeist. Arianne didn't know what had happened, but she knew with every ounce of her breaking heart that it wasn't Keston who stood between her and Leon.

"Kes?" she squeaked, her mortification finding a way through Instinct's bloodlust.

"Instinct, meet Upgrade," Leon and Keston said in haunting unison.

Hera beamed proudly. "Two solutions in one. We have a way to control a particularly unpredictable weapon, *and* without his consciousness holding him back, we can unlock feral-like abilities. It's not a natural enhancer like Instinct, but it's close." She tapped her temple. "Almost like a Simulator collar, but vastly more versatile. Takes a little more effort to implant the chip in the brain stem, but the results are fabulous."

"You didn't think we would make a weapon without an off-switch, did you?" Cassius asked, showing a disgusting lack of remorse for his supposed son.

Granted, Arianne had first-hand experience with that award-winning parenting style.

"*Give him back.*" Her voice was guttural.

"How about you join him instead?" Leon and Keston said.

There was nothing human in Leon's smile.

Before Arianne could move, Keston shot forward. His body was a blur. Arianne jumped skyward, but he was too fast. She bellowed in annoyance as he grabbed her ankle and ripped her from the air, sending her tumbling down and cracking the marble floor.

The impact didn't slow Keston. He landed above her, his feet crushing holes in the floor. Instinct gave her just enough speed to sweep his feet from under him and retreat. But nothing slowed his pursuit.

If Instinct was the supernova, Upgrade was its black hole. In his perfectly timed attacks, Keston moved with machine-like, emotionless precision.

And the worst part: Instinct wouldn't let her harm her mate.

If Leon or Hera hadn't guessed the connection Arianne had formed with Keston, she couldn't let them know. So she leaned into Instinct's rage, using the corresponding rush of energy to defend against the onslaught of attacks.

"Can't you see?" Leon screamed over the commotion of the two angels locked in holy war. "With the two of you together, the war is ours."

Arianne absorbed a bone-quaking blow to her crossed forearms, fighting with all her might to stand tall against the sheer force of Upgrade's power. "Keston, wake up! It's me, come on!"

"I'm sorry, dear," Leon pouted. "This isn't a fairy tale. True love's kiss won't wake him up."

With every hit, with every reminder that Keston was gone, Instinct faded. She was exhausted, injured, and emotionally drained. Her energy had burned too high for too long—almost a year too long. And there, fighting to stay alive against Leon's newest horror, she was finally reaching her limit.

I can't do this anymore.

Keston's fist drew backward. Part of her didn't have time to dodge. Part of her took the hit willingly. His fist careened into her temple. The world spun as her knees buckled underneath her, positive she'd blacked out for a second. When her blurred vision refocused on reality, she was face-first on the ground. Her ears rang, blood's coppery taste filled her mouth, a ghostly haze surrounded everything she saw, and a raging headache nearly made her vomit.

Hands grabbed her wings, hauling her from the ground. Arianne was too dazed to scream as the joints of her wings dislocated. She reached deep down to find some kernel of willpower to keep fighting, but any flame was thoroughly doused when she looked up into the face of the love of her life, her mate, and saw *nothing*.

Even struggling out of Keston's grasp proved impossible. Her body had stopped responding. If the agony in her wings was any indicator, she had no hope of escaping either.

Fight and flight were no longer options. She was left with something she rarely did: freeze.

As she was dragged on her dislocated wings toward her father, she caught a flash of purple hair. Her eyes met Jaya's. The Chameleon's face was set in a hard line, and despite her best acting, her fingertips had started to turn fire red. Jaya looked seconds away from launching into an attack. Brave, righteous, Jaya was ready to get herself killed for her oldest friend.

A friend who'd lied to her and abandoned her.

Love sparked to life in her chest for her former friend. She quickly covered it with a healthy dose of novacaine. Emotion of any kind wouldn't serve her where she was going. The familiar numbness from her nightmares coldly clawed at her. She was almost thankful for it.

Arianne slowly shook her head. Fighting was pointless. No one else needed to get hurt.

I'm sorry, Jaya mouthed as tears welled in her bloodshot eyes.

No, Jaya. I'm sorry.

Arianne didn't lift her head again. She didn't want to see, she hardly wanted to think. Luckily, she could feel her mind shutting down.

Keston dropped her at Leon's feet. She distantly registered that her hands and wings were cuffed behind her back. Not that the cuffs mattered, she could hardly lift her arms.

Tired. She was so tired.

Leon knelt before her. In a movement reminiscent of what he'd done before her execution in Citadel Hospital, he used one finger to lift her chin until her rolling head was facing him. His scarred and painfully familiar face filled her vision. The victorious smile on his lips was one she was cursed to see in the mirror every day. So similar... even then, she couldn't ignore how many parts of her greatest enemy lived inside of her.

"Oh, Arianne, don't look so sad," Leon whispered lovingly. "We're going to change the world together, just like it was always meant to be. Welcome home, my daughter."

Epilogue

The Caged Beast

Arianne's prison was a pristine white rectangle, its front constructed of perfectly waxed plexiglass. The winged warrior sat with her head down in the middle of the cell, her bloodied clothes leaving a stain on the polished floor—the one imperfection that would need to be cleansed.

Jaya wanted to scream, cry, *something*, but she couldn't. In a military base full of enemies, she couldn't afford to make one mistake if she wanted to remain alive. So she stared at her oldest friend at the lowest point in her life and forced herself to feel nothing. She needed to be robotic, seemingly enslaved by the collar's control.

Like Keston.

She risked a glance to her side, and nausea rose in her throat. Still in his ruined suit, Keston was another disheveled stain in the stunning perfection of Hera's lab. Her focus lingered on his eyes: two golden orbs shining with their own infernal light. One singular tear fell down his cheek, glistening as it passed over his smiling lips.

Tears of joy. She would know: her own control simulations had taken her to Citadel Island's beaches, some of the best days of her life. What did Keston see? Her heart broke for him and what he'd feel when he finally woke and learned those dreams were simply honey to help his psyche swallow the rancid taste of his actions.

Leon paced in front of his daughter's prison, his blue eyes hungry as he took in his newest weapon. He paced for a minute, two, three, but Arianne wouldn't look up. Even broken beyond repair, Arianne—stubborn Arianne—refused to give her father the satisfaction of her attention.

Jaya's throat constricted at the control collar strapped to her neck. In a few short moments, Arianne's consciousness would be stolen, her body forced to rip the world to shreds at her father's command. As that fate rapidly approached, she didn't plead or beg. She just stared at the ground.

Maybe her silence wasn't stubbornness. Maybe Arianne had finally hit her limit. Jaya wanted to scream at her friend, but she clamped down on that desire before it got her thrown in the neighboring cell.

"What are we waiting for?" Leon barked impatiently.

At a set of computers to the left, Hera's gloved hands typed furiously across the touchscreen as her ice blue eyes reflected the vital charts on the display. The scientist General was silent for a few moments, her focus locked on the myriad of flashing signals across the screen. "We must be careful," she warned. "We've never attempted this protocol on a Level Two mutant before."

Cassius glanced from the cage to his son curiously. "What could happen?"

Her typing paused. "We're attempting to manipulate her mind—there's a real possibility Instinct will rise up to defend."

Leon crossed his arms. "Her energy stores are depleted. Turn on the collar."

"Sure, her ability to call on Instinct voluntarily is depleted," Hera said through clenched teeth, "but Instinct is a natural protective ability. Like a hand on a hot stove, this reaction would be involuntary and far more powerful. All data I have points to the strong possibility of a near feral retaliation."

Cassius brightened. "Like an allergic reaction."

"Sure," Hera said flatly.

Jaya felt herself bracing at Hera's concern. From her extended stays with the mad scientist, very few things unnerved Hera. If the professional was cautious, they all should be.

"And if she's allergic to the treatment?" Leon pressed.

"We go to Phase Two," Hera replied, pulling up a chart of Arianne on her screen. The room was silent as the neon green of the silhouette slowly turned blue. "Gene therapy. We systematically turn off the *Fera* mutation in every cell in her body. Once Instinct can no longer turn on, we'll have a short window to insert a control chip into her brainstem and put her into the trance. When her abilities return, they won't know they must protect her because the change was already made. I would prefer to avoid that process. It will be long and not particularly *pretty*."

At that, Arianne looked up. "You can't take my abilities away. *You can't.*"

Her words started as a command reminiscent of her father, but that last sentence lacked the confidence her bloodline boasted. *You can't.* A desperate plea.

Jaya almost threw up. Looking down, her fingertips turned ivory white, and she quickly shoved them into her pockets.

Happy to explain her methods, even to the subjects she performed her ungodly science on, Hera brightened. "Gene therapy isn't permanent, but if we're lucky, we'll get a short period where your abilities are completely turned off. Think of it like chemotherapy, but instead of treating cancer, we'll treat all of you."

Arianne's upper lip curled. "You're acting like what we are is a disease."

"A disease I cannot cure, yet. But once we have you in our arsenal, who knows what we can do?"

Arianne didn't get a chance to convince Hera of her humanity before the scientist began.

She pressed a button on the screen. The entire room went silent as the collar on Arianne's neck began to flash. At the same time, a blue smoke drifted into the cage: a gas form of Cindy to suppress her abilities more.

Before the gas consumed her, Jaya caught her gaze. Eyes red with tears, Arianne mouthed the plea that shattered Jaya's heart: *Kill me.*

The gas surrounded Arianne before she could witness Jaya's grief-stricken, slow shake of her head.

Jaya wouldn't. She *couldn't.*

Tears stung her eyes as Arianne's silhouette fought the vapor, her chest puffed and hands braced on the glass. But she could only hold her breath for so long. Jaya saw the exact moment her friend lost the last of her willpower. With a defeated slump of her shoulders, she was finally forced to inhale the gas with a choking gasp. Cindy took control, and it was enough to get the collar to take over her mind. Without so much as a sound, Arianne fell face-first to the floor, blue clouds swirling around her in ominous whisps.

Jaya was seconds away from bellowing at the top of her lungs.

Leon, on the other hand, had never seemed so satisfied. He inclined his head. "Arianne, to my side," he ordered in a voice powerful enough to bend mountains to his will.

The room was dreadfully silent.

Jaya heard the exact moment Hera's breathing caught. Arianne's once limp body tensed, and the silhouette of her figure rose slowly, predatorily, in the fog.

Then one hand slammed into the plexiglass with startling force. Her fingers curled into talons and scraped hungrily down the window.

"*To your side?*" the beast grumbled from within.

"We need to evacuate. *Now,*" Hera screamed.

"*To your side?*" the beast repeated in an incredulous bellow.

Arianne's shoulder slammed into the glass. Her roar of rage was so guttural that it woke a primal fear in Jaya's nerves. The room quaked, and Hera slammed her fist down on a flashing red button next to her computer. Alarms blared, accompanied by flashing yellow lights washing the room in a sickly amber hue. Hera ran toward the doors, Leon and Cassius quickly following behind. Jaya barely had a moment to orient herself and follow, her feet scrambling desperately to flee whatever ancient horror tried to escape behind her.

The speaker system in the lab announced loudly, "*Oxygen shutdown in five...four...three—*"

Keston remained behind, golden eyes glowing ever brighter as he braced to hold back the natural disaster preparing to level that lab.

The glass cracked.

Jaya ran through the lab doors just as a nuclear-grade steel door began to close over the entrance. She watched long enough to see a demon built of rage, blood, and fury crash through the walls of a prison too mortal to hold her. Keston intercepted her rampage, slowing her for only a millisecond. But the millisecond was enough to keep the beast at bay as the steel security doors locked shut.

An earthquaking bang rattled the walls as Instinct fought to escape. For a moment, Jaya feared the combined efforts of Keston and those steel doors wouldn't hold her back. Her hands quivered in anticipation at the sounds of struggle on the other side.

Hera, Leon, Cassius, and Jaya watched the lab entrance with the reverence of a vigil as the warning lights erected above them continued to flash. A sign reading *Oxygen Shutdown Protocol* blinked above the doors, warning that the lab was being drained of oxygen. It wasn't until two simultaneous thuds sounded on the other side of the doors and the flashing lights stalled that they let out a breath of relief.

They'd contained the cataclysmic threat... for now.

"This is far beyond anything I've dealt with," Hera gasped.

Leon's eyes sparked with glory, victory, and pride, the very passions of a man who believed he was leading the charge into a new age of gods and mortals. "Exactly. Prometheus brought fire and separated us from animals, altering the course of human history—the fire starters, the steam engineers, the nuclear scientists, software coding, and now this. Whoever commands evolution commands the next era of this world. And it will be us."

All Jaya could picture was Arianne mouthing those two words.

Kill me.

Kill me.

Kill me.

ENJOY THIS STORY?

PLEASE CONSIDER LEAVING A REVIEW!

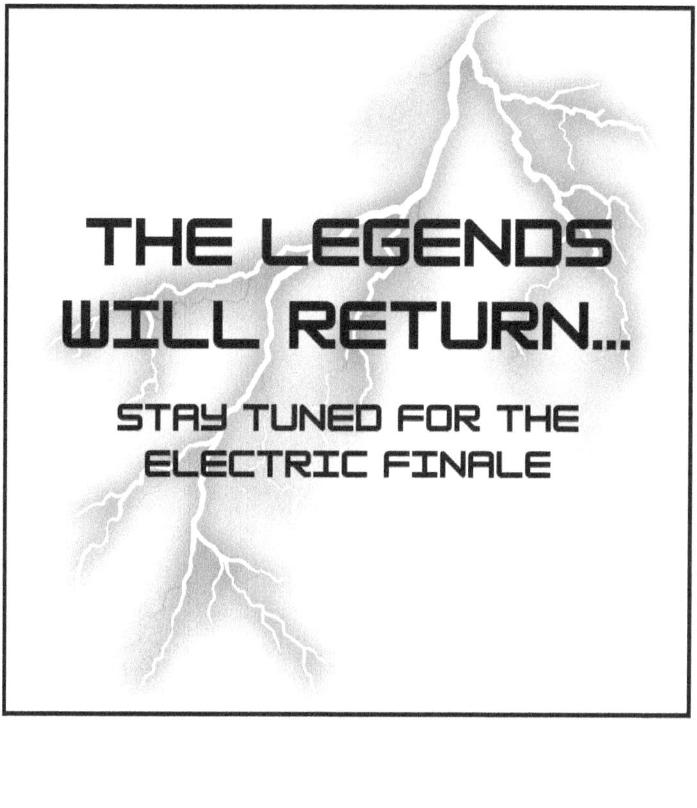
THE LEGENDS
WILL RETURN...
STAY TUNED FOR THE
ELECTRIC FINALE

www.ingramcontent.com/pod-product-compliance
Lightning Source LLC
Chambersburg PA
CBHW060214030726
47499CB00004B/1046